There was no sound from t ... difficult and dangerous. On ... thought wryly. The darkness was almost complete, with only a faint glimmer from the leaden sky to help her along the way. With Hughie's hand held firmly in her own, she hurried along the narrow lane.

Her hand was on the front gate leading into the tiny garden when a shadow detached itself from the bushes nearby and a voice spoke into the thick, murky silence.

'You are home at last, Mrs Knight,' said a voice in the clipped tones of someone speaking very correct English. 'I have been waiting. Please may I come in and talk to you?'

BY LILIAN HARRY

April Grove Quartet

Goodbye Sweetheart
The Girls They Left Behind
Keep Smiling Through
Moonlight & Lovesongs

Other April Grove novels

Under the Apple Tree
Dance, Little Lady

'Sammy' novels

Tuppence to Spend
A Farthing Will Do

Corner House trilogy

Corner House Girls
Kiss the Girls Goodbye
PS I Love You

'Thursday' novels

A Girl Called Thursday
A Promise to Keep

Other wartime novels

Love & Laughter
Three Little Ships
A Song at Twilight

Burracombe novels

The Bells of Burracombe

Other Devon novels

Wives & Sweethearts

Lilian Harry's grandfather hailed from Devon and Lilian always longed to return to her roots, so moving from Hampshire to a small Dartmoor town in her early twenties was a dream come true. She quickly absorbed herself in local life, learning the fascinating folklore and history of the moors, joining the church bell-ringers and a country-dance club, and meeting people who are still her friends today. Although she later moved north, living first in Herefordshire and then in the Lake District, she returned in the 1990s and now lives on the edge of the moor with her two ginger cats. She is still an active bellringer and member of the local drama group and loves to walk on the moors. Her daughter lives nearby with her husband and their two children. Her son lives in Cambridge. Visit her website at www.lilianharry.co.uk.

A Song at Twilight

LILIAN HARRY

An Orion paperback

First published in Great Britain in 2006
by Orion,
This paperback edition published in 2007
by Orion Books Ltd,
Orion House, 5 Upper St Martin's Lane,
London WC2H 9EA

1 3 5 7 9 10 8 6 4 2

A CIP catalogue record for this book is available
from the British Library.

ISBN-13 978-0-7528-8125-6

Typeset by Deltatype Ltd,
Birkenhead, Merseyside

Printed and bound in Great Britain by
Clays Ltd, St Ives plc

The Orion Publishing Group's policy is to use papers that
are natural, renewable and recyclable products and
made from wood grown in sustainable forests. The logging
and manufacturing processes are expected to conform to
the environmental regulations, of the County of origin.

www.orionbooks.co.uk.

To my editor Yvette Goulden,
always patient, encouraging and willing to help.

Acknowledgements

As always I have received much help in the research and writing of this book, and I would like to thank the following and apologise to anyone not included:

The Harrowbeer Special Interest Group, who have been assiduously uncovering the history of Harrowbeer Airfield (you can find their excellent website at www.rafharrowbeer. co.uk); Richard White, who entertained me for an afternoon in his cottage with stories of Milton Combe during his childhood (and who makes a great Dame in our local pantomimes); 'irene', 'SeaNymph', 'Basia,' 'Peet' and all those others in Old Mustardland, who gave me so many ideas for titles, Polish names, etc, and even told me how to stop my computer printing out 350 copies of an entire book one day (I actually just wanted one copy of page 350); and last but not least all those at Orion who worked so hard to turn my typescript into a published book, with a lovely jacket.

Chapter One

October 1943

'So this is Harrowbeer.'

Alison Knight stepped out of the Morris 8 and gazed at the hastily erected collection of sheds, huts and hangars. At the far side, she could see aircraft standing on the runways or parked in bays, protected by grass-covered ramparts. Airmen, mechanics and WAAFs were everywhere, driving trucks, walking or cycling briskly along the paths or lounging in the autumn sunshine outside their huts. Lifting her eyes, Alison could see planes tumbling in practice aerobatics over the rolling Devon moors. The air was filled with the roar of their engines.

She stared up at them, wondering if the man who had confessed to her that he was growing more terrified every day was in one of those planes. Throwing it around in the sky with such apparent nonchalance; hiding his fears from his fellow pilots; living a nightmare in his mind.

'Alison?' Andrew asked, concern in his voice. 'Are you all right?'

She shook herself out of her thoughts and smiled at her husband. 'Yes, I'm fine. Just taking it all in. What was here before?' She turned to help Hughie out of the back seat and he stood beside her, stocky and square, his thumb in his mouth and one hand clutching her skirt, gazing up at the aeroplanes. Alison brushed a fair curl back from his forehead and he twitched away from her with exactly the same impatient gesture that Andrew sometimes used. Although as fair as his mother, all his actions and mannerisms came directly from his father.

Andrew came round the car and stood with his arm across her shoulders. 'Nothing much, as far as I can make out. It was just empty moorland. Nothing between Yelverton, over there –' he pointed at a stubby grey church tower rising from a huddle of buildings '– and a few small villages on this side. Buckland Monachorum, where there's a decent little inn, Buckstone, which is really just a hamlet near the perimeter, and Milton Combe down in the valley. Our cottage is just outside the village on top of the hill. The nearest town is Tavistock, about six miles away.'

'Plymouth's quite near too, isn't it?' she asked, and he nodded.

'About the same distance in the other direction, but it was more or less flattened during the Blitz. I hope you won't feel too isolated, darling.'

'Of course I shan't. Not with all this going on, and you coming home whenever you can.'

Andrew squeezed her shoulders. 'Even if I can't stay every night, we're close enough for me to be able to come home pretty often. You'll see plenty of me, don't worry.' He ruffled his son's fair curls. 'Have to keep an eye on this young man.'

Alison leaned her head against him. 'I could never see too much of you.' She looked out across the airfield again and watched the planes in the sky, repressing a shudder as she thought of the terrifying weeks of the Battle of Britain, with Andrew in the air almost all the time, fighting somewhere over the Channel or France. In the end, he had been shot down over Kent, so help had been swift in reaching him, but the broken leg and ribs and other injuries he had suffered had kept him in hospital for nearly three

2

months, throughout much of the Blitz of 1940 and 1941. Although he hadn't crashed in the three years since then, Alison could never quite forget that it might happen again.

Andrew, however, seemed to think that he was now invincible. 'I've had my crash,' he would say cheerfully. 'I won't have another one.' And he had been back in the air the moment the doctors had given him the all-clear.

As she stood beside him now, looking out past the huts and hangars at the Devon countryside, Alison could feel the vitality quivering through him. She twisted her neck to look up into his face and saw that abstracted expression that meant he was already, in his mind, somewhere in the sky.

'Are you going to show me where we're living, then?'

Andrew pulled himself back to earth again and grinned down at her. 'Of course, darling. I just hope you'll like it. It's not awfully big.'

'I don't mind that. It's not as if we've got masses of furniture, anyway. Just our crockery and cooking things, and bedding. They'll be arriving tomorrow, so I'll need somewhere to stay tonight. Oh, and my bike's coming as well, so I'll be able to get about.' She looked beyond the airfield towards the village of Yelverton with its square-towered church, and past that at the hills of Dartmoor, topped with their rocky outcrops. Nearer at hand was a sharp escarpment which seemed, like a brooding Sphinx, to be keeping a watchful eye on these noisy intruders. 'I shall be able to explore the moor and villages. It'll be fun.'

'It'll be hilly, too,' he warned her. 'The village itself is at the bottom of a really steep valley. And I'm not sure I like the idea of you cycling about all on your own, with Hughie on that little seat. Dartmoor Prison's not too far away, don't forget – and remember the Sherlock Holmes story. You don't know what might be lurking out there!'

'I don't imagine there are giant hounds, anyway,' she laughed. 'But I'm sure I'll find someone to go with.

3

There'll be other wives coming down too, won't there? And you might get a bike and come with me sometimes, when you're off-duty.'

Andrew went back to the other side of the car and slid into the driving seat. 'Not if I can help it! As long as I can scrounge some petrol, we'll use this little beauty. Anyway, a lot of the moor's out of bounds now. Get in, and we'll go down to the village pub for a drink before I show you your new home. And I've fixed for you to stay at a farmhouse until you've got the place sorted out.'

He started the engine and the car chugged off down a narrow lane between high, grassy banks with hedges growing from the tops. Behind the hedges, Alison could see tall trees, fields and the occasional cottage. They came to a sharp left-hand turn and shot down a steep road into the village, with rows of old stone cottages on either side and a narrow stream bubbling beside the road. An old inn stood at the bottom of the hill, with a low wall running along in front of it.

'What a lovely village,' Alison said as she stood in the narrow street. She could hear the sound of children's voices coming from nearby and the singing of birds from the trees that towered above the steep valley sides. An old man was sweeping up leaves along the edge of the road and the innkeeper was rolling a barrel along in front of the inn. 'You'd never think there was a war on, it's so peaceful.'

'Well, it was until they built the airfield,' he grinned. 'I think we must have made quite a difference to the rural atmosphere. Anyway, shall we have a snifter now that we're here? We can sit outside with Hughie – they've got a bit of a garden with a few seats. You're not in too much of a hurry to see the house, are you?'

'I have to admit I'm thirsty after that long train journey,' she said as Andrew carried out a pint of beer for himself and lemonade for herself and Hughie. There were a few

4

other customers already there, sprawled on benches in the sunshine – pilots in flying jackets and two or three WAAFs in their soft blue-grey uniform. Alison leaned back and let her eyes travel round the old stone walls of the inn and the nearby cottages, wondering what stories they could tell.

Andrew glanced up as one of the pilots approached them. 'Here comes Tubby Marsh to say hello. Come on, Tub, park your bottom here and try to behave yourself.'

Alison followed his glance and felt her heart move a little. The man coming towards them was about the same age as Andrew, in his late twenties, and Alison had known him ever since before the war had started. For a long time, he and Andrew had flown in the same squadron but now they were both Squadron Leaders, although still in the same Wing. He wasn't married but he'd had a string of girlfriends, and Alison could see the attraction. Chubby he might be, but his fair, boyish face had an engaging cheekiness that came as a relief from the serious business of fighting a war. Most of the pilots, especially when going through the major battles, treated life with a flippancy that masked their real fears, but with Tubby it had always seemed natural and unforced.

The rotund pilot beamed at Alison and sat down beside her. He took a sip from his tankard and said, 'I see you're still going in for self-denial and punishment. Why you ever married this buffoon, when you could have had me, I've never been able to understand.'

Alison smiled. 'I didn't know you then,' she pointed out, and he thought for a moment, then nodded.

'That must be it, then. Knew you must have some reason. Pity, though.' He drank again and winked at Hughie. 'And how's this young feller-me-lad, eh? Remember your Uncle Tubby, do you?'

'She married me because she knew a good bet when she saw one,' Andrew told him. 'And because I knew the minute I set eyes on her that I wasn't going to let anyone else have her.'

Alison looked from one to the other, then turned away, afraid that her thoughts might show. She nodded towards the inn sign, painted along the front of the long, low building. 'That's an unusual name – the Who'd Have Thought It. D'you know why it's called that?'

'Probably because the whole village is the last thing you expect to see when you come down that fearsome hill!' Andrew said. 'It's pretty old. Francis Drake used to live nearby, at Buckland Abbey – remember we passed it just up the road? All the land hereabouts, and this village, would have been part of the estate. This old inn must have quite a history.'

'It'll get a bit more, now that the RAF's moved in,' Tubby observed with a grin. 'Especially the Poles! I gather half of them are counts or princes or something, and they're *all* a hit with the ladies. You'll have to watch this pretty wife of yours, Andy.' He looked at her with frank admiration. 'That lovely frock is exactly the same shade as your eyes, and exactly the same as the sky when we're flying above the clouds. How do you always manage to dress like a princess, when other women are cutting up old clothes?'

'I'm cutting up old clothes too,' she told him. 'This was one of my deb dresses. In a year or two it will be a blouse and it'll probably finish up as a scarf. Or even a handkerchief,' she added ruefully, 'if this war goes on for as long as Mr Churchill seems to think it will.' She changed the subject. 'Are there many wives here?'

Tubby set down his tankard. 'Well, not many of the blokes are married. Didn't have the sense that old Andy here had when he snapped you up. Anyway, ninety per cent of them are only about nineteen or twenty – haven't had time to get caught yet. There are the WAAFs, though.

They're having a camp built just up the road from Buckland Monachorum – the next village. There's a handy little footpath from there down through the fields to the Drake Manor Inn.' He winked. 'I dare say a few will be using that – quite a lovers' lane, it'll be. Probably give it a try myself, one fine evening.'

'Tubby!' she remonstrated. 'Don't you ever think of anything but girls?'

'Not when I'm down here with my feet on the ground,' he said. 'Don't give 'em a thought when I'm in the air, though.'

Alison bit her lip. She had begun to relax in the banter but Tubby's words were a sharp reminder that the war was still being fought and that he and Andrew would be fighting it. She still had nightmares about the day Andrew had crashed – the realisation that he hadn't returned from the sortie, the anxious wait for a phone call telling her that he had landed safely somewhere else, and then the news that he was injured. Guiltily, she had hoped that he would be kept out of the air completely, but she'd known as soon as she saw him in his hospital bed that he would be flying again at the first possible moment.

'Look at Douglas Bader,' he'd said. 'If he can fly with tin legs, I'm darned sure I can with real ones. A few broken bones aren't going to beat me. Anyway, the docs say they're stronger after a break.'

She caught Andrew's eyes on her now and knew that he understood what she was thinking. He gave her a little nod and said, 'Come on, darling, you must be dying to see our new home. And Hughie's getting tired. You've had a long train journey. Let's be on our way, shall we?'

'You mean you don't want to sit here making conversation with me,' Tubby said mournfully. 'Well, I don't blame you. I know I wouldn't want to hang about with my pals if I were old Andy here, with a lovely wife to take home.' He

7

picked up his tankard again. 'Run along, children. Enjoy yourselves. Don't worry about poor old Tubby, left here all alone to cry into his ale.'

'If you're here all alone it'll be for the first time,' Andrew told him heartlessly, tossing back the last of his own beer. 'We'll not be halfway up the street before you're flirting with the barmaid. Come on, Alison, let's leave the old phoney to drown his sorrows. You'll be seeing plenty of him, more's the pity.'

'You certainly will,' Tubby said, winking at Alison. 'I'm expecting a permanent invitation to *chez* Knight once you're settled in. Parties every night, that's what Andy's promised us.'

'You'll be welcome any time,' Alison said sincerely, getting up to follow Andrew to the door. She looked down at him and their eyes met for a moment. 'You know that.'

The village street was quiet. A couple of women stood outside the little shop across the road, holding baskets over their arms as they chatted. The sides of the valley rose towards the blue sky, the trees tinged with auburn and gold. It seemed impossible to believe that there was a war on; that not far away, in another country, people were killing and being killed; that her own husband, whose arm she was holding now, would soon be back in the thick of it, risking both his life and their happiness; and that without those risks, taken by so many young men, all such happiness and freedom, and the very peace of this tiny village, might be lost for ever.

She glanced again at Tubby, remembering the last time they had met, only a week or two ago, before he and Andrew had been moved from Manston in Kent to this newer airfield in Devonshire. Then she turned back to her husband.

'Let's go and look at the house,' she said. 'Let's go and see where we shall be living.'

Chapter Two

'RAF Harrowbeer?' John Hazelwood frowned slightly, as if trying to remember something. 'Where's that?'

'It's near Plymouth,' Ben said. 'On the edge of Dartmoor. They were going to build Plymouth Airport there but they hadn't got round to it when the war started, and now they've put an RAF station there instead. D'you know it, Dad?'

'I know where it is. I used to go out to Tavistock on the bus when the regiment was at Crownhill, in Plymouth. A friend of mine was vicar at the church there.' John had been an Army chaplain before retiring to become a vicar in the Hampshire village of Ashdown. 'Isn't it somewhere near Yelverton?'

'That's right. Funny sort of place – not what you'd expect of a Dartmoor village at all. It looks more like a spa, with Georgian houses all round a big village green.' He grinned. 'The ones on the south side are mostly shops, and guess what they've done? Taken off the top storeys of every one, so that the planes won't hit them on take-off! They look like a collection of shacks now, while the houses on the other side are still all right.'

'Is it an operational airfield?' his mother asked. She already had two sons serving – Ian, who had followed in his father's footsteps and joined the Army as a chaplain, and Peter, now a Lieutenant-Commander in the Royal Navy, while her daughter Alexandra was a VAD nurse in a naval hospital near Portsmouth. All were facing danger, either from fighting or bombing and, like so many other mothers, she lived in dread of the orange or brown envelope that would bring a telegram telling her her son was missing or dead. She caught herself up and shook her head. 'I'm sorry, that's a silly question. Of course it's operational. Don't take any notice of me. I hope you'll have good accommodation, anyway.'

Ben laughed and John looked at his wife with understanding and took her hand. 'He'll be better housed and fed than a lot of people in their own homes. The Services look after their men – if only because they're valuable pieces of equipment!'

'Like a plane or a lorry,' Ben said, grinning. 'They're not going to let me go rusty, Mum, don't worry.'

'You don't sit still long enough to go rusty,' Olivia Hazelwood said. She looked at him with resignation. 'I can see you don't regret having joined the RAF, anyway.'

Neither John nor Olivia had wanted their youngest son to volunteer so quickly, but Ben had refused to wait until he was called up. He had signed on the moment he left school at eighteen, his ambition right from the start to be a pilot, and he'd passed his training with honours. Since then, he seemed to have led a charmed life, coming through unscathed where many of his friends had been killed or badly injured. He took it blithely for granted, never dreaming how many sleepless nights his mother had spent, thinking of him and her other children and wondering which she would lose first.

Her son's eyes glowed. 'Mum, it's the best thing I ever did. You can't imagine what it's like – being up there, above the clouds, all on your own in the sky. It's like being in another world. I can't think of anything better, I really can't. And to be able to do that *and* have a crack at the Germans – well, I still have to keep pinching myself to make sure it's true. And the others are a grand bunch – all about the same age as me, nineteen or twenty. We're all dead keen to get down to Harrowbeer.'

'Well, make the most of the time you've got with us, won't you,' Olivia said quietly. 'Have you told Jean where you're going?'

'Haven't seen her yet. I came straight in to you. Is she around?'

'She's taken Hope down to the Suttons'. Why don't you go and meet her? I expect she'll be on her way back by now – it's almost Hope's teatime.'

'Might as well.' Ben uncoiled his long body from the armchair and loped out through the French windows. His parents watched him cross the garden and let himself out through the tall wooden gate set in the stone wall, and then looked at each other.

'Oh, John,' Olivia said, her voice trembling a little, 'he's so young. Just a child, still. And the way he's talking about the others being young as well – doesn't he realise, even now—?' Her voice broke and she put her fingers to her lips as if to control their quivering. 'Doesn't he realise that it's because so many have already died?'

John Hazelwood squeezed her hand. 'I know, my love. But that's the way the young have always been. They all think they're invincible, even when there's overpowering evidence that they're not. Ben is quite confident that nothing will happen to him, and perhaps that's his protection. After all, he's been flying for two years now and nothing *has* happened to him. As for us – we have to put our faith in God.'

'And how many others have done that?' she asked bitterly. 'Hundreds – thousands – who have done just the same and yet still been killed. You've been in the Army, John – you served in the Great War. You know just how much protection God gives!'

There was a brief silence. Tears slid down Olivia's cheeks. Her husband lifted his head and met her anguished eyes.

'John, I'm sorry. I never meant to say that . . .'

'It's all right,' he answered quietly. 'You're not the only one to ask such questions. And the only answer I can give you is to remind you of the way in which His own Son died – one of the most cruel and agonising of deaths. There's no more I can say than that.' He paused, then added, 'I had to remind myself many times in the trenches. Watching fine young men die in the most squalid circumstances. Trying to give them strength. Writing to their families . . . Many, many times.'

'But you still kept your faith,' she said. 'You never lost it.'

'Didn't I?' he said ruefully. 'Well, I think I mislaid it a few times! It was certainly very hard to find. But there was nothing I could do but act as if it were still there – and one day I woke up and found it back, as strong as ever. The dying, the killing, the suffering – they'd almost destroyed it. But the courage and the cheerfulness and the stubborn, stalwart faith of some of those young men – *they* were what saved it. And saved me as well. After that, I could go on and do my job, and feel in touch with my God again.'

'And now you never question it.'

'Oh yes,' he said, 'I question it. When I hear about the bombing and think of all those innocent people killed, when I think of all that terrible suffering, happening all over again, I can't help questioning it. But it's always happened, hasn't it? There have always been wars. And what's the use of a faith that falters when it doesn't understand? I ask my questions, just as we all do, and then I remind myself again of the Cross. And somehow that helps me to go on.'

'And so we have to let Ben go,' she said. 'And Ian, and Peter, and Alexandra. I just want to protect them, John. I want them to be back in their prams, like little Hope, where I can keep them safe. I know it's stupid – we brought them up to be independent and strong, and we have to let them go. But it's so hard, and it seems hardest of all with Ben. He's our baby.'

'Not any more. He's a grown man now, and we can be proud of him. Try to think of it that way, my love. We can be proud of them all.'

'I am,' she said, and smiled at him. 'And I'm proud of you, too. *You're* my strength, John. And I won't ask that question again.'

'Ask it as often as you like,' he said, and leaned across to kiss her.

Ben sauntered along the lane, his hands in his pockets, whistling a snatch from Glenn Miller's 'In the Mood'. He glanced up through the dark, coppery leaves of the beech trees at the sky and thought about flying. It really was, as he had told his mother, a different world up there. Looking down on the countryside laid out like a colourful map far below, spotting the things you knew so well on the ground, soaring like a bird and throwing your plane around the sky in a tumble of aerobatics. It was the biggest and best game in the world and he could still hardly believe his luck at being allowed to play it. He had never, in all his life, been so happy as he was when he was in the sky.

He knew, of course, that there was a serious side to this too. The skills he had developed, the handling of an aeroplane in all conditions, even the 'circus acts' – the somersaulting, flips and rolls – were all part of a deadly purpose: that of engaging with an equally skilled enemy, seeking to kill and avoiding being killed. Already, Ben had seen squadrons leave the aerodrome in strict formation and return in a ragged skein, like hunted geese. He had seen pilots come into the mess, red-eyed with exhaustion, ridden with anxiety for their friends who had not come back. He'd watched them as they waited for the phone call that would tell them that someone had come down safely miles away and would be returning, or that they were injured but alive. He'd seen their shock as they received the news that some would not be coming back; he'd seen the look on the face of a pilot who had watched his own best friend spiral into the sea in a ball of flame. He'd suffered it all himself, in the past two years – the exhaustion, the shock, the grief. He knew just what it was all about.

But it was all quickly covered up; it had to be. Next day, perhaps sooner, they would be called into the air again. They could not afford either the time or the energy for grief or fear. It must all be buried while they got on with the job of fighting the war.

'Ben!'

He came to with a start and found that he had been standing quite still, staring up through the coppery canopy at the infinity of blue. A young woman was walking towards him with a small girl trotting beside her. He grinned and waved.

'Hello, Jeanie. How are you? And how's my little Hope?' He squatted down and held out his arms and the toddler broke into a lurching run and fell into them. He swung her in the air, and she squealed and laughed.

'Do you remember me, sweetheart?' he asked, holding her above his head. 'Do you know your Uncle Ben?'

'Well, she should do,' Jean remarked. 'You're her godfather, after all. Anyway, it's not that long since you saw her.'

'It's three months.' He set her down gently on her feet and touched the little girl's smooth cheek with the tip of his finger. 'And she changes every time I see her. I can't believe she's the same tiny thing she was when she was a baby, all red and wrinkled.'

'She never was!' Jean said indignantly. 'She was never wrinkled.'

'Well, red, anyway.' He turned and they began to walk back to the vicarage together. 'And how is everything with you, Jean?' he asked. 'Are your mum and dad really all right now? Are they happy about Hope?'

'I don't know about *happy*, exactly. Having a baby without being married – well, you know what people can be like. And they always told me I'd be out of the door if I ever brought trouble to the house. But they've come round to the idea now, and nobody could be cross with Hope, could they?' The little girl caught both their hands and laughed with pleasure as they swung her between them. 'I mean, look at her. She's the sweetest baby there ever was. And they know Terry and me were going to get married. If it hadn't been for the war and him going off so sudden, we would have done. And if he hadn't been killed . . .' They were silent for a moment, then she went on more brightly, 'It's your mum and dad who saved us – having me out here and letting me stay at the vicarage and all that. I honestly don't know what I'd have done if it hadn't been for them.'

'I think you've been just as much help to them,' he said seriously. 'I know they didn't want me to join the RAF – not so soon, anyway. I could have waited for call-up. But having you around the place, and now Hope – well, it's given them something else to think about. I suppose you'll stay here for the rest of the war now. You won't want to go back to Portsmouth, although the bombing does seem to have stopped.'

'Oh, I'll stop here as long as they'll have me. Can't take this little one back to Pompey, with the state it's in.' She touched the baby's soft hair again, her fingers gentle and caressing, and Ben glanced at her face, remembering the pinched misery and fear that had been there when he had first met her. Now there was a tender motherliness in the curve of her cheek, and a calmness and contentment that he hadn't noticed before.

'I'll still work my way, though,' she added, glancing up and misinterpreting his expression. 'I won't take advantage. I'm doing all I can to help your mum, and I'm doing some war work as well. Making scrim and collecting sphagnum moss, like Judy did when she was here. I can do all that. I take Hope along with me, she's as good as gold.'

Ben nodded. He had met Judy – Terry's sister – when she was in Ashdown, staying at the Suttons' farm where her young cousin Sylvie was evacuated while she recovered from the effects of bomb blast. It was through her that Jean had come to Ashdown when Terry was killed and her pregnancy was discovered.

'Anyway, what about you?' she asked. 'You're still flying Spitfires and Hurricanes all over the sky, and killing Germans for us?'

'Well, only Spitfires,' he said with a grin. 'Actually, that's why I'm home this weekend – I'm going to a new airfield in Devon. Some of the blokes I've been with are going too, but we're joining a new squadron. I've got to be there first thing Monday morning so I'll be off on Sunday night. Catching a train.' He stopped. 'I'm not sure how much I should be telling you.'

'Go on, I'm not a spy!' She laughed at him. 'Still, you'd better not say too much. I know all those posters say walls have ears, but I reckon trees could have as well. And you know that song about whispering grass!' She glanced around at the woods that lined the narrow country road. 'I still think it's a bit creepy out here, you know. The first time I heard an owl, I thought it was a ghost – I was scared out of my wits. And then another night I was sure someone was being murdered, but your dad told me it was just a fox. What an awful noise!'

'You're just a townie,' Ben said affectionately, and they

16

walked on together, chatting, swinging Hope between them. Now and then they passed someone they knew – a villager or an evacuee – and everyone smiled and said hello, most stopping to speak to the toddler as well. 'You don't get that in Portsmouth,' Ben observed after the fourth person had done this. 'Nobody even looks at you in a town – it's as if everyone's invisible.'

'Well, there's just too many people, aren't there. You can't say hello to everyone you meet. And people spoke to each other in the Blitz, all right – everyone mucked in then and helped each other. I don't think townies and country people are any different really, not when it comes down to it.' They reached the vicarage gate and Ben opened it for Jean to go through. She paused and looked at him. 'It's nice to see you back again, Ben. I've missed you while you've been away.'

Ben sat down on a garden bench and watched her go into the house. It was true that she had brought new life to the vicarage, more than repaying the kindness of his parents who had taken her in when her own parents had cast her off. But even though the baby's birth had brought her parents round, he couldn't help wondering what would happen to her in the future. While the war was on, she would have a home here in Ashdown, working as a maid at the vicarage, but what about afterwards? Would she want to stay in Ashdown or go back to Portsmouth? What would her life be then, as a young unmarried mother with a daughter to support?

He thought back to the first months when Jeanie had been with them, arriving a young and frightened girl, grieving over her lost fiancé and carrying his baby. Her parents had been too ashamed to let her stay at home and it had been Judy Taylor, the sister of the boy Jeanie had hoped to marry, who had suggested that she come to

Ashdown. It had been here, in this very garden, that Hope had been born under the apple tree.

Jean and Ben had been friends from the start and he'd been proud to stand as Hope's godfather. By the time the christening took place in the little grey church, Jean's parents – now more accustomed to the situation but still uncomfortable with the fact that their daughter was an unmarried mother – had been there, and so had Terry's family.

Ben still remembered the moment when his father, holding the baby in his arms over the old stone font, had asked the godparents to name the child. Everyone present knew that the baby was to be called Hope, but Jean had said nothing about a second name. She didn't have to have a second name, of course, but Ben knew that if the baby had been a boy he would have been named after his father. Terry's family too must have been thinking that as John asked his question, and then Judy Taylor, the chief godmother, took a very small step forward.

'Hope Teresa,' she said clearly, and there was a tiny sigh from everyone present. Ben saw Terry's mother turn and look at her husband with brimming eyes and then John dipped a small silver cup into the water. He poured it over the baby's thick, dark hair and made the sign of the Cross upon her forehead. 'Hope Teresa, I baptize thee in the Name of the Father, and of the Son, and of the Holy Ghost. Amen.'

Hope woke with a start. She drew in a deep breath and opened her mouth wide, letting out a yell that could have been heard in Southampton. Everyone smiled, Judy giggled and Jean blushed scarlet with embarrassment and went to take the baby back, but John lifted one hand and shook his head reassuringly. Cradling the baby against him, he conducted the rest of the service against a crescendo of furious screams, and then it was over and Jean was allowed to have her baby again and calm her.

'I'm ever so sorry, Mr Hazelwood. It was getting her head wet all of a sudden, like that.'

'It's all right, Jean. It's supposed to be a good sign for the baby to cry. It shows that the Old Adam's being driven out, or so they say.'

She gave him a doubtful look and turned to find Ben at her side. 'Well, you're her godfather now, Ben. I hope you're going to do your duty by her – help me bring her up properly, and all that.'

Ben remembered how he had looked down into her eyes, seeing the sadness there and the need. Already, he could feel a rapport between him and this girl, and a bond between himself and her daughter.

'I'll do my best,' he said quietly. 'I'll do my best to help you.'

That was almost two years ago now, and he'd always sought Jeanie out when he came home on leave. Their friendship had grown and he felt a deep fondness for the little girl. Sometimes, as they strolled in the woods and fields, taking a simple picnic with them and playing with Hope, he felt almost as if they were a family.

His mother came out of the house and found him there. She sat down beside him on the bench.

'Jeanie's looking very happy,' she said. 'Has anything happened, Ben?'

He looked at her, wondering what she would say if he said 'yes'. He knew that she liked the girl, but would she welcome her as a daughter-in-law? He didn't know. His mother was no snob, and neither was his father – but he still didn't know the answer.

'No,' he said. 'Nothing's happened. I think she's just happy to be here.'

Chapter Three

The cottage that Andrew had found was one of a pair beside the road, a short distance from the top of the hill that led down into the village. Alison stood at the gate and looked at it.

'I thought it would have a thatched roof and eyebrow windows and roses round the door.'

'There's not much thatch hereabouts,' Andrew told her. 'And I'm afraid it's not as sheltered as the houses down in the valley – we'll get all the winds straight across from Plymouth Sound here. But it's got electricity and its own water supply. Most of the cottages still have to use a standpipe, and I'm not sure you'd be too keen on collecting your water in a bucket!'

Alison screwed up her face. 'No, I don't think I would.' She stood in the tiny front garden and looked across the road. Beyond the cottage she could see a wide view stretching into the far south-west, with the glitter of water in between, while in the other direction she could see rolling hills and distant villages surrounded by what looked like tall chimneys.

'Are those factories over there?' she asked, frowning. 'I didn't know there was a lot of industry down here.'

'I think it's old mine-workings. That's Cornwall you're looking at, across the Tamar estuary. It's riddled with mines – tin, mostly – though I don't think they're all working now. Those chimneys are part of them.' He dumped her case on the path and pushed open the door, then turned to swing Alison into his arms. 'Got to do it in style.' He set her on her feet on the stone-flagged floor and turned to lift Hughie in as well. 'What d'you think?'

'Well, I haven't had a chance to look yet.' Alison brushed back her fair hair and gazed around with interest.

The door opened into a small, square hallway which in turn opened into a long room that might once have been two smaller ones but now went the depth of the cottage, with windows at each end. In the front part there was an old stone hearth with an iron basket where a pile of logs was laid ready to be lit, and in the back a smaller fireplace which didn't appear to be in use. The ceiling was crossed with beams of oak so aged the wood was almost black.

'A piano!' Alison's eyes lit up as she saw the instrument standing in one of the alcoves. She opened its lid and played a few notes. 'You never told me about this.'

'I wanted it to be a surprise. It's not all that special, mind.'

'It's not bad, though.' She ran her fingers up and down the keys. 'I can keep up my practice and it'll be lovely for parties.' She closed the lid again. 'What else is there?'

'There's a kitchen – more of a lean-to scullery really, but it's got an electric cooker and running water. And there's a lavatory outside. We've got our own septic tank as well, so there are no problems there.' Andrew unlocked the back door to take her out into the yard. 'And not a bad little garden either. A bit of grass for Hughie to play on, and vegetable patch. But wait till you see upstairs.'

Alison followed him up the narrow stairway, with Hughie tugging at her hand. So far, she was pleasantly surprised by what she had seen. The cottage had obviously been looked after and improved, the downstairs room would be marvellous for the parties Tubby had told her he was looking forward to. And there was furniture, too – a sofa and two armchairs in the front part of the room and a big kitchen table and six chairs in the back, as well as the piano.

'Here's our bedroom.' Andrew opened the door to the front room and stood back. Alison went past him and gave a little cry of delight.

'Andrew, it's lovely!'

'Thought you'd like it.' He beamed as proudly as if he'd done the furnishing himself.

'I adore the beams. And the blue curtains,' Alison said, moving across the room to look out of the window. 'And look at the view! It's even better than it is from the garden. It's a really nice, sunny room, isn't it?' She turned to him, her eyes glowing. 'I'm going to love living here.'

Andrew put his arms round her. 'That's good. Because I hope we'll be here for quite a long time. As long as the squadron's here, anyway.'

There was a slight pause as they both thought of the reason for their being here. Alison leaned her head against his chest and he lifted her chin with his fingers and kissed her lips. 'Don't worry, darling. I'll be all right. I've had my crash, remember.'

'I know.' She did not share his belief that he was now invincible. Others had crashed more than once, and usually the second time had been their last. She moved away from him. 'How many other bedrooms are there?'

'Two. One's furnished, so we'll be able to have people to stay, and the other one will do for a nursery. We'll need to get you a bed,' he told his son, who was gazing around him, wide-eyed. 'But you can sleep in the guest-room to begin with.' They went into the back bedroom with its two single beds, each stripped like the one in the front room. 'You can choose which one you want.'

'This one!' Hughie jumped on to the bed nearest the window. 'I want this one!'

'That's the one I'd choose too, so that I could see out from my pillow,' his mother said. 'It's a nice view down into the garden.' She moved back to the landing. 'What's in this room?'

'Ah.' Andrew stepped back and gave a flourish with one hand. 'This is the *pièce de résistance*. Another small convenience that you might not expect in a cottage.'

'A bathroom!' Alison exclaimed in delight. 'Oh, how wonderful! I thought we'd have to bring a tin one in every Friday night. Andrew, you're so clever to find this place. It's lovely.'

'Well, I was rather pleased with myself,' he admitted. 'And it's not too far away from the airfield. They've issued everyone on the station with a bike, so it's really only a few minutes away. Bit noisy for you, though, with the planes flying over.'

'I shan't mind that. I'm used to aircraft noise.' She went back into the bedroom and stood gazing out of the window. 'Oh, I can't wait to move in.'

'Well, as soon as our stuff arrives, we can.' He glanced at the bed. 'Pity it's not here now. You don't happen to have a couple of pairs of sheets about your person, do you?'

'No, I don't,' she said ruefully. 'And we really ought to go to wherever it is Hughie and I are staying tonight. But if the luggage arrives tomorrow, I can get everything ready during the day and we can spend the evening in our very own home. I'll even cook you supper!' She collected Hughie from his bedroom and shooed him down the stairs. 'Come on, I want to drive all round the perimeter, so that I can see exactly where you'll be. And then we'll go to the farmhouse. All right?'

'Yes, Miss,' Andrew said obediently, like a small boy. 'No, Miss. Three bags full, Miss. But I won't forget what you've promised for tomorrow night – don't think I will.'

'And what was that?' she enquired innocently. 'All I remember saying is that I'd cook you supper.'

'No,' he said, and caught her in the doorway. 'You promised more than that. You know you did.' He ran his fingertips down her face, from eyebrows to throat. 'You didn't have to say it – your eyes told me. And your lips.' He bent and kissed them again.

Alison wound her arms around his neck and said in a whisper, 'I wish we had those sheets. I really do.'

'Tomorrow,' he murmured. 'Tomorrow, in our own new home. We'll have all night, then. All the time in the world.'

Much later, as she sat in the window of the farmhouse listening to Hughie's regular breathing as he slept, Alison thought back over the day. As Andrew had said, it had been a long one, starting with the railway journey from Kent to Devon, and she was tired. Yet she had been unable to go to sleep straight away, and had got out of bed to gaze out of the window at the rolling fields, silvered with moonlight. She could not forget the look in Tubby's eyes as he had glanced up at her outside the village inn. And she could not forget that conversation with him a week or two earlier, in the rented house at Manston.

'It's like a huge black shadow looming over me,' Tubby had said. He was lying back in the big armchair by the fireplace. Most of their personal possessions – their books, a few ornaments, Andrew's rowing trophies, their wedding photographs and the painting of Alison that her father had commissioned when she was presented at Court – had been packed, ready for the move to Devon, and the room seemed bare and cheerless. Alison had been busy wrapping glass and china when Tubby arrived, but when she saw his face she had put them down at once.

'Whatever's the matter?'

'I'm sorry. I shouldn't have come – shouldn't be

24

bothering you with this. But I've got to talk to someone.' His normally cheerful, rosy face looked pale and a little drawn, and there was a hunted expression in his eyes. 'I don't know what I'm going to do. I just don't know—'

'Tubby!' Really alarmed now, she came to his side and caught his arm. He stared down at her and she guided him to the chair. 'Sit there, and tell me what's the matter. Take your time, there's no hurry. Hughie's asleep and Andrew isn't coming home till later. Tell me what's happened.'

'Nothing's actually happened.' He sat forward, his hands clasped between his knees. 'It's just that – oh hell, I don't know how to put this.' He beat his fists against his mouth and then started to get up. 'I'm sorry, I shouldn't have come. I'd better go.'

'No.' Gently, she pressed him back. 'No, don't go, Tubby. Look, you don't have to tell me if you don't want to. Just sit there for a while. I'll make you some tea. Or coffee – which would you like? Or there's a bottle of sherry we haven't packed yet. I expect I can find a glass somewhere.' She glanced at the box she had been packing when he arrived, but Tubby shook his head.

'Better not. Oh, Christ – sorry, Alison, I'm forgetting my manners. Coming into your house and swearing . . . Look, forget it, will you. Forget I ever came.' His face was working and she saw beads of sweat on his forehead. Once again, she pressed him back into the chair.

'You're staying here. And I'm making some tea. It seems to me you really do need someone to talk to.' She hesitated, then said, 'I'm quite safe, you know, Tubby. I won't pass it on, whatever it is.'

He glanced up at her from under his brows. 'Not even Andy?'

'Well . . .' She hesitated again. 'I've never had any secrets from Andrew.'

'That's just it,' he said gloomily. 'Andrew's the one

person who must never know. That's why I can't tell you – I should have thought of it before I came.' He let his shoulders sag. 'I'll have a cup of tea, and then I'll go. Let you get on with your packing.'

'So who will you tell?' she asked quietly.

Tubby sat silent for a few moments, staring at the floor. Then he lifted his shoulders, and looked up into her face.

'No one.'

Alison waited for a moment. Then she knelt before him and looked into his eyes, shocked by their darkness. Normally a bright, laughing blue, they were almost black with despair. She took a breath and said, 'Tubby, there's something badly wrong. If you want to tell me what it is, I promise I won't tell a soul.' She took another breath. 'Not even Andrew.'

'I can't do that,' he said. 'I can't ask you to keep secrets.'

'It's wartime,' she said. 'People are having to keep secrets all the time. Andrew has to keep secrets from me, I know he does. Tubby, I trust you not to tell me anything I ought to tell him. Trust me, too.'

'That's just it,' he said wretchedly. 'It *is* something you ought to tell him. But if he knew . . .' He met her eyes again and then drew in a ragged breath. 'Oh, to hell with it. I'm scared, Alison. That's what it is. I'm scared stiff. And if Andrew knew – if anyone on the station knew – they'd have me grounded before you could say Jack Robinson. Whoever he was,' he added with a wry attempt at humour.

Alison sat back on her heels and stared at him. A small frown gathered between her brows.

'Scared? You mean, of flying?'

'That's right. Scared of flying, scared of meeting Jerries, scared of fighting. Scared of being shot down, burning to death or drowning in the Channel. I'm scared of everything, Alison, but the worst thing is that I'm scared of anyone knowing. That's why you mustn't tell Andy. You mustn't tell anyone.' His eyes bored into hers. 'I can't be grounded, Alison. I can't.'

'But why not?' she asked helplessly. 'If it's that bad . . . Tubby, you know what they say. A frightened pilot is a dangerous pilot. You *shouldn't* be flying.'

'It's not true,' he said. 'I'm not dangerous. If anything, I fly better. It's like walking a tightrope – I'm more careful than I've ever been before. I'm a good pilot, Alison.'

'I know you are. Andrew's told me that. One of the best he's ever flown with. But all the same . . .' She shook her head, and then asked, 'How long have you been feeling like this?'

'A few weeks. Four or five. It came on quite suddenly, one day. Nothing had happened, nothing out of the ordinary. It just suddenly hit me – a wave of fear, like a huge wall of water sweeping over me. I wasn't even fighting at the time, just stoodging along over the Channel. We haven't been fighting all that much lately, you know that. It seemed so stupid – I wouldn't take any notice of it. Thought maybe I was just a bit tired, you know.'

'I expect that's all it is,' she said. 'You need a rest. Don't you think that's it, Tubby? Don't you think that if you told Andrew, or the Wing Commander, or went along and saw the doctor, that's what they'd say? A week or two off flying duties, that's probably all you'd need.'

'I can't. Once I started to talk about it, they'd know – they'd see me shaking. Look at me now.' He was indeed beginning to shake, his hands trembling violently, then becoming a shuddering which crept over his whole body. His teeth chattering, he stared desperately at Alison and she gazed back, horrified.

'Tubby, you must see someone—'

'*No!*' he shook his head emphatically. 'I've told you, I can't. I'd be grounded for good, and there's no need. It's

27

not interfering with my flying. I can still do my job. I just don't enjoy it any more,' he ended in a dispirited tone.

The shuddering had eased as quickly as it had begun. Alison looked doubtfully at him. He grinned weakly and said, 'How about that cup of tea?'

Slowly, she got to her feet and gave him another anxious glance as she went out to the kitchen and filled the kettle. As she found cups and saucers, warmed the pot and made the tea, she wondered what she should do. Her instinct was to tell her husband, yet she had given Tubby her promise. She went back to the sitting room with the tray of tea.

Tubby was in the same position as when she had left him, staring hopelessly at the floor. She put down the tray and poured two cups of tea. 'Drink this. It'll make you feel better.'

He gave her that wry grin again. 'If only it were that easy.' But he took the cup and lifted it to his lips, and a little colour came back into his cheeks. Alison sat on the floor near his feet and sipped her own. She felt shaken and slightly sick. She looked up at him.

'Tubby. Please, won't you let me tell Andrew?'

His mouth twisted a little. 'Can't really stop you, can I?'

'Of course you can! I gave you my promise. I won't break that, Tubby, but I'm asking you to release me. Please. For your own good. It frightens me, seeing you like this.'

'I'm a bastard,' he said. 'I shouldn't have come. Piling all this on you. Not fair, not fair at all.'

'Don't worry about that,' she said. 'I just want to help. Why don't you want to rest? Surely it would be better. Andrew would understand, I know he would. Everyone would. It happens. It happens to the best of pilots.'

'I've told you,' he said dully. 'If they once saw me like – like I was just now, they'd take me out of the air at once. I'd be flying a desk for the rest of the war. I'd be useless.' He

28

looked at her again and she saw the determination in his eyes. 'If that happened, I wouldn't want to go on.'

A ripple of cold ran through her body. She put down her cup. 'You mustn't talk like that.'

'There's no point in talking at all,' he said, 'unless I tell you the truth.'

There was a small silence. Then, feeling as if she were walking on eggs, she said carefully, 'But I still don't understand why. You don't have to be ashamed.'

For a moment or two, Tubby didn't answer. Then he said, 'Maybe I don't. But it's not just me, you see. It's my family. My mother and father.'

'Surely they'd understand. They'd want you safe.'

He sighed. 'Yes, I expect they would. But if I were to die, they'd rather it was as a hero than a coward.'

'I don't understand.'

'When I said I wouldn't want to go on,' he said, 'I meant that I wouldn't want to go on living. Because however much they might try to understand, they really wouldn't. They'd always be disappointed in me. Deep down, they'd always think I was a coward.'

'But—'

'I had an uncle,' he went on, cutting across her protest. 'My father's younger brother. He died in the First World War.' He took in a deep breath. 'He was executed for cowardice.'

'Oh, *Tubby* . . .'

'He was only in the trenches for a few days. He couldn't stand it. He tried to run away. His officer could have shot him there and then, but instead he went for court-martial. They did it there, the next day. He wrote to my grandparents from his cell and told them he was condemned to death. He was only fifteen.'

'*Fifteen?* But why was he—'

'A lot of boys lied about their age to join up,' Tubby

said. 'Nobody bothered to check. They just wanted men – more and more of them. They didn't much care if they were really boys.'

Alison put her hands to her face and found that her cheeks were wet with tears. She shook her head blindly. 'That's dreadful. Dreadful.'

'So you see,' he said, 'I can't let them have another coward in the family.'

'He wasn't a coward. He was just a boy.'

'But I'm not. And I've been flying for ten years.' He finished his tea and looked at her. 'Well, there it is, Alison. Are you going to tell?'

'I don't know,' she whispered, and then caught herself up. 'No, of course not. Not if you don't want me to. But – oh, Tubby, I can't bear to think of you up there, feeling like that.'

'I'm sorry,' he said gravely, and reached for her hand. Regarding it intently, he said, 'If it ever gets too much for you, then you can tell Andrew. I don't want you burdened by this. But, if you *can* keep my secret, well, I'd be grateful. You see, I always feel that as long as I can keep flying, I can do some good. Kill some Jerry who might otherwise go on to do something appalling to us. It's possible, isn't it?'

'Yes, I suppose so,' she said in a small voice. Then she gave him a small nod. 'All right, Tubby. I'll keep your secret for as long as I can. I won't say a word until I have to.'

Their eyes met again in understanding, and then he let go of her hand and began to get to his feet. 'I'll go now. And – for what it's worth – it *has* helped, to talk to you. You're a dear, Alison. Thanks.'

He dropped a kiss on her bent head and she closed her eyes. Once again, the tears began to slip down her cheeks, and when she opened her eyes again he had gone.

Slowly, she began again to pack, ready for the move to Harrowbeer.

Andrew left his wife at the farmhouse where she was lodging that night, and drove back to the airfield. As requested, he had driven her all round the perimeter. The air was filled with the noise of aircraft taking off and landing, and they could see Spitfires, Hurricanes and Blenheims on the runway or standing in the bays, protected from blast by high grassy bunkers. Inside the bunkers, Andrew told her, were air raid shelters, and there were others scattered between the buildings. The whole area must be very different from what it had been only a year or two earlier.

The officers' mess was in a large house on the edge of the aerodrome, opposite the watchtower. By the time he arrived, most of his squadron were either stretched outside in the autumn sunshine or indoors, lounging in armchairs and chatting or reading newspapers. A few were playing cards in one corner. Tubby Marsh looked up as he came in and took his pipe from his mouth. The smoke curled lazily upwards.

'Those new bods have turned up. They're getting sorted out. I told them to come along here when they were ready. We've warned them that you're an ogre.'

'That's good.' Andrew glanced out of the window at the planes, standing ready by the runway. The squadron was on two days' rest, but tomorrow they'd be back on operations and the new members would need some practice before being allowed to fly with the rest of them. 'We'll take 'em up, see what they're made of. How did they strike you?'

Tubby shrugged. 'How do any new bods strike us? Think they're here to save the world.' He spoke with the weary resignation of one who had seen it all before – young pilots, often fresh from training, desperate to get into the sky and prove themselves as the finest flyers yet, here to save the squadron, to save their country, to save the entire world. He'd seen them leap into their aircraft on their first sortie; he'd seen them in the air, swooping and diving, heard their voices filled with exhilaration as they threw their planes around in the sky. And he'd seen them shot down, spiralling in flames towards the sea or the earth. Killed before they'd had a chance to live; unable to save themselves, let alone the world.

Yet some did survive. Some became fine flyers. Some, like Andrew, even seemed invincible. Perhaps these two youngsters would be the same.

He felt the familiar darkening of his private nightmare begin to creep upon his mind, and thrust it away, in his habitual fashion, with a joke. 'I expect they'll teach us all we need to know.'

The door opened and in they came, two boys of twenty or so who looked as if they should still be at school, yet had probably had a good two years' flying experience. All the same, Tubby heard someone give a muffled groan and someone else muttered the word 'kindergarten'. The taller of the two newcomers, a fresh-faced lad with fair, curly hair, flushed scarlet and then set his jaw.

Andrew stepped forward, holding out his hand. 'Afternoon. You must be Hazelwood and Sinclair. I'm your Squadron Leader – Andrew Knight. You don't need to take any notice of these characters. They were all green once – some still are.' He waved his hand dismissively around the mess and the other pilots cheered sardonically. 'OK, let's see what you're made of, shall we? On your feet, Tubby. You can take one, I'll take the other.'

Tony Sinclair and Ben gazed at him. 'Take a plane up now, sir? Right away?'

'Well, you're not here to drive buses. At least we've got a

chance to play around for a bit. We're back on ops tomorrow, so there wouldn't be much time then.' Andrew was already making for the door. 'Come on. No time like the present.'

The two boys stared at each other, half excited, half nervous. Tubby grinned at them and put a hand in the small of each one's back, propelling them towards the door. 'Been to Dartmoor before, have you? Bit different from Lincolnshire. Just got to watch out for the sheep and ponies when you fly low, that's all. And try not to crash into any of the tors. We've even got one of our own at the end of the runway, for practice.'

They were outside now, striding towards the aircraft. Ben felt his heart thud in his chest. Flying was no longer new to him; he had already proved that he was competent and confident in the air. But he had never got over this sudden attack of nerves when he flew for the first time with the man who was to be his Squadron Leader – the man who would lead him in operations against the enemy, expecting nothing but the best from him. This man would hold the life of the squadron in his hands, and his own life might at times *depend* on the squadron's actions. On *Ben's* actions.

He swallowed, feeling the familiar weight of responsibility as the two men were marching so purposefully and yet so casually towards their planes. Suddenly, his confidence seemed misplaced. What did he know about flying, even after two years? What did he know about anything at all?

Tony Sinclair, walking beside him, muttered, 'This is it, Benjamin. In an hour's time we could be on our way back to Cranwell to start all over again.'

'Thanks,' Ben said wryly. 'I love your sense of humour.'

They parted to go to the two aircraft standing a little way from the watchtower. Ben found himself with Andrew and Tony walked off with Tubby. The mechanics waited, ready to carry out the last-minute chores of helping them strap themselves in, swing the propellers and whisk the chocks out from under the wheels. Ben's heart was in his mouth.

Andrew said nothing. He swung himself up into the cockpit and motioned to Ben to take the seat in front. Silently, they fitted their helmets and goggles over their faces and Ben looked at the controls. For a panic-stricken moment, they seemed to swim before his eyes, and then his vision settled and he realised with a great rush of relief that he recognised and understood them. There should be no problem.

The propeller began to turn, seemed to hesitate and consider turning in the opposite direction, then settled into a blur. Still trembling a little, Ben began to taxi out on to the runway and set the nose into the wind.

'Watch out for the rock,' Andrew's voice said laconically in his ear.

'The rock?' He searched the tarmac with his eyes, and then saw it – a craggy outcrop almost blocking the end of the runway. It looked enormous; a huge jagged lump like a hand pointing dirty fingernails at the sky. He opened up the throttle and the nose lifted just in time – so close that he almost expected to feel the rough granite scraping the belly of the plane. Lurching a little, they rose higher and then he felt the aircraft steady and let out his breath in a sigh of relief.

'Just made it,' Andrew observed. 'Well done.'

'Can't it be shifted?' Ben asked, relaxing slightly. 'It's right in the damned way.'

'Shift it? It'd take half a ton of dynamite to move that. Why should it be shifted, anyway? It's good practice. Keeps the chaps on their toes. Cheaper to use a drop or two of extra fuel than bring in the bulldozers. Keep going south, we'll have a look at Plymouth.'

The airfield was built close to the edge of the moor and soon they were over Plymouth. Ben looked down, sobered by the devastation he could see below. The whole of the city centre appeared to have been flattened. Where once he imagined there had been shops and streets and houses, there was now little but rubble. The church still stood, albeit with no roof, and there was a lone clock-tower not far away, but apart from that there was almost nothing.

'My God,' he said. 'When was the blitz here? I can't remember.'

'There've been so many, we lose count,' Andrew said grimly. 'It was in April 1941. The usual hammering – several nights of heavy bombing. They say the fires were so intense that the windows melted, and the gold in one jeweller's shop was running down the road like a stream. There were barely two bricks left standing on each other when it was over.'

'They're clearing it up, though,' Ben said, looking down.

'Yes, and I'll tell you something else – a lot of the rubble was brought out to build our airfield.' Andrew gave a short laugh. 'They say it's an ill wind that blows nobody any good!'

They flew out over the Sound. Devonport Harbour was crowded with ships, brought in for repairs and revictualling. Ben, whose home was near the ports of Portsmouth and Southampton, gazed down with interest. All naval ports were alike, he thought, and yet each of them was different too. In Portsmouth, there was a huge natural basin, entered by a narrow neck of water between the twin bastions of Sallyport and Fort Blockhouse. Here, the harbour lay in the wide estuary of the River Tamar, with the green shores of Cornwall on the far bank, and the protective shelter came from a long breakwater stretching across the mouth.

In another moment they were out over the Channel, looking down at a blue sea, flecked with white foam. A few ships were moving below, and he saw some aircraft on patrol, but everything seemed peaceful.

'Why wasn't the airfield built sooner?' he asked, and Andrew's voice crackled back through his earphones.

'Because they didn't think the Germans could reach this far – and until they took France and got all their airfields, they couldn't. Dunkirk changed everything.' His voice was sombre. 'Turn inland. We'll have a look at Dartmoor and you can show me what you can do.'

Dartmoor was a wide expanse of moorland, spread with a rolling quilt of fading brown bracken and purple heather. Topping the hills were the rocky tors for which Dartmoor was famous, and bright rivers snaked their way through the valleys. A few villages huddled in deep combes, their grey church towers standing out like beacons, and surrounded by fields and woods before their slopes rose again to open moorland. And, almost in the centre of the wide expanse, stood a vast circle of grey, forbidding buildings, hemmed in by a high, blank wall.

'Dartmoor Prison,' Andrew said briefly, and Ben shivered, remembering the stories he had heard about this grim place, and the criminals who were kept there – and sometimes escaped. Indeed, the whole of Dartmoor, sunlit though it was today, had a dark, sinister aspect, alien to the boy who had grown up on the fringes of Hampshire's New Forest. He thought of mires and bogs that could suck a man to his death, of swirling fogs and driving snow, of strange sounds and hauntings. It was a relief when Andrew told him to head back towards Yelverton.

'Right, you can show off a bit now,' his Squadron Leader told him. 'A few rolls, whatever you like. Only not over the airfield itself. That's strictly forbidden, and don't you forget it.'

Ben concentrated on remembering all he'd learned, during both practice flying and operations. The dogfights between him and other pilots – almost a form of wrestling in the sky, diving at each other, flying head-on and turning away at the very last moment, all the aerobatics designed to increase their skills when it came to real fighting. *Choose a point on the horizon, then roll your plane around it. Make sure the plane's nose is above your chosen point, get your speed up, keep the stick hard over and just touch the rudder, and over you go into the roll, gliding upside down and almost hanging out of the cockpit, held in only by the harness strapped to the seat . . .* This was the moment when he used to have a brief flash of fear that he might forget what to do next, but he had done it so often now that he reacted as easily as if he were opening a door, applying the opposite rudder now, thrusting the stick well forward and coming out of the roll and upright again.

'Not bad,' Andrew said, and Ben performed his second roll and then went on to some more of the manoeuvres he had felt so proud of, still nervous in case he wasn't passing muster with his new Squadron Leader.

After a little while, they turned back towards Harrowbeer. Ben saw Tony's plane coming in to land just ahead of him, and they brought their craft in together, taxiing to a stop and climbing out with shaking legs.

As they came close enough, Ben and Tony looked at each other and then at their mentors. To their relief, Andrew and Tubby were nodding and grinning.

'You'll do,' Andrew said, and clapped Ben on the back. 'Not a bad show at all. A few rough edges to iron out, but nothing a bit of beating and starvation won't cure . . . Come back to the mess and have a drink. I'll introduce you to the others.'

As they walked back together, Ben glanced over his shoulder at the two planes, now the property of the mechanics once more. It's going to be all right, he thought. It's going to be all right at Harrowbeer.

Chapter Four

Alison quickly settled into her house above Milton Combe. It was a real picture-postcard village, she thought, with its cottages clustered deep in the narrow valley and the stream bubbling down the centre. There was a tiny church with a little bell in an open turret, a Wesleyan chapel, and two shops apart from the one Alison had seen near the inn on her first day, which was also a tea room. The tiny Post Office consisted of a cardboard box kept under a table, and when Alison went in on her first visit to buy stamps for letters home, she found that the entire stock was made up of one of each sort.

'Us don't need to write many letters, maid,' the elderly woman who ran the shop told her. 'Us all lives round here, see. And the airmen and sailors, they get theirs from their NAAFI.'

'But there must be people who have gone away to serve in the war. Surely their families need to write to them?'

'Oh, I knows how many to have in,' the shopkeeper said. 'These is just spares, see.'

Alison and Hughie walked on through the village. You could walk all the way along to the other end and come out on the main road, climbing the hill back to the ridge. From here the road was so steep that it seemed almost to stand up on end as you approached it, and Hughie screwed his face up in dismay. Alison took his hand and encouraged him.

'I expect this is the hill Jack and Jill fell down, don't you?

You can just imagine them rolling all the way down to the bottom, bumpity-bumpity-bump. They wouldn't have much water left by the time they got there, would they!'

They climbed slowly, pausing every few minutes to look at something in the hedgerow or on the high banks, listening to the roar of aircraft engines only a mile or two away, and wondering what the local people thought of this intrusion into their tranquillity. It must have been so quiet and peaceful here, in these leafy lanes with only the sheep and ponies to roam the empty moorland; now, with the airfield spread over such a vast area, with all the huts and hangars and other buildings sprawled over the grassland, with the planes themselves taking off and landing at all times of day or night, and the airmen thronging the pubs and inns, the villagers must feel as if they'd been suddenly transported to the middle of a city. And they were just as much at risk, she thought. Safe though this part might once have been – and she knew that people had trekked out from Plymouth every night, to sleep in barns or sheds or even under hedges, rather than stay in the threatened city – the fact that there was an airfield there was bound to attract the Germans' attention.

The sun seemed particularly bright this morning, she thought as they reached the top at last, and the air especially fresh. There had been a light shower of rain during the night and the autumn reds and golds of the trees along the edge of the narrow road glowed like the colours of a rich tapestry. There were blackberries, swollen by rain and ripened by the sun, growing in the hedge, and Alison picked a few and gave some to Hughie, wishing as they ate that she had brought a basket. As she paused, she realised that there was someone on the other side of the hedge and a moment later, a round, pretty face peeped through the branches and a voice, warm with the local Devon accent, said, 'Hello! I didn't know there was anyone there. Be you picking too?'

'Only a handful,' Alison said. 'I was just thinking how nice it would be to take some home, but I didn't bring anything to carry them in. My husband loves blackberry and apple pie.'

'You can have some of mine if you like,' the girl offered. 'I've got plenty.'

'Oh, I couldn't take yours! I only live a few minutes' walk away, anyway. I can come back later.'

The girl disappeared and a few seconds later Alison saw her coming through the gate from the field. They walked to meet each other, and Alison looked at the basket she held over her arm. It was almost filled with gleaming black fruit.

'We'm going to make jam,' the girl said. 'And bottle some, too. You can't let good food go to waste these days.' She smiled at Hughie. 'Do you like blackberries, my handsome? It looks as if you do!'

Alison looked down and laughed. Hughie's face was smeared with purple juice. 'He loves all sorts of fruit, but we don't get much these days unless it's home-grown. I ought to make jam too – I made quite a lot last year. Would it be all right to pick some?'

The girl nodded cheerfully. She looked a year or two younger than Alison, small and plump, with dark hair curling round her rosy cheeks, and brown eyes that flashed. 'Course it's all right. They'm free for all.' She gave Alison a curious glance. 'Have you just come to live here, then? Are you evacuated?'

'No, my husband's a pilot on the airfield. We're renting a cottage just along the road. You're local, aren't you?'

'Lived here all my life, in one of the farm cottages.' She indicated along the lane. 'My name's May. May Pretty-john.'

'What a lovely name,' Alison said, and held out her hand. 'I'm Alison Knight, and this is Hughie.'

May looked at her own hand, stained with blackberry juice, and laughed again. 'I'm too sticky to shake hands! Why don't you come home along of me, and I'll lend you a basket for some blackberries. You can meet Mother too. She'll be waiting to start the jam.'

'Oh yes, I'd like that.' They turned and began to walk along the lane, with Hughie capering along in front of them. Two aircraft flew over and they both looked up at them. Alison could see that neither was the familiar Spitfire or Hurricane, and remembered that Andrew had told her some of the newer Hawker Typhoons were arriving today and wondered if he were already up in one, trying it out. The squadron had been in two minds about the new planes, eager to try something new yet reluctant to let their beloved Spitfires go, and she knew he would be in the air at the very first opportunity.

'The airfield must have made a big difference to this area,' she remarked, trying to turn her mind away from the spurt of anxiety she always felt when she knew he was 'up'. 'Do you notice the noise much?'

'We did to start with. We'm used to it now.' May shrugged her plump shoulders. ''Tis war, isn't it? At least we've not been bombed out of house and home, like they poor souls in Plymouth. Terrible what's happened there, it is – terrible.'

'I know.' They walked in silence for a moment or two, then Alison said, 'Don't you have to go away, for war work?'

May shook her head. 'No, because I've got parents to look after, see. Father worked on the farm till he had an accident and hurt his back, and Mother can't look after him on her own, and Grandpa lives with us too so I've got exemption. But I do as much as I can for the war effort. I do some sewing for the Marine barracks down Plymouth, and I help collect sphagnum moss and lambswool for field dressings. 'Tis good for healing wounds, sphagnum moss.'

'Is it?' Alison wasn't even sure what sphagnum moss was. 'I don't think we have it in Lincolnshire, where I come from.'

'Lincolnshire?' May opened her eyes wide. 'That's right over on the other side of the country! Is it very different from round here?'

'Very different,' Alison said. 'Not nearly so hilly, for a start, and we don't have your moorland. But it's pretty in its own way.' She looked around, taking in the wide views down to Cornwall, with the tall chimney stacks of the mines standing out like pillars against the sky. 'It's beautiful here, though. I just wish it hadn't been a war that had brought us here.'

May gave her a sympathetic glance. 'It must be a worry for you, knowing your man's up there in the sky, fighting. Makes my heart turn over, it do, whenever there's an alert.'

'Yes, it does mine as well. But we have to get used to it, don't we. And at least our men come home at night.' She paused, leaving the words *if they're lucky* unspoken. 'Not like soldiers and sailors, away all the time.'

May nodded. 'I've got two cousins in the Navy. We never know where they be.' They arrived at a cottage with a garden in front of it filled with vegetables and flowers, and May laid her hand on the gate. 'Here we are. It'll be nice for Mother and Father to see someone new.'

The cottage was set back a little from the road, with a garden in front of it. At the back, the valley sloped down towards the village, although Alison could see a few fruit trees behind it and guessed there was a garden there too. No doubt every inch of it was productive, and she thought of the garden at her own cottage – the only part that seemed neglected – and made up her mind to do something about it as soon as possible.

She followed her new friend to the door. The path was paved with grey local stone and the plants on either side spilled over in profusion. Even though it was now autumn, there was still plenty of colour from the yellow poppies and dahlias that still grew amongst neat rows of newly sown winter vegetables. Along one edge there were soft fruit bushes and two apple trees, with red and golden fruits lit like lanterns, leaned towards each other over the gate itself.

'Who looks after all this?' she asked.

'My dad's an invalid, so Grandpa does a lot.' May nodded towards the cottage wall and Alison realised that there was an old man sitting there on a bench, a gnarled stick at his side. She paused and he narrowed his eyes and peered out through a network of wrinkles. He looked as if he had been lovingly carved from a piece of old oak.

'Who be this, then, maid?' His voice was surprisingly deep and gravelly, like the sound of a horse tramping over shingle.

''Tis a lady from the airfield, Grandpa, and this is her little boy, Hughie. Her husband's a pilot.' May showed him the basket of blackberries. 'Look at all these.'

He nodded with approval. 'Ah, good pickings. You want to get in as many as you can before the end of the month, mind. Devil spits on 'em then. Be there many sloes, did you see?'

'Yes, there's a good crop. I'll go out for them next. Is Mother in?' She turned to go through the low doorway, and Alison smiled at the old man and followed her into the cottage, blinking in the dim light.

The front door led straight into the living room, which was larger than she had expected, with stone-built walls and a large inglenook fireplace. Beyond that she glimpsed a kitchen, with a cooking range and a deep white sink. A large dresser stood along one wall, its shelves brightened by an array of coloured crockery, and a jug of chrysanthemums stood on the wide windowsill beside a pie which was gently steaming through a hole in its golden crust, as if it had just been taken from the oven.

A comfortably built woman was preparing vegetables at the sink, and as she turned, Alison saw that she was an almost exact replica of May, as round and rosy as an apple but with white curls instead of dark. The same smile beamed out, and Alison felt instantly at home.

'My dear soul!' May's mother exclaimed, wiping her hands on her flowery apron as she bustled through. 'You didn't tell me you were bringing visitors, May. Come you in, my dear, and sit down. I'll make a cup of tea. And I dare say this young man would like a glass of milk, wouldn't you, my handsome?'

'Oh no,' Alison protested. 'I don't want to take your rations. But I'd like a cup of water, if that's all right.'

'Well, you couldn't do better than our water,' Mrs Prettyjohn declared. 'Fresh from our own well, it be. But why don't you have a drop of good milk, from our own cow? You look as if you could do with some building up, if you don't mind me saying so.'

'Oh, I can't resist milk,' Alison said, laughing. 'Especially the milk you have here. It's so rich – no wonder you have such wonderful cream.'

'And we still make our own,' the countrywoman nodded, pouring milk from a large blue and white striped jug. 'You must take some back with you.' She handed Alison a brimming cup and took a plate from the dresser. 'I've just this minute taken a few rock cakes out of the oven. Here you are, young man, you can take these outside and share them with May's Grandpa. I dare say he'll find something interesting to show you. I'll carry the milk, in case you spill it.' Hughie glanced at Alison, who nodded at him, then followed her out to the garden. Coming back, she said, 'I heard young May here tell her Grandpa that you're from the airfield. You'll be living in Coombe Cottage, I reckon. I heard as someone had taken it on.'

'Yes, that's right. I thought there might be more of us wives renting houses in the village, but I haven't met anyone else yet. Most of the pilots aren't married, of course. They're all so young . . .' Her voice faded as she thought of the boys, no more than eighteen or twenty, who made up most of the squadron. So many had been killed already, without ever having the chance to marry. And there were frighteningly few of those who were older, like Andrew and Tubby, who had been in the RAF before the war began.

'There, you'm cold!' Mrs Prettyjohn exclaimed. ''Tis coming in out of the sun. Come and sit near the fire, do.'

'No, really. I'm not cold – just a goose walking over my grave.' Alison sipped her milk. 'May told me you're going to make jam with the blackberries.'

'That's right. I expect you know the Government lets us have extra sugar for jam. I've made a lot already this summer.' She opened the dresser door. 'There you are – strawberry, raspberry and gooseberry on that shelf and plum and greengage on that one. And there's the bottled fruit as well. That should see us right through the winter.'

'It looks lovely.' Alison thought of her own cupboards, almost empty but for a few tins and jars from the village shop. 'I couldn't get much fruit to bottle this year. I could still make some jam, though, if I can get the sugar.'

'Of course you could, my dear. 'Tis too late for the soft fruits, but you can pick some blackberries, like our May here. They go best with a few apples, mind, to help the jam set. We'll let you have a few off our tree, there's plenty to spare. And take a pot of raspberry jam home with you.' She took one from the cupboard and set it on the table.

Alison gazed at her helplessly. 'You're so kind. But I can't take your jam. I really can't.'

'Bless you, my dear, 'tis only a pot of jam. Of course you can take it.' Mrs Prettyjohn paused and looked at her seriously. ''Tis little enough to do, my dear, when your man's fighting for us all. You take it, and welcome.'

'Thank you.' Alison felt her eyes mist with tears. She looked at the pot of jam, gleaming with ruby colour. Outside, she could hear Hughie's piping chatter and the deeper tones of the old man. She realised suddenly how lonely she had felt for the past few days, so far away from all she knew, and leaned her head on her hand.

Mrs Prettyjohn looked at her with understanding. Her voice was as soft and warm as a buttered scone. 'That's all right, my dear. You'm welcome whenever you want to drop by. There's always someone here.' There was a sudden banging on the ceiling above their heads and she looked up. 'That's my hubby, that is. I dare say he wants to know who's down here. Perhaps you wouldn't mind popping up to say hello later on. He do love to see a visitor.'

'Yes, of course,' Alison said a little nervously. She hadn't had much experience of sick people, and had no idea how ill May's father might be. Still, she couldn't refuse, not after May and her mother had been so kind.

'He'm all right in himself,' Mrs Prettyjohn said, as if reading her mind. 'But he fell off a haycart, see, and broke his back. Paralysed from the waist down, he be, but there's nothing wrong with his head. We'd like to get him downstairs so he can be more part of the family, like, but if we put a bed down here there won't be any room for the rest of us! So us has to ask visitors to go upstairs to give him a bit of company.'

'Yes, of course I'll go,' Alison said, feeling slightly ashamed of her reluctance. She set down her cup and made to stand up.

'Oh, no need to go right away,' Mrs Prettyjohn said, gesturing to her to sit down again. 'Plenty of time to see he another day. You'll be wanting to get home for your dinner. Do your man come home for his?'

'No, he stays in the mess. But you're right, I should go – you're getting your own meal ready.' She got up and hesitated. 'Will you be making your jam this afternoon?'

'We will. You come along too if you like, maid, and you can help. Then, if you like to pick some of your own fruit, our May can come and help you – that's if you'd like her to. Us don't want to push in.'

'Oh, you wouldn't be!' Alison turned to the girl. 'Would you do that, May? Or would it be taking up too much of your time? I know you've got your job as well.'

'Oh, I can find the time,' the dark-haired girl said, smiling. 'But you need to make sure you can get your sugar first. And you'll need to get it soon, because the black-berries will be over by the end of the month.'

'I know – the Devil spits on them!' Alison moved towards the door. 'It's been lovely to meet you, and thank you for the milk. I'll be back this afternoon.' She ducked out into the sunshine, and found Hughie with the old man, clearing leaves from the path and heaping them in a corner of the garden. 'Come on, Hughie, we've got to go now. Say thank you. We'll see you again soon, Mr Prettyjohn.'

The bent figure straightened. 'And welcome you'll be, whenever you like to call,' he said. 'We'm happy to see you, maid, and the liddle tacker, too.' He nodded, and once again she felt the tears prick her eyes.

Walking back along the lane, she felt as if the sun had suddenly grown warmer. I hadn't realised how lonely I felt, she thought. Even though Andrew's home most evenings, and he often brings some of the others with him, I've had no friends to pass the days with. And I haven't even been into another house here until today.

She looked at the hedgerows, with their thick clusters of black, juicy berries. I'll go along to the shop as soon as they open after lunch, she thought, and ask about sugar. And I'll take a basket with me when I go back to the cottage this afternoon. At the very least, I can make a blackberry pudding for Andrew's dinner tonight.

The low thrum of an aircraft engine sounded in her ears and she looked up to see the two Typhoons coming in to land. Well, if one had been Andrew, he was safe for the moment. And as she opened the gate to her own tiny front garden, she felt a little surge of relief lift her heart.

She hoped that the other one had been Tubby.

'Home-made jam!' Andrew said a few days later, gazing at the little row of jars, filled with purple preserves. 'That's marvellous, darling. And a blackberry and apple pie as well. What a clever wife I've got!'

His words were cheerful enough, but there was an odd, brittle edge to his voice and Alison gave him a curious glance, aware at once that something had happened on the airfield. Briefly, she wondered whether to ask him, but dismissed the idea. Andrew would tell her in his own time, if he meant to tell her at all. She knew that there were some things that he would never tell her – things he *couldn't* tell her – and she remembered Tubby's words about secrets.

She'd been disappointed that so far the rotund pilot hadn't taken up her invitation to come and see her. He'd been to the cottage once or twice, with Andrew and some of the other pilots, but she had never had a chance to be alone with him, to ask him if the nightmare was still with him or if, with the change of airfield, it might have receded. She'd tried to catch his eye the last time he'd been here, but he'd simply grinned cheerily at her, as if there had never been any conversation between them, and she'd known that she couldn't introduce the subject. It had to be left to Tubby himself.

She picked up one of the jars of jam. 'Next year, I'll make more. And bottle some fruit, too. I was thinking, Andrew, we could dig up the back garden and grow our own food. It's what we're supposed to be doing anyway, isn't it? Digging for Victory. D'you suppose the owners would mind?'

'I could find out.' He kissed her and drew her into the living room. The edge was still in his voice, and she could feel the tension in his body. 'What are you thinking of growing? And who's going to be doing all the digging? I can't promise that I—'

'No, I know you couldn't do that,' she said quickly. 'You don't get enough time at home as it is.' Andrew was only able to come home in the evenings, and seldom even stayed all night. 'May says her grandfather will come and dig it over for me, and after that I'll be able to manage it for myself. He'll tell me what to plant and when.'

'You seem to have made some good friends there,' Andrew observed, throwing himself into a chair and pulling her on to his lap. 'You'll have to take me along to meet them sometime soon.'

'They'd like that. They really appreciate what you and the others are doing, you know, even though the airfield has made life rather noisy for them.' She rested against him. 'Is anyone else coming round tonight? Tubby, or the new ones?'

'No, I thought we'd have some time to ourselves.' His arms tightened around her. 'I don't get enough time with you to want to share you every evening. I just want a quiet few hours on our own, like an old married couple.'

'That's lovely.' She wished he would talk to her, tell her what was wrong. There was something she needed to tell him, too, but she couldn't do it while there was this hidden

49

tension between them. She made her voice bright. 'Just what I want, too. And I'll let Hughie stay up a bit later than usual – it's lovely for him to have his daddy at home.' She leaned her head on his shoulder. 'I was wondering today if we should have a party at the weekend, if there aren't any alarms. What do you think?'

Andrew paused for a moment before answering, then nodded. 'Yes. It's a good idea. These new youngsters, Hazelwood and Sinclair, could do with a bit of a breather. They've been practising with the Typhoons till their ears drop off.' He frowned. 'The chaps aren't all that keen on this new plane, you know. There've been a lot of problems with it – carbon monoxide in the cockpit, for a start, just as if it weren't already too hot inside, and quite a few engine failures. They'll get sorted out eventually, I know, but we feel a bit like guinea pigs at the moment. Still, it's good to be flying a fighter-bomber at last. Gives us the best of both worlds.'

Alison heard this with some disquiet. Andrew usually kept problems like this to himself. Perhaps he was aware that she knew there was something wrong, and hoped to distract her with talk of difficulties with the new aircraft. She decided not to comment and asked instead, 'Are the two new boys ready to go out with the squadron yet?'

'Next week. That's why it'd be a good idea to give them a bit of a shindig. Not that the chaps don't have a brawl in the mess most evenings, but something more civilised might go down well. What are you planning?'

'Well, I thought I might get May to come in and help me with the food. She might do some baking beforehand, if we can get the rations.'

'That's the stuff. They'd sell you a pat or two of butter too, wouldn't they, and a few eggs and some cream?'

'They might. They'd rather give it to me, though. Honestly, you've no idea how generous they are, Andrew. I know they have their own cow and hens but they don't have to give it all away. I hardly dare mention a thing for fear Mrs Prettyjohn will wrap it up and press it into my hands.'

'Well, why not come to an arrangement? Tell them that if they offer you something you'll accept it – as long as it's not too much – but if you actually ask for something, they've got to sell it to you. And then don't give them too many opportunities to offer first!'

Alison laughed. 'I'll do that. And I'll pay May for her help. How many shall we ask?'

'Well, all the squadron, of course. Robin and Jackie, and all the rest – you know them already. But we've got some Poles coming soon – might ask them along, if they're here by the weekend.'

'Poles?' She looked at him blankly for a moment, then her face cleared. 'Oh, you mean Polish airmen! Oh yes, ask them as well. I just hope we've got room for everyone.'

'You don't need enough room at a party,' he said. 'You need not *quite* enough – much more fun! It'll be quite a celebration. A welcome, I mean, for the new bods.'

'Mm.' Alison looked at him, a small smile tugging at the corners of her mouth. 'Actually, it might be more of a celebration than you think.'

'Why?' He twisted his neck to peer into her face. 'What's happening? Is someone coming to stay? Your parents – mine? You haven't said anything before.'

Alison gave him a mysterious look. 'Someone's coming to stay, but it's not my parents, or yours. Still, it's not quite certain yet. You'll have to wait and see.' She kissed his nose and swung her feet to the floor. 'And now you can go out in the garden and play with your son while I get our dinner ready and start thinking about the party. You do realise we're on rations, don't you. It won't exactly be a lavish spread.'

'Some of Mrs Prettyjohn's bread and your home-made jam will do,' he said, trying unsuccessfully to pull her back on to his lap. 'And I want to know who's coming to stay. It's not fair, keeping me in the dark like this. I shouldn't have to worry about things when I'm flying my new Typhoon.' His plaintive tone had no effect on Alison, who merely ruffled his thick, dark hair.

'It's nothing to worry about,' she said heartlessly. 'You'll be pleased, I can tell you that – and that's all I am going to tell you. Just wait and see.'

She whisked away into the kitchen, leaving her husband lying back in the armchair, warmed by her affection. I don't know what I'd do if I couldn't come home in the evenings, he thought. I don't know what I'd do if I hadn't got Alison to make things bearable.

It had cost him enormous effort to come into the house that evening as if he were a normal man, coming home from a normal day's work. As if nothing bad had happened. As if he'd enjoyed every moment, just as Alison seemed to have enjoyed every moment of her day, picking black-berries, making jam and pies, planning a party. And this surprise visitor, who was presumably going to be here in time for the party.

Well, whoever it was, she had obviously made up her mind it was to be a nice surprise, and God knew he could do with one of those at the moment. And somehow he was going to have to tell her what had happened today.

He closed his eyes, seeing it all again in his mind and trying to find the right words. He knew just what a shock it would be. Their cosy evening would evaporate into sadness; at the very least, she'd probably want to cancel the party. But Andrew knew they must go ahead with it. Nobody could be allowed to grieve for too long, or they would never take to the air again.

That afternoon, he and Tubby had been on patrol along

the Channel and had been surprised by a pair of enemy Heinkels. In the ensuing fight, Tubby Marsh had shot one down into the sea. But even as his yell of exultation had sounded in Andrew's ears, a third had dived on him, straight out of the sun.

His aircraft disintegrating in a ball of flame, Tubby had spiralled into the waves below.

'Tubby?' Alison said in a small, disbelieving voice. She stared at Andrew as if she suspected him of playing a cruel joke. 'It can't be true. Not Tubby.'

'I'm afraid it is,' Andrew said. She was back on his lap and he held her in his arms but she lay stiffly against him, not responding. 'I saw him go down myself. There was no chance.'

'But you've been together since you first started at Cranwell,' she whispered. 'He's never even had any accidents. He's a brilliant flyer, you've always said so.'

'Not in his hearing!' Andrew said, thinking of the insults and banter he and Tubby had shared over the years. He pulled his wife's head gently down to his shoulder and stroked her hair. 'Darling, I'm afraid it doesn't make any difference how good a flyer you are, when someone comes out of the sun and shoots you down.'

He stopped, wondering if he had said too much. Alison knew the dangers he faced, but they seldom discussed them. Like the pilots, she ignored them and pretended to herself that they didn't exist. But when something like this happened, pretence was impossible and sometimes it couldn't be recovered. Andrew had known pilots – excellent flyers, too – who had broken down at that point and been unable to face it again. Some had finished up in hospital, some were now working at desks, and one had shot himself.

It was as bad for wives and families, and they had no control over it at all. They just had to endure.

'You don't have to worry about me, you know,' he said. 'I've had my crash.'

Alison was silent for a moment. Then she said, 'You know that doesn't make any difference.' She raised her eyes and gave him a steady look. 'It's all right, Andrew. I understand the risks. Every time I say goodbye to you, I wonder if it might be the last time. But there's nothing we can do about it. We've just got to go on.' She paused. 'What about the party? We can't possibly have it now.' She looked at him accusingly. 'You knew this, and you let me go on chattering about parties. Oh, Andrew!'

'No,' he said forcefully. 'We must have it. Cancelling it would just make everyone even more miserable, and that's dangerous. A miserable pilot isn't taking the care he should, and if he's upset over something like what happened to Tubby, he's likely to be frightened as well. His reactions aren't as good, he's not in the right frame of mind, and he's at even greater risk. A frightened pilot is a dangerous pilot – how often have you heard me say that?'

Alison stared at him, remembering how she had quoted those very words to Tubby. How she had tried in vain to persuade him to confess his fears, to tell Andrew or to go to the station doctor. But in the end, it hadn't been fear that had killed him. As Andrew said, it didn't matter how good a flyer you were, if someone came out of the sun and shot you down.

If Tubby had had time to know anything, he must have known that. He had known, in the end, that he hadn't died a coward. She hoped that it had been some comfort to him, in those last terrible moments.

'We've got to have the party,' Andrew repeated quietly.

'Yes. All right.' She looked at him, trying to gauge the

depth of his own distress. 'Oh, Andrew, it's awful. Poor Tubby. He was your best friend.'

'I know.' But he was still taut, his sorrow held like a tightly wound ball of elastic deep inside him. She knew that he would not let go easily. He was too used to this, too used to keeping his emotions under control when pilots were killed. It happened too often.

But this was Tubby. This was the man he had started his RAF career with, the man he had stayed with all these years, the man who was as close to him as a brother.

She made up her mind. He would have to hear her own news sometime, and perhaps it would help him to hear it now. She wound her arms loosely about his neck and smiled at him a little tremulously. 'Well, perhaps I won't wait till then to tell you who our visitor is. I'll tell you now. Although I'm not sure we can really call him a visitor. Or her.'

'You mean there are two of them?' He seemed relieved to have the subject changed. 'Why can't we call them visitors, then? How long are they staying?' A sudden thought struck him. 'We're not getting evacuees, are we?'

'No – and there aren't two of them, either. Not as far as I know, anyway.' Her lips twitched. 'It's just that I don't know yet whether it will be a him or a her.'

'You don't know?' He stared at her. 'What on earth are you talking about? For heaven's sake, you must know who it is!' He gave her a suspicious look. 'Come on, out with it. What are you laughing at?'

'Can't you guess?' she asked, her joy bubbling up even through the sorrow she felt for Tubby. 'Someone coming to stay – not a visitor but someone coming to *live* with us – and I don't know whether it's going to be a him or her?' She laid some extra emphasis on the words. 'I don't know if it will be a *boy* or *girl*.'

There was a brief silence. Then Andrew said, 'Are you telling me that we're – we're having another baby?'

'*Yes*!' Her smile spread over her face. 'Yes, we're having another baby, Andrew! It's due next May. Or early June.' Her smile turned to laughter. 'What do you think? Isn't it wonderful?'

'Wonderful,' he said. 'Yes, it is. It's wonderful.' He kissed her and rested his cheek against her head. 'Another baby. Another little boy or girl that *we've* made . . . it's terrific news, darling. And an even better reason for having our party.'

Chapter Five

Alison wasn't the only one to wonder if they ought to be having a party so soon after Tubby's death.

Ben and Tony discussed it as they sat in the mess over a pint of beer. Neither had been in the air at the time, but they'd known as soon as the squadron came back that they'd lost someone. Often, when this happened, the missing pilot telephoned from somewhere else in the country where he'd been forced to land, and returned – with or without his aircraft – to jeers and catcalls. But this time, everyone knew that Tubby would not be coming back.

'He was Andrew's best friend,' Tony said. 'I don't know how he can still laugh and joke with the others. I don't know how anyone can.'

'No, but we've got to do it just the same,' Ben replied. 'You know that as well as I do. We've seen it so many times already. There's no time to sit around weeping and wailing. We have to get up there and fight, and thinking about what happened to Tubby – and what might happen to us – isn't going to help.'

'I know.' They were silent for a moment or two, then Tony asked, 'Have you lost anyone yet, Ben? Friends, or anyone in your family, I mean?'

Ben shook his head. 'We've been lucky so far. But there are four of us in it now . . .' His voice faded slightly as he thought of the odds against all four of them coming through the war unscathed, then he said, 'What about you?'

'I had a cousin in the Navy. He went down in the *Hood*. My aunt, his mother, died soon afterwards. She was widowed in the 'flu epidemic in 1918 and he was the only child. She just didn't seem to be able to go on living.'

Ben could find nothing to say. Behind every death, there must be an equally tragic story. It wasn't just the men – the soldiers, the sailors, the airmen – who lost their lives, it was the huge gap they left behind, in the lives of those who loved them. And some of those people would never recover.

'I know a girl whose fiancé was killed,' he said after a minute or two. 'She was pregnant – they'd been going to get married, but he went away without even knowing about the baby. Her parents turned her out and she came to live with my people as a maid.'

'I suppose she had to give the baby away,' Tony observed. 'That's what usually happens, isn't it?'

'No, she didn't, as it happens. She kept it – it's a little girl – and they're still with my father and mother.' Ben hesitated. 'I'm her godfather, actually. She's rather a nice girl – the mother, I mean. And Hope's a little sweetheart.'

Tony gave him a curious look, but before either could speak again, Andrew came over, bringing a tall, fair-haired man in the uniform of a Polish pilot. He was very upright and correct, standing almost to attention as he came to a halt beside their chairs.

'This is Stefan Dabrowski,' Andrew said, and they stood up to shake hands. 'He's joining the squadron.' He didn't need to add, *in Tubby's place*. The three men nodded at each other and sought for something to say.

'Have you been in England long?' Ben asked at last.

'Since just after the beginning of the war. As soon as Hitler invaded, we came here so that we could fight him and win back our country.' His English was very precise and he spoke with a quiet purpose that slightly startled Ben. He was used to the jovial bravado of the British and Canadian pilots he had met, with their breezy enjoyment of flying, as if it were still all rather a game, despite the fact that the 'game' was deadly enough to kill their fellow pilots on a regular basis, and he shared their desire to score as many 'kills' as possible. But this Pole seemed to have a deeper motivation. It was as if he understood more than Ben about war and its meaning.

'I can't imagine what that would be like,' Ben said at last. 'Losing your country, I mean. I know we're fighting to stop Hitler invading us, and I know he's nearly done it once or twice, but he's not succeeded and I hope to God he doesn't. But for you . . .'

Stefan Dabrowski nodded. 'It's different when you have seen your neighbours overrun, and know that it's your turn next. The march of jackboots through your streets – the raiding and the killing, having nowhere to hide.' His pale, ice-grey eyes glittered. 'I mean to kill as many of them as I can,' he said quietly. 'And so do my friends. They may have taken our country from us, but we shall take it back, and with interest.'

There was a brief silence, then Andrew said, 'And good luck to you, Stefan. Now, the reason I've brought you to meet these two characters is partly to get it over with as quickly as possible, and partly to invite you all to my house for a bit of a knees-up on Saturday night. It's time you saw civilisation again. My wife's going to lay on some bread and jam, maybe a sausage or two, and we'll put on some music and roll up the carpet for some dancing. Not that there's much room, but I dare say you won't mind having to cuddle up a bit.'

'So long as you ask some girls as well,' Robin Fairbanks observed, joining them with a pint in his hand. 'I'm not cuddling up to any of these oiks.'

'Oh, there'll be girls,' Andrew said airily. 'I'm asking a few of the WAAFs. But no hanky-panky, mind. This is to be a refined party, not the sort of brawl we have here in the mess.'

Ben grinned. He'd been startled at his first encounter with a mess 'brawl', with the airmen hurling themselves at each other rather as they hurled their planes about in the sky, somersaulting over rows of chairs and tables and ending in a struggling heap on the floor. It had all seemed rather juvenile to the eighteen-year-old not long out of school, who had expected a little more gravitas from senior officers. But he'd soon come to recognise that this was a vital way of letting off steam, recovering from the strains and tensions of risking your life in the air, watching a plane you had destroyed explode beneath you, and coming back to find that yet another of your friends had lived his last day.

'Will your wife mind having a lot of idiots invading her house?' Robin enquired seriously. 'Does she realise what she's letting herself in for?'

'Oh yes, she's got plenty of experience. We've been married four years now, you know – been at Manston and Tangmere and one or two other stations. She's well used to RAF types.'

'And she's *still* prepared to let us into her home?' Robin said, shaking his head in mock wonder. 'Well, so be it. I'll do my best to keep order.'

Andrew grinned. 'You won't have to. Alison can keep order. In fact, she'd make a very good Group Commander. Now look, I'll leave Stefan here in your capable hands. Treat him gently, mind – they're damned good flyers, the Polish.' He went off, leaving the small group to settle themselves in armchairs and look at each other.

'So how long have you been flying?' the Pole asked Ben and Tony. 'You look very young.'

'I'm twenty,' Ben said with dignity. 'And Tony here's an old man of twenty-one – had his birthday on our last station. Got the key of the door and everything. We've been flying two years.'

'Only just joined here, though,' Tony added. 'Haven't started ops flying yet. Hoping to do so next week.'

'I don't think there's any question about that,' Robin observed, filling his pipe with tobacco. 'All three of you will be up.' He glanced at Stefan. 'It's unusual to have one of you chaps in with us, though. You usually stick with your own squadrons.'

Stefan looked across at the far corner of the mess, where some others wearing the same uniform were drinking steadily, as though competing for some prize. 'Andrew asked if he could borrow one of us. I volunteered.'

'Volunteered!' Robin exclaimed. 'It's easy to tell you're not English. That's the first thing we learn when we join up – never volunteer for anything.'

The Pole gave him an unsmiling glance. 'I volunteered because your squadron is the best on Harrowbeer and I want to fly with the best. There is then much more chance of killing Germans.'

'Well, yes, of course there is,' Robin said, slightly taken aback by the pilot's intensity. 'That's what we all want to do.' He glanced at the other two and then said, 'I'd better be off too. Things to do, you know. Find a clean shirt for Saturday night, that sort of thing.' He stuck his pipe into his mouth and sauntered off, leaving the three newest members of the squadron together.

Stefan watched him. 'I'm afraid your friend doesn't like me. I take it all too seriously – I let my feelings show too much. I don't have the British stiff upper lip.' He drank from his glass and then set it down with a small thump. His voice shook a little. 'But if he had seen what I have seen – people forced to wear yellow stars on their sleeves and live

61

behind brick walls, people shot down in the streets, just for daring to walk along them – then perhaps he would take the same attitude. You don't really know what war is in this country. You have no idea at all.'

'Hold on,' Ben protested. 'We might not have been invaded, but we've been through some pretty foul times. Our cities blitzed almost out of existence, thousands of civilian casualties, men lost at sea. And Dunkirk too, when our whole Army could have been lost if we hadn't managed to rescue them. Not to mention the Battle of Britain. I think we've got a pretty good idea of what war is about.'

They regarded each other for a moment, and then Stefan inclined his blond head. 'Yes. You have an idea, certainly. But at least you know your families are as safe as everyone else. You don't live with the fear that they may have been taken to concentration camps. You can write them a letter and they will answer. You can pick up a telephone and hear their voices.' His voice shook a little, and he stood up and clicked his heels together. 'I'm sorry. This is not the place for such talk. We're supposed to relax here, not upset each other. I'll go to my room.'

He turned and walked away, his back as stiff as if an iron rod had been inserted in his jacket. The other two looked at each other and Ben blew out his cheeks.

'Well!' he said. 'I know he's right, but he's not exactly the sort of company you want at a party, is he? I just hope he leaves his cloak of misery behind on Saturday evening.'

They got up and drifted over to join a crowd of pilots who were roaring with laughter at Duncan Aird, a tall, rangy Scotsman with a pawky sense of humour and an inexhaustible fund of dirty jokes. For a while, they tried to forget about Tubby Marsh's death, and the passionate intensity of Stefan's words. But it wasn't long before Tony wandered off and disappeared through the door, and a few minutes later Ben followed and found him making his way towards the huts where they had their rooms.

Above them, the stars hung in a huge, inverted bowl of darkest blue. There was no 'bomber's moon' and except for the occasional hoot of an owl the night was silent. There were no lights to be seen anywhere, either on the bleak wilderness of the moor, or from the towns of Tavistock to the north and the ruins of Plymouth to the south. The darkness was almost solid.

Yet there was no sense of peace. It was as if the profound darkness and silence were a threat rather than a reassurance. At any moment, the alarm could sound and send men scurrying to their aircraft. Or a flight of enemy planes could come screaming out of that huge inverted bowl, scattering bombs and gunfire over the entire airfield. The men they were growing to know, the men they would fly with, even they themselves, could all be killed in the moment it took to visualise the scene.

'I think we know what war is,' Ben said at last.

May was delighted to help out at the party and accepted the offer of payment without demur. Alison understood that the situation between them was now accepted; on the one part was friendship, with favours given and received on both sides, on the other a purely business relationship. Apples, eggs and cream could be offered as gifts, or requested and paid for, and the servant was worthy of her hire.

'Not that I think of you as a servant,' Alison said quickly. 'We had a cook and a couple of maids at home – my parents' home, I mean. But that was before the war. My mother doesn't have any help now, except for a village woman who comes in three days a week. Most of them are doing war work.'

They had been making bread in the Prettyjohns' kitchen

as they talked. It was a long-drawn-out but satisfying process, with time while the dough was 'resting' to complete other tasks, such as bottling plums or making more jam.

Although Alison had known the family for less than a fortnight, she felt almost as at home in their cottage as she did in her own. The rooms were comfortably cluttered, with old-fashioned ornaments and china on the shelves and a row of gleaming horse-brasses hanging from the oak mantelpiece. Sagging armchairs stood on either side of the fireplace, piled with cushions and, as often as not, occupied by the two cats, Ginger and Blackbird. The kitchen was always warm and smelled of cooking, either the bread they were making now, the fruit and sugar for jam, or whatever was being prepared for that day's dinner.

Hughie, too, enjoyed going to the Prettyjohns' cottage. He had struck up a firm friendship with old Mr Prettyjohn and the two spent hours out in the garden, tidying and digging, or just sitting in the sun holding long conversations. Alison often thought that Hughie sounded like an old man himself, earnestly discussing the ways of birds and animals or other mysteries of the natural world.

'My daddy flies up the sky,' she heard him say one day. 'He can go right up to the sun. He fights Germans.'

Alison paused in what she was doing, wondering how on earth he knew that. She and Andrew never discussed the war in front of him, thinking that at three years old he was too young to understand. But it was inevitable that he would pick up something from the talk that was all around, from the people they met in the village street and the airmen who came to the house to drink tea, to the wireless with its talks and news and comedy programmes like *ITMA* and the Charlie Chester show. It might seem to go over his head, but he was bound to hear and repeat some of it. He probably didn't even know what a German was.

By now, Alison had also met May's father, William Prettyjohn, who spent his time in bed upstairs. She had been relieved to find that his room wasn't a bit like a sickroom – his wife and daughter had done their best to make it as much like a living room as possible, with chairs for the rest of the family to sit in when they were spending time with him. The bed was close to the window so that he could look down into the garden and across the fields, and his view stretched all the way across the Tavy valley to Cornwall. Beside the bed was a small table and a bookshelf, and it was obvious that he was a great reader. He also oversaw the work in the garden, planning what would be grown and where it should be planted, and conferring with his own father, the gnarled old man who did most of the work.

'I may be paralysed,' he said to Alison the first time they met, 'but that don't mean I can't do my bit.' He looked at her with bright eyes. 'I dare say you'm somethin' of a reader, too.'

'Well, I do like reading,' she agreed, surprised by some of the titles on his bookshelf. He had all Dickens's works and most of Trollope's and Jane Austen's, as well as Wilkie Collins and Conan Doyle. He caught her glance and his mouth twitched.

'Us was lucky to have a teacher down in Buckland school that knew what a good book was,' he said. 'Not like they read today, all these comics and Enid Blyton. And I've had time to catch up since me fall.'

'Have you read all of them?' she asked. Although she had read Jane Austen and some of Dickens, she had never tried Collins or Trollope and felt slightly ashamed.

'Over and over again,' he answered. 'You can always go back to a good book, you know.'

Since then they'd had several chats. Alison had borrowed *Barchester Towers* and promised to look out for books for him. He wanted some more of Eden Philpotts' books, explaining that this was a Devon author who wrote very fine tales about Dartmoor. ''Tis good to read about places you know,' he said. 'And he've got good things to say, too. *Understanding* things. He makes you think a bit. I get plenty of time for thinking, these days.'

Alison had time for thinking too, as she picked black-berries, made jam and bread, played with Hughie and tried to dream up interesting meals to give to Andrew when he came home in the evenings. It wasn't always easy, because she never knew for certain that he would be in. Sometimes the squadron was kept busy flying almost all day, and as soon as the mechanics had made sure the planes were fit to fly again, they could be back in the sky. Mostly, they were patrolling the Channel, guarding both naval and merchant ships, but an alarm meant they were up within minutes, and then a battle would ensue and those on the ground could do no more than wait anxiously until it was over and the planes were safely back. Since Hitler had invaded Russia, however, there were fewer raids over Britain and the work of the fighters was mostly confined to patrols, shipping protection and accompanying bombers on their own raids.

Still, as often as not, there would be one or more missing when the squadrons returned. And although, as now, the loss seemed almost too painful to bear sometimes, she had learned, as they had all had to learn, to put away her sorrow and concentrate on the joy.

It was all anyone could do.

Chapter Six

There were no alarms on Saturday evening, but the squadron had been flying all day and by the time Andrew arrived home, Hughie was fast asleep in bed and Alison and May had laid out a spread of sausage rolls and sandwiches. There was plenty of beer and a couple of bottles of sherry, together with two large jugs of orange squash. The gramophone was ready, with some fresh needles and a pile of dance records beside it, and the square of carpet in the front part of the living room had been rolled back to expose the floorboards, which May had insisted on polishing.

'I don't want you coming here to clean and polish,' Alison protested, trying to take the cloth away from her hand, but May held on to it firmly.

'If you'm going to pay me to be here, I ought to be doing something. I don't want to be paid for sitting doing nothing.' She glinted a look at Alison from her dark brown eyes. 'Besides, you didn't ought to be doing this sort of work, in your condition.'

'My condition!' Alison exclaimed, feeling the blush rise up from her neck. 'What are you talking about?'

'Well, I didn't want to say anything because I might be talking out of turn, but Mother thinks you'm expecting. She can always tell, she says, when a woman's in her third month. So you can ask me to mind my own business if you like, but—'

'No, it's all right. I'm just surprised, that's all.' Alison glanced down at her slim figure. 'I'm sure there's nothing to see yet, and I haven't been sick or anything – in fact, I didn't really think I could be pregnant, until I saw the doctor. But you're right. Perhaps I ought to have come to see your mother first!'

May sat back on her heels and beamed up at her. 'Well, there's some nice news. So it's all right if I tell Mother, is it? She'll be well pleased, and so will Father. And Grandpa, too. 'Twill be nice to have another little tacker about the place.' She hesitated, then added a trifle anxiously, 'You'm pleased about it, I hope? And Mr Knight?'

'Oh yes, we're thrilled. We hadn't intended it to happen just yet, not with the way things are, with the war and everything. I mean, you wonder if it's right to bring children into the world just now, don't you? But it all seems to be going on for so long, we just didn't want to wait any longer to give Hughie a brother or sister. And so here I am.' She laid her hand on her flat stomach. 'It's rather hard to believe, that's all. That there's a new human being just starting to grow in here. It's like a sort of miracle.' She laughed, feeling suddenly embarrassed. 'I suppose everyone thinks that, yet it's happening every day. It's not even as though it's my first time.'

'That don't stop it being a miracle.' May finished her polishing and got up. 'If you ask me, all life's a miracle and that's why we've got to try to look after it. From a tiny baby to the whole world.' She took her cloth and tin of polish out to the kitchen and put them away in the cupboard. 'There, that's done, and it looks all the better for it. Smells good, too.'

'It's lovely. Thank you, May.' Alison went to the window and looked out along the narrow lane. 'They should be arriving any minute – oh, here comes Andrew now.'

Andrew wheeled his bicycle up the path and leaned it

against the front of the house. The Morris 8 had been put into a corner of one of the barns at the nearby farm, for use only on high days and holidays, and only then when the petrol could be obtained. Most of the time, like all the other men on the station, he used the cycle he'd been issued with.

He had taken his time cycling home this evening. His mind had been filled with thoughts of the friend he had lost, the gap that had been left in his life. He had been disconcerted by the depth of his feeling for Tubby Marsh, and didn't really know how to deal with the grief he was experiencing. Accustomed as he was to losing pilots – particularly during the Battle of Britain, when he had had his own crash, but also since then – he had also grown accustomed to buttoning his feelings down tightly beneath the surface. But with Tubby, it was different. With Tubby, he had lost his best friend – almost, as Alison had said, a brother – and, it seemed, a part of himself.

To make it worse, he had seen that last desperate downward spiral into the sea. And he had heard Tubby's screams in his ears.

Cycling home along the darkened lane, Andrew had found himself trembling, so violently that he had been forced to stop and lean on a field gate for support. He rested his arms along the top rail and bent his head, wondering if he was going to be sick. The nausea passed slowly, and he lifted his head again, staring out over the twilit landscape. The hedges were filled with twittering birds, settling down for the night, and he wondered dully what the war meant to them. Did they notice the noise, or did they accustom themselves to it? Did they begrudge the loss of so much habitat on the moor, when the airfield had been built, or did they welcome the increase in food scraps from the kitchens and canteens? Did any of the things that humans did, to the world and to each other, matter to them or did they simply adapt?

He became aware of a snuffling and snorting in the field. It was part of a large farm and pigs were kept here, to provide bacon and pork for Harrowbeer and for the national meat ration. The farmer and his son collected the waste from the kitchens at the airfield, and Alison had told him that the farmer would often find cutlery mixed up with it. You could hear the pigs playing with the knives and forks in the troughs when they had eaten the swill. Sometimes, when the wind was in the wrong direction, you were all too aware of the pigs not far away, but usually the smell blew the other way.

As he stood there, leaning on the gate, Andrew tried to force his mind away from thoughts of Tubby and into these other byways – birds, pigs, the twilit fields, the glitter of the sea far away in Plymouth Sound. But however hard he tried, he could not forget. The rosy, cheerful face kept returning to his mind, and the shadow he had sometimes glimpsed in the twinkling blue eyes.

Andrew had known all the time. He had known that Tubby was afraid, and he had done nothing about it.

He came into the cottage at last, rubbing his hands and beaming. 'Everything ready? The others'll be along pretty soon. I say, this all looks terrific. Can I have one of those sausage rolls now?'

'No!' the two women said in unison, and Alison slapped his hand away. May coloured up with confusion and said, 'I'm sorry, Mr Knight. Fancy me shouting at you in your own house. I don't know what came over me!'

Andrew laughed, aware that it was a little too loudly.

'I deserved it. And don't call me Mr Knight – Andrew will do.' He overrode her embarrassed dissent. 'You call Alison by her name, don't you? Well, then.'

The doorbell jangled and May went to answer it, still blushing. There was an immediate outburst of laughter and chatter as the first of the pilots came in, stamping their feet on the mat, and then Robin Fairbanks and Brian Summers shouldered their way into the room. To Alison's relief, they were as breezy as ever; it had obviously been tacitly agreed that there would be no shadows cast over the evening.

'Alison, you look more beautiful each time I see you,' Robin declared as more young men crowded through the door. 'Andrew's told us your good news. I must say, if you've got to marry someone like him, you may as well make the most of it and bring in reinforcements.'

'So long as the sprog doesn't actually *look* like him,' Brian Summers stipulated. 'It's got to have some sort of chance in life.'

'Alison's looks and my brains, that's what we've agreed,' Andrew said, handing round glasses of beer, but the others shook their heads.

'Alison's looks *and* Alison's brains, that's what it'll need.' Brian lifted his glass. 'Anyway, whichever it turns out to be, here's to the new little Knight. What's the proper name for the son of a knight – a viscount, or something?'

'Don't be more of an idiot than you can help.' Andrew glanced over to where Ben and Tony were hovering uncertainly in the doorway. 'Come on in, you two, you make the place look untidy. Who's that lurking behind you?'

'It's Stefan.' Ben hauled the Polish airman in, and Andrew pushed his way through the throng and gripped them both by the arms.

'Come and meet Alison. You too, Tony.' He carved his way back and stood them in the nearest approximation he could manage to a row. 'Look at these three erks, darling, and hope never to see them again! Ben Hazelwood, Tony Sinclair and Stefan Dabrowski. We've borrowed him from the Polish squadron. He's a nice bloke, you'll like him. Got better manners than our mob.'

Alison held out her hand and the three young men shook it in turn, Stefan giving a little bow as he did so. She smiled at them.

'Has Andrew given you a drink yet? There's some food, too – help yourselves whenever you want to. Is this your first posting?'

Ben shook his head. 'We've been flying a couple of years now. Been on quite a few courses lately. Can't wait to have a crack at the Hun. Stefan here's an ace, got a couple of dozen kills to his name.'

'I trained before the war began, with the Polish Air Force,' Stefan told her seriously. 'It's good to be here, and it's very kind of you to invite me to your party. Thank you.'

'Oh, that's quite all right,' Alison said, a little flustered by his gravity. He seemed older than most of the pilots – probably about the same age as Andrew, she thought. She wondered if his family were still in Poland, but decided it was better not to ask, at least until she knew him better. 'You will have a drink, won't you? And something to eat.'

'Of course he'll have a drink,' one of the other pilots butted in, handing him a glass. 'The difficulty will be getting him to stop. These Poles train fish to drink, you know. And he can eat too, though you might not believe it to look at him. We stood him behind a lamppost the other day and he completely disappeared!' He lifted his own glass to her. 'Your very good health, Alison, and thanks for organising this. I'm afraid we're a rowdy mob to have in your house. Not sure my wife would do the same.'

'I didn't know you were married, Ozzie,' Alison said in surprise, and the pilot laughed.

'I'm not! Nor likely to be, unless I catch some poor lass looking the wrong way. But if I *were* married, I'm not sure my wife would agree to have a crowd like this invade her domain. Well, did I hear you mention food? I'd better nab some before these greedy gannets eat the lot.' He disappeared into the crowd, leaving Alison and Stefan looking at each other. Ben and Tony had vanished too, and there seemed to be a tiny oasis of quiet amongst the babble.

'How long have you been in England?' she asked.

'Since soon after the war began. It was necessary to be in a place where we could fight.' He looked down at her. Their glances locked and she caught her breath at a sudden, disturbing glimpse of passion simmering somewhere beneath the ice of his light blue eyes. With difficulty, she looked away and then found herself drawn back again.

'If you ever want a quiet place to be,' she said, 'you're always welcome here.'

Their eyes met again and he nodded with the stiff little bow with which he had first greeted her. 'Thank you. That's kind. It's often noisy in the mess. I have my own room, of course, but even so . . .' He hesitated. 'As long as your husband wouldn't mind.'

'Andrew won't mind,' she said. 'He wants all the pilots to be able to come here and feel at home.' She smiled. 'Of course, you might find it just as noisy as the mess at times!'

'Even with all of the others here now,' he said, 'it seems peaceful. I think you are that kind of person, the kind who brings peace with her wherever she goes. My mother is—' he stopped, then went on again '—my mother is that kind of person too.' There was just the faintest discernible emphasis on the word *is*.

There was a brief silence and then he glanced around the room and said, 'You have a piano.'

'Well, it's not really ours. It's part of the furnishings. But it's nice to have it there – I play it sometimes in the afternoons.'

'You're a pianist?' he asked, his eyes sharpening.

Alison laughed. 'I wouldn't go so far as to say that! But

73

we all had to learn at my school, and there's one at home too, of course. Do you play, Mr—'

'Stefan,' he said. 'You English can never pronounce our names. Yes, I play. We're a musical family.' He lifted one hand and flexed the fingers, and she noticed how long and slender they were. 'We have a piano of sorts in the mess. I play that sometimes, but the others – they all want something not so serious. I play jazz for them.'

'You could come and play ours if you like,' she offered, and his eyes lit up.

'You'd let me do that? I must warn you, I play serious music as well as jazz – Bach and Beethoven, Chopin too, of course. You may not wish to hear it so much.'

'It would be lovely,' she said, meaning it, and touched his arm. Before either could speak again they were interrupted by Andrew. 'Some of the WAAFs are here. We're going to put some records on and have a dance. That's all right, darling, isn't it?'

'Of course.' She gave Stefan another quick smile and then moved away to greet the latest batch of newcomers. They were all young girls, not much more than twenty, she guessed, and were grouped shyly together in one corner. She started to talk to them, asking their names and where they were from, and before long they were chatting like old friends.

Stefan was still watching her and Andrew followed his glance.

'Alison's a marvel at putting people at their ease. Just the right person for dispensing a bit of tea and sympathy – you can talk to her about anything.'

'I know,' the Pole said slowly. 'I can see it in her eyes and in her smile. You're a lucky man, Andrew.' He moved away, towards the table where the sandwiches and sausage rolls were fast diminishing. 'A very lucky man.'

A lucky man. Andrew watched him move away, the

words still sounding in his ears. I know I am, he thought. I know it's true. Yet, just at this moment, he could not quite believe it. It was as if the Andrew Knight that Stefan had been talking to were someone else – someone quite different.

He drained his glass and went to refill it.

'There's not really much room for dancing, is there?' Ben said, holding May a little tentatively. He was very much aware of her warm body and soft curves close to him. He glanced at Tony and wished he could be as suave and self-assured. Tony was always going to dances and seemed to acquire a new girlfriend every time.

'Not really,' May agreed. 'Still, it's nice of Mr Knight – I mean Squadron Leader . . .' she recalled her instructions and amended her words again, '*Andrew* and Alison to ask us all here. Specially me.'

'Why especially you?' he asked. 'You're Alison's friend, aren't you?'

'Yes, but I've only met her these past few weeks, and I've come to help tonight. I'm not really a guest. I don't know that I ought to be dancing at all.'

'Oh, I'm sure they want you to enjoy yourself. You've done all that food, and I know you were washing up just now – you deserve a bit of time off.' He held her a little closer and, since she didn't seem to object, closer still. She really did feel very pleasant, nestled comfortably against him. 'Do you live quite close, then?'

'Just down the road.' She told him about her family and the cottage they shared. 'Prettyjohns have always lived there. Father worked on the home farm at the Barton till he had his accident, but Squire never turned us out, he said us could stay in the cottage as long as we liked. Grandpa still helps out with the stock and does a bit of milking now and then, and Mother works up at the house a couple of mornings a week.'

Ben nodded. His own home was in a small village and he understood about farms and tied cottages. Generally, in such circumstances, a farmer would allow a family to remain in their home, but if he needed it for another worker he could give them notice. A family like the Prettyjohns could be in real difficulties if that happened.

The music stopped and they waited for Andrew to change the record. He had been playing some of Victor Sylvester's records but now he put on one of Ambrose's, with Vera Lynn singing about bluebirds over the white cliffs of Dover. People began to join in with the words as they danced, and Ben heard May's soft voice in his ear.

'You've got a lovely voice,' he said when the record stopped. 'Did you know that song's about us – the Air Force? We're the bluebirds, in our aeroplanes.'

'I didn't know that!' she said in surprise. 'I thought it meant real bluebirds.'

'No, it's us. That's what I've been told, anyway.'

They stood together in the middle of the room. The sky was dark now and Andrew had put up the blackout curtains and lit a few lamps which cast a soft, mellow light. There were small groups of people wedged into every space and several sitting on the stairs. May glanced through to the table and disengaged herself from Ben's arms.

'Don't go,' he said, trying to draw her back. 'Andrew's putting on another record.'

'I ought to see to the food.'

'There's none left. We've eaten it all. Come on, let's have another dance.'

'Yes, but the table needs clearing and there'll be more washing-up to do. That's why I'm here.'

'We'll do it together, then.' Still keeping hold of her

hand, he followed her to the kitchen and closed the door behind them.

Andrew, setting the needle on a Glenn Miller record, watched them go. He'd seen the young pilot dancing with Alison's friend and knew the look on the young man's face. He wasn't flirtatious like Tubby or knowing like Tony Sinclair; he was more serious, the sort of youngster who would fall in love properly, as Andrew had with Alison. And that was the most dangerous kind of all.

Restlessly, Andrew went to fill his glass again. He had lost count of how many beers he'd had – in fact, he'd never counted at all. It didn't seem to matter. They weren't having any more effect than water – he wished they would. It might help him to forget.

He slipped into the passageway and out of the door. The garden was cool and quiet, the darkness lying like a blanket over the fields. He stood for a moment breathing in the chilly night air and thinking about Tubby.

I knew he was frightened, he thought. I knew and did nothing about it. And yet, what could I have done? He wouldn't have thanked me for it. He wouldn't have wanted to be grounded. He'd have hated me for doing that to him. Hated me.

And he would still have been alive.

Andrew took in a deep breath. He tilted back his head and stared up at the sky, searching for a star, some kind of light, as if searching for a signal. For a moment, he laughed bitterly at his fancy – did he think that Tubby was sending him a sign? Yet he still went on searching.

There was nothing.

He let his head drop forward again and raised his glass to his lips. It was almost empty. The beer had disappeared as if he'd tipped it on to the ground.

Andrew swore, silently and at length, using every word

that he had ever known. Then he went back into the cottage to fill the glass again.

In the little kitchen, May started to run the tap while Ben picked up a tray and went back to the dining room. Most of the plates had been emptied now, and he piled them on the tray, added a few glasses and carried them all back. They washed up together, the kitchen feeling cosy and companionable.

'You don't have to do that,' May said after a moment or two. 'You're supposed to be enjoying the party.'

'I'm enjoying being here. It feels like being at home.'

She laughed at him. 'Go on! I bet you don't ever wash up at home. You'll have a maid or something.'

'Not really. Well, I suppose we do, in a way.' He told her about Jeanie. 'She helps around the house in return for her board and keep, and Mum pays her as well, so I suppose she is a maid. But she seems more like one of the family. I'm the baby's godfather,' he added proudly.

'Well, that's lovely. I bet you'll make a smashing godfather.'

'I ought to,' he said. 'My father's a vicar.'

They finished the washing-up. The music was softer now and it sounded as though almost everyone had gone. The door opened and Alison came in with another tray of glasses.

'Goodness me! I didn't realise you were here. May, you've done enough – you've been slaving away all evening. You'd better go home now or your mother will think we've kidnapped you.'

'I haven't been working all the time,' May said. 'I was dancing with Ben some of it.'

'And very nice it was, too,' he said, folding his tea-towel and draping it over the wooden rack. 'I'll see you home.'

'Oh, there's no need! I don't mind walking along the lane

78

in the dark – I'm used to it. It's only about ten minutes' walk.'

'I'll see you home, all the same,' he said firmly, and waited while she fetched her coat. He and Alison looked at each other for a moment and he said, 'It's all right. I'll look after her.'

'Yes, I'm sure you will,' Alison said, her lips twitching a little. May probably knew the lanes like the back of her hand – it was more likely that she would look after him. But she gave him a warm smile and waved goodbye as they walked away down the lane.

Andrew came and stood beside her, his arm over her shoulders. He felt heavy, leaning on her a little, and she glanced at him in concern.

'It's been a good party, hasn't it?' His voice was slow and slurred.

'I think so.' She decided not to notice. 'And I hope they'll all feel they can drop in any time they like. It must be good for them, to have a proper home to come to now and then, instead of staying in the mess all the time.'

'Oh, I don't think they'll do that!' he said with a grin. 'They've practically taken over the pub at the Leg o' Mutton, and there's the Drake Manor as well, and the Rock at Yelverton. They're not short of places to go. But I expect we'll get a few knocking on the door from time to time.'

Everyone had gone now and he drew her inside. May and Ben had done a good job of clearing and washing-up, and Tony and Robin had rolled the carpet into place and set the chairs back more or less where they came from. As Alison began to shift them into position, he caught her hand.

'Leave that for now, darling. It'll wait till morning. Let's go to bed.'

She looked at him doubtfully. 'Andrew, are you all right? You sound—'

'I sound drunk,' he said. 'Well, maybe I am. God knows, I've tried hard enough. That beer's got too much water in it – wouldn't put a baby to sleep.' He swayed a little and Alison put her hands on his arms and propelled him to a chair. He collapsed suddenly and buried his head in his arms. 'God, I feel awful.'

'Oh, Andrew,' she said, and knelt beside him. 'Darling, what's the matter? I've never seen you like this.'

'I've never let you,' he said thickly. 'Not that it happens very often, but when it does – well, I've got more sense than to come home then. But tonight . . .' He shook his head and then groaned. 'Oh, hell. *Hell.*'

'It's Tubby, isn't it?' she said quietly after a moment.

Andrew was silent. He lay back in the chair, his eyes closed. His face was white, etched with pain. She stroked his hands and waited, her heart filled with pity.

'Tubby was scared,' he said at last. 'He was scared. I knew it, and I let him go on. I could have grounded him, but I didn't. I let him go on flying, and now he's dead.' He sat up a little, his face buried in his hands. 'It's nothing new, for God's sake. Look how many young pilots I've seen killed – either shot down, or got caught out by engine failure, running out of fuel or crashing on landing or take-off, and some poor blighters even killed by our own ack-ack fire. I've been upset by every one of them. But you can't let it affect you. You've got to push it aside and concentrate on the job.' He paused, then added in a voice racked with pain, 'Only this time, I can't. With Tubby, it's different.'

'Andrew,' she murmured. 'Darling . . .'

He went on as if she were not there, talking more to himself than to her. 'I keep looking for him. I look for him in the air, in the mess – all the time I'm walking or cycling round the airfield. I look for him in the pubs. And every time, it's like another shock when I remember I'm not going to find him. He's at the bottom of the sea, all mixed up in the wreckage of his aeroplane.'

Alison tightened her fingers around his wrists. She pulled his hands away from his face and stared into his eyes, seeing the grief there, the haunting regrets. She knew now what had been tormenting him during these past few days. It was more than grief for his friend, more than the sense of bereavement at the loss of a man who had been like a brother to him; it was remorse. Remorse and guilt at having let Tubby down, at not having grounded him and kept him safe.

'Andrew,' she said. 'You are not to do this. It wasn't your fault that Tubby died. Yes, you knew he was afraid, and maybe if you'd gone by the book you'd have grounded him. But you didn't, because you knew that wasn't what he wanted. It didn't matter how afraid he was, he still wanted to go on flying. He wanted that more than anything else. And if he'd known that you realised how he felt and still let him fly, he'd have thanked you for it.'

'Maybe you're right,' he said sombrely. 'But we'll never know, will we? We'll never know how he really felt, because he never told anyone. He never talked about it.'

Alison took a deep breath. She told herself that the promise no longer held good, that Tubby would have wanted her to break it now; that he would have wanted this burden lifted from Andrew's shoulders.

'He did,' she said. 'He talked about it to me.'

Andrew stared at her. 'To you? But why – when—?'

'It was just before we moved here,' she said. 'He came to see me. He didn't mean to let me know, but somehow it all came out. He was in a dreadful state – shaking all over, almost crying – and he told me everything. How scared he was – how it came over him all of a sudden, when he was on Channel patrol one day. He'd thought it would pass, but it didn't. It got worse.'

'But why didn't he say?' Andrew asked, bewildered. 'I'd have got him rested.'

'That's just what he didn't want. He was terrified of being grounded. He said if that happened, he – he wouldn't want to go on. He made me promise not to tell you. There was nothing I could do about it.'

'You should have done, all the same.' He looked at her with accusing eyes. 'If you had done—'

'I know!' she cried. 'He'd still be alive now. Or maybe he wouldn't. Maybe something worse would have happened. He really meant it when he said he wouldn't want to go on, Andrew.'

'Oh, that's just talk! People don't mean those sort of threats.'

'Sometimes they do,' she said quietly. 'I think Tubby did. He couldn't bear to think of his parents knowing he was a coward, you see.' Briefly, she recounted the story Tubby had told her, of his young uncle, executed by firing squad during the First World War. 'He was only fifteen, he shouldn't even have been in the Army, but he was called a coward just the same. It affected the whole family. And if anything killed Tubby – apart from this war – it was that. He couldn't bear the thought that they might think he was a coward too. It wasn't you, Andrew. You must believe that. He was grateful that you let him go on flying. It was what he wanted.'

'Poor devil,' Andrew said, rubbing his forehead. 'Poor bloody devil.' He sat up straighter in his chair and looked back into her eyes. 'Well, it seems to me there's only one thing I can do now – and that's to go on flying myself. Kill some more bloody Huns, and get this whole damned war over and done with.'

Chapter Seven

It was probably, Andrew thought, a good thing that the squadron was due to return to night-flying in a week or two. Although the squadron had either had previous experience or been on several training courses, he and Tubby had never done night-flying together, so there would be no memories to distract him. Distractions were perilous; they could be a sign that a pilot was due for a rest, but Andrew didn't want to rest. He wanted to stay in the air, leading his squadron, fighting the war and helping to win it. He wanted to bring peace to his country and to his family, and now that there was a new baby on the way he wanted it even more.

He broke the news about the night-flying to Alison the day after the party. They'd talked far into the night, drinking enough tea to wash away the effects of the beer, and then slept as late as Hughie would allow. In the afternoon they went for a long walk into the valley and beside the river, through a wood of huge old oaks, chestnuts and beeches. Hughie ran ahead, kicking up a deep carpet of gold and brown leaves.

'Night-flying?' she echoed, straightening up with a prickly chestnut case in her hand. Her eyes told him that she knew the dangers but was too controlled to let them show. Instead, she said, 'Are you pleased?'

'I'm pleased about anything that will help us bring this war to an end.' He glanced at Hughie, trampling through the leaves and throwing himself into a heap that had blown into a pile against a bank. 'I don't want my children growing up with the kind of life we've endured for the past four years. I want them to have peace and freedom – all the things we thought the First World War was going to bring us.' He gave a short laugh. 'The war to end all wars, that's what they called it! Well, it didn't work – but this one *must* put a stop to it, or it will get worse and worse, and the world will be a more dangerous place than we can even begin to imagine.'

Alison stared at him, shocked. She had never heard Andrew speak like this before. He had always throbbed with energy and eagerness to get into the air, but at the beginning there had been a kind of elation in him – a vibrant pleasure in the act of flying, in using the skills he had developed and using them to good purpose. Gradually, over the years, that elation had changed to a burning determination to wring the best he could from his machine, his men and, above all, himself. He had seen death and destruction, he had played his own part in bringing it about yet he knew that it was only by continuing with it that the war could be brought to an end.

Now, there was a new note in his voice – a bitter fury that she had never heard before. It was because of Tubby, she thought. Andrew had grieved over all the men he had seen go to their deaths, but he had thrust his grief aside and used it to go on, stepping on it like the rungs of a ladder. But Tubby's death was a rung too high. It had shocked him more deeply than he had ever been shocked before.

It would make him even more dangerous in the air, she thought – more dangerous to the enemy. But would it also make him more dangerous to himself?

She glanced from him to their son, scooping up the leaves in his arms and tossing them high, laughing with pleasure as they fell about him in a brilliant shower of red and gold.

'Let's go home and have a cup of tea,' she said, taking Andrew's arm gently. 'We'll light the fire, and have a quiet evening together.'

Night-flying was a different world.

Instead of soaring into clear blue sky above the clouds, using their eyes to search for enemy aircraft, the pilots floated in a huge black hemisphere, peppered with stars. Sometimes the darkness was pierced by the beams of searchlights, like bright swords slicing through the sky; sometimes it was almost absolute, a dense shadow that could conceal the raiders that might lurk within. At dawn or at dusk, you could get into position in order to see the enemy against the glimmer of light on the horizon; or, if there were a moon, you might catch him flying down the glittering pathway it flung on the surface of the sea, or silhouetted against a big sheet of cloud.

The main task of the fighters was to accompany bombers deep into France or Germany. For many months now, the Allies had been waging a bitter offensive against the core of industrial Germany. But the losses had been heavy until the Americans learned what the British Bomber Command already knew – that even the great Flying Fortress could not survive over Germany without the protection of fighters. More squadrons were to be brought in for the task of escort, and Harrowbeer was to be one of the airfields to provide them.

Andrew was deeply satisfied. He called his pilots together and gave them a vigorous talk about their new duties. 'It's our chance to show what we're made of,' he said. 'We've had our rest, we've had our fun pootling about the sky having a pop at the occasional reconnaissance plane – now we'll be back in the thick of it. It's our chance to get a few of these bastards and show them what's what.' His glance settled on Ben and Tony. 'You've both done some night-flying, haven't you?'

They nodded. Ben said, 'I was in the Med for a while. I saw what they did to Malta. I'll be glad to do a bit more towards getting rid of them.'

'I too,' Stefan said, and the others joined in with their agreement. The whole atmosphere of the mess was changing already, Andrew noted with approval. They hadn't been fed up, exactly, and they'd all needed the rest that pilots had to take every now and then, but they'd been growing impatient and were eager to be back in real action. Combat was what they wanted, to test and use the skills they had so finely honed; combat which would help to win the war as it had already won the Battle of Britain.

'You'll all have a forty-eight-hour leave pass before we start,' Andrew told them finally. 'If you can get home, do so. Otherwise, I dare say you'll find ways to pass the time!' They laughed and he fixed them with a mock glare before adding, 'And don't think you'll be spending it round at my house. I consider myself on leave too!'

'Will you go home?' Tony asked Ben as they stood in a corner of the mess later, each with a pint of beer in his hand.

'Oh yes. The parents will want to see me. We all try to get back whenever we can, although it's not so easy for my brothers. And there's Jeanie too,' he added, half to himself.

Tony gave him a curious glance. 'That's the girl with the kiddy, isn't it? I didn't realise she was your girlfriend as well.'

'She's not!' Ben's reply came quickly and he felt himself colour a little. 'It's just that she's part of the family now – they both are – and I'm Hope's godfather . . .' His voice trailed away and Tony cocked an eyebrow at him.

'Sounds like it's a bit more than that. You'd better watch

your step, young Benjamin, or you could find yourself drifting into something you might regret. You know what they say about repenting at leisure.'

'For Pete's sake, Tony! I'm not thinking of marrying her!'

'Then what are you thinking of?' Tony asked shrewdly. 'Because you certainly had her on your list of people you need to see.'

'And who's on yours?' Ben demanded, deciding that attack was the best form of defence. 'Half a dozen different girls, I suppose. Will you have time to see them all?'

'Shan't even try.' Tony finished his drink and wiped his mouth with the back of his hand. 'It's too far for me to go home on a forty-eight so I'll just loll about here. Get the train into Plymouth or Tavistock and see what's going on. And maybe look in on a couple of popsies.' He grinned. 'Safety in numbers, you know – you ought to remember that. Now I'm off to find my address book. See you later.'

He strolled away and Ben, shaking his head, finished his own drink. He glanced at his watch and tried to remember the times of the trains from Yelverton to Plymouth. If he got his skates on, he could be home by teatime.

Chapter Eight

'What a lovely surprise.' Olivia Hazelwood stepped back and held her youngest son at arms' length. 'You should have let us know – we'd have done something special for supper.'

'A fatted calf?' he grinned, and she gave him a wry smile.

'Well, a few eggs, at least! They're the equivalent of a fatted calf these days. Anyway, you're not a prodigal son.' She linked her arm through his and led him into the house. He had met her as she strolled home from her WI meeting; humping his kitbag, he had walked from the tiny railway station through the familiar lanes, sniffing woodsmoke from cottage chimneys and listening to the caws of the rooks on their way back from the fields to their roosts in the tall elm trees growing in the churchyard. He had known the footsteps belonged to his mother as soon as he heard them treading softly through the fallen leaves, and he had waited at the gate, whistling quietly so as not to alarm her.

'I knew it was you the moment I heard that tune,' she said affectionately. 'How long have you got?'

'Forty-eight hours. That means I've got to leave straight after breakfast the day after tomorrow. There's a good train to Plymouth and then I can get the branch line to Yelverton.' He hesitated, then decided he might as well tell her straight away. 'We're going on to night-flying.'

'Oh.' She was silent for a moment or two. They stood in the hall, taking off their coats and gloves, then she raised her eyes to his. She knew quite well how dangerous it was, and that there was really nothing to be said about it, and after another minute or so she remarked briskly, 'Well, we'd better have a look in the kitchen and see what Jeanie's doing. The hens are laying well at the moment – we had six eggs this morning, so they're nice and fresh. You can have one for your breakfast tomorrow.' She was talking at random as she walked past him and through the kitchen door, and he heard her say to Jeanie, 'Guess who's come home? Come and see who's here, Hope. It's your Uncle Ben.'

'Ben!' Jeanie came through the door, her eyes bright and her round, pretty face beaming. She came to a stop a foot or two away, holding out her hands, and he took them in his, smiling with pleasure.

'You've got flour on your nose,' he said, and let go of one of her hands to brush it away.

Jeanie blushed and said, 'I'm making a rabbit pie for supper. How long are you staying?'

'Everyone asks me that,' he complained. 'It's just another way of saying "When are you going back?" You can't wait to get rid of me.'

'Yes, we can!' she protested, and blushed again when he laughed. 'Oh, you know what I mean. We just want to know how long we can have you here.'

'Don't tease her, Ben,' Olivia said, appearing in the doorway with Hope, who immediately squealed and flung herself at him, wrapping her arms around his legs and burying her face in his knees. He laughed and swung her off her feet.

'How's my favourite girl, then? How's my little princess?'

Jeanie moved back towards the kitchen. 'I'd better get back to my pie. And I expect you'd like a cup of tea.'

'A huge one,' he nodded, and followed her, still carrying

Hope in his arms. Olivia busied herself putting the kettle on and taking cups and saucers from the dresser. She looked in the cupboard.

'We've no cake, I'm afraid, but I got some broken biscuits in the village shop.' She put the tin on the table and Ben fell upon it.

'Broken biscuits! Any chocolate ones? Or custard creams?'

He pulled off the lid and Jeanie said smartly, 'Now, you're not to go ferreting about in there, looking for all the best ones. As for chocolate biscuits – I haven't seen such a thing for years. I don't think they make them any more.'

'Never mind. I'll make do with Rich Tea. And here's a bit of custard cream for Hope.' The little girl climbed on to his knee and he fed her the scrap of biscuit, then leaned back in the chair, letting his eyes roam about the big, warm kitchen. The curtains were drawn, the blackouts in place and the lamps lit, making a cosy cocoon filled with the warm scent of baking. Jeanie had made some rock cakes and a Victoria sponge, which were cooling on a wire rack on the scrubbed wooden table, and she had now returned to rolling out the pastry for the rabbit pie. The meat was in an enamel pie dish beside her.

'I came home on the right night,' he said, sipping his tea as he watched her. 'Nothing like a bit of home cooking to feed the starving hordes.'

'Go on,' she said, curling the pastry round the wooden rolling-pin and draping it over the dish of meat. 'I bet you get fed like fighting-cocks. I've heard all about it – eggs and bacon for breakfast every day, roast beef for dinner. Most people in Pompey have forgotten what a real egg looks like.'

'Well, we have to be properly fed if we're going to win this war,' he said. 'No good letting our tummies rumble while we're flying – we might mistake it for enemy gunfire.' He stopped, remembering that he intended to play down the dangers he faced in the sky. 'Not that we get much of that on daylight patrol.'

'You will when you're on night-flying, though,' John Hazelwood said, coming into the kitchen. He had let himself in through the back door and Olivia had gone to meet him as he took off his boots in the outer scullery. He slapped his hand on Ben's shoulder. 'Good to see you. How long are you here for?'

Ben and Jeanie burst out laughing. 'You see?' he said to her, and then grinned at his father. 'Till the day after tomorrow. Then we start the new routine. I'm looking forward to it. Night-flying has something special about it – you're in another world, a world of your own, up there with the moon and the stars all around you, and nothing but darkness below. Well, except for the neutral countries, of course. It's odd to see all their lights shining when everywhere else is blacked out. But it's hard to realise, sometimes, that there's a war on. If it weren't for that, I think I could fly for ever at night.'

His own eyes shone as he described it, and Olivia, watching him, could see that in his mind he was there now, flying amongst the stars, searching the glittering pathways of the moon on the shifting sea, far removed from the world below . . . She shivered. In peacetime, she would be able to share in his excitement, sense the thrill of it and imagine herself in that other-world where he felt so much at home. But this was war, and she knew that death could come blasting from that darkness; that the ethereal peace was false and concealed a bitter danger.

John glimpsed the shadow in his wife's eyes and said quickly, 'Well, I've got another surprise for you all too. Alexandra's coming home tomorrow.'

They turned to him, all talking at once . . . 'How do you know?' 'When is she coming?' 'How long can she stay?'

'Why didn't you tell us before?' until he lifted one big hand and called for them to quieten down.

'She rang up while you were at the WI meeting,' he said to Olivia. 'And then I went to see old Norman Stanley – you know he's ill – and when I came back Ben was here. And I've only just walked through the door, anyway! I haven't had much chance.'

'Well, tell us now,' Ben said. 'I haven't seen Alexie since the middle of summer. How's she getting on?'

'Oh, much as usual, from what I can gather. They keep the VADs pretty busy at Haslar, and a lot of them went out to Egypt, you know. Anyway, we'll find out more when we see her. She'll be here about eleven, she thinks, and she'll have to go back in the evening.'

'Well, it will be good to see her.' Olivia sighed. 'If only Peter and Ian could be here too. It's such a long time since we had the whole family together.'

'I know.' John took her hand. 'And I'm afraid it will be a long time before we're all together again. This war's going to go on for a while yet, although I do think the tide's beginning to turn. Russia's making a good job of fighting the Germans off, and with Italy turning against them too they're in a difficult position. I think the next year could see us looking towards the end of it all.'

'Another year!' Olivia said. 'John, it's been going on for over four years already. That's even longer than the First World War.'

'I know,' he said. 'But we won that, didn't we? We'll win this one too. You'll see.'

Olivia said no more, but they all knew that her mind was with all those still fighting, and with her children especially: her son Ben, about to start night-flying, which could only mean accompanying bombers on their desperate missions deep into Germany, and her other sons – Ian, an Army chaplain somewhere in Italy and still in danger despite that country's change of heart, and Peter, commanding a ship in the waters of the Pacific.

Even Alexandra, working at the Haslar Royal Naval Hospital in Gosport, had been in danger from the relentless bombing of Portsmouth and Gosport earlier in the war. And although that bombing had stopped, there had been disquieting talk of a 'secret weapon' and everyone was afraid that it might start again, even worse than before.

Jeanie had put the pie into the oven as they talked and was now busy with the vegetables. Olivia finished her tea and got up to help her, and Ben lifted Hope from his lap and set her on the floor.

'I'll take my kit upstairs.' The bedrooms were always ready for any of them who came home unexpectedly, although it was a long time since Peter's and Ian's beds had been slept in. Followed by Hope, who had attached herself to him like a limpet, he hauled his canvas kitbag up to the room he had occupied ever since he was a baby and, before switching on the lamp, he stood for a moment looking down into the twilit garden. There was still just enough light to see the rows of vegetables where once his mother had grown flowers, and the little patch of orchard with its tiny lawn and the apple tree where he'd first met Judy Taylor, deafened by bomb blast, and where Hope had been born. He remembered climbing the tree when he was a small boy, eating so many of the windfall apples that he'd had a stomach-ache all night and, later, being allowed to pick those still on the tree when they were ripe. There had always been one or two just too high to reach, and they'd been left there all winter, to ripen and glow like scarlet lanterns against the sky.

He'd spent hours under that tree, first as a baby in his pram and then on a blanket with a book in front of him. He'd done his homework and holiday tasks there, he'd played noughts and crosses, draughts and chess with his brothers, and he'd just lain there in the dappled sunlight, thinking of nothing much and drifting off to sleep.

He had known this garden all his life, and to him it was the essence of England, the essence of all he was fighting for.

Hope tugged at his jacket; he drew the blackout curtains and turned away from the window to switch on the light. He had dumped his kitbag on his bed and, grinning at the little girl, he began to unfasten the ties around its neck.

'I know what you're after. Well, let's see what we can find, shall we?' Ferreting about inside the bag, he pulled out a bar of chocolate. 'There, is that what you want?'

'Chocolate,' she breathed, her eyes widening. She took it almost reverently in both hands and Ben laughed.

'You'd better not eat it before supper, or I'll be in trouble.' He began to unpack the few bits and pieces he had brought with him. Hope ran out, calling for her mother to show her what she'd been given and Ben flung himself down on his narrow bed and lay back, letting his eyes move slowly round the room.

It was the smallest of all the rooms in the vicarage except for the tiny box room where the family dumped all the things they had no room for anywhere else. Ben didn't mind this at all – he enjoyed not having to share, as Peter and Ian did in their larger room. Here, he could spread his clutter around as he liked, without fear of anyone either moving it or complaining that he was taking up more than his share of space.

Apart from being tidier than it was when he was living at home, the room was much as he had left it. There on the chest of drawers were his treasures – the fossil he had picked up on the beach near Swanage during a family holiday; the sea-urchin shell his mother had brought back from Cornwall; the wooden model of a Spitfire he had made himself at school, soon after the beginning of the war, when he had just started to dream about becoming a pilot.

His cricket bat was still propped in one corner, and on the mantelpiece of the little fireplace stood the photographs of the various teams he had played in at school – the cricket and rugger teams, the rowing eight. On the walls hung three pictures – a photograph of his grandparents, looking stiff and stern in their Victorian clothes, one of his whole family taken just before the war started, and a rather gloomy picture in which you could just make out three Highland cattle standing up to their knees in a bog amongst shadowy mountains. It had been on the point of being taken to a village jumble sale when the ten-year-old Ben had rescued it and insisted on its being hung in his room.

On his bookshelf were a row of books from his childhood that he still couldn't bear to part from – his *Rupert* annuals, other books on such diverse subjects as bees, internal combustion engines and volcanoes, and the set of Biggles stories by Captain W.E. Johns which had first fired his desire to learn to fly.

Ben closed his eyes for a moment. Faintly, he could hear the sounds of people talking in the kitchen or hallway. Hope's excited babble was interspersed with Jeanie's light voice and John Hazelwood's deeper tones. The sounds were a comfort to him, reassuring him that there was another world, a world that wasn't about fighting and killing other men. For although Ben lived for flying, although he revelled in the use and development of his skills in the air, somewhere in his heart was the dark knowledge that those skills were used to deal death to people he had never met and might even like.

These short visits home reminded him that peace was the ultimate aim, even of war. Peace, and the freedom to live in harmony and contentment.

A knock on the door roused him and he heard Jeanie's

voice. 'Supper's ready, Ben. You haven't gone to sleep, have you?'

'Not far off.' He swung his legs off the bed and opened the door. As she stood there, small and pretty in her flowered pinafore, he was suddenly filled with affection for her. Pulling her into his arms, he gave her a smacking kiss, and she squealed with surprise.

'Ben! Whatever are you doing?'

'Giving you a kiss,' he said, looking down at her. 'And what's more, I'm giving you another one, too.'

This time the kiss was gentler and lasted a little longer. As he released her, they looked at each other, suddenly solemn. Then Jeanie gave a little laugh and stepped away.

'Come on, Ben. The pie will be getting cold.' She turned and ran down the stairs and he followed, slowly and rather thoughtfully.

Sitting round the kitchen table eating rabbit pie, Ben was suffused with warmth and affection. He glanced at Jeanie once or twice, remembering their kiss, and caught her peeping at him through her lashes. Each time, she blushed and looked away quickly, and his heart gave an odd little twist. Afterwards, he helped her wash up and felt the same comfort that he had experienced while helping May Prettyjohn with the same task.

'We're going to listen to the wireless in the drawing room,' Olivia said. 'You're welcome to come in as well, Jeanie.'

'Oh, no – you'll want Ben to yourselves. Anyway, I've got to put Hope to bed and there's some mending I ought to be getting on with.' Her voice was flustered and Olivia glanced at her curiously. As she followed her son into the large, pleasant drawing room, she said, 'I hope you haven't been upsetting Jeanie, Ben.'

'Of course I haven't! How could I have upset her?'

'I don't know,' his mother said, 'but you should remember that she's had quite a hard time. It wouldn't be kind to give her the wrong idea.'

Ben felt the warmth creep into his face. He bent to put a log on the fire and let the heat redden his cheeks, then straightened up. He said, 'It's all right, Mum. I won't do that.' He met her grey eyes. 'I like Jeanie. That's all.'

'I wouldn't mind if it *weren't* all,' Olivia said, 'so long as you're honest, and sensible. I'm very fond of Jeanie myself. I just don't want either of you to be hurt.'

They were still standing there when the door opened again and John came in, carrying the daily paper. He glanced at them and said breezily, 'Hasn't anyone turned on the wireless yet? We'll be missing half the programme.' And he walked over to the set and began to twiddle the knobs.

As the whistling and burbling sounds of the wireless warming up filled the room, Olivia and Ben moved apart. Ben dropped into an armchair and his mother settled herself on the sofa. The signature tune of their favourite comedy programme began and they smiled at each other and prepared to enjoy themselves.

Jeanie didn't come downstairs again. She stayed in her bedroom, sewing and listening to her own wireless, and thinking of her lost fiancé, Terry.

Chapter Nine

Alexandra arrived on the eleven-fifteen train from Portsmouth next morning and almost fell from the carriage into Ben's arms. She exclaimed in surprise and flung her own arms around him for a hearty hug.

'Why didn't anyone tell me you were going to be here?'

'They were afraid you wouldn't come if you knew that,' he said, grinning, and she made a face at him.

'They were probably right. What's happened? Has the RAF come to its senses and thrown you out?'

'Not at all,' he said with dignity. 'We were just given a forty-eight-hour pass, that's all, before going on new duties. Night-flying.'

'Oh.' Her tone told him that, like their mother, she understood exactly what this meant. 'I expect you'll enjoy that.'

They fell into step, strolling back through the lanes to the vicarage. Alexandra lifted her head and sniffed. 'It's lovely to smell fresh country air again. Not that we don't get plenty of fresh air at Haslar, being right on the sea, but country air's different.'

'There's more muck, for a start,' Ben said, stepping round a pile of horse dung.

Alexandra laughed. 'Well, there's that. But it's *nice* muck – except when it's pigs', of course. And I get plenty of that smell at Haslar – there's a pig farm not far from the hospital. How d'you like your new station, Ben?'

'It's good. Right on the edge of Dartmoor – plenty of fresh country air there, I can tell you. Plenty of good fresh food, too. We get quite a lot of stuff from local farms, and there are even places where you can get clotted cream.'

'*Proper* clotted cream?' she asked, and he nodded. 'I haven't had proper clotted cream since we went to Cornwall on holiday before the war.'

'You ought to come down to Devon for a few days next time you get leave,' he said. 'There are some nice villages around Harrowbeer. I'm sure we could find you somewhere to stay. There's a girl—' He stopped suddenly and his sister gave him a quizzical glance.

'There is, is there?'

'It's nothing like that!' he said quickly. 'It's just a girl I met at a party at the Squadron Leader's house. She helps his wife – they're friends. Anyway, I don't think they'd have room,' he finished, remembering the situation in the Prettyjohns' cottage. 'But there must be plenty of other places.'

'It's an idea,' she said thoughtfully, 'as long as Mum wouldn't mind. I know she likes me to come home whenever I can.'

They arrived at the vicarage gate and went into the house. Jeanie was polishing the hall floor and sat back on her heels as they came in, beaming. From the kitchen came the warm aroma of freshly baked bread, and they could hear Olivia chatting to Hope, who was kneeling up on a chair and watching as she stirred cake mixture in a brown and white earthenware bowl. She looked round as they came in and left the mixture at once to come and hug her daughter.

'Alexie! You're looking well. Come and sit down and I'll make some coffee. Only Camp, I'm afraid, but it's all we've been able to get for ages now. Take your fingers out of the cake mixture, Hope. I'll let you scrape out the bowl when I've finished.'

'Oh, I was hoping to do that,' Ben said at once, and Jeanie bustled in from the hall and swooped on the little girl.

'Come on, naughty. We'll take you out into the garden and leave Mrs Hazelwood in peace. No,' as Hope let out a roar of disappointment, 'it's no good screaming at me. We're going to feed the chickens.'

'It's all right,' Ben said as they departed, 'I'll leave the bowl for you.' He went to put the kettle on and Olivia returned to her mixture. Alexandra sat down in the chair Hope had vacated, and stretched her arms above her head.

'Oh, it's good to be here. We've been terribly busy at the hospital. A lot of patients came in from that ship that went down in the Channel a week or so ago, and I've been working in theatre almost non-stop. We're all exhausted – it's the busiest we've been since Dieppe. Are there real eggs in that cake mixture?'

'One,' Olivia said. 'The rest are dried. Ben had two for his breakfast.'

'Greedy gannet,' Ben's sister said automatically. 'Are the hens off lay, then?'

'No, not yet, but I wanted to save some for you to take back with you. They're in that bowl.' Olivia nodded towards a bowl containing three brown eggs and Alexandra kissed her fingers at them. 'You've got somewhere you can boil them, haven't you?'

'We can use the stove in the dormitory. You're an angel, Mum. But will there be any left for Ben's breakfast tomorrow?'

'Not that you care!' he said, pouring a teaspoon of dark brown Camp coffee liquid into each cup and adding boiling water. 'What you're really asking is whether you can have those too. You can if you like – we get fed pretty well.

Won't do me any harm to go without an egg for one morning.'

'You're both angels,' Alexandra told them. 'I come from a family of angels. That's probably why I'm as nice as I am. Where's Dad?'

'Over in the church, being an angel,' Ben said, and she drank her coffee and fished in the tin of broken biscuits, then pushed back her chair and stood up.

'I'll go and find him. Coming, Ben?'

Ben looked at her. As the only girl in the family, Alexandra had a special relationship with their father, and he knew that she really wanted some time with him on her own. He smiled and shook his head.

'You go and be angels together, Sis. I'll come over and tell you when lunch is ready.' He slid into the chair she had vacated and stretched a tentative finger out to the mixing bowl.

Olivia slapped his hand away. 'Honestly, Ben, you're as bad as Hope.' She sighed a little and he knew that she was thinking of her other two sons and wishing they could all be here together. 'Sometimes, I wish you were all little again, playing around my feet and squabbling over who was going to scrape out the bowl or have the skin off the custard. It all seemed so safe, then. Nothing seemed to go wrong. The Great War was over and done with, the Twenties were in full swing and there was no sign of the Depression. It was a charmed time.'

'It was an unreal time,' he said. 'Nothing was going wrong, but it was all there under the surface, waiting to happen. Like a pullover with one dropped stitch, waiting to unravel. And once it starts, there's nothing you can do to stop it.'

'Oh, Ben, that sounds terribly gloomy.' She turned the mixture out into a cake tin and opened the oven door. 'Even an unravelling pullover can be mended.'

'Yes, I suppose so.' He ran his finger round the bowl and licked it. 'I'm not so sure about an unravelling world, though.'

Olivia shut the oven door and straightened up, turning to face him. 'You don't think it's that bad, do you? Oh, I know it's dreadful – the whole war is dreadful. But surely we can put it right, eventually? It's got to come to an end one day. Nobody can go on like this for ever.'

Ben looked at her. He wished he had not said anything – he wasn't even sure why he had. The thoughts he had just expressed were those that came to him in the night, when he couldn't sleep, when his fears about the dangers he faced every time he took off in his aircraft outweighed his joy in flying. And when men like Tubby Marsh were killed. Tubby, and all those others he had seen go to their deaths during the past two years.

'No,' he said at last. 'Of course they can't. It'll come to an end one day, and we'll sort it all out and put it right then. And it can't be too long before that happens. Not after all we've been through.'

'I hope not,' Olivia said, staring with troubled eyes at the cluttered table. 'Oh, Ben, I do so hope not.'

John and Alexandra returned in time for lunch, strolling arm in arm up the path that led from the churchyard. Jeanie and Hope had had their lunch first and gone for a walk, despite Olivia's protests. 'You want your family to yourself,' Jeanie had said. 'It's only right. We're going down to the Suttons' farm to see Sylvie and the others – we'll be back by teatime.' She pulled on her coat, wrapped Hope's scarf around her neck and departed.

Olivia shook her head. 'She really doesn't need to do that. She's one of the family now.'

'Is she?' Alexandra asked. She hadn't seen as much of

Jeanie as Ben had done. 'Does she have her meals with you all the time, then?'

'Of course. She does most of the cooking, after all, and we usually eat in the kitchen these days. It would be silly for her and Hope to have their meals separately.'

'I suppose so. Still, it's nice to be on our own.' Alexandra sat down at the table. 'Mm, stew. It smells lovely – better than we get at Haslar.'

'It's always more difficult to cook large amounts.' Olivia spooned out a helping of rich brown gravy, filled with carrots, onions and meat. 'It's rabbit again, I'm afraid, Ben, but it's almost impossible to get any other meat now, except in tiny amounts. I don't know what we'd do without Percy Fry bringing us rabbits. He brought two beauties this week – must have known you were coming.'

'I like rabbit, anyway,' Ben said, helping himself to mashed potato. 'That pie Jeanie made last night was scrumptious. She's turned into a really good cook, Mum, and all due to you.'

'Oh, she wasn't a bad cook when she first came. She just hadn't had much chance, that's all.' Olivia served the rest of the stew and sat down. Alexandra looked impatient.

'Do we have to talk about Jeanie all the time? After all, she's only the maid, isn't she? And if she didn't have that child she'd be doing proper war work, like the rest of us have to.'

There was a brief silence. Ben opened his mouth indignantly, but before he could speak his father said quietly, 'We don't look on her as a maid, Alexie, but I'm sure she wouldn't want us to be talking about her anyway. Tell us what you've been doing with yourself in your spare time.'

Ben glanced at his sister and saw the flush on her cheeks. He knew that she wouldn't like being reproved by her father and hoped she wouldn't go into a sulk. There was little enough time for them to spend together as it was.

Swallowing his own annoyance at her remark, he said encouragingly, 'Yes, what films have you seen lately? Or have you been dancing on your nights off?'

Alexandra ate in silence for a moment or two, then she said reluctantly, 'I went to see *Jane Eyre*, with Joan Fontaine and Orson Welles. That was good. And Ingrid Bergman in *For Whom the Bell Tolls*.'

'I saw that, too,' Ben said. 'I thought it was rather good.'

'I've been to a few dances as well,' Alexandra went on. 'We go over to Southsea mostly. They have Joe Loss sometimes, and Ambrose – all the big bands. And sometimes we push back the beds and do a bit of jitterbugging in the dormitory – one of the girls brought in her gramophone. I'm collecting Frank Sinatra's records. I've got "You'll Never Know" and "My Heart and I".'

'I like Glenn Miller best,' Ben observed. 'Have you heard his new one, "American Patrol"?'

They went on chatting and Jeanie was forgotten for the time being. Later, however, as they sprawled in armchairs in the sitting room in front of the fire, drinking tea and reading newspapers, they heard Hope's voice piping on the pathway, and a moment or two later the front door opened. Alexandra glanced up from her paper and said, 'Do they make themselves at home everywhere? I mean, will they be coming in here?'

'No, I don't expect so,' Ben said. 'Jeanie understands that Mum and Dad want us to themselves. I think she sits in here with them sometimes when they're on their own, though. It makes sense, after all. There's no point in having two lights burning.'

'I suppose not. I hope she realises how lucky she is, falling on her feet like this.'

'I think she earns her keep,' Ben said quietly. He looked at his sister and said, 'You're a bit jealous of her, aren't you?'

'Jealous? No, of course I'm not!' Alexandra flung down her newspaper and glared at him. 'Why on earth should I be jealous?'

'Well, *I* can't think of any reason at all,' he said, 'but *you* might have one. Like, she's here all the time, and you're not. And you've never had to share your home, or Mum and Dad, with another girl before.'

'Share them? I'm not sharing them! She's a *maid*, that's all – and I think it's a pity she doesn't know her place. She's certainly nothing to be jealous of!'

'That's all right, then, isn't it?' Ben said. He was having some difficulty in keeping his temper under control. 'Because I happen to like Jeanie. I like her a lot. And she isn't "just a maid". So I'm glad you're not jealous of her.'

Alexandra stared at him. 'You're not falling for her, are you, Ben?'

'I just think she's a nice girl, who's a help and a comfort to Mum and Dad, and she doesn't deserve to be treated the way you're treating her, that's all.'

'I'm not treating her in any way at all! I've hardly spoken to the girl!'

'All right, I don't like the way you've been talking *about* her.'

'That's easy to put right then, isn't it? I won't even mention her again.' Alexandra picked up her newspaper and held it in front of her face. Her hands were shaking and Ben reached across and pulled the paper away.

'I'm sorry, Sis. Don't let's argue – we've only got a few hours at home and we don't want to upset the parents.' He looked at her pleadingly and she pulled a wry face and shrugged her shoulders.

'I suppose not. But honestly, Ben, don't you think she's got her feet under the table a bit too much? She and her brat—'

'My goddaughter,' he said quietly, feeling his temper begin to simmer again, as Alexandra sighed with exasperation.

'There you are, you see! Oh, all right, I'm not going to start again. We'll forget all about her, if we can. And you needn't worry, I won't be rude to her. How about a game of draughts?'

'Good idea.' He fetched the board and they set the pieces out and settled to their game. Gradually, their irritation diminished and when Olivia opened the door to bring in a tray of fresh tea and a loaf of bread to be sliced and toasted on the fire, they were laughing.

'Oh, that's so good to hear,' Olivia said, setting down the tray. 'My children, playing together just like when they were little. If only Peter and Ian were here, it would be just like old times.'

Ben and Alexandra glanced at each other. He gave her a rueful grin, and she replied with a tiny shrug. The quarrel was over – but the questions it had raised lingered in both their minds, and Ben wondered again what Jeanie would do once the war was over.

The visit was all too quickly over. They all walked through the village later that evening to see Alexandra off on the ten o'clock train and, after an enormous breakfast next morning, Ben went reluctantly upstairs to bring his kitbag down. His parents and Jeanie, with Hope clutching her mother's skirt, stood in the hall waiting for him.

'I'm sorry I can't come to the station with you,' John Hazelwood said, already in his cassock, 'but old Mrs Turnbull would never forgive me if I didn't get back in time for Matins.'

Ben grinned. 'It wouldn't do to get on the wrong side of old Mrs Turnbull. Your life would be a complete misery.'

They all laughed, though their laughter was a little uncertain. Saying goodbye was always difficult; the thought was never far away that this might be the last time they would see each other.

Ben and his father shook hands and the vicar walked

through the garden to the church gate. The rest of them set off along the lane to the railway station.

It was a cold November day, not exactly raining but full of a heavy damp that hung around the trees and turned the fallen leaves to a slippery mush. A few rooks flew overhead, cackling to each other, and a magpie crossed the lane in front of them. Jeanie watched it anxiously and gave a sigh of relief when it was followed by another.

'That's two for joy, anyway. I know you're not superstitious,' she added to Olivia, 'but it don't do no harm to be on the safe side.'

Apart from the ancient porter, the little station was deserted. As they arrived, he shuffled out of the waiting-room with a bucket and began to shovel coal into it from the pile at one end of the platform.

'Morning, Mrs Hazelwood.' His voice sounded like the coal he was shovelling. 'Morning, young Ben.' He glanced at Jeanie and nodded, his seamed face cracking into a smile at sight of Hope. 'And how's the little lady, then? Come to see Master Ben off, have you?'

Hope was busy looking for the elderly cat who spent his days sunning himself on the platform or dozing by the fire in the stationmaster's office. She found him crouching by a small hole in the ground beneath a rose bush, and immediately scooped him into her arms.

'No, don't,' Jeanie said, trying to loosen her grip. 'He doesn't like it.'

'He does like it.' Her arms tightened and the cat squirmed and objected loudly. Jean prised her daughter's fingers apart and he dropped to the ground and scurried away, stopping at a few yards' distance to wash himself as if he felt contaminated.

'He did like it,' Hope said mutinously. 'He likes me.'

'Well, he was too busy to be picked up. He was waiting for a mouse.' They looked along the line as the train chuffed slowly into view. Both women turned to Ben and Olivia drew in a small breath while Jeanie took hold of Hope's hand.

'He wasn't busy.'

'Be quiet, Hope,' Jeanie said distractedly, but the other two weren't listening. Olivia had taken both her son's hands in hers and he was looking at her with sudden gravity. He'd meant to be cheerful – meant to leave his mother with a smile and a wave – but somehow, now that the moment had come, he was filled with sadness. Almost a premonition, he thought suddenly, and thrust the idea away.

The train drew up beside them, the steam and smoke from the engine enveloping them in a warm, damp cloud. As it began to clear, the porter opened a carriage door and heaved Ben's kitbag inside. There was only a minute or so left. Ben glanced at Jeanie and saw that her eyes were bright with tears. He turned hastily to his mother and put his arms around her.

'Cheerio, Mum. Take care of yourself, won't you.'

'It's you who must take care of yourself,' she said. 'I know I shouldn't say this, but I do worry about you, Ben.'

'I know.' He didn't tell her there was no need to worry; they all knew that there was every need. Everyone worried, all the time. Mostly, the worry was kept hidden, but it was always there. War brought worry with it, like a many-clawed creature that fastened itself into your heart and mind and refused to be dislodged.

He turned back to Jeanie and hesitated, remembering the kiss they had shared on the landing. He glanced at Hope, staring up at him with huge brown eyes, and bent to gather her in his arms.

'Goodbye, little princess.' He buried his face against her soft, warm neck, then set her on her feet again and now it seemed quite natural to take Jeanie in his arms as well and kiss her gently on the cheek. 'Goodbye, Jeanie.'

'Goodbye, Ben,' she whispered, and turned her face to return his kiss.

There was a moment of silence and then he gave them all a distinctly shaky grin and stepped up into the carriage. He leaned out of the window and reached down and they both reached up to take his hand. Then the engine snorted and gave a preliminary jerk before starting off again. Ben leaned a little further out, then let go of their hands, gave them a final wave and was gone.

The three of them stood there for a few moments and then Olivia straightened her back and said, 'Well, that's that, then. I must go back. I'll be too late for church, but I can start the lunch. Are you coming, Jeanie, or do you want to take Hope for a walk?'

'I'll come with you,' Jeanie said, guessing that Olivia wanted her company. She felt sad and empty, as if something precious had been taken away from her. The kiss Ben had given her on the landing had remained with her during the whole weekend, and she had been half afraid, half hopeful that it would be repeated. Now, she didn't know whether to be glad or sorry that it hadn't, and she knew that she still hadn't forgotten Terry.

They walked along the lane together, each absorbed in her own thoughts. Hope dragged on her mother's hand, still looking for the cat. When the boy came round the corner of the lane by the vicarage gate, riding his red bicycle, none of them realised at first what it meant.

Then Olivia put her hand to her throat. She stared at him, and then at the envelope he was holding out.

'No,' she said in a dry, hopeless whisper. 'Please. *No* . . .'

Chapter Ten

It was Peter who was missing. His ship had gone down in the Far East, with only a few saved and taken prisoner by the Japanese. There was no word yet as to who had survived but, like the Taylors when they heard that the *Hood* had gone down with only three survivors, the Hazelwoods knew that Peter's chances were slim.

'Even if he was picked up,' Olivia said, her voice husky as if the tears she had shed had left her throat dry, 'he'd be a prisoner. And you know what they're saying about Japanese prisoners of war. They're treating them dreadfully.' She covered her face with her hands. 'I can't bear to think of our Peter being tortured.'

'We don't know that for certain.' John took her in his arms and she leaned against him, fresh tears coming as if she had discovered a new well deep inside. 'It's hearsay only.' But he spoke without conviction. 'Olivia, my dear, we mustn't despair. He's in God's hands.'

'And so were all the others,' she cried bitterly, lifting her hands away to stare at him. 'All those who have died, died horribly – all those who are suffering now, never mind which side they're on. The Germans are Christians too, or supposed to be – are *they* in His hands? And the Japanese themselves – is He looking after them too, even if they don't believe in Him? You say He's an all-merciful God, but who is it who receives His mercy, when all the people on earth are fighting one another like spiders in a jar? Is He going to let thousands of others die, yet save Peter, just because he's ours? I'm sorry, John, I can't believe it. I can't believe any of it any more.' She pressed her hands to her face again.

John sighed. He could find no words of comfort or reassurance; in truth, he needed them too badly himself. All he could do was cling to his own faith, the faith that had been so severely tested during the First World War, and it was as if he too could feel it slipping from his grasp. He was like a drowning man, clinging to a lifebuoy and feeling the waves tearing it from his numbed fingers.

Olivia felt for her handkerchief and blew her nose. 'I'm sorry. I shouldn't be giving way like this. I should be more like you, strong and sure of myself and my God.' I should have some courage – I should set an example. I'm not the only mother to have lost her son this morning. Or any morning, come to that.' She shook her head sadly. 'There are people receiving telegrams like this every day. Every single day.'

'Yes,' he said, 'and some of them in this very village, too. Wasn't young Billy Watson on Peter's ship?'

Olivia stared at him in horror. 'Of course he was! Oh, John, that poor woman – he was her only child. And she lost her husband only last year. Oh, we must go and see her at once.'

'I'll go,' he said. 'As long as you're sure you'll be all right. I'll get Jeanie to make you some more tea—'

'No. I'll come with you.' She rubbed away the tears. 'It's the least I can do. Just give me a few minutes to wash my face.' She was on her feet, deathly pale but determined. 'It's all right, John. I shall feel better to be doing something.'

He watched her go, her slender back straight again, and felt the love and admiration bloom in his heart. Whatever her own feelings, Olivia would always put others first. This news about Peter was what they had both dreaded ever since the war began – their eldest son, missing, believed killed – and he knew the anguish she was suffering, because he suffered it with her. Yet because he must go and give comfort, she would put that pain aside and go with him. Because her pain was so sharp and deep, she was all the better able to share that of another woman.

At some time, he would have to try to help her with the loss of her faith as well. But he was very afraid that it was as unlikely to survive as Peter was.

Ben was told the news when he arrived back at Harrowbeer. Andrew called him into his office the minute he appeared in the mess and Ben, wondering what could be the matter, followed him into the small room on the first floor of the big, gracious house.

'I'm not late back, am I? The trains were all on time for once.'

'No, there's no problem there.' Andrew sat behind his desk and look gravely at the young pilot in front of him. 'Sit down for a minute, Ben, and take off your cap. I'm afraid I've got bad news.'

'Bad news?' Ben looked at the sheet of paper his Squadron Leader was holding. 'Have I been posted to another squadron?'

'No. Nothing like that.' Andrew hesitated. He hated breaking news like this – it was even worse than when one of the pilots was killed. At least everyone knew about it then and didn't have to be told in this horribly cold, formal way. 'I'm afraid it's news from home – your home, I mean.' He stopped. Ben was on his feet, alarm creasing his face.

'From home? What – who is it? Mum? Dad? Alexie? Jeanie? It's not Hope, is it?'

Andrew didn't know who all these people were. He had Ben's particulars in front of him and knew there was a sister, but the other two girls' names were unknown to him. He shook his head.

'It's none of those, Ben. It's your brother Peter. He's in the Navy, I understand.'

'Yes.' Ben sank down again on to the chair. His face was ashen and his cap was crumpled between his fingers. 'He's in the Far East, commanding a frigate.' He met Andrew's eyes. 'What's happened?'

'I'm afraid the ship has gone down,' Andrew said quietly. 'There were a few survivors, picked up by the Japanese, but—'

'But Peter won't have been one of them,' Ben said in a dull, flat tone. 'He was in command. He'll have been last to leave the ship. He probably went down with her.'

'We don't know that.'

'I know my brother.' Ben sat staring at his cap for a few moments. Then he looked at Andrew again and said, 'I ought to go home.'

'Yes, you should. You can go tomorrow – take another twenty-four hours. After that, I'm afraid you'll have to come back. We're going to be pretty busy now, you know.'

'I know. Could I go tonight? There's a late train from Plymouth and I can probably hitch a lift or something from Southampton. Or walk, if I have to. The sooner I get there, the better. There's only me and my sister in the country, you see.'

Andrew thought for a minute. 'Yes, you can. I'll drive you into Plymouth myself. Better still, do you have a driving licence? Take my car – we'll scrounge some petrol from somewhere. You can be there in a few hours.' He opened his drawer and took out a bunch of keys, removing one of them from the ring. 'Here you are. You know which one it is, don't you?'

'Yes – the Morris 8.' Ben looked at the key Andrew was

offering him. 'Sir, are you sure? You don't even know if I'm a good driver.'

'I know you're a fine pilot,' Andrew told him, 'and that's good enough for me. Get some food inside you before you go, and stop for a rest if you feel tired. And be back here without fail by eight on Tuesday morning, understand?'

'Yes, sir,' Ben said, standing up and saluting. 'Thank you very much. Thank you very much indeed.'

He spun on his heel and hastened from the room. Andrew sat at his desk a moment longer, looking after him, and then sighed and closed the drawer.

The boy would be all the better for driving through the night to go back to his family. It would give him a sense of doing something, when in fact there was nothing to be done. It would be some comfort to all the family.

Like John and Olivia, he thought of all the other families up and down the land who would be in need of comfort that night.

'Poor Ben,' Alison said to May the next afternoon. 'He had to turn round and go straight home again. Andrew lent him his car. I feel so sorry for him.'

'He seemed a nice young chap,' May said. 'I liked him. I hope this won't hit him too hard.'

The two young women were sitting in front of the range in the Prettyjohns' kitchen, knitting gloves and balaclavas in Air Force blue wool. Mrs Prettyjohn had gone to the Women's Institute meeting and Hughie was upstairs with the two men, playing Happy Families. Outside, the November mist was as chill and drear as it had been the day before, but indoors the logs burned brightly and the kitchen smelled, as it always did, of fresh bread and cooking. Alison felt wrapped around with warmth and friendship.

'He's the youngest of the family, so he told me,' she

remarked. 'Two older brothers and a sister – all serving, of course. His poor mother must live in dread of this happening.'

'Mum lost a brother in the last war,' May said thoughtfully. 'His name's on the memorial cross, up at the corner. She never talks about him, but I reckon she missed him sorely. It's always the parents us thinks of, isn't it, not the brothers and sisters, but it must be a hard blow to them as well.'

'Yes, it must.' Alison had no brothers or sisters, but she had always wished she had, and even the thought of losing family members she had never actually possessed made her heart ache. 'Andrew has a brother, but he's much younger – only sixteen. Everyone was hoping the war would be over before he was old enough for service, but if it goes on for much longer, he'll be in it too. Andrew's mother's dreading it – he seems so young, just a child still.'

''Tis a terrible thing,' May said soberly, and they worked in silence for a while, the only sounds the crackling of the fire and the piping of Hughie's voice, set against the deeper, rumbling tones of the two men, in the room above. After a while, May put down her knitting. 'I'll put the kettle on. Mother'll be back soon and us could all do with a cup of tea.'

'And I'll have to be going after that. It gets dark so early these afternoons.' Alison looked at the calendar on the wall. 'Do you realise it's the fifth of November today? We ought to be having fireworks and bonfires out in the garden!'

'Oh, I love fireworks.' May was busy at the sink. 'Father and my Uncle Ted used to buy one each every week as soon as the shop got them in, and bring them home. They'd buy a rocket one week or a Catherine wheel, or a squib, and us liddle tackers – me and my cousins, that is – would crowd round and look at them in the tin and imagine what they were going to be like when they were set off. It were nearly as good as on the night itself.'

'Hughie's never seen fireworks,' Alison said wistfully. 'I hope he's not too old before we can have them again.'

May set the kettle on the top of the range. 'I don't reckon the children will enjoy them like we did though, do you? They've seen too many bombs. A few rockets or Roman candles aren't going to seem much to them.'

Alison laid her knitting in her lap. 'What a sad thought that is. I hope you're wrong, May. And at least they'll know they're not meant to hurt people.'

May came and sat down again, to knit another row or two as they waited for the kettle to boil. 'There be that. But, you know, I don't reckon as children are going to be the same when all this is over. They'll have seen and heard too much. If you ask me, even when the war's finished and done with, it'll still be going on in a way. In people's minds, I mean. What it's done to them, and the little ones, especially – that's going to last for years.'

Alison looked at her. May's round, pretty face was grave and the usually merry eyes solemn. For a moment, the warmth of the cottage seemed to recede, as if someone had opened a door and let in the dank November fog. And then the door did indeed open. A swirl of mist seemed to billow in before it was swiftly closed again, and Mrs Prettyjohn's voice broke the spell.

'My stars, 'tis a miserable afternoon and no mistake! 'Tis good to get in home, out of the cold. Have you got the kettle on, May? I'm parched for a cup of tea. We were going to have one at the hall, but us couldn't get the boiler to work. I'm chilled right through to the bone.' She came over to the fire and held her hands out to its warmth. 'And how be you, Alison? You'm looking very serious, the pair of you. Not had words, I hope?'

'As if we would!' Alison said, laughing. 'No, we were just

setting the world to rights as usual. And there was some bad news at the station yesterday. One of the pilots – Ben – had to go home suddenly because his brother had been killed.' Her smile faded. 'It's upset us all rather.'

'Oh, my dear.' Mrs Prettyjohn turned at once and came over to lay her hand on Alison's shoulder. 'Oh, how sad. And there's me prattling on about cups of tea and boilers, for all the world as if there was nothing worse than being a bit cold. I'm sorry.'

'There's no need to be.' Alison wound the wool around her needles and stabbed them through the ball. May had made the tea as soon as her mother had come in, and was already pouring it into the cups. 'I'll have that and then I'll go, I think. You're right, it's not very nice out now and I don't want Hughie getting cold.'

They drank companionably together and then Alison took cups up to the two men and fetched a reluctant Hughie away from their game. She wrapped him up warmly in the winter coat her mother had made him, wound his scarf around his neck, and pulled on her own coat and gloves before stepping out into the lane.

There was no sound from the airfield; the fog made flying difficult and dangerous. One thing in its favour, Alison thought wryly. The darkness was almost complete, with only a faint glimmer from the leaden sky to help her along the way. With Hughie's hand held firmly in her own, she hurried along the narrow lane.

Her hand was on the front gate leading into the tiny garden when a shadow detached itself from the bushes nearby and a voice spoke into the thick, murky silence.

'You are home at last, Mrs Knight,' said a voice in the clipped tones of someone speaking very correct English. 'I have been waiting. Please may I come in and talk to you?'

Chapter Eleven

'Stefan!' she gasped after a moment of frightened bewilderment. 'You nearly made me jump out of my skin. Whatever are you doing here?'

'Waiting to speak to you.' He moved a little closer and she instinctively backed away. 'I apologise, Mrs Knight. I did not mean to frighten you. I thought you could see me.'

'See you? It's almost pitch dark.' She fumbled for her door key. 'You'd better come in so that I can draw the blackout curtain across.' She drew Hughie in behind her and the three of them stood in the narrow hallway, uncomfortably close. Stefan Dabrowski came in last and closed the door, and Alison reached past to draw the curtain, brushing against him as she did so. Feeling even more uncomfortable, she turned on the light and moved away.

'How long have you been waiting?'

'I don't know. Half an hour, perhaps. It doesn't matter – I knew you would come back soon.'

'Half an hour? You must be freezing! Look, you go into the front room and put a match to the fire and I'll make you a cup of tea. Hughie, keep your coat on until the fire's going, it's cold in here.'

She went through to the kitchen. Hughie followed her, a little nervous of this tall stranger who had loomed so suddenly out of the darkness. Alison herself felt oddly uneasy. It's just because he startled me, she thought. He's perfectly all right – he's one of Andrew's pilots, he came to our party. All the same, there was something about him that bothered her slightly, and she wished that he had let her know he was coming. Accustomed though she was to the casual ways of airmen, she would have felt more comfortable meeting him on a more formal basis.

By the time she returned, the fire was burning and Stefan was lying back in an armchair, his eyes closed. She stood still for a moment and looked at him. His long legs were stretched out in front of him and his face was pale beneath the thick, blond hair. There was a bluish tinge to his eyelids, as though they were so delicate that the colour of his eyes showed through the skin, and his finely chiselled lips were compressed as though he were feeling pain somewhere deep inside.

Alison's unease receded. She felt a deep compassion for this man, not much older than herself, who was so far from his own country yet fighting desperately to save it. Why he had come here this afternoon she had no idea, except that he was accepting an open invitation that had been made to all the pilots. And he had been waiting in the cold, and looked tired and unhappy. In that moment, her heart went out to him.

She put the tray down on a small table and at the sound he opened his eyes and sat up.

'I am sorry. I think I must have dozed off.'

'It's all right.' She sat down in the chair on the other side of the fireplace and began to take off Hughie's coat and scarf. The room wasn't properly warm yet, but as long as he was close to the fire he would be all right. She put the fireguard in front of the flames and tipped his wooden bricks on to the hearthrug for him to play with. 'There's tea there – drink it while it's hot. I haven't put any saccharin in, they're in that little bottle.'

'No, I like it as it is.' He picked up the cup and sipped,

closing his eyes again. 'This is something I have learned to enjoy since I came to England. We don't drink tea at home. We prefer coffee.'

'Oh, I could make you some. It's only Camp, but—'

He laughed. 'No, no! Tea is good. I told you, I like it now. As for your Camp . . .' he screwed up his nose '. . . that is nothing like coffee!'

'I don't like it much either,' Alison confessed, smiling. 'But it's better than acorns. I've heard that's what the Germans use.'

'Ah,' he said. 'The Germans.' And he turned his face away and looked into the fire.

Alison waited for a moment and then said, 'Have you had some bad news?'

Stefan did not reply at once. Then he turned back to her and said, 'I have had no news. That's the problem. There is no news. Sometimes I feel as if I am starving, just to hear a word or two from my family, to know if they are all right, but there's nothing.' His eyes looked into hers and she saw with a shock that they were blazing, as if a fire burned behind them. 'Nothing! My father, my mother, my sisters, my aunts and cousins and nieces – nothing. I do not even know if they are still alive.' He spoke the last words in a low voice so that Alison had to strain to hear them.

'Oh, Stefan . . .' she said at last, feeling how inadequate a response it was. She put out her hand and reached across in front of the fire towards him. 'Stefan, I'm so sorry. I'm so terribly sorry.'

He nodded, but made no reply. His pale face was set and cold, only the bitter line of his mouth and the fire in his eyes betraying his torment. She tried to imagine what it must be like for him. How would she feel herself, exiled in a foreign country, away from Andrew and her parents and friends. Away from Hughie . . . Instinctively, she put her hand down to her son's head and trembled as she felt his hair beneath her fingers.

'Would you like to tell me about your family?' she asked. 'Or do you just want to sit here quietly?'

He didn't answer directly. Instead, staring into the fire again, he said, 'I was in the mess when Ben came in. He was so happy after his leave at home. And then Andrew took him into his office and told him about his brother. When he came out, he looked different. Older. It was all gone – the life, the joy, everything. Killed by this filthy war, as his brother was killed.'

'It's dreadful,' Alison said, wishing that her words didn't sound so inadequate. 'I feel so sorry for his mother. She must be worrying all the time. I know what it's like.'

He turned his face towards her again and his voice was bitter. 'You do not know what it's like,' he said. 'You have no idea what it's like.'

Alison felt a little spurt of anger. 'I think I do, as a matter of fact. I worry whenever Andrew is up. He had a bad crash two years ago, you know. He was very nearly killed. And I know what dangers you face, all of you, when you're flying. I do know what it's like.'

He snapped his fingers. 'Oh yes, you know that. I didn't mean to say that you didn't understand worry. I'm sorry. I was speaking of my own family.' He lay back again in the chair and let his eyelids close over the burning eyes. 'My mother doesn't even know where I am. She has not heard from me since I left Poland. She doesn't know if I am alive or dead, any more than I know whether she is still alive – or the rest of my family.'

Alison bit her lip. 'I'm sorry. No, you're quite right – I don't know what that's like. But I think I can imagine it, a little.' She glanced at him, lying there as if exhausted by his pain. 'If you want to tell me about it, I'll try to understand more,' she said softly.

'I know you will,' he said. 'I saw it in your eyes, on the night of the party.'

There was a short silence. The fire crackled and Hughie murmured to himself as he built his bricks into a castle. Stefan had switched on a table lamp when he came in and it cast a pool of soft light over his face. She felt a great wash of pity for him and for a brief moment felt that she caught a glimpse of the dark world that lay beyond those pale eyelids; the memories of events so terrible they had driven him from his home to fight for the survival of his country, events that must have been going on ever since, were still going on.

There was a sound at the front door. Alison heard it open and close again, and then Andrew's voice in the passageway. Hughie jumped up, knocking his bricks to the floor with a clatter, and Stefan opened his eyes and sat up abruptly.

Andrew opened the door and came in, swinging his son into his arms.

'Hello, darling! Foul afternoon out there.' He saw Stefan and stopped. 'Dabrowski – I didn't know you were here. Dropped in for tea?' He glanced at the tray. 'Any left?'

'It's only just been made,' Alison said, getting up to kiss him. She smiled down at the Pole, apologising silently for the interruption. 'I'll freshen up the pot. Are you ready for another cup, Stefan?'

'No, thank you.' He began to get up. 'I should go. I didn't mean to intrude.'

'Don't be a fool,' Andrew said, pressing him back into the chair. 'You're welcome. Have another cup. Stay for supper. I don't know what it'll be, mind.' He glanced at Alison. 'Pot luck!'

'No, I can't do that.'

'You can,' Andrew said firmly. 'Look, I've told you all, this is open house. I dare say some of the others will drop in later anyway, since there'll obviously be no flying tonight. No point in you going back, only to turn round and come straight out again. We'll put a few records on.'

Stefan looked towards Alison, and she nodded. 'Yes, please stay. And call in any time you like. As Andrew says, the door's always open to you.' She smiled at him, hoping that he understood that she would be ready to listen to him whenever he felt like telling her about his family. 'You could come and play the piano, if you wanted to.'

And as he gave her a small nod and the little half-bow that was so characteristic of him, she knew that he did understand; and that he would return.

When Ben came back to Harrowbeer, he came as a changed man.

'I just feel so *angry*,' he said to Tony. 'I know I've seen lots of blokes go down – friends of mine, most of them. I've seen them crash into the sea or over land. I've seen them shot down and I've been bloody nearly shot down myself. And it's always made me all the more determined to get the buggers who did it, or some like them. It's them or us, isn't it? But this was my *brother*. He taught me to climb trees and swim. He showed me how to kick a football and hold a cricket bat. He used to take me to collect conkers and he showed me the stars at night. He knew all the birds we ever saw, and he'd sit for hours at night, watching for badgers. He was Head Boy at school, and cricket captain. He got a Blue at Oxford . . .' The hand holding his pint tankard was shaking, and he set the glass down on the table and clenched his fists together. 'And now it's gone. All of it – gone. Lost for ever. Just because of some madman wanting to rule the world. Just because we didn't stop him sooner. And now all these lives are being thrown away, wasted, before they've had a chance to be lived.'

Tony looked at him. Ben's face was drawn together in a

dark scowl, his body tight with anger. He said, 'How about your people? How are they taking it?'

'How d'you think? Mother's nearly out of her mind. I mean, she's always known it could happen, but up till now we've all got through OK. Now one of us has gone, and she's terrified it'll happen to the rest of us as well. That's when she's not just crying her heart out over Pete. I tell you, Tony, she's completely broken up. She won't even go to church.'

'But your father's a vicar, isn't he? Can't he help?'

'Doesn't seem like it,' Ben said gloomily. 'He's just as upset, but going to church seems to help him. Well, you'd expect that, wouldn't you? But Mum – well, she seems to be angry about that too. As if she thinks he's abandoned her.'

Tony hesitated. He went to church because they were all expected to, but left to himself he wouldn't have bothered. He wasn't sure how Ben felt about it; religion wasn't something they'd ever discussed between themselves. After a moment or two, he said, 'What about you? What do you think?'

'I just think,' Ben said in a quietly ferocious tone, 'that I want to get up into the sky and kill as many bloody Jerries as I can. I just wish I could have a go at the Japs as well – they're the ones that sank Peter's ship. But since I can't do that, I'll go for the Hun. *They're* the ones who started it all.'

Andrew saw the change in Ben and watched him carefully.

'He's like a piece of thin, brittle glass,' he said to Alison. 'He could break at any minute. Or he could be fired into something really tough. It could be the making of him as a pilot.'

'That seems an awful thing to say,' Alison said. 'As if his brother getting killed is a good thing.'

'I'm not saying that, but when a man gets the kind of

anger Ben's feeling now – well, sometimes it seems to concentrate his mind even more. I've seen it before. It makes a good pilot a fine one.' He paused. 'I've felt it happening to myself as well. I've seen so many pilots die, but when Tubby went – it was different. I feel much angrier over his death, and it's made me even more determined.'

'Determined to kill,' Alison said.

Andrew looked at her. 'Yes. That's what we're here for. It's war, darling, you know that. It's not new.'

'I know.' She felt suddenly very tired. 'It's been going on for too long, that's the trouble. She laid her hand on her stomach. There was no swelling there yet, not even the smallest flutter of movement, yet she knew that there was a new life beginning deep inside her. 'It makes me feel different too. I can understand how all those mothers feel – Ben's and Tubby's and all the rest. I just don't know how I could bear it if our children – Hughie, and this new one coming – had to go off to war. I really don't, Andrew.'

There were tears in her voice and Andrew pulled her into his arms. 'Hey, come on, darling. That's not going to happen. This war will be over long before they're grown up. It'll be over even before they start school. The tide's turning, you know that. It's just a matter of time now.'

'And is this going to be the last war?' she asked. 'There have been two already this century. How can anyone say there won't be more, and worse ones? When Hughie's twenty-one and the new baby's eighteen – it'll be 1961 then. How can anyone say we won't be at war again?'

'I hope to God we're not,' he said. 'And it's up to us to make sure we're not. We need to finish the job that didn't get properly finished in 1918, and make sure the Germans don't get another chance. And that means killing now. Killing as many as we can.'

'Yes,' she said sorrowfully, 'that's what it comes down

to, isn't it? Killing as many people as we can. Never mind who they are – men, women, children, tiny babies. Just so that in the end one side will give in, because they haven't got anyone left to kill.' Her slender body trembled in his arms, and then she said, 'I'm sorry, darling. I know you have to do it and I'm proud of you, I really am. It's just that sometimes it all seems so futile.' For a moment, she sat silently looking into the fire, then she withdrew from Andrew's arms and stood up. 'I'm just feeling a bit low, that's all. I think I'll go to bed.'

She left the room quietly and closed the door. Andrew heard her footsteps on the stairs and then overhead as she went softly into Hughie's room to see that he was asleep and covered up. After a few minutes, he heard her go into the bathroom and then to their own bedroom.

He sat for another half-hour, watching the fire go down. Tomorrow night he would be flying, escorting bombers to deal death and destruction to innocent people in foreign cities. Without any doubt, they would be attacked themselves and he would make every effort to shoot down the enemy planes. To kill. And, quite possibly, to be killed himself.

Alison knew all this as well as he did. He knew that she supported him in his work. She knew that the war must be won, and what they must do to win it. Yet he could understand her feelings, her fears and her sorrows. It was part of the burden of being a woman.

It made no difference to his determination to hunt and shoot down every enemy plane that came within his range.

Chapter Twelve

By Christmas, Bomber Command had spread its grey wings over all of industrial Germany, and the fighter squadrons were kept busy escorting vast formations of bombers on their deadly missions.

Andrew and Ben, both still burning with white-hot anger, felt no mercy for the pilots they sent to their deaths, nor for the people below who received the fury of the bombs themselves. They knew that many of those killed must be innocent, helpless to affect the war one way or the other, yet somehow they were able to set that knowledge aside, as if thrusting it into a darkened room and slamming a heavy metal door on it. They ignored it because they had to, in order to do their job, and because they needed to avenge those they had lost. One day, perhaps, they would have to take it out of its dark, silent room and look at it again, but that day was somewhere in the future, and might never come.

On the morning of Christmas Day, Andrew came home exhausted, just in time to see Hughie open his stocking. He watched the little boy's delight as he pulled out the few bits and pieces they had been able to find for him – a wooden model of a Typhoon, a bag of marbles, some plasticine, a few sweets and an orange which was tucked into the toe. He had some bigger presents too, pushed into a pillowcase which bulged excitingly – a couple of picture books, a toy train which had been Andrew's, a tennis ball, some crayons and a colouring book. May had knitted him a bright red jumper, made with wool unravelled from an old pullover of her father's, and a pair of mittens to go with it, and these he insisted on wearing at once, when Alison took him down to the village church for the service.

'I won't come if you don't mind,' Andrew said. 'I'll get some sleep, or I'll be fit for nothing later on.'

'That's all right.' Alison looked at his grey face and red-rimmed eyes. They had invited some of the squadron to come round in the evening and no doubt they too would be spending most of the day in bed. 'You sleep as long as you like. We'll have dinner when you wake up.'

There was no turkey this year, nor even a chicken. The Government had promised that every American serviceman in the country would have turkey, to remind them of home and thank them for their presence, and civilian quotas had been so small that even the large town butchers were getting fewer than a dozen birds. The Prettyjohns were having one of their own fowls, fattened especially, and had been apologetic that they couldn't offer Alison one as well, but she'd brushed aside their regrets.

'We can't expect you to feed us. You've only known us a few months.'

'It's just that we promised Uncle John and Aunt Betty one as well, and then there's Mum's cousin over to Sampford Spiney, she always has one, and we only had the three cock birds spare. We haven't even got an old hen.'

'I told you, it's all right. You've got your own family to think of. We'll be quite happy with whatever we can get.' Rabbit again, she thought, but was grateful for it. At least there were plenty of them out here in the country, eking out the meagre meat ration.

The sound of the little bell ringing in its turret welcomed Alison and Hughie to the church. The ban on bell-ringing, declared soon after the war had started, had been lifted once the threat of invasion was thought to be safely past and a few months ago it had been announced that church bells could be rung again on special occasions. Even so, a lot of churches remained silent because there were no ringers, but the bellrope at Milton Combe needed only to be pulled, and the choirboys competed for the honour. Today, the young son of one of the local farmers was tugging away at it, a beaming smile on his face, and as the parishioners walked up the church path, they turned, wishing each other a happy Christmas, and Alison smiled back, feeling warmed by their friendliness.

Most of those at the airfield would be at Yelverton, where there were a Methodist chapel and a Roman Catholic church as well as St Paul's, but Alison liked to join in whatever went on in the village. She had already begun to wonder if she and Andrew might settle here once the war was over and he left the RAF, but that seemed to be too far in the future to consider seriously. All the same, she played with the idea that she belonged here, in this pretty, stone village, and that these people singing carols with her really were her friends and neighbours.

May and her mother and grandfather were just across the aisle. They nodded and smiled as Alison and Hughie took their seats, and she felt warmth and peace touch her heart. There was something about this small church that gave her comfort in an increasingly troubling world, and she knelt to pray, with Hughie beside her.

Afterwards, she walked up the steep hill with the Prettyjohns. They parted at the corner with a kiss and good wishes, and then Alison and Hughie walked on alone towards the cottage.

'Uncle Stefan!' Hughie said suddenly, and she looked up to see the tall, fair-haired Polish pilot strolling towards them. She quickened her pace and they stopped, facing each other.

'Happy Christmas,' Alison said, and he nodded and bowed his head slightly.

'And I wish you a happy Christmas too, Alison.' He glanced down at Hughie. 'And did Saint Nicholas come to visit you last night?'

Hughie looked doubtful. 'Is that the same as Santa Claus?' His face cleared when Stefan nodded, and he said eagerly, 'Yes, he did. He brought me lots of presents. I've got a Typhoon, look.' He took the wooden toy from his pocket and swooped it through the air. 'I'm going to have a real one when I grow up, like my daddy.'

Stefan looked down at him gravely and Alison caught the thought behind his eyes. 'I know,' she said quietly. 'I hope not, too.' She hesitated, then said, 'Weren't you flying last night? I'd have thought you'd be in bed now, making up for lost sleep.'

'I slept for a few hours. Then I woke up and thought, It's Christmas Day. I began to think about home . . .' He paused. 'When that happens, I find it's best to go for a walk.'

'Oh.' Alison looked at him. The pale face was drawn and the fine grey eyes shadowed. 'You're thinking about Christmas with your family.'

He inclined his head again. 'I know I shouldn't, but I can't help remembering happier times, when we all spent Christmas together. The decorations, the music. It all seems so far away – so long ago.'

Alison rested her hand on the top of the gate. It was a cold morning. The ground was hard and frozen, and a bleak wind blew across from the Sound. She looked at the pilot and said, 'Why don't you come in? I'll make some coffee. We'll have to be quiet, because Andrew's asleep, at least, he was when we went out, but we can talk in the living room.'

He hesitated. 'I don't want to intrude on your Christmas.'

'Don't be silly,' she said warmly. 'You've been invited to come this afternoon anyway, and I expect some of the others will drop in too. We're hoping for a party tonight. It will be nice to hear more about your Christmases at home – that's if you don't mind talking about them.'

His eyes met hers. They were the colour of ice on the sea – a pale grey with tiny flecks of green and blue somewhere in their depths. He looked away from her, out towards the broad, cold horizon, and then said simply, 'No. I don't mind talking about Christmas at home. Perhaps it will bring my family closer for a while.'

They went through the door and Hughie immediately tugged Stefan by the hand, taking him into the living room where Alison had set up their tiny Christmas tree. There were no lights, but there were a few bright glass baubles kept from former Christmases, and she had made gingerbread biscuits and hung them amongst the branches, together with a few scraps of coloured paper cut into the shapes of stars. The room was strung with paperchains that she and Hughie had spent hours glueing together during the past two or three weeks, and there was a row of Christmas cards propped along the oak beam over the fireplace.

When she came back from the kitchen, bearing a tray with coffee and warm milk, Hughie was still showing Stefan his presents. She set the tray down.

'Do you have Christmas trees as well?'

'Oh, yes,' he said. 'We have very tall ones in all the public squares and smaller ones in our homes. All of them are lit and decorated – we use biscuits, like these, and wrapped chocolates and fruits and nuts. And on the top we put a shining star. The star is a very important part of

Christmas, because it was a star that led the Three Kings to the stable where Jesus was born.'

'And do you have presents on your tree?' Hughie asked. He cast a longing look towards the tree standing on the deep windowsill. 'There are some presents on ours, but Daddy says we're not to have those until tomorrow.'

'That's just because he thinks it will be nice to have something else to look forward to,' Alison told him and he pushed out his lips but said nothing.

Stefan said, a little apologetically: 'We have presents from our tree on Christmas Eve. Saint Nicholas comes to us then – he's dressed in the same way as your Father Christmas, but we call him the Starman. We have our main celebration then, you see – *Wigilia*, we call it. The whole family comes together to eat good food at supper. We begin as soon as the first star appears in the sky. Remember that the winter is very cold in Poland, with deep snow on the ground by Christmas, so many of the guests will arrive by sleigh.'

'With real reindeer?' Hughie asked, his eyes enormous as he listened, and Stefan laughed.

'No, we use horses, with little bells fastened to their heads.'

'Jingle bells!' Hughie cried, hopping up and down with excitement. 'I know that song!'

'I do too,' Stefan said. 'The others have been singing it in the mess.'

'Do you have carols? We've been singing carols in church. I like "Once In Royal David's City" best, because it's about a boy,' Hughie said, and when they both looked at him he added impatiently, 'The boy *David*. He killed a giant.'

'Well, not at Christmas,' Alison began, but Stefan laughed and she decided to shelve Hughie's religious instruction for the time being.

'Yes, we have carols. We call them *Koledy*.'

'Tell us some more about — what was it you said Christmas Eve was called?' Alison asked.

'*Wigilia*,' he said. 'Well, there's a lot of preparation for it, just as there is here. We start during Advent, with special church services every morning at six. And the women bake the *peirnik* — a honey cake which they make in all kinds of shapes, like stars and animals and hearts, and little models of Saint Nicholas himself. We hang mistletoe over the door to ward off evil, and place wheat in the corners of the room to drive away unhappiness and to remember that our Saviour was born in a stable. And the *Gwiadorze* — the star-carriers — wander from village to village, singing carols or putting on puppet shows and nativity scenes.'

'We used to go carol-singing round the village at home,' Alison said. 'And there used to be Christmas mummers' plays as well. What else happens on Christmas Eve?'

'We start our supper with a specially baked bread, with a holy picture on the top. It's passed around the family, and as each person breaks a piece off, they forgive any hurts or grievances that have happened over the past year and wish each other happiness. *Wigilia* is a time for forgiveness and fresh starts.'

'Christmas is here, as well,' Alison said. 'At least, it's supposed to be. I'm not sure that it always works out that way.'

He laughed. 'It can be a difficult time, I know. There are some members of the family who will never get on! But most of them try to, at least for this short time, and if there's a quarrel that hasn't been healed, it often helps to mend the breach. Well, after we have shared our *optalek*, and sung some carols, we begin our meal. There are eleven courses—'

'*Eleven*?' Alison repeated in astonishment. 'How can you possibly eat all that?'

133

'Well, we have fasted all day,' he said. 'But most of them don't contain meat. We will have almond soup, and perhaps beetroot soup, and then fish and vegetables – sauerkraut in pastry and fried millet in cabbage leaves – very different from your vegetables. And many sweets, of course – children everywhere love sweets.' He smiled at Hughie. 'But again, they're not much like yours. Poppyseed cakes, perhaps, and ginger cakes and sweet pastries. And fruits – dried fruits and oranges and apples. And plenty of wine and mead to drink.'

'It sounds lovely,' Alison said, thinking of pre-war English Christmases, with sherry before the turkey and a good burgundy or claret to drink with it. Then Christmas pudding with brandy butter, crackers to pull and maybe a piece of Stilton and a glass of port for her father afterwards. Pastry filled with sauerkraut didn't have the same attraction somehow, but if it was what you were used to . . .

'But what about the presents?' Hughie asked impatiently. 'You said Father Christmas comes and gives you presents.'

'Ah yes, Father Christmas – the Starman. The children are all taken to another room to meet him. Perhaps their father has dressed up or perhaps it is the parish priest himself, who examines them on their catechism and asks about their behaviour over the past year. Some of the children may feel very uneasy about this!' He grinned, and Alison surmised that he had had his own moments of discomfort. 'But once this is over, he takes them back to the dining room and there they find the lanterns lit and the Christmas tree filled with presents and, good or bad, you may be sure that they are all well satisfied.'

'I wish the Starman would come here,' Hughie said wistfully.

'Well, he did, didn't he?' Alison told him. 'He came last night, while you were asleep, and filled your stocking.'

'I'd like to *see* him, though. I'd like him to come to supper like he does at Uncle Stefan's house.'

'What happens then?' Alison asked. 'Do you have a party, with games and songs and stories?'

'Oh yes. We gather round the fire and sing, and sometimes we visit each other with more presents, and at last we go to midnight mass. That's the church service,' he added to Hughie. 'We go in our sleighs, all wrapped up warmly, and give thanks for all the good things we have.'

There was a moment's silence. Alison saw his face settle into more sombre lines and knew that he must be thinking of those happy times, and wondering if his family were still able to celebrate Christmas – if they were even still alive to celebrate at all. She reached across and touched his hand, and he gave her a quick glance and a small smile.

'Sing us some carols now,' Hughie commanded, oblivious of the moment of sadness.

'Hughie!' Alison protested. 'Uncle Stefan may not want to sing carols.'

Stefan got up and went to the piano. 'I will play you some, very quietly so as not to wake your father.' He sat down and began to pick out a tune, very softly, one note at a time.

'Why, we know that tune!' Alison exclaimed in surprise and, at the same moment, Hughie said, 'It's "Twinkle, Twinkle, Little Star"!'

'It's a nursery rhyme,' Alison explained to the Pole, and Hughie chanted it. 'It never occurred to me that it might mean the Star over Bethlehem. And you have it too!' It seemed to bring them even closer together.

'Play another one,' Hughie said, and this time the Pole began to sing as well, very softly.

'*Wsrod nocnej ciszy, Glos sie rozchodzi,*
Wstancie pasterze, Bog sie wam rodzi.

135

> *Czym predzej sie wybierajcie,*
> *Do Betlejem pospieszajcie,*
> *Przywitac Pana!'*

'Do you know it in English?' Alison asked, and he began the tune again.

> *'Angels from heaven sang a thrilling psalm,*
> *Waking the shepherds from their drowsy calm.*
> *Rise, ye shepherds, hurry onwards,*
> *Greet the newborn Son of David,*
> *King Emmanuel!'*

The song drifted into silence as his fingers caressed the last few notes from the keys, and he sat motionless for a moment. Alison glanced at his face and saw there the pain of all that he had lost and might never find again, and wished she had not asked him to talk about his memories. Then Hughie said, 'I *knew* it was about the boy David!' and they both laughed.

'All the Christmas stories are about a boy,' Stefan said, closing the piano lid, and as he turned Alison caught a glimpse of movement from the corner of her eye and saw Andrew standing in the doorway.

'Oh, darling! Did we wake you?' She got up and went over to him, needing suddenly to make a link with her husband, to feel the warmth of his skin. 'We meant to be quiet.'

'No, I was waking anyway. It was rather nice, hearing the piano.' He glanced at Stefan. 'Good to see you. Are you staying for lunch?'

'Not at all.' The Polish pilot got up hastily. 'We met by chance and your wife invited me in for coffee. But I won't intrude any longer – you want your family to yourself now.

And I'm poor company, especially at Christmas. I think too much, so the others tell me.'

'It's easy for them to say that,' Andrew said. 'Most of them can get home now and then, and even the Canadians can keep in touch with their families. You can't.' He came further into the room and dropped into an armchair, reaching out his arms for Hughie to scramble on to his lap. 'You may as well stay. Some of the others will be coming in later – no point in you going all that way, only to turn round and come back again. And I'm sure Alison is providing us with a feast.'

'A feast!' she said with a rueful laugh. 'Rabbit – that's what we're having. Again. But better than lots of people will be having, I'm sure.'

'Yes,' Stefan said. 'Better than many, many people will be having.'

Behind his clouded eyes, Alison seemed to catch a glimpse of hungry people, driven from their homes, living in squalor and desperation, and she shivered.

As Andrew went out to the little garden shed to fetch vegetables from the store Alison kept there, she turned to him and said, 'Thank you for telling us about your Christmases, Stefan.' She hesitated for a moment, then went on, 'At the party we had a couple of months ago, you said you'd like to come and talk to me. To tell me about your home and your family. You never did.'

'I've come to your house many times since then,' he said.

'But not to talk. Not like that.'

'It's too much. I can't burden others with my troubles.'

'I wouldn't mind,' she said, meeting his grey eyes. 'I really wouldn't mind. If it would help.'

There was a short pause. Then he said slowly, 'It has helped, talking to you this morning. Yes. Perhaps I will do it again, one day.'

The back door opened and slammed again as Andrew

and Hughie came in, bringing a gust of cold air with them. Stefan turned away, and Alison went to start the preparations for their Christmas dinner. Later, the other pilots would come and the day would grow merry, but she knew that she would not forget this hour of quiet, nor this glimpse she had been given of another kind of Christmas.

Ben was the only member of the squadron who didn't take up Andrew's invitation that Christmas Day.

He went to dinner that evening in the mess, sitting at the long tables with the other pilots without really noticing what he was eating – it could have been roast beef, turkey or fish and chips for all he was aware. He drank steadily, listened to some jokes and speeches without taking in anything that was said, and finally got up, pushed back his chair and excused himself.

Outside, the darkness was lightened by the moon which had enabled them to see their way to Germany last night. He stood for a few minutes in the narrow road, letting his eyes get accustomed to the stark black and white, and then turned to walk along beside the perimeter fence. He didn't want to go inside the airfield – there was too much chance of bumping into someone he knew, even on Christmas night, or having to explain himself to some sentry. Instead, he stayed outside, trudging along the moonlit ribbon of roadway, his thoughts far away from the quiet shadows of the moors.

He had still not come to terms with his brother's death, partly because his mother was unable to accept it. He had managed one more quick visit home a week ago, hitch-hiking part of the way, and found her moving through the days with a blank face. She had greeted him with a kiss, but her smile had been pallid and forced, as if it were no more than a crack in the face of a marble statue, and when he talked to her he wasn't sure that she heard his voice. She seemed abstracted, as if listening for something – or someone – else, and when she replied it was with a cool, remote tone in her voice, as if she weren't really interested in what she was saying.

She made Ben a cup of coffee and offered him a biscuit, talking all the time as if he were a stranger. He sat at the kitchen table with her, watching her pale face and noting the pink rims of her eyes, and felt as if a fist were clutching his heart.

'Mum,' he said at last, breaking into a flat-voiced monologue about the Sunday School Christmas party. 'Mum, tell me how you are.'

'I'm very well, thank you, Ben,' she said after a moment during which he wondered if she'd heard him. 'And how are you? Are they feeding you properly? You look thinner.'

They were all the things she always said to him, yet they sounded different now, as if they were lines in a play that she'd learned and was now repeating to his cue. She didn't sound as if she wanted to know the answers.

He hadn't known what to say to her. He had the feeling that she was made of thin glass and the slightest clumsy movement might break her. He mumbled something and she went back to what she had been saying. Little Sylvie, the evacuee at the Suttons' farm, had won the prize for best attendance, but she wouldn't be at the Christmas Eve carol service because she was going home to Portsmouth for the holiday . . . All the Bagshaw children had turned up for Sunday School on the last two Sundays before the party, to make sure they were invited, even though everyone knew they wouldn't be seen in the church again until next November . . . Freddy Phillips had got into a fight with Micky Morrison and almost knocked over the Christmas tree . . . It had been even more difficult than usual, finding presents to give the children . . . Old Mr Merryweather had decided his arthritis was too bad to allow him to play Santa Claus this year, so Bert Mullins had done it instead . . .

It was all the sort of news she would have told him at any other time, but the flat voice in which it was delivered made it seem again like lines from a play – a play she wasn't interested in and just wanted to have over and done with, so that she could go back to that deep place somewhere inside her, where she could hear and talk to that other person – the one she really wanted to hear.

'Mum,' he said again, reaching across the table for her hand. She looked down as if she had never seen hands before and he felt the fist squeeze a little more tightly around his heart. 'Mum, please. Look at me. Talk to me.'

She met his eyes and he wished he hadn't asked. It was like looking into two pools of emptiness, with nothing but desolation at their heart, and he felt suddenly as he had felt once as a little boy, when the night-light had blown out and he'd been left in the dark. 'Mum, please!' he repeated shakily. 'I know we've lost Peter, but you've still got the rest of us – Ian and Alexie, and me. Doesn't that help at all?'

The hollow grey eyes seemed to look right through him and then she said in that flat voice he was beginning to hate, 'I know I've got the rest of you, Ben. I don't know what I'd do if I didn't. But I haven't got Peter, have I? I haven't got Peter, and I'm never going to see him again.'

Her pain tore at his heart. He shook his head helplessly, and said, 'Oh, Mum, isn't there anything at all I can do to make you feel better?'

The back door opened, quelling any words that she might have spoken, and his father came in. John Hazelwood's face lit up at the sight of his son and then the smile faded as he saw the look on his wife's face. He shucked off his Wellington boots and came quickly across the cold brown quarry tiles in his socks and put his arms around her slender shoulders.

'Olivia. I'm here, my dear.' He looked at Ben. 'It's good to see you. How long can you stay?'

For once, Ben didn't make the usual response, that what his father was really asking was 'How soon are you going back?' He said, 'I've only got the day. I'll have to catch the train this evening.' He felt his eyes slide towards his mother again and saw that she was still sitting upright, making no acknowledgement of her husband's hands on her shoulders. 'Can we have a – a bit of a talk sometime, Dad?'

'Of course. Come over to the church with me. I only slipped back for some papers.' John Hazelwood glanced down at his wife. 'You'll be all right, won't you, my dear? It's a pity Jeanie's not here to keep you company.'

With a small shock, Ben realised that he hadn't given Jeanie a thought; he'd been so alarmed by the sight of his mother, so pale and remote, that he'd forgotten all about her and Hope. He looked around now, as if expecting her to step out from behind the dresser. 'Where is she?'

'She's gone to Portsmouth for a day or two,' Olivia said in the cold, dry voice that seemed so different from her usual soft, silvery tones. 'Her mother and father wanted her to spend some time with them.' She put her palm to her forehead and began to get up. 'I think I'll go and lie down. I've got such a headache . . .'

'I'll bring you a cup of tea,' John suggested, but she shook her head.

'I don't want anything. I just want to sleep.' She drifted out of the room and they heard her feet climbing slowly up the stairs.

Ben and John looked at each other. At last, Ben said, 'Is she ill, Dad?'

John sighed and spread his hands on the table. 'Not ill, no. Not in the usual sense. Just grieving. But I'm afraid—'

He stopped, as if he didn't want to voice his fear, but Ben couldn't let him leave it.

'Afraid of what? Tell me, Dad. Please.'

'I'm afraid she doesn't know how to grieve properly. To let it out – to *use* it, even, to stop it going bad inside her. She's holding it inside.'

'She seems like a spring,' Ben said. 'Tightly wound up. I was almost afraid to say anything in case she snapped.' He looked at his father's kind, worried face. 'What would happen, Dad, if she did snap?'

'I don't know. I'm afraid to think about it.'

For a few moments, both were silent. John looked at the table and Ben noticed that he hadn't finished his coffee. He drank it, even though it was cold and unpleasant, and then asked, 'What about church, Dad? Doesn't that help?'

The silence this time was longer. Then John shook his head.

'No, it doesn't. It can't.' He looked up and met Ben's eyes. 'She doesn't give it a chance to help. She won't go inside the door. She's lost her faith, Ben – lost it at the very moment when she needs it the most.'

Chapter Thirteen

Ben thought of this visit as he walked alone through the moonlit lanes of Harrowbeer on Christmas night. He had gone over to the church with his father and they'd discussed the situation without coming to any answer. 'If we were in a Victorian novel,' John had said, 'I'd have said your mother was going into a "decline", and there doesn't seem to be a thing I can do about it. But I'm sure it will do her good to have you home for a few hours. We both appreciate your coming, Ben.'

Whether it had really done his mother any good, Ben didn't know. She had drifted around the house like a ghost, lost in her own world. His father had assured him that his visit had helped, that she was better for it, but all Ben could do was wonder just how bad she had been before. Towards the end of the day, she had seemed to make an effort, smiling at him, joining in their conversation, and hugging him when he left. But as he walked away down the lane towards the railway station, he had felt again like a little frightened boy, crying because his mother had left him alone in the dark.

He'd written to Alexandra, asking what she thought about their mother, but there seemed to be nothing else he could do. Nothing, other than put all his energies, all his grief, into his flying. Nothing, but avenge his brother and all those friends he had lost, in the only way he knew.

All this while, he had been walking fast along the

perimeter fence, with no real purpose or direction. He came to one of the gateways and hesitated, debating whether to go inside and call it a day. The moon shone brightly down from the cold, clear sky and he could see the outlines of the huts and hangars, the shapes of some of the planes and, away in the distance, the dark silhouettes of the hills with their rocky outcrops – Sheepstor, Cox Tor, Vixen Tor. There were no lights showing, but he knew that in some of the huts men would be playing cards, perhaps singing a few songs, celebrating their own Christmas. In his own mess, there would be someone to drink with, to share a joke with. He thought about it a moment longer, aware that the sentry must be watching him, and then, feeling suddenly weary of it all, sick of war and of everything that would remind him of it, he turned abruptly and walked away, the airfield at his back, still half inclined to call in at Andrew's cottage after all.

The lane was narrow, the hedges towering on either side. Tall trees whispered softly in the breeze, high above his head. The moon was higher too now, a gleaming silver bauble in the sky, and he realised that he had passed the Knights' cottage and was approaching the Prettyjohns'.

As he came to the gate, the door opened and someone came out, drawing the blackout curtain quickly. Ben paused, and the figure stopped and said, 'Is someone there?'

'May!' he said, feeling an unexpected surge of pleasure. 'It's me – Ben Hazelwood. Sorry, I didn't mean to startle you.'

''Tis no matter.' She came down the path and rested her hands on the gate, looking up at him. Her face was pale in the glimmering light and her eyes no more than shadows beneath the dark curls. 'Were you coming to see us?'

Ben felt confused and embarrassed. 'No – I mean, I was just out for a walk. I didn't really notice where I was until I found myself here. I wouldn't have disturbed you, not on Christmas night.'

'Why ever not? We'm happy to see you any time.' She began to open the gate. 'Would you like to come in now, and have a Christmas drink? Grandpa's opened a bottle of elderberry wine.'

'Oh no! I really didn't mean – I was just out for a walk.' He paused and looked up at the sky. 'It's a lovely night. Usually, we'd be flying on a night like this, but . . .'

'Tell you what,' May said as he paused, 'I was just thinking of a walk myself. I've been indoors most of the day. Why don't I come along of you now, and then you can come in for some of Grandpa's elderberry when we come back? He and Mother would be pleased to see you, and so would Father. We decided to bring him downstairs for Christmas and he's having a lovely time.' She paused, then added quietly, 'Or did you want to be on your own? I heard about your brother.'

'Yes,' he said after a moment, 'it was a bad show. But there's plenty of others in the same boat.' He looked down at her again and then smiled. 'That sounds a really good idea. If you're sure they won't mind?'

'Of course they won't. I said I was coming out for a breath of fresh air anyway. I'll just pop back and get my coat and tell 'em I'll be about half an hour, if that's all right.' She beamed at him and slipped back through the door. In a few minutes she was back and he held the gate open for her. They walked on along the lane together.

'I suppose you know all the fields and footpaths for miles around,' Ben said after a moment.

'My stars, yes. Played on all these fields as a little maid, went for picnics in the woods, down to the river at Double Waters, and swimming at Lopwell, and on the common, everywhere. I don't reckon there's a blade of grass I don't know. Mind you, 'tis very different now, with the airfield there. Used to be able to walk for miles, us did, before that were built, and it was so quiet too. You could go outside and hear nothing but birds singing.'

'I shouldn't think the local people were very pleased about that,' he remarked. 'It's not exactly quiet now.'

'Well, there was talk of building an airfield here before the war. A proper airport, you know. But it didn't come to anything. I suppose now that it's here, it'll stay, once the war's over. Yelverton and Milton Combe and Buckland won't ever be the same again, but what can you do about it?'

They walked on in silence. Instead of keeping to the roads, as Ben would have done, May led him along footpaths through moonlit fields and shadowy woods. They came to a stile and paused for a moment, gazing down at the broad ribbon of the estuary streaming away to the sea. A few miles further down were the naval docks at Devonport, so often a target for the German bombers. People said that the Germans found them by following the river, May said, and Ben knew it was true. A shining silver pathway like this was a godsend to a pilot.

'I suppose people came out here to be safe,' he said thoughtfully, and she nodded.

'They used to come out in buses and sleep in the old school and the Reading Room. Then they'd go back to Plymouth next morning. Some of us took them in as well, if us had room, and us had the liddle tackers as well, to stay all the time. Most of them have gone back now that the bombing's stopped.' She turned her head to look into his eyes. 'I was real sorry to hear about your brother, Ben.'

'I know. Thanks.' He laid his hand on the top of the stile, looking down at it. 'I know there are a lot of people who've lost relatives. It ought to make it easier, somehow, but it doesn't. I just can't seem to get it into my head.'

'Of course that doesn't make it easier,' May said. 'He was

your brother. Everyone who loses someone feels just as bad. Why should you be any different?' She thought for a minute and then added, 'If you ask me, I think it makes it harder, knowing there's all these people been killed already, and still being killed. Thousands of them – millions, even. And what for, eh? What's it all about?'

Ben gave a short laugh. 'You ought to ask Stefan Dabrowksi that. You know, the Polish pilot. It was because Hitler invaded Poland that we went into it in the first place. I don't suppose anyone thought it would spread the way it has.'

'It's like a horrible disease,' she said. 'Spreading all over the world, breaking out like sores. All we're doing is treating the sores – cutting them out or cauterising them. But that doesn't do any good to the disease itself. The germs still go on underneath.'

'Yes,' Ben said, 'that's just what it's like. But what else can we do? We've got to try to stop it spreading. And we'll win in the end. We must.'

'I hope so,' she said. 'I really do hope so.'

They stood quietly for a moment. Then May curled her fingers in his, and lifted her face. Looking down, he could see the dark pools of her eyes and the pale glimmer of her teeth as she smiled at him.

''Tis Christmas night,' she said softly. 'Let's just think about that, shall us?'

Ben looked into the dark eyes. The gleam of the moon was reflected in them like twin stars. Her full lips were parted slightly over the glistening white teeth and he caught his breath and bent towards her. He felt her fingers curl into his palm, and he slid his other arm around her waist and drew her against him as she raised her face to his and their lips met, softly, in a kiss that was no more than a whisper in the breeze.

They stood together for a moment without speaking. Then, very quietly, Ben said, 'Happy Christmas, May . . .'

By the time they returned to the cottage, Mabel Prettyjohn had laid out a supper of cold chicken and ham, with some home-made pickles and bread and cheese. Her father had set a second bottle of elderberry wine on the table, the fire glowed and the cottage was a cosy fortress against the winter's night and all the sorrows of the war.

'There you be!' she welcomed them, her face wreathed in smiles. 'My, you do look all bright and glowing – that's the cold air, I dare say.' She drew them inside and held out her arms for Ben's coat. 'Come and sit by the fire, my handsome, and get warm.'

'It's lovely out, Mother,' May said, taking off her own coat and hanging it behind the door. 'The brightest moon you ever saw, and the fields are all white with frost. It's like fairyland.'

'At least there's been no snow this year – so far.' Mrs Prettyjohn took Ben's cold hands between her warm ones and rubbed them gently, something nobody had done for him since he was a small child. After a moment, she held her hand out to the fire to warm the palm again, then rubbed his hands once more. It was strangely comforting and he remembered how he had been feeling like a frightened little boy, and then took himself severely to task. I'm not a little boy! he thought crossly. I'm a grown man, fighting a grown man's war, and I'm fighting it for my brother now as well as my King and country. And for these people, too – who hardly know me, yet welcome me into their home on Christmas night because they know I'm fighting for them.

All the same, it couldn't do any harm to let go for a little while, to relax in this cosy living room with its stone walls and warm fire, and let these strangers envelop him with their kindness. And there was May, as well, and the kiss they had shared by the stile. It wasn't Ben's first kiss, yet it had somehow seemed like it. Somehow special . . .

May's mother let go of his hands and moved over to the table. 'Now, my lover, you'll help yourself to whatever you fancy. There's plenty here and us've got plenty for tomorrow's dinner, so you needn't worry that you'm taking our rations.'

'Well, I had dinner in the mess,' he began, but the sight of the simple, homely meal laid out on the table with the best lace cloth and willow pattern china because it was Christmas, woke a fresh hunger in him and he was pleased to take some of the crusty, home-made bread and the mellow cheese and a slice or two of meat with some of Mrs Prettyjohn's pickles.

'That's good to see, a healthy young appetite,' William Prettyjohn said. He was sitting up in a makeshift bed along one wall, wearing a proper shirt and tie instead of his pyjama jacket, and already had a plate on his lap. He was rather pale but didn't seem ill otherwise, and Ben remembered that May had told him that he had had an accident which had left his legs paralysed, and spent most of his time upstairs.

'He needs to keep his strength up,' Mabel said, heaping some more cold meat on to Ben's plate and waving away his protests. 'I told you, it's not taking our rations. Our own cock bird, this was, fattened up for Christmas. Horace, we called him,' she added.

'Horace?' Ben looked at the meat which had once been so much part of the family that it had had a name. 'Er . . .'

'Oh, 'tis all right,' Mrs Prettyjohn assured him. 'He had a happy life.'

Old Mr Prettyjohn lifted the dark brown bottle of wine and tilted it over Ben's glass. 'Try this, my handsome. My own elderberry, this is. Or I've got a drop of rowan, four years old and ready to drink. And there be cider as well, made of apples from our own orchard. Try them all!'

Ben scarcely knew where to start. 'Maybe some cider first, to go with the cheese,' he suggested, and a large glass was poured out and handed to him. He took a sip and felt his face screw up at the dryness. The others laughed.

'You've not tried home-made Devon scrumpy before,' William Prettyjohn said. 'Takes you by surprise, doesn't it. Better not drink too much, specially if you'm going to try Dad's wines as well. He's a master at winemaking, is Dad.'

They sat round the fire, their plates on their laps, and the talk passed to old times, before the war. 'Many's the winter's night us've spent sitting round this very fire, roasting chestnuts and telling stories,' William went on. 'Good times, they've been.' He turned to the old man. 'Father, tell this young chap a few of your old Dartmoor tales. I dare say he'll not have heard them.'

'He'll be the only one in the world who hasn't, then,' May remarked and her mother shook her head at her. She grinned unrepentantly.

Ben looked at the grandfather, sitting in his wheelback chair by the fire. He had finished eating and was filling his pipe. 'I'd like to hear them.'

Old Mr Prettyjohn sucked hard on his pipe to get it going, then took it from his mouth. 'Well, now, which shall I start with? Have you heard the tale of the Hairy Hands? Or the lady who drives out from the gatehouse down by Fitzford Bridge at midnight with her carriage? Or old Dewer – the Devil hisself – driving his hounds over the Dewerstone Rocks one dark, stormy night? Or—'

'I haven't heard any of them,' Ben said eagerly, and the old man sucked his pipe again and began.

'Well, I'll tell 'ee about the Hairy Hands first.' He lowered his voice and they all leaned forwards, even those who had heard the story so many times before. ''Tis out on the road across the moor, between Princetown and Two Bridges that it happens. Mostly motorbikes, the Hairy Hands go for. They appear out of nowhere and grip hold of the handlebars and drive the bike off the road. The prison doctor from Princetown was killed there, twenty years or so ago, and there were another feller too, thrown to the side of the road. He didn't live neither, but he had a pillion passenger who said he'd seen the hands hisself, just before the crash. And then there was a couple once sleeping in a caravan – around the same time, it were, give or take a year or two – and the young woman woke up sudden-like, sensing danger, and saw these two huge hands, all covered with thick hair, crawling up the window, which was open at the top. Her knowed at once 'twas her man they were after but she made the sign of the Cross and prayed, and they slipped down again and disappeared.' He looked gravely at Ben and added, 'Take my word for it, young chap, don't 'ee go roaming over the moor at night, now. There's stranger things happen on Dartymoor than ever was told.'

Ben felt a shiver run down his spine. He glanced at May and she gave him a small smile and moved a little closer on the settee. He could feel her warmth against him.

'Then there's the ghosts of prisoners,' the old man went on. 'There's a little man with long dark hair, been seen many a time, running through the grounds of the prison. Even one of the Governors saw un once. And then there's another, David Davis he were called, spent fifty years behind bars there and looked after the prison sheep. When it came to un being turned loose, he didn't want to go – couldn't stand the thought of living outside – and he begged the Governor to let un stay but Governor said he had to go. So poor old David Davis, he said, "Well, keep the job open for me, will ee, because I'll be back for certain," and sure enough not a fortnight later un was back again and stopped there for the rest of his life. Folk've seen un since, driving his sheep about, happy as a sandboy.'

'Well, that's not quite so frightening,' Ben said, but the old man shook his head.

''Tis never good luck to see a ghost. But the worst one of all be only a few miles from here, down by Meavy. That's where the Devil drives his black Hounds of Hell over the rock – the Whistle Hounds, they'm called hereabouts. Old Dewer, he is, though some call him the Midnight Hunter, and he rides a huge black horse with fire breathing out of its nostrils. Every hound has eyes of fire as well, and great slavering jaws, and to see them means you'll die within the year. Some say they'll hound you off the rock there and then, and leave you dead at the bottom. On a stormy night, you can hear them howling ... howling ...' He paused dramatically. 'Come you hear that, boy, you don't want to be outside. Better to stay indoors.'

'Grandpa!' May protested, half-laughing. 'Ben'll be afraid to go back to the airfield if you go on like that.'

'Oh, I'm not scared of ghosts,' Ben declared. 'Anyway, I'm not going that way tonight. The airfield's only just up the road. Mind you,' he added, 'there are a few tales of haunted airfields. I knew a man who swore that at one station he was at, there was a ghost of an airman who used to appear in the officers' mess.'

'Ah,' old Mr Prettyjohn nodded. 'There's nowhere safe from ghosts.'

There was a short silence, then Mrs Prettyjohn got up briskly. 'Time for a cup of cocoa, I think. And maybe while I'm making it we could have a song or two, to help cheer us up. Ghosts are all very well, but they do leave you a bit gloomy.'

The others laughed and William began to sing. He had a good voice and they listened in silence as he sang 'Where E'er You Walk' and one or two Edwardian ballads, then joining in as he went on to some of the popular wartime songs like 'The White Cliffs of Dover' and 'We'll Meet Again'. By the time Mrs Prettyjohn brought in the cocoa they were roaring their way through 'Daisy, Daisy', 'My Old Man Said Follow the Van' and 'Waiting at the Church'.

'That sounds better,' she said, setting down the old tin tray with the cups of cocoa steaming on it. 'I've brought in a few biscuits as well.'

'I'll be too full to move after all this,' Ben said, but she shook her head.

'You need something inside you for the walk back. It's a good two mile or more, that is, back to Ravenscroft. Now, help yourself. I won't take no for an answer, mind.'

As Ben looked at her warm, homely face, he thought of his mother, sitting at home grieving over her lost son and unable to find comfort anywhere, even in her faith, and felt a sudden twinge of guilt. This had been such a pleasant, cheerful evening, so different from the way it had started. It doesn't mean I've forgotten, he thought. It doesn't mean I'm not still grieving myself. It's just that life has to go on, and would Peter want us to mourn him for the rest of our lives?

'Thank you,' he said to Mrs Prettyjohn. He finished his cocoa and stood up. 'I really ought to go now. Thank you all so much. You've made it a wonderful Christmas for me.'

May's mother gave him an understanding smile, as if she knew just what thoughts had passed through his mind. 'You'm always welcome here, my handsome. Just you remember that. Come in any time you'm passing. Us'll all be glad to see you.'

May came outside with him to the gate. They stood together for a moment, watching the moon slide slowly across the sky, and then she said, 'I hope you'll do what

Mother said, Ben. Come and visit us again. It's been lovely to see you.'

'It's been lovely to see you too, May.' Shyly, he touched her cheek with his fingers. 'Thank you. Thank you very much.' And then he bent and kissed her again.

As he made his way back to the airfield, he had the sensation that he was walking on the moonlight itself.

Chapter Fourteen

As the New Year opened, Alison read the papers with a sinking feeling that the war was never going to end.

'It's not all bad news,' Andrew said, trying to comfort her. 'Look how the Russians are kicking the Germans out. They've chased them all the way back to Poland. Hitler must be wishing he'd never gone into the country. It was far too much for him to take on.'

'Poland,' she said. 'Poor Stefan – he must be so worried. He has family still there.'

'I know. He doesn't say much in the mess, though. Talk about the British stiff upper lip – I think some of these Poles starch and iron theirs! Well, I have to admit I'd be worried too, in his position. God knows what the Germans have been doing in Poland, but it's not going to get much better with the Russians chasing them back there as well.'

'I thought you said that was the good news,' Alison said sombrely, and he made a wry face.

'I did, didn't I. Well, it is when you realise that the Germans are losing something. It's just a pity that a lot of other people have to lose as well. I'm sorry, darling. I don't always think of it like that. Can't really afford to, I'm afraid,' he added ruefully.

'No, I know you can't.' Alison understood that once he was in the air, Andrew was, like all those engaged in this war, as much a fighting machine as his aircraft. 'Is there any other good news?' she asked, without much hope.

'Oh yes, I almost forgot! You'll like this. You know that film actor you like – James Stewart? He's over here now – a major in the US Air Force, flying Liberators from a base in Norfolk. Well, the buzz is that he was coming back from a daylight mission over Germany a few days ago, when he saw that the lead group had gone off in the wrong direction and were heading out over France, right across the enemy airfields. So he went off after them to give cover. There was one hell of a battle, by all accounts, and they lost eight Liberators, but it would have been much worse if he hadn't spotted them. We had a bloke in the mess from over that way today, that's how I know.'

'Goodness me. So he's a real hero, not just a film-star one. We saw him in *Philadelphia Story*, do you remember, Andrew? He looks a really nice man.'

'He's no nancy-boy, that's for certain.'

There were other things Andrew could have told his wife as well, but he stuck to stories that she would read in the newspapers or hear on the radio. Implicitly though he trusted her, the less information was discussed, the less likely it was to reach the wrong ears.

'Has Stefan been over to see you yet?' he asked. 'You said you'd invited him. It would do him good to talk to you on his own. He's too buttoned up – needs to let things out a bit.'

'I know. That's what I thought, too. But I haven't seen him since Christmas.' She sighed. 'I've told him I'm here if he wants to talk, but I can't keep on saying so. It starts to look like prying. Perhaps he's just being polite and wishes I'd stop.'

'Who knows?' Andrew stretched his arm out and drew her close. 'Best not to worry about it any more, darling. He'll come if he wants to. In the meantime, you've got to think about yourself and our baby.' He touched her stomach gently. 'You're not doing too much, are you? You're not letting yourself get tired?'

'No. I rest every afternoon, and—' She stopped suddenly and caught her breath. 'Andrew!'

'What? What's wrong?' He sat up straight, alarmed, and she laughed a little shakily.

'Nothing. There's nothing wrong. It's just . . .' She caught her breath again. 'There! I'm almost sure . . .'

'Sure of what? What are you talking about? Darling, are you sure you're all right?'

'Very all right,' she said, and a smile broke out over her face. 'It's the baby, Andrew. It just moved. For the very first time. Here.' She caught his hand and placed it over the soft roundness of her stomach. 'Keep very still and see if it happens again.'

He saw the small flame of excitement leap again into her eyes. 'Was that it? I can't feel a thing.'

'It's very slight. More a sort of flutter, really. Like having a butterfly in my stomach. But I know that's what it is.' She lifted his hand and held the palm to her cheek. 'You'll feel it soon enough, don't worry – when it starts to kick and punch with its fists. But it's lovely to feel it. It makes it seem so real. Oh Andrew, why are we so lucky?'

'I don't know,' he said, and pulled her close into his arms. 'But we are. And let's be thankful for it.'

For the rest of the evening, they sat before the fire, letting its flames light the room as they savoured each other's closeness and talked quietly of the future. A future when there was no more war; when they could watch their family grow up in peace. The peace they were fighting for now.

Stefan finally came in the last week of January. There had been no flying the night before and Andrew was busy at the station. Alison, who had developed a cold, was indoors by the fire with Hughie.

'Stefan! Come in – that's if you're not afraid you'll catch my cold. It's getting better now, but I'm still a bit snuffly.'

'I don't catch colds.' He followed her into the front room. The fire was burning brightly with logs that May's uncle had brought along just before Christmas, and Hughie was on the floor with his bricks and the bag of marbles he'd been given for Christmas. Alison had been reading.

'Would you like a cup of tea? I was just about to make one.' She went out to the kitchen, leaving Stefan on his knees with Hughie. When she came back, carrying a tray with the tea and a plate of scones, they were constructing a castle with turrets.

'Oh, that's pretty,' she said, putting the tray on a small table. 'Like a fairytale castle.'

Stefan gave her a sombre glance. 'Not a fairy tale now, I am afraid. It's the kind of castle we have in my homeland. Probably the Germans are living in it, or using it as a prison – if it's standing at all.'

'Oh – I'm sorry.' Alison was nonplussed and he got up, immediately apologetic.

'No, it is I who should be sorry. How could you know? I built it just because it's the kind of castle I know.' He looked down at the little boy on the hearthrug. 'Knock it down, Hughie, and build one of your own castles. Let's forget fairy tales.'

'But I like fairy tales,' Hughie objected, and began to add another turret.

Stefan laughed, and Alison thought what a difference it made to his face. The fine skin around his grey eyes crinkled and his chiselled lips curved in a smile of great charm. She smiled back and gestured towards Andrew's armchair.

'Please – sit down. Have a cup of tea. Hughie, there's some orange juice for you, and a biscuit.'

'Orange juice?' the Pole said. 'It's very good for him, but I thought it was difficult for you to get oranges.'

'Oh, this is what the Government issues to children under five. It's quite strong – you have to dilute it. Hughie loves it.'

Stefan nodded. 'Your Government looks after you very well.'

'I think they do their best. We all complain about rationing, but it's the fairest way, and we all seem to stay pretty healthy on it. Not too many sweets or fatty foods!' she added with a smile. 'And we're encouraged to grow as much as we can ourselves. Andrew and I have got quite a few vegetables in the back garden already.'

'I would like to think that my family are as well off,' he said sadly.

Alison took Hughie's empty cup from him and the little boy went back to his bricks. She looked at Stefan.

'Don't you know anything at all about how they are?'

'Nothing. I told you, I left Poland soon after Britain declared war. It was plain to see that we could not fight the Germans in our own country and I could be most effective here. But it was hard, leaving them all behind; my mother and father are both in their sixties now, and then there are my sisters and their families. I felt as if I were being torn into pieces. I almost didn't leave, but they urged me to come to Britain. They said it was their only chance, for those of us who had the skills to fight to come to a place where we could use them.'

'What could you have done if you'd stayed?' Alison asked gently, and he shrugged.

'Nothing. I would probably have been killed trying to resist. I wouldn't have been any use at all then, and might even have caused their deaths as well.' He glanced down at Hughie. 'Perhaps I shouldn't be talking like this.'

'I don't think he notices. He's in a world of his own.' She hesitated, then said, 'Tell me about your family. How many sisters do you have?'

'Four. All older than me. I am the baby of the family. Irena is the eldest. Then there is Kataryna and then Urszula. The youngest, Krystyna, is just a year older than me and got married only a year before the war began. She is the one I worry about the most.'

'Why?'

'Because,' he said, 'her husband is Jewish.'

'Oh.' Alison frowned a little. 'And Hitler doesn't like the Jews, does he?'

'He thinks they should be exterminated,' Stefan said.

Alison drew in a sharp breath. '*Exterminated*?' She gave Hughie a quick, involuntary glance but although he looked up at her exclamation he returned at once to his bricks. 'But – that's not possible! How could he—?'

'I don't know,' Stefan said. 'But with that man, nothing is impossible. He's evil.' He regarded her thoughtfully, as if making up his mind whether to go on. Then he said, 'Have you not heard of *Kristallnacht*?'

'*Kristallnacht*?'

'The Night of the Broken Glass,' he said. 'It was in November 1938. The Nazis ordered that the houses of Jews – *all* Jews – be searched. Thousands were arrested and sent to internment and concentration camps. Synagogues were destroyed – set on fire, many of them. Jewish shops were looted and closed, their windows smashed. In Vienna, fires raged everywhere and Jews were hustled along the streets, jeered at and assaulted by crowds of hooligans. People in their apartments and homes found their doors kicked in by the SS and their belongings destroyed or stolen before their eyes. If they protested, they were shot. Some were thrown from the windows of upstairs apartments and lay broken and screaming on the pavement, and nobody dared help them. Those who tried were also shot. In the morning, the streets were covered with broken glass from the many windows, and that is where it got its name.'

Alison felt sick. In a whisper, she said, 'But this was almost a year before the war began. What happened to the Jews who weren't killed that night? Were they all taken away to these camps?'

'Not all. Some were left behind, but life became almost impossible for them. They had to remain in their homes, if they still had homes, except for a few hours each day when they were allowed out. Even then, they would be jeered at in the street or have stones and bottles thrown at them. And the children were not allowed in public places like swimming pools or playgrounds. They were expelled from their schools. High walls were built and they were herded behind them, to live apart from the rest of the community. Many people killed themselves.'

Alison shuddered and looked away. The hard lines of Stefan's face softened. 'Perhaps I should not be talking to you like this. Perhaps I should go.'

'No!' she said sharply. 'Of course you should talk about it. I ought to know. We *all* ought to know. I feel ashamed that I didn't know before, but I was too busy having a good time, going to dances and parties and getting married. I wasn't interested in what was going on in the rest of the world.'

'That's part of the problem,' he said. 'Even in Poland – in Germany itself – in all the countries of Europe, I think people were too busy dancing to see what was happening behind the stage.'

There was a short silence. Hughie had finished building his castle and was driving a small toy car through the passageways he had created. Some of the bricks fell down and he made an exclamation of annoyance. Stefan replaced them.

'They weren't balanced properly,' he said. 'You see, you mustn't have one too far out from one underneath it, or it will fall. Put them like this.'

Alison glanced at Hughie, wondering how much of this he understood, but he was absorbed in his game, driving his little car in and out of the castle, and murmuring a story to himself. She caught the words 'prince' and 'princess'. She looked back at Stefan.

'And – and do you think this might have happened in Poland as well?'

'I know it did,' he said quietly. 'Within three weeks of the invasion of my country, Warsaw – our proud city, our *capital* – was crushed. The Jewish Ghetto was formed there. My sister Krystyna's husband, Benedykt, was in fear of his life but he was still safe when I left, sheltered by the family. Krystyna wanted him to come with me, but she was expecting their first child and he wouldn't leave her. In any case, he wouldn't have been allowed to leave. He would have been discovered.'

'And you don't know what's happened to him? To any of them? '

'I have never heard any more,' he said. 'When this war is over, I will go back and try to find them. But . . .' He shrugged, a simple gesture with a world of hopelessness.

Alison looked down at Hughie again, playing so unknowingly with his toys, and thought of the new baby. 'What a world this is. What a world to bring children into.'

'And yet we cannot stop. We have to have children. It's the way of the world. And if those of us on the side of right and goodness stopped, that would leave the way for evil to walk all over the world. There would be nobody to prevent it.'

'I know. It's just that you can't help thinking about your

own. Thinking what they might have to go through . . .' She shivered and then said, 'What about you, Stefan? Are you married, or do you have a sweetheart – someone special?'

He was silent for a moment, looking into the fire. Then he said, 'No. There is no one special.'

'Would you like another cup of tea?' she asked gently after a moment, thinking at the same time how mundane and trivial a question it was after all he had told her, yet aware that it was time to return to the present day. 'And one of my scones? I made the jam myself – it's blackberry and apple.'

He turned and smiled at her, as if coming back from some inner journey, and reached for a scone. She poured him a second cup of tea.

'Tell me about yourself,' he said. 'Have you always lived in Devon? Is this your home?'

'Oh no – I come from Lincolnshire.' She told him how she and Andrew had met, when Andrew was at Cranwell, and about her year as a debutante. 'It seems like another world now. I know people were talking about war for quite a while before it started – they were even delivering air-raid shelters and digging trenches in Hyde Park – but we kept hoping it wouldn't come to anything. I think we even pretended it wouldn't.'

'We couldn't pretend in that way,' he said grimly. 'When you see your neighbours being overrun and you know that evil is casting its eye over your land, you don't have the luxury of pretence.'

His eyes were haunted and Alison knew that he was back with his memories again. She said, 'I meant it when I said you'd be welcome to talk to me about anything you like. If it would help at all . . .'

Once again he turned his eyes towards her. 'I know. Some of the time, I feel I want to do that. I feel I need to talk about it with someone else, to share the horror, not to have to carry it alone – and then I think how unfair that would be. To burden you, or anyone, with all that is in my mind, would be simply spreading the sadness, and what good does that do to this broken world we've created?' He looked down at the scone he was holding, gleaming with purple jam, and shook his head. 'I'm poor company in return for your hospitality. Perhaps I should go.' He made to get up.

'No!' Alison cried, surprising herself with the strength of her dismay. 'No, you mustn't. And you mustn't feel you have to be good company, either. Stefan . . .' She slipped off her chair and knelt on the rug beside Hughie, reaching up a hand to turn the Polish pilot's face towards her. 'Stefan, look at me. Please. And listen. I've grown up a lot since the days when I tried to pretend there wasn't going to be a war. I've had to. I've had to wait at home while Andrew flies, knowing he's in danger every time he goes up. I've had to sit beside him in hospital after he crashed. I've had to see him go back, knowing he could crash again, that he could be killed. And I know that there are millions of people who have suffered much worse than any of that. People like Ben, and his mother and father. Why should I sit here in my warm, cosy little house, cocooned from all of that?' Her hand slipped from his face and she gripped his wrist tightly. 'We *ought* to share it,' she said passionately. 'We ought to know what's happening, however awful it is. Otherwise, how can we ever stop it?'

There was a silence. The fire crackled. Outside, she could hear the sweet, high voice of a robin making his last brief song before twilight fell. Stefan's face was close to hers, his eyes burning with the light of the flames. His wrist was strong and warm beneath her fingers.

'Mummy!' Hughie exclaimed with outrage. 'You're knocking over my castle.'

'Oh – I'm sorry, sweetheart.' Flustered, she broke away and scrambled back to her seat, glad of the heat of the fire to hide the sudden colour in her cheeks. Hughie gave her a reproachful look and began to pick up the scattered bricks, and Stefan knelt to help him.

'Perhaps you're right,' he said at last, over his shoulder. 'I feel that myself. People ought to know. Yet it's hard to talk about some of these things.'

'It's hard because they matter so much to you,' she said quietly. 'But it must be harder still to carry them in your heart all alone.' She paused for a moment. 'Why don't you come round one evening – some time when you're not flying? Andrew wouldn't mind. Or I could ask May to have Hughie one afternoon – he often goes there. I really would like to help, and it's not so easy to talk with him here. I don't want him upset or frightened.'

The Polish airman sat up in his chair again and regarded her with sombre eyes, as if assessing her capability. 'Would you?' he asked.

She had a sudden flash of insight and realised that if he did decide to talk to her, she would be taking on her own responsibility for his memories and his fears. It was not, she knew, a responsibility to take lightly.

She met his gaze. 'Yes, Stefan. I really would.'

Chapter Fifteen

On the first Saturday of the new year, Ben cycled down to the Prettyjohns' cottage to take May to a dance.

The dance was being held at the old school, which now did duty as a village hall. May had told Ben how families from Plymouth had slept there at night during the Blitz, arriving in double-decker buses that had groped their way carefully along the narrow lanes and down the steep hill. 'Slept in rows, they did, on camp beds or mattresses on the floor, and us used to come in of a morning with fresh milk from Mr White's farm and make tea for 'em before they went home again.'

They walked down the hill together. The cottages were all darkened by blackout curtains but Ben could imagine how it would look in peacetime, with the stars above and the lights shining from each cottage along the tiny, twisting streets. The valley was so deep and narrow that the cottages looked almost as if they'd slipped down the two sides, landing in a higgledy-piggledy heap at the bottom, with those on the higher terraces clinging on by their fingernails. The inn, standing at the end, faced them as if trying to call them to order, but those windows too were blacked out.

'It used to be really jolly down here of a winter's evening,' May said, evidently thinking along the same lines. 'All the windows bright, and yellow lamplight in the pub. They'd leave the door open if it weren't too cold, and if someone got a sing-song going you could hear the voices all through the combe. Now, us daren't leave a door open even a crack in case Tom Prior, the air-raid warden, starts shouting the odds.'

'Well, it's his job,' Ben said. 'And they're right, it's amazing how you can see even a tiny pinpoint of light when you're in the sky. You don't want bombs dropped on the village.'

'Oh, we've had a few. There were some dropped up the hill, and you know there's an anti-aircraft gun up in the top fields. Us knows all about there being a war on, even down here in Milton Combe.'

The village was filled, as usual, with servicemen, some on their way to the dance, others to the inn. Just lately there had been a lot of Americans who were camping in the grounds of Bickham House. There were black as well as white soldiers – the first time many of the villagers had ever laid eyes on a black man – and although Mrs Stamp, in the pub, was willing to serve either, there seemed to be some rule that if the blacks were there first, the whites wouldn't come in, and vice versa. May shrugged her shoulders impatiently at this. 'Us don't make no difference between them. They'm all fighting on the same side.'

'Is the shop still open?' Ben asked, noticing someone emerge from the little tea room on the other side of the road, carrying a heavy shopping basket. 'What time does it close?'

'When Miss Kirby goes to bed!' May said with a laugh. 'Opens at eight in the morning, her do, and don't shut up shop till eleven. You can always knock on her door for something you've forgotten. Haven't you ever been in there?' Ben shook his head and she laughed again. 'You ought to! She's a real character – smokes cigarettes in one of they long holders. Used to organise all the village trips, her did, before the war, and if you go in there for your

Christmas shopping she'll give you a glass of sherry. Real piece of Milton Combe, she be.'

'Strikes me the village is full of characters,' Ben said, and May nodded.

'I reckon it is. But us don't know no different – us've growed up with them. I dare say all villages are much the same, when it comes down to it.'

'Probably.' Ben thought of his own village in Hampshire, and chuckled suddenly. 'There's a bloke in ours who rides round on an old bike, towing a brazier behind him. We call him Smoky Jack.'

'A brazier? One of those things roadmen use?'

'That's right. He keeps it burning, too. He lives in a shack in the woods and does odd jobs round the village, and it's his fire and cooking stove. He never lets it go out. Not unless the weather's very hot, anyway.'

They had passed the church now and crossed the little bridge to the old school. Like every other building, it was dark, but as they walked up the path they could hear the music of an accordion and a piano, and when they pushed open the door and thrust aside the blackout curtain, they were met with a kaleidoscope of bright lights and whirling colour.

'That's a shilling each, please,' said the plump woman sitting at a rickety table just inside the door. 'Oh, hello, May, didn't see as it were you. And who be this, then?'

'His name's Ben,' May said, shrugging off her old tweed coat to reveal a dark green skirt and white blouse with flowers embroidered on the front. It was an old school blouse and the skirt was cut down from her gymslip, but both were still serviceable, and not many people had anything special in the way of clothes by this stage in the war. And she was pleased to see by the expression in his eyes that Ben thought she looked nice, anyway.

'From up the airfield, I dare say,' Mrs Carter observed,

taking Ben's money. 'You can put your coats over there, my handsome. We've got Minnie on the piano tonight, so you'm sure of a good time.'

She was right too, they found as they joined the couples on the floor. The two musicians, their fingers busy on their respective keyboards, hardly seemed to need a rest and certainly didn't intend to give the dancers one. From foxtrot and waltz, to quickstep and tango, they scarcely took a moment until the interval, when the breathless dancers fell upon the tables set out with lemonade and sandwiches. Ben, who had never thought of himself as a good dancer, found that with a partner like May, as light as a feather in his arms, his feet seemed to take on a life of their own and soon he was steering her round the floor and twirling her at the corners as if he'd been born to it.

The evening passed so quickly that soon it was ten o'clock and time for everyone to go back home. As they made their way out into the crisp night air, Ben kept his arm around May.

'I wish you lived further away,' he said.

May giggled. 'Well, that's not much of a compliment! Would Scotland be far enough?'

'I don't mean that,' he said, laughing in his turn. 'I mean, I wish we had further to walk tonight so that we could spend longer together. I don't want to say goodnight, May.'

'Neither do I,' she said, suddenly solemn. 'But – I don't know as we ought to be getting so serious, Ben. We only met a few weeks ago. We hardly know each other.'

'Yes, we do.' He stopped and drew her into a corner. The other dancers passed by, chattering and laughing. Ben stroked May's cheek with one hand and then kissed her gently on the lips. 'I feel as if we know each other very well. I feel as if we've *always* known each other.'

They stood quietly for a moment, then she raised her

face again and he could see the faint glimmer of the starlight in her eyes.

'I feel like that too,' she whispered. 'But don't let's go too fast. Let's go slowly, Ben, can we? Please?'

He touched her face again. 'A stroll through the meadows rather than a mad dash up the mountain – is that it?'

'That's it,' she said, and he could feel her smile. 'A stroll through the meadows. I like that.'

'Then that's what it'll be.' He kissed her again. 'With a few stops along the way, though. I insist on that.'

May chuckled and kissed him back. For a moment or two, he could feel her soft body against his, muffled by the thick tweed coat. Then she pulled away and he drew her out of the corner.

They walked on along the darkened village street, their hands held tightly together, and began to climb the steep hill back to the Prettyjohns' cottage.

In February, the Germans started to bomb London again. Alison's heart turned cold as she listened to the news on the radio and thought of Andrew and the squadron, on readiness last night. Had they been sent to fight off the raiders, or had he been on yet another escort mission with their own bombers?

As she gave Hughie his breakfast, the icy dread she felt seemed to match the grey chill of the February morning outside. When they had finished eating, she wrapped him up in his thick coat, scarf and gloves, pulled on her own jacket and set off for the airfield. To her apprehensive eyes, there seemed to be the normal number of aircraft standing in the bays or outside the hangars, but from the fence she could see only a part of the whole area, and she had no idea where Andrew's plane might be.

The sentry knew her and shook his head at her anxious

enquiry. 'No, we didn't have no losses last night, not that I've heard of – and I would have heard. You go home in the warm, Mrs Knight, and don't worry, he'll be back for his dinner as sure as eggs is eggs.' He thought for a minute, his humorous face screwed up a little. 'Well, sure as eggs *used* ter be eggs, anyway. These days, they're just yellow powder!'

Alison laughed and thanked him, feeling her heart lighten. She turned away from the gate and walked back, but instead of going home she continued on to the Prettyjohns' cottage. 'We'll go and say hello to May and the others,' she said to Hughie. 'We haven't seen May's daddy for a week.'

William Prettyjohn had stayed downstairs after Christmas. It was warmer for him, and more companionable, although his wife complained that she was lonely upstairs in their bed by herself at night. 'Still,' she added philosophically, 'I'm the one that can run about, so I shouldn't complain.'

Old Mr Prettyjohn was in the living room, with the door open into the kitchen, when Alison and Hughie arrived. He pulled the door wide to usher them in.

'Here's a sight for sore eyes! Have you come to help me with a bit of mending?' he asked Hughie.

'What mending? I can't darn socks, Mummy does that.'

'No, my handsome,' the old man told him. 'I'm not mending socks, but you'm not far off. 'Tis shoes I'm mending this morning, down in the shed.' He held out his hand. 'Come with me, tacker. Have you ever seen anyone do a bit o' cobbling?'

Hughie shook his head and looked at his mother. Alison nodded at him. 'You go along, Hughie. I'll stop here and talk to May's daddy for a while. Unless you were doing anything else?' she added to the man in the bed.

William Prettyjohn laughed. 'I'm not going anywhere!

Got me war work to do.' He looked towards the scraps of leather scattered over his bed. 'Making bags for service-women. Even an old crock like me can be a bit o' use in wartime.'

'You're not an old crock,' Alison protested, but he just patted her hand and called through the open kitchen door to his wife, who was busy preparing a stew with carrots, turnips and swedes from the garden and a few scraps of shin beef from the butcher in Yelverton.

Mrs Prettyjohn came hurrying through, wiping her hands on her apron and beaming. 'Well, here be a nice surprise. Is Father taking Hughie down the shed? I'll make him a cup of cocoa in a while. You'd better have one too, maid, you look shrammed. Come over to the fire – 'tis raw cold out there.' She pushed the big black cat from the armchair where he had settled for the day. 'Get off, Blackie, you lazy great lump. Sit you down here, Alison, and I'll put the kettle on.'

Alison did as she was told and leaned her head back against the chair. The warmth of the cottage and the welcome she always found there lapped around her like a balmy sea. After the anxieties of the night, which she always felt when she knew Andrew was 'up', and the news of the fresh wave of bombing over England, she felt suddenly exhausted and grateful to be looked after.

William Prettyjohn glanced at her and said, 'You'm looking a bit washed out, maid. Taking care of yourself, are you?'

'Oh yes. I'm just a bit tired. You've heard about the bombing, I expect?'

'Ah, had it on the news this morning. Bad job, but I can't say it's a surprise. We been giving they Germans such a hammering, they were bound to hit back sometime. Tell you the truth, maid, and I don't want you to be upset about this, but I wonder if all this bombing really works. I mean, look at it. Look at the way they blitzed London and Coventry and Plymouth and the rest – all those big cities, smashed to bits. But has it stopped us? No. We've just gone over there and done the same to them. And it hasn't stopped them, neither. They'm coming here again. Seems to me nobody's going to stop till there's nothing left at all, and what good's that going to do, eh?'

'I don't know,' Alison said wearily. 'I don't know at all.'

'I'll tell you summat else,' he said. 'What our boys have been doing – and I'm not saying a word against them, mind, not a single word, brave lads every last one of them and deserve every medal going – but what they been doing, bombing factories and such – well, that's not working either. We're supposed to be going for their production – stop them building planes and making ammunition, but from what I heard this morning on the wireless, they've got plenty of planes and plenty of bombs too. We haven't stopped them at all. So what's the point of us sending our boys over there to be killed? I can't see it meself.'

Alison felt a cloud of dread settle over her. He was saying what she had been thinking, or trying not to think, for months. Perhaps ever since the war had begun. Was Andrew risking his life every day, every night, for something that had no end, no achievement but the destruction of the world they were actually fighting for? The warmth she had felt seemed to recede, leaving her cold and shivering as if she had come out of the sea to find the weather changed and an icy wind blowing.

Mabel came out of the kitchen, bearing two steaming cups of cocoa.

'Now, what are you doing, Will? I heard you, frightening the poor girl and making her all moithered and miserable. That's unpatriotic, talking that way, and you know it. I'm ashamed of you, I am really. You ought to know better.'

Alison opened her eyes. 'It's all right, Mrs Prettyjohn. I

often think that way myself. Sometimes it seems as if this war's been going on all my life. It doesn't seem as if it'll ever end.'

'Well, it will,' the countrywoman said stoutly. 'They Germans aren't going to have things their way much longer. Look at how they'm being driven out of Russia, and Italy. I know it's awful, the fighting there, same as everywhere else, but they can't hold out much longer. We'm winning, you mark my words. Things are getting better.' She picked up that morning's copy of the *Western Morning News* and flipped through the pages. 'Look at this. Men's suits can have turn-ups and pockets again, and us ladies can have all the pleats we wants in our skirts. If that's not good news, I don't know what is!'

Alison stared at her and then began to laugh. 'Pleats in skirts? Turn-ups and pockets? Oh, Mrs Prettyjohn!'

'There, that's better,' the plump little woman said comfortably. 'Now, don't you go talking like that no more, Will. Alison didn't come here to be made miserable.' She went back to the kitchen, leaving the door open so that they could chat through it. 'May'll be sorry to have missed you. She've gone over to the Leg o' Mutton to do a few hours as Betty's been took poorly.'

'The pub isn't open this early, surely?'

'No, bless you, they'm not open, but they asked May to go in and do a bit o' cleaning before dinner-time. Then she'll be behind the bar, ready for all they airmen. Talking of airmen . . .' She came back into the living room, holding a swede that she was peeling. 'Have you seen much of that young Ben Hazelwood? He'm in your man's squadron, so I understand.'

'Ben? Yes, he pops in sometimes during the evening. He's a nice boy. Why?'

'It's just that I think he's a bit sweet on our May, that's all. He came round on Christmas night – not deliberate, he were just walking past when May went outside for a breath of air and she asked him in for a bite of supper. He seemed a bit low – upset about his brother – 'tis only natural. He's been a few times since then and he took her to the picture show at the garrison theatre, up at Buckstone, and they've been to a dance or two together in the village. I wondered if she'd said anything to you about him.'

'No, she's never mentioned him. It's not serious, is it? He *is* a nice boy,' Alison repeated. 'His father's a vicar. You don't need to worry that he'd take advantage of her, or anything like that.'

'No, I don't think he would. It's just – well, like you said, he's a vicar's boy, and we'm just plain, ordinary folk. And May's two or three years older than he. To tell you the truth, I think she'm just sorry for him, what with losing his brother and all. I don't think she'm likely to let her head get turned, but as I said, he'm just a young chap, and you know what it's like in wartime – folk gets muddled up a bit, specially the young ones, away from home and all.'

Alison thought about this, then said, 'Well, if you want my opinion, I'd say May was good enough for any man. But I don't suppose it's serious anyway. I expect you're right, she's just being kind to him.'

The door opened and Hughie and the old man came in, carrying armfuls of shoes and boots. Mabel Prettyjohn went back to the kitchen to make more cocoa and Hughie dumped his load on the floor.

'Look, Mummy, we've mended all these. Grandpa's got a foot in his shed, all made of iron, and he puts the shoes on them and takes off the old sole and he makes a new one out of leather, and nails it on with a hammer, and there it is, all mended. Isn't he clever?'

'He is indeed.' Alison picked up one of the shoes and examined it. The workmanship was neat, the shoe as good as new. 'Would you have time to mend mine as well?' she asked. 'I've got a pair of old shoes with holes in. I was going to take them in to Tavistock to the cobbler there.'

'You bring 'em to me, my pretty,' the old man said. 'You don't want to go to no cobbler – charge you the earth, he will.'

'Oh, I'd want to pay you, though. I can't ask you to do it for nothing.'

'Us'll see about that when 'tis done,' the old man said easily, but Alison shook her head.

'No, you've got to say a fair price and let me pay it, or I won't bring them. You all do far too much for us as it is.' She lifted her chin and Mabel, coming in with more cocoa, laughed at her determination.

'Met your match there, you have, Father. Now, here's me been chattering on about us and never asked you how you were. How you'm feeling in yourself, maid? Keeping well, are you? Feeding yourself right? Eating for two now, you be.'

'I think I'm eating for three or four,' she said, smiling. 'Poor Andrew would be starved if he didn't get fed in the mess.'

She stayed for a while longer, drinking cocoa and talking to William about the books they were reading, and then she wrapped herself and Hughie up in their coats and scarves again and set off for home. The clouds had lifted a little and the air felt milder. Suddenly, it seemed as if there were a touch of spring in the air.

'Look, Hughie,' she said. 'Some of the leaves are starting to come out along the hedge. And there are some snowdrops – see those little white flowers? And the birds are starting to sing as well.'

'Will summer come back?' he asked, trudging along beside her. 'Does it come every year?'

'Every year,' she said, and felt her heart lift. 'Spring comes every year and so does summer.'

Now that she had seen the first signs of spring, there were others – the bright colours of some early crocuses along the edge of someone's vegetable garden, a few primroses like golden coins on a bank. A blackbird sang from the corner of a roof. It all seemed to add up to hope.

She thought of Ben, mourning his brother, and Stefan who didn't even know if his family were still alive, and wondered whether spring would bring them such comfort.

Chapter Sixteen

In all these weeks, Stefan had not come near Alison. It was, she thought, as if he regretted their conversation; she wondered a little sadly if he wished he had not opened his heart to her.

He came at last, on a bright, windy afternoon with shreds of clouds flying like clean white washing across a pale blue sky.

Alison and Hughie were just about to step out of the front door when he opened the garden gate. They stood staring at each other for a moment, then she began to unwind her scarf.

'Stefan! How nice to see you. Come in.'

'No.' He hesitated, his hand still on the gate. 'You're just going out.'

'Only for a walk. Come with us if you like.' She smiled, feeling unexpectedly glad to see him. 'Then we'll come back here and have some tea. Please.' She held out her hand.

'Yes,' he said after another hesitation. 'I'd like that.' He stepped back and she and Hughie followed him. They walked along the road, passing the entrance to Buckland Abbey where once Sir Francis Drake had lived, and then turned down a lane that curved between high Devon banks. The lane was as deep as if it had been trodden for centuries, with hedges growing from the tops of the banks, sprinkled thickly now with primroses and tiny wild daffodils.

Looking up through the branches of the trees, still waiting for their canopy of new leaves, Alison could see the wide blue sky and hear the sound of birdsong.

'It's very beautiful here,' Stefan said. 'And very peaceful too, when the planes aren't flying.'

'I know. But it must have been very noisy once. There were mines all around here, you know. I've seen some of the adits in the woods.'

'Adits?'

'The openings of the shafts. Not big ones, going straight down like coal mines. Just like small tunnels, going into the sides of the hills. They used to mine tin and copper, I think, and arsenic as well. Oh, and someone told me there were silver mines not far away.'

He nodded. 'It would have been very busy. We have mines in Poland as well. Coal, mostly. They're not pleasant areas to live in.'

'Like South Wales, I suppose, and the English Midlands. I heard the other day that some of the boys being called up now are going to work in the mines instead of going into the Forces. They don't have any choice – it's being decided by ballot. The luck of the draw.' She shivered. 'It would be bad luck for me. I'd hate to work underground.'

'I've never really thought about it, but I think I would, too,' Stefan said. 'Perhaps that's why I like flying.' He looked up at the feathery white clouds. 'To be up there, all alone in the blue, is a very wonderful thing. To ride your aeroplane like a horse amongst the clouds; to play between the thunderheads; to dance with the stars. It's like a miracle.'

Alison stared at him. 'You make it sound like poetry.'

'It is like a poem,' he said simply.

They walked in silence for a few minutes, with Hughie running ahead along the quiet lane. The February air was mild, the rawness of the winter softened for the time being.

No doubt it would come back, Alison thought. There was still the rest of this month and most of March to get through before you could really say it was spring. But today, here in this sheltered lane with only the softest of breezes blowing, you could almost imagine that summer itself was around the corner.

Another summer of war.

After a moment, she asked, 'Have you heard any news of your family?'

'No.' His tone was abrupt and she stole a glance at him, hoping that he wasn't offended. 'Nothing.'

'I didn't mean to pry. You don't have to tell me anything if you don't want to.'

'It's all right.' He paused for a moment and then went on, 'I would like to talk to you. I haven't come before, because I felt it was wrong to burden you with my troubles. But I keep thinking about it. I keep thinking about you. I feel that you would understand. I feel that I can tell you what is in my heart.'

'Oh.' Alison was a little startled by his intensity. Then she reminded herself of his words about flying. He was different from the Englishmen she knew, more passionate, more poetic, quite unlike the practical, pragmatic Andrew. And he had kept whatever memories he had to himself all this time. He must be burning up inside.

'You can tell me whatever you like,' she said.

'We lived in the city of Warsaw,' he began. They had come back to the house and Alison had lit the fire and made some tea. Hughie was curled up in the corner of the sofa, looking at the Rupert Bear annual he'd been given for Christmas. He loved the stories of Rupert and firmly believed that he lived nearby and that one day he would be lucky enough to meet him.

Alison waited. She knew it wasn't easy for Stefan to

begin his own tale and she could only let him tell it at his own pace and in his own way. He had fallen silent already, his eyes full of memories as he gazed into the fire, and she wondered what had happened that made it so painful for him to talk about. Even now, she wasn't sure that he would be able to tell her.

'My father was a music teacher,' he went on, breaking the silence. 'He taught in one of the big schools and he also played in the city orchestra. The violin was his main instrument but of course he could play many others – the piano, the harp, all the stringed instruments. He taught us all to play. It was as natural as learning to read.'

'Did your mother play too?'

He nodded. 'The flute. Our house was always full of music. My father, learning a new melody on the violin. Or the sound of my mother's flute, like the silver water of a cascade. And every day was a party in our house. My mother was so full of life, always inviting people in, and she'd make little sweetmeats and biscuits to serve with their wine, and we children would have to give little concerts.' He smiled. 'It was how I imagined our life would always be, with more children coming along and learning their own instruments until we had enough for an orchestra of our own!'

'It sounds wonderful,' Alison said, and he nodded.

'We did not know how wonderful until it came to an end.'

He fell silent again, and Alison refilled his cup. Hughie asked for another biscuit and she looked in the tin to find one he liked. Stefan reached down to the log basket and put another piece of wood on the fire, which crackled and flared as the flames caught the slivers of bark.

'We knew it was coming to an end, of course,' he said at last. 'We had watched Hitler march over Europe all that year. We saw him enter Prague in March, stripping the banks of their gold to rescue his own destitute economy. We knew he was coming closer to us.'

'You knew that he would invade Poland?'

'Those who understood the situation did. Others buried their heads in the sand and refused to see the signs. And we were unprepared. Our army relied on cavalry still, and our air force had only antiquated planes. We could never stand up to an attack.'

'Wouldn't Russia help?'

He made a swift gesture of repudiation. 'Poland has been dominated by Russia before! We didn't want them on our soil.' His shoulders slumped a little as he added, 'Perhaps that was a mistake. But whatever might have happened, Germany invaded on September the first and so it all began. A second world war, only twenty-one years after the end of the first.'

There was a short silence, broken only by the crackle and hiss of the fire and the soft murmur of Hughie, telling himself the stories as he gazed at the colourful pictures in his book. Alison said, 'What happened then? After the invasion?'

'We were prepared, up to a point,' he said. 'Our army was in position along the borders, ready for defence. But how could we, with our old-fashioned methods and equipment, hope to stand up against the might of the Germans with their tanks and their armaments? By the end of the month, they had completely overrun our country. Along with many others, I came to England and I've been here ever since.'

'And you've never heard from your family in all that time?'

'No. How could I? They are in enemy hands.' A small spasm of pain twisted his features. 'But we hear things. We hear of the atrocities being committed there. People starving. People killed for no reason. There are many of these stories.'

Alison thought of her own parents, living comfortably in Lincolnshire in their own home. Like everyone else, they were deprived of many of the pleasures of peacetime, but they had enough to eat and sufficient warmth. They might be bombed from the skies, but they could feel secure within their own community. They weren't afraid of soldiers in the street. They didn't have to live behind high walls.

And she would hear very quickly if anything happened to them.

Silently, she reached out and touched his wrist. He turned his hand over so that their palms met, and he curled his fingers around hers. She felt their warmth and strength, felt the sensitivity in his long, musician's fingers, and a strange, warm ache ran up the inside of her arm directly into her heart.

It was growing dark when they stirred at last. Hughie had fallen asleep over his book and the only light in the room came from the smouldering fire. Alison, feeling as if she had woken from a deep sleep, turned her head and looked into Stefan's face. He was lying back in the chair, and she knew that telling his story had been almost too much for him.

He had stopped talking at last, and laid his head back in the chair, drained and exhausted, and Alison had remained quiet, feeling his hand in hers and not wanting to let it go. But now it was almost dark and she knew she must move.

Gently, she withdrew her hand and murmured, 'I have to draw the blackout curtains.' She stood up and drew the heavy curtains across, then switched on the lamp. Hughie, feeling the light on his eyelids, moved and whimpered a protest, and she laid her hand on his cheek. Stefan sat up slowly and looked at her.

'I'm sorry. I've taken up your whole afternoon, and made you unhappy.'

'No. You've made me sad, but not unhappy. And I'm glad you told me. I'd like you to come again, and tell me more. Talk for as long as you like.' She looked down at his pale, tired face. 'I'd like to hear more about your family.'

'Thank you.' He leaned forward and put another log on the fire. 'And now I think I should go.'

'Oh, no,' she protested. 'Stay for supper. Andrew will be home soon – he's not on readiness tonight. He'll be pleased to see you.' She hesitated, then said quietly, 'You said once you would like to play on our piano, but you never have. Would you like to play now – some of your favourite music, the kind you used to play at home? Would it be any help at all for you to do that?'

He was silent for so long that she feared she had offended him. Then he nodded his head.

'Yes. I would like to do that. It would be good, I think.'

He went over to the instrument and lifted the lid. For a moment or two his fingers drifted softly over the keys, barely touching them. Then he sat down and began to play.

From the first note he struck, Alison recognised that this was no ordinary piano-player. Stefan was a true virtuoso. She listened, enthralled, as he went into the intricacies of one of Beethoven's sonatas, and even Hughie stopped his game and fell silent. From there, he moved on to some Chopin and then, lightening the mood, to some jazz. And then he struck a note that went straight to Alison's heart.

It was the piece written especially for his country – for his city. A piece that had been written after the war had begun, a piece that his family and all those at home – if they were still alive – had probably never heard, and yet it seemed to speak both to them and of them, and of all the dangers they had faced and were still facing.

It was the Warsaw Concerto.

Chapter Seventeen

'You'm keeping well,' May observed one morning as she threw used tea leaves on to the living-room carpet. 'Were you like this with Hughie?'

'Mm, I hardly knew I was expecting.' Alison touched her swelling stomach. 'Except for this, of course, and all the kicking. They're both going to be either footballers or boxers, I'm sure.'

'Everyone always thinks that,' May said. She knelt on the floor and began to brush up the tea leaves, bringing dust and fluff up with them and leaving the carpet clean and bright. Andrew had suggested a month or so ago that Alison should ask her to help with some of the housework, and May had been pleased to do so for a few shillings a week. She had several jobs around the village now, as well as her war work sewing for the Marines and her voluntary work, but she always seemed to have time for a cup of tea and a chat, and she often took Hughie for a walk to give Alison a rest.

'Have you thought of any names yet?' she asked, sweeping the tea leaves into a dustpan. 'I expect you'd like a little girl this time, wouldn't you? Pigeon pair.'

'I don't really mind. I like little boys.' Alison looked through the window to where Hughie was playing in the back garden. It was a fine March morning, with a light breeze tossing the yellow-headed daffodils in a ballet dance beneath the hedge. She was darning Andrew's socks as she spoke, May having firmly taken away the newspaper with which she'd been about to polish the windows. 'I think Andrew would like a girl, though.'

'Ah, men like to have a pretty daughter.' May sat back on her heels. 'And you stay friends with your daughter, too. You know what they say: *A son's your son till he takes him a wife. A daughter's a daughter the whole of her life.*'

'Oh, I can't believe I'd ever lose Hughie,' Alison protested, looking out of the window again. Hughie was crouching down, watching something in the grass – a beetle or a worm, probably. He was fascinated with all wildlife just now. 'In fact, Andrew says he's too much of a mummy's boy.'

'I'm not saying you'd *lose* him. Just that he'd have to put his wife first and she'd go to her own mother. 'Tis only natural.' May glanced up and saw the expression on Alison's face. 'Here, don't you go looking like that! 'Tisn't going to happen next week. You've got twenty years or more before young Hughie starts to think about getting wed.'

Alison laughed. 'I know. It's just that I can't quite bear to think about him growing up at all, let alone leaving home. Well, all I can say is that when he does think about getting married, I hope he finds someone as nice as you, May. I'm sure I'd be very happy about that.'

May smiled but then got up and picked up the dustpan, taking it outside to tip the contents into the bin at the bottom of the garden. Alison watched her pause to talk to Hughie, stooping to examine whatever it was he had found, and then return to the house.

'You'll never believe what that boy's studying. It's a snail with its horns out. He says it's his pet and it's called Oscar and he's going to keep it in his bedroom.'

'Oh, is he indeed? I'll have to search his pockets when he comes in.' Alison looked at her friend. 'May, I hope you don't mind me asking, but you looked a bit odd when I mentioned Hughie marrying someone like you. Have I touched a sore spot?'

May began to shake her head, then sighed and went to put the dustpan and brush away. She came back and sat down opposite Alison.

'To tell you the truth, I've been meaning to talk to you about that. I didn't know how to put it, like, but now you've brought the subject up . . .'

Alison stared at her. 'Don't tell me you're asking for Hughie's hand in marriage! You'll have to wait a while, I'm afraid.'

May laughed a little and said, 'No, it's not that. It's about Ben.'

'Ben Hazelwood?' Alison remembered May's mother asking her if May had said anything to her about him. 'Are you having any problems with him?'

'Not problems, exactly. But us've been out a few times together – to the picture show on the airfield, and he's taken me to a couple of dances, and us goes for a walk now and then. And – well, us likes each other.' Her cheeks coloured. 'Us likes each other a lot. But I don't know if I ought to let it go on. I mean, I'm just an ordinary maid, I don't have no education or nothing. I don't even talk right, I know that. I couldn't ever fit in with his sort of life.'

Alison looked at her thoughtfully. May was sitting upright in her chair, her fingers busy pleating the folds of her pinafore. Her face was pink and her eyes very bright.

'What does Ben think about that?' she asked.

'I don't know. He don't seem to have thought about it at all. Tell you the truth, I don't really know *what* he thinks, but I do know he's getting too fond of me. And I can't tell him to stop, can I, not when he's putting himself into danger night after night, and he's lost his brother and his poor mother's so upset still.' May lifted her head and a tear rolled down her cheek. 'I can't hurt him now, but if I lets it go on any more he might be even more hurt when – when . . .' She sniffed and felt in her sleeve for a hanky, then burst into tears.

'May!' Alison came out of her chair and went to put her arms around the sobbing girl. May leaned her head against her.

'I'm sorry. I didn't mean to come over all unnecessary.' She blew her nose. 'It's just that I've been worrying about it, and I keep thinking I must tell him we didn't ought to see each other no more, but I haven't got the heart to do it. And I *wants* to see him,' she finished piteously. 'I wants to go out with him and – and all that. Even though I know it isn't right.'

'But why isn't it right?' Alison asked. 'I know you're from different backgrounds, but I don't think that matters so much these days. Not with the war on, and everything. People are getting all mixed up now, they're not so separated as they used to be. And Ben's a nice boy.'

'That's another thing,' May said. 'He'm still a boy really, for all he goes up fighting in the air. He'm three years younger than me, and it ought to be the man that's older.'

'I don't think three years matter all that much,' Alison said. 'It's not like ten or twenty. What do your parents say?'

'I haven't talked about it to them. I haven't talked about it to anyone, to tell you the truth. It's not as if Ben's *said* anything, you see. I might be reading more into it than there really is. Maybe he just wants a bit of fun.'

'I don't think Ben's that sort,' Alison said. 'And I think you know how he feels, without having to ask, don't you?'

May nodded. 'I just don't know what to do about it,' she said despondently.

'Do you have to do anything? Can't you just enjoy it, and let things develop as they will?'

'But I'm going to have to stop it in the end. I know his

parents wouldn't want me as his wife, I know it! His father's a vicar. They've got education. They've got a lovely home, I've seen photographs of it. I wouldn't fit in at all. They wouldn't think I was good enough for Ben. And my mum and dad – they'd tell me to stop putting on airs and keep my place. They'm beginning to think something's going on as it is.'

'But they like Ben, don't they?'

'Of course they like him! Everybody likes him. That don't mean to say they want me *marrying* him. I tell you, Alison, they wouldn't want that at all and it's me they'd be annoyed with. They'd think I'd led him on, or set my cap at him, or something.' She blew her nose again. 'I tell you, I'm proper mazed with it all.'

Alison felt helpless. 'I don't know what to say. I think you and Ben would be very happy together. I don't think the differences matter at all, but I know they would to a lot of people, and that might make it hard for you both.' She sighed and moved back to her chair. 'If only you could just forget all the problems and enjoy the time you have together.'

May glanced across at her. 'And that's another thing, isn't it ?' she said quietly. 'Us don't know what time us do have together. I might tell Ben it's all over and the next day he might go and get killed, and I'd never know . . .' She began to cry again. 'All I'd know would be that I'd made his last day miserable. I can't do that. I *can't*.'

'Of course you can't.' Alison wanted to take the girl in her arms again but at that moment Hughie burst in through the back door, his face scarlet with distress. Both women moved automatically, but he ran straight to his mother and buried his head in her lap.

'What is it? What's the matter? Have you hurt yourself? Stop crying, sweetheart, and tell me what it is.'

He raised his face. It was wet with tears and contorted

with fury. 'It's Oscar!' he bellowed. 'My snail! He's all broken up! He's all smashed! A bird came down and pecked him and now he's dead! My snail's *dead!*'

May and Alison gazed at him, then each other and their mouths twitched. Then May got up and went out to the kitchen.

'Come on, Hughie,' she said. 'It's time for your milk. And I brought some of Grandma Prettyjohn's special biscuits with me this morning. You can have one of those.'

He hesitated, still snuffling, and Alison got up too and took his hand.

'Let's go and see if we can find another snail, shall we? You remember how we saw them all sleeping in the cracks in the wall? I expect they're all waking up now – Oscar must have been the first – so there'll be lots in the garden and you can give them names as well.'

May gave her a wry look. 'Don't let Grandpa hear you say that,' she cautioned. 'He've got only one name for snails, and it's not one you'd want Hughie to hear!' She smiled, looking a little more cheerful now that she'd unburdened herself. 'Thanks for the talk, Alison. I still don't know what to do for the best, but I feel better for talking about it. And I suppose there isn't anything much I can do, for the time being anyway. I'd best just let things take their course, like you say.'

'I'm sure it's the best thing,' Alison said gently, touching May's arm as she passed. 'Why not make a cup of tea now, while I take Hughie out into the garden and look for snails?' She smiled. 'It might be a good idea to collect a few up in a bucket anyway – we don't want them on our cabbages!'

She went out into the fresh March air. A thrush was singing on a nearby branch – probably he was the culprit who had killed Oscar – but even as she listened, his song was drowned by the roar of aircraft taking off from the airfield. She lifted her eyes and watched as a formation of

Typhoons flew overhead, climbing steadily into the pale spring sky.

May was right. How could she possibly tell Ben their friendship was over, when he might be killed at any moment?

May walked home without noticing the primroses that spangled the grassy banks, nor the violets nestling like purple shadows beneath them. She scarcely heard the birdsong that filled the air once the roar of the planes had faded into the distance nor revelled, as she usually did, in the unfurling of the pale, fresh green leaves along the hedges. Her mind was completely taken up with Ben.

She hardly knew how they had fallen so deeply in love. It had begun at Christmas, of course; she didn't count the party at Alison's house where they'd met, but on that Christmas night, with the stars so thick across the sky that you could have pulled them down in handfuls, when Ben had kissed her by the stile, she'd known what was going to happen. It already had happened – the touch of his lips, so firm yet so soft and sweet, had set her whole body tingling. It was like a moment of revelation, as if she had been waiting for this all her life, and only now understood what had been missing. She felt as if she had been made whole at last.

And he'd felt the same. She'd known it from the shock that sprang between them and by the tone of his voice as he whispered her name. '*May* . . .'

There had been more kisses after that, yielding and tremulous, before they'd walked back to the cottage hand in hand, both a little shaken by the feelings that had swept over them. And when Ben had finally left, after the supper and games and songs they'd shared round the fire, May had walked to the gate with him and they'd shared another kiss.

'I can see you again, can't I?' he'd whispered into her hair, and May had nodded. 'Soon? Tomorrow?'

'I can't,' she said regretfully. 'Uncle Percy and Aunt Mary are coming round. They always do on Boxing Day. And it's a Sunday, so there'll be church in the morning. I'll have to stay home.'

'Can't you even come out for a walk?' he asked, but she shook her head. 'The day after, then.'

'I'm working in the morning.'

'The afternoon. The evening. We'll go out somewhere. We'll catch the bus and go into Tavistock and have some tea. There'll be places open, won't there?'

'Well, Perraton's might be, I suppose. But it's only just after Christmas.'

'There must be somewhere,' he said, and she touched his cheek.

'I don't mind if we don't go anywhere. Let's just go for a walk.'

'So long as we're together,' he said, and she nodded in the darkness.

'So long as we're together.'

After that, they had spent as much time as possible together, walking the fields and the parts of the moor not taken over by the airfield, occasionally going to the picture show or to a dance but happy to be on their own. For May, it was a magical time, a time of frosty mornings and starlit nights, of scarlet and orange sunsets, of the gradual awakening of spring and the song of birds at dawn and at twilight; a time of the tender blossoming of love, even though its delicate tints were shot through with the dark knowledge that it could all be taken away at any moment; that Ben could be lost to her. That one day, it would all come to an end.

She never thought for a moment that it could last. Even if Ben survived the war, he would leave her when it was over. He might come to see her once or twice after that, but then he would go back into his own life and it would be no more than a memory, to be carried in her heart for the rest of her life. And at first, she'd believed that it was the same for him.

But then, one day in March, things had changed.

They'd been deep in the valley, where the two rivers Tavy and Walkham met in a tumble of rocks and foam. Once, long ago, there had been mines down here and you could still come across the narrow adits, leading deep underground, and the low hummocks of spoil heaps, grown over with furze and silver birch. The valley rose high and steep on either side and on the opposite bank there was a heronry in the tall trees. The nests swayed high in the branches, an untidy jumble of sticks; soon, the birds would be back to start their families again and the air would be filled with their harsh, guttural voices.

It had been frosty for several days and the rocks glistened with half-frozen water. Icicles hung in fringes on their shaded sides, the tips constantly washed away by the broken water. The sunlight filtered down through the branches of the trees, glittering on the flying spray and turning it to diamonds in the cold, bright air.

'There's a kingfisher!' May exclaimed in a low voice, and pointed up the river. 'There – see?'

The blue flash was like a swift bolt of electricity, gone in an instant, but Ben nodded. 'I just caught a glimpse. And there's a dipper on that rock, see him? Like a robin with a white breast. This is a nice place, May.'

'We used to come here for picnics a lot when I were a little maid. Double Waters, we call it. Must have been a bit different when the miners were here, but 'tis quiet enough now. Pretty, too.'

'It's very pretty,' he said quietly. 'But not as pretty as you, May.'

'Oh, Ben! Don't be so foolish, now. How can you compare me with a place?'

'I can compare you with anything I like, and you'd still come out best.' He slipped his arm around her waist. 'You know how much I think of you, May.'

She was silent for a moment, her heart beating fast. 'I know, Ben. I think a lot of you, too.'

'Not just a lot,' he said. 'You're the whole world to me, May.'

May turned her head and looked into his eyes, her heart turning over as she saw the darkness in them. She opened her mouth but, before she could speak, his lips were covering hers and she gasped as she was caught up in his kiss. The sound of the tumbling water combined with the rush of her own blood in her ears and she felt herself melt in his arms. They lay back on the moss and Ben ran a trembling hand over her body.

'Ben . . .'

'It's all right,' he whispered, though his voice sounded ragged. 'I won't do anything you don't want. I love you too much.' He lifted his head and looked down into her eyes, repeating in a tone of wonder, 'I *love* you, May.'

'I love you too,' she returned, her own voice shaking, and buried her face against his chest. They lay together, not speaking, hearing the rustle of the wind in the branches above, the splash of the water at their feet and, in their ears, the whisper of the grass. The sweet trill of a robin sounded from a nearby bush and the faint cry of a buzzard, like the mew of a lost cat, from high in the sky. For May, it was a moment of perfection, one she wished would never end, one which would stay with her for ever.

After a little while, Ben raised himself up on to one elbow, and looked down at her.

'We'll always be together, May, won't we?'

'As long as we can be,' she said, though her heart had

already sunk a little. How could they always be together?

'As long as you want me, anyway.'

'Then that's always!' His arm tightened around her. 'I'm going to want you for the rest of my life, May. You know that.'

'Ben, that's silly.'

'*Silly*? What's silly about it? We love each other – we've just said so. We're going to be together for ever, for the rest of our lives. It's what we both want.' He looked at her again, his eyes dark with anxiety now. 'It *is* what you want, isn't it?'

'Yes, of course it is. It's just – well, I don't see how it's possible, Ben. There's your mother and father . . .'

'What do they have to do with it?' he asked, genuinely puzzled.

'They have a lot to do with it. They won't want you taking up with a girl like me – an ordinary country girl. They'll want you to settle down with someone of your own sort. Someone who can live the kind of life you live at home. Someone like Alison, for instance. I wouldn't even know what knife and fork to use,' she finished miserably.

He stared at her. 'What do knives and forks matter? I don't see what you're worrying about.'

May was silent for a moment. Then she said, 'Don't let's talk about it now, Ben. Let's just go on having a nice time, like we've been having ever since Christmas, and not think about the future. Let's just have what we can for now, and be thankful for it.'

He looked away from her, over the river, and she was afraid that she had angered him. Then he turned back and kissed her again, lightly.

'All right. We'll leave it for now. But I love you, May, and I want to share my life with you. That's not going to change, whatever else may happen. You'd better make up your mind to it.'

He kissed her again, more passionately this time, and May closed her eyes and gave herself up to it. She pushed her anxious thoughts out of her mind and let herself be swept away, like the rushing stream, on a tide of love and longing. This is the day I'm going to remember, she thought as her senses swirled. Ben's right. Whatever else may happen, this is never going to change.

Later, however, her fears and anxieties returned, nagging at her mind during the day and haunting her sleep at night. I can't believe it's going to be all right, she thought as she walked home from Alison's house after pouring her heart out to her friend. I can't believe it will last for ever.

One way or another, she was sure that her dreams would be shattered.

Chapter Eighteen

All along the south coast, something new was happening.

On 1 April, an order was made to close a ten-mile-deep belt of coastland from Land's End to the Wash. Nobody who lived outside the restricted area on that date would be permitted to enter it unless they were vital to the war effort, and those who lived inside must carry their identity cards at all times. Once again, the smell of invasion was in the air.

This time, however, without it being talked about much, everyone knew that the invasion would come from the British shores. This time, the Allies would be invading Occupied France.

'And let's hope they make a better job of it than they did at Dieppe,' Andrew said grimly.

The RAF losses were still heavy, and every night, as the bombers and fighters took off, Alison would listen in dread, knowing that Andrew and his squadron were on another dangerous mission; she was always awake with the first distant snarl that meant they were coming back. After that, she stayed awake, unable to settle to anything until she heard Andrew's key in the door and his voice calling down the passageway.

Her parents came to stay for Easter, her mother fussing and anxious.

'Why don't you come home with us for a while, and have your baby there? We could look after you and help with Hughie. You can come back as soon as you're ready.'

Alison shook her head. 'I can't leave Andrew. He needs me here. And it's not as if I were in any real danger. We get the occasional German plane over, but the boys soon see them off. And I'd never forgive myself if anything happened to him and I wasn't here,' she added quietly.

Her mother sighed. 'I knew you'd say that, of course, but I had to try. If only I could stay here, but I'm so tied up with committees and the WVS and the rest of my war work.'

'It's all right, Mummy. It's not as if this is my first baby. I've booked into a nice little maternity home in Horrabridge, so even if Andrew's not here I shall be all right. And May's promised to come and sleep here when it's nearly time, and she'll take Hughie home with her when I go in. Everything will be all right.' Alison got up and went indoors to put on the kettle. Her father had taken Hughie for a walk around the perimeter and Andrew was on readiness, so the two women were enjoying some peace and quiet in a patch of spring sunshine in the garden.

'You do seem to have it well organised,' her mother admitted when Alison came back, carrying a tray of tea. 'I still don't like being so far away, though. And you should have let me do that. I'm not here to be waited on.'

'I had to go in anyway.' Alison put down the tray. 'And at least we're still able to write to each other. I've been talking to one of the Polish pilots just lately. He hasn't heard from any of his family since just after the war started. He's afraid to write to them, in case the letter brings them trouble. He doesn't even know if they're still alive.'

'Yes, that's awful.' Elizabeth accepted a cup of tea. 'What about that other young pilot you told me about – the one who lost his brother? How's he getting on?'

'Ben's all right.' Alison wondered whether to tell her mother about May, but decided against it. 'I don't think his mother's getting over it at all, though. He's gone home for a couple of days. Apparently, his father's very worried about her.'

'I'm sorry to hear that,' Elizabeth said. 'There are so many mothers losing their sons that I'm almost glad I never had one. At least I have a good chance of keeping my daughter, and my grandchildren. You will take care of yourself, won't you, darling? Don't work too hard. Let May do the heavy work – she told me she's quite willing to. And I don't think you ought to be lifting Hughie up. He's getting too big and heavy.'

'I know, but he's still my baby for the time being. It won't be long now before the new one's born, and everyone will be telling him he's a big boy and has got to look after his sister – or his brother,' she added with a smile. 'I keep forgetting we don't get a choice, and Andrew's so determined it's going to be a girl I've begun to think so too.' She sat down on the garden bench.

'Have you chosen any names yet?'

'Oh, you know how it is – we keep making lists! I don't know why we don't just use the ones we thought of last time, but I can't remember what they were. At the moment, Andrew wants Morag for a girl and Alistair for a boy – both Scottish, of course. I'd rather have Caroline, myself.'

'But Andrew's not Scottish, surely.'

'His grandmother was. She came from the Highlands. Anyway, by the time it's born I don't suppose I'll care what we call it so long as it's well and healthy.' Alison rubbed the small of her back. 'These last two months are the worst, aren't they, when you're getting bigger and heavier every day. I remember with Hughie, they seemed to drag on for ever.'

'Well, while we're here you're not to do any more chores,' Elizabeth said firmly. 'Not even making a cup of tea. You're to have a good rest.'

Alison lay back on the cushions they'd brought out into

the garden. It was nice to be fussed over, she thought, provided it didn't go on for too long. Since marrying and leaving home she had developed a strong streak of independence, needed by any Service wife, but she had to admit that she was very tired these days and a respite would be welcome. It was nice to have the company of her father and mother, too – almost like peacetime. They were lucky not to have lost anyone close to them in this war yet.

A cold finger touched her spine as the last thought drifted across her mind, and she shivered. Don't tempt Fate, she thought. Don't think about it at all.

The sound of her father's deep tones, with Hughie's chatter like birdsong twittering amongst church bells, sounded from the pathway at the bottom of the garden, and a moment later the gate opened and they came in.

'I've brought you some flowers,' Hughie said, and dumped a handful of primroses, their stems crushed by his fist, in her lap. The cold finger dropped away from her spine and she leaned forward and kissed him.

They were indeed very lucky.

Olivia Hazelwood didn't feel at all lucky.

'She can't seem to find any bright spots in life at all,' John told his son when Ben came home on a twenty-four-hour leave pass. 'I know we've lost Peter – I'm as grieved about him as she is – but we do still have you and the other two. But if I say that to her, she simply replies, "But we haven't got Peter", and there's nothing I can say to that. It's not that he mattered any more than the rest of you – it's just that he *did* matter, for himself. I can understand that, of course – I feel just the same. But we have to rise above the loss, and your mother doesn't seem able to. I don't know what to do about it.'

He ran his hand over his thick, greying hair and Ben looked at him. He had never seen his father like this, unable to find the right words of comfort, almost in despair. His dread of meeting his mother grew, and with it an unexpected sense of grievance. What was he supposed to do to help these two middle-aged people, when they couldn't help themselves? He was still only twenty years old – how could he know how to comfort his parents over the loss of his own brother?

'I can't stay long,' he said uncomfortably. 'You do know that, don't you? I was lucky to get a leave pass at all, as all leave's been stopped. I don't really know how Andrew managed to wangle it for me. I've got to be back by two tomorrow afternoon.'

'Yes, I know. Well, it'll do her good to see you, even if it's only for a few hours.'

They were standing in the church as they talked. Ben had gone straight there, hoping to find his father before he met his mother. John's telegram had sounded desperate, as if Olivia were seriously ill, and although even this shouldn't have been enough to obtain a leave pass at this tense moment, Andrew had moved heaven and earth to get it for him. Now it seemed as if it was just unhappiness that was making her ill, and Ben couldn't really understand the urgency.

'She will get better, won't she?' he asked doubtfully. 'I mean, she will get over it. It's not as if she's the only one. Thousands of people—'

'I know. But I don't advise you to tell her that.' John rubbed his face, covering his eyes for a moment. 'People have their own ways of dealing with this. Some people are stronger than others; some just refuse to believe it and go on expecting their sons or husbands to come home after all. It's quite common, even when you know that someone has died, even when you've been to the funeral and seen the coffin lowered into the grave, to be hardly able to believe it. People dream – they dream that it was all a mistake, that the person who's died has come back. I've done it myself.' He paused, his face wrinkled with sadness. 'It can be almost a comfort in itself. A little piece of extra life, given like a gift. But then you wake up . . .'

Ben was silent. Then he said, 'What do you want me to do, Dad?'

'I don't really know. Perhaps I shouldn't have telegraphed you, but it was all I could think of. Alexie can't leave Gosport, with this ten-mile zone and all travelling forbidden, and of course Ian's in Italy – he was at Monte Cassino, you know. All I knew was that she needed to see one of you, just to be reassured that you hadn't all died and I was keeping it from her.' He caught Ben's indrawn breath and nodded at him. 'Yes. She's even accused me of doing that.'

'Oh, Dad . . . I don't know what to say.'

The vicar touched his arm. 'Perhaps there's no need to say anything at all. Just be here. Just spend some time with her – tell her things about yourself, good things, *happy* things if you've got any. Try to show her that there is still a life, that there is still hope for the future.'

Hope. The word reminded Ben of Jeanie and her child. 'Are they still here? Doesn't having a little one about the place help Mum at all?'

'Yes, she helps a lot. Dear little girl. But then there are times when even she seems to remind your mother of what she's lost.' He shook his head. 'You know, I think it's rather like the shellshock men suffered in the last war. She's been so brave all this time, and worked so hard for the war effort – and now I think she's just had enough. More than enough; more than she can take. But you can't say you've had enough, can you? You can't turn your back and walk away, because the war's there and it's not going to stop just because you want it to. You've got to live through it to the end, whatever the end may be.'

He sighed and passed his hand along the end of a pew. It was worn and polished smooth by centuries of use. Ben watched him look around his church and knew that he was thinking of all the people who had worshipped here down the years, of their hopes and joys, their sufferings and pains. Gone and forgotten now, most of them, yet they had left their imprint here. You could, if you sat and closed your eyes and emptied your mind, feel their presence. And it was, on the whole, one of harmony and tranquillity, as if whatever they had suffered they had, in the end, found peace.

'Let's go over to the house,' he said quietly. 'I haven't got long and I want to make the most of it. And I do have something happy to tell you, so maybe I will be able to make her feel a little bit better after all.'

'Married?' Olivia echoed faintly. She put a long, slender hand to her throat. 'You want to get *married*?'

Ben looked at her, disconcerted by her reaction. He had waited until after supper, when they were in the drawing room with a tray of tea, to tell them about May, realising that his mother needed time simply to get used to seeing him again. Although she had known he was coming, had even prepared for it by asking Jeanie to put some extra vegetables in the stew (there was, of course, no extra meat even though it was no more than scrag end of lamb) and had seemed pleased to see him, there was a strange kind of vagueness about her manner, as if she were always thinking of something else. And I suppose she is, he'd thought sadly. She's thinking about Peter.

He had been dismayed by her appearance. The cool elegance had disappeared and her dress looked limp and drab, hanging loosely on a figure that had once been slender but now looked gaunt. Her silvery hair, always drawn back into a smooth knot, now looked grey and wispy, and the porcelain skin was muddy. The calmness in her eyes had given way to a bewildered pain that even Ben's arrival had not been able to dispel, and he wondered with a sinking heart if she was really ill – and if she would ever get better.

Jeanie wasn't having supper with them. She had had her tea at the same time as Hope and then gone up to their room to read and listen to the wireless. When Ben had protested, she'd merely smiled and said, 'Your mother needs you to herself for a bit. Anyway, it's *ITMA* tonight – you wouldn't want me to miss that, would you!'

'I'll want to see you tomorrow, though,' he warned her, putting out a hand to hold her back as she made to go upstairs. 'No sloping off to the village in the morning. I'll have to be on my way by ten.'

'Oh, I shall be around at breakfast-time,' she assured him. 'And we can walk to the station with you, if you like. Make sure you're safely off the premises.'

'That's a date, then.' He'd looked at her, seeing the plump, pretty face as if for the first time. 'I'm glad you're here, Jeanie. You're a real help to my mother. Almost as good as a daughter, in fact.'

Jeanie lowered her eyes. 'It's nice of you to say so, but I'll never be that. I do my best, though. I'll never forget how kind your mum and dad have been to me, taking me in when my own parents didn't want to know me. But that's all past now,' she finished, looking up at him again. 'Hope's really won their hearts, bless her. They dote on her. It's right, what people say – babies bring their love with them. And Hope brought enough for ten babies, I reckon.'

'I think so too.' He'd smiled at her and there was a tiny moment of silence as their eyes met. Then it was broken as his mother came out of the drawing room, and Jeanie turned and went up the stairs.

Now, after their meal of Irish stew and bread pudding,

they were in the drawing room and Ben had taken a deep breath and told them about May.

'I don't understand,' Olivia said, staring at him with bewildered eyes. 'Who is this girl?'

'She lives near the airfield. Her name's May Prettyjohn and she helps Andrew Knight's wife in the house – does a bit of cleaning and looks after their little boy, that sort of thing. I met her at a party they had before Christmas. And then I was out one night – Christmas night, it was, as a matter of fact – I didn't feel like joining in the shenanigans in the mess and I went for a walk and happened to pass their cottage and she'd just come out to get some logs or something. And we went for a walk across the fields . . .'

'On Christmas night? She went out with a strange man on Christmas night, across the fields?'

'Yes,' Ben said. 'What's wrong with that? And I wasn't "strange". We'd already met, at Andrew's house.'

'But it must have been dark.'

'There was a good moon. We could see perfectly. And May knows all the footpaths for miles around.'

'That's not what—' She looked at her husband. 'John . . .'

'Let's just hear what he has to say first, dear,' the vicar said, his voice calm, though his eyes were wary. He pulled at his pipe and nodded at Ben. 'Go on.'

'Well – that's it, really,' Ben said lamely. 'We've seen each other quite a bit since then. I go round to the cottage or we go for a walk or to the picture show, that sort of thing. We get on well – we did right from the moment we met. You'd like her, Ma, you really would. She's pretty and nice, and she's a marvellous cook. She can do anything in the house and she helps her grandfather in the garden—'

'Why isn't she in the Services?' Olivia asked in a sharp tone, her bewilderment disappearing so suddenly that he was brought up short.

'Mostly because of her father, I think. He was paralysed in a farm accident and they need her at home. But she does war work in the village – making scrim and collecting sphagnum, all the things you do here, and they all do sewing and knitting, even her father. They all pull their weight.' He was conscious of a slightly resentful note creeping into his voice, and strove to modify it, although he couldn't help feeling hurt at the reception of his news. 'You'd like them all,' he repeated.

'I'm sure we would,' Olivia said without conviction, and turned to her husband again. 'John, I don't know what to say. It's all so sudden.'

John Hazelwood took his pipe from his mouth. 'Ben, have you really thought about this? Marriage is a serious business, you know. It's for life. And you're only twenty. You could be tied to this girl for the next fifty or sixty years . . .'

'I know. That's what I want.'

'It may be what you want now, but will it still be what you want in ten years' time? Twenty? Thirty? People change, Ben, and they change most while they're young. You've still got a long time ahead of you.'

'Well, we don't actually know that, do we,' Ben retorted, and bit his lip as his mother made a small sound of distress. 'Sorry, Ma, I didn't mean to say that, but it's true, isn't it? We've got to face up to it. People aren't going in for long engagements any more. They're getting married while they have the chance.'

'And you know what they say.' John was trying to lighten the tense atmosphere. 'Marry in haste, repent at leisure.'

'That's if you're lucky enough to have the leisure.' Ben's lips were set in the stubborn line both his parents recognised. He'd looked like that when he'd told them he meant to join the RAF and become a pilot, instead of waiting for call-up. He'd looked like it all through his childhood whenever he had set his heart on something he thought might be denied him. Usually, when he looked like that, he got his way – but not every time.

However, he was no longer a child. He had come to manhood by a hard, brutal route and they knew that any battles would be all the harder to fight.

'Ben,' Olivia said, her voice trembling, 'tell us the truth. There isn't any – any *reason* why you should get married, is there? You haven't done anything,' she hesitated, searching for the right word, '*foolish?*'

'Foolish?' He stared at her, now truly indignant. 'No, I haven't! May's a decent girl. And I'd have thought you'd know me better!'

'We do, we do.' John's voice was calming again. 'All the same, it does happen. We all know that.' There was a pause while everybody thought, but nobody said, *Look at Jeanie*. 'And you also know that your mother and I wouldn't judge anyone it happened to.' Again, they thought of Jeanie, taken into the vicarage when her own parents had turned her out. 'You must admit, it's rather sudden.'

'I don't think so,' Ben said. 'It seems to me as if I've known May all my life.'

There was a short silence. Then Olivia said in a quiet, rather piteous voice that indicated that she was retreating again into her own sorrow, 'But Ben, you're so young. And this girl – what is she, seventeen, eighteen? Neither of you have had a chance to grow up yet.'

'As a matter of fact,' Ben said, 'May's twenty-three.'

'Twenty-three?' Olivia stared at him, aghast. 'But that's three years older than you!'

'Nearly four, as it happens. I don't see that that matters.'

'And what are her family? You talked about a cottage. What does her father do – what *did* he do, I mean, before he was injured?'

'He worked on the farm; so did her grandfather. They're

plain, honest country people, Ma, like dozens around here. The sort you always call "salt of the earth".'

'I see,' she said, and his anger flared up again.

'I hope you're not going to be a snob about this. May's a lovely girl. You haven't given her a chance! You haven't even seen her but you're taking against her already. I thought you'd be pleased that I'd found someone so – so good and so nice and so pretty. I never thought—' He stopped abruptly as his mother began to cry. 'Oh Lord, I'm sorry, Ma. I've done this all wrong. Maybe I shouldn't have said anything, but – but I had to.' He waited, looking apologetically at his father, while his mother regained her fragile composure, then said, 'I had to tell you, because – well, look, we all know something big's blowing up. We don't know when it's going to happen, but it's on the cards that we'll be invading France before long. And I'd like to be married before that happens.' He looked at them both, and this time there was pleading in his eyes. 'And I need your permission.'

'Our permission . . .' Olivia said faintly. 'Yes, of course. You're not twenty-one until June. But surely you can wait until then!'

He sighed. 'I can't, Ma. We don't know what's going to happen or when. Look,' he reached out and put his hand on hers, 'I know this isn't the way you wanted it. I know you'd have liked to plan a wedding with the bride's mother and have a big do and everything. But it just isn't like that these days. Nobody can wait that long. And May's family wouldn't want that kind of wedding anyway. They're ordinary, simple people. They'd just want their family and friends in the village church and then go back to the cottage for a ham tea. That sort of thing.' He looked at his father. 'I'd want you both to come, of course. I'm sure the local vicar wouldn't mind you officiating.'

There was another short silence. Then Olivia said, 'You talk as if we've given our permission already.'

'Sorry, Ma.' He gave her his most engaging grin. 'That's me all over – jump in with both feet. But you are going to, aren't you?'

The Hazelwoods looked at each other. There was something in Olivia's eyes and expression that Ben couldn't read. At last, his father said with a sigh, 'This isn't something we can decide all in a few minutes, Ben. We've got to talk it over first.'

'But, Dad, there isn't *time*.'

'There has to be. I'm sorry, Ben, but you can't expect us to rush into this. You talk about jumping in with both feet, and yes, that's always been one of your problems. Perhaps because you were the youngest we've always allowed you a little too much of your own way. But we've always tried to guide you in the right direction, and on the whole you've accepted that guidance. This time, though . . .'

'Dad, for God's sake!' Ben caught his father's sudden frown and apologised hastily. 'Sorry, but you're still treating me like a child. I'm a *man* now, fighting a man's war. I fly an aeroplane. I'm trusted to make life-or-death decisions. It's ridiculous that I can't also be trusted to make a decision about my own life. This asking your permission – it's just a formality. I didn't even think we'd bother to discuss it.'

'But why are you in such a hurry?' Olivia asked. 'You'll be twenty-one in a few weeks, you won't need our permission then. Why not wait? Give yourselves time to plan something. I'm sure May's parents would rather you did that anyway.'

'Yes, that's a good point,' John said. 'What do May's parents think about all this?'

Ben looked down at the floor. 'As a matter of fact, they don't know. We haven't talked to them about it yet.' He hesitated again. 'What's more, I haven't even asked May. I wanted to be able to tell her we could go ahead as soon as possible. But I know she'll say yes!' he added fiercely, raising his head again. 'I *know* she will!'

'If you don't mind my saying so,' his father said mildly, 'nobody knows for certain what someone else will say until they ask them.' He looked at his son. 'Why don't you do as your mother suggests? Plan – if May agrees to marry you at all – for a June wedding. You won't need anyone's permission then. The RAF's not like the Army. And we'll come down, and Alexie too if she can get away, and if the local vicar really doesn't object, I'd be delighted to officiate. Don't you think that would be best?'

'No,' Ben said doggedly, 'I don't. I've told you, there's something big brewing and we don't know what will be happening or where we'll be in June. There's a war on, Dad, in case you haven't noticed.' He stood up, hurt and misery in every line of his face and body. 'I'm sorry to have upset you both – especially you, Ma. I never meant to do that. I thought I was bringing you good news. I thought you'd be pleased. I think I'll go to bed now.' He paused. 'I've got to go back in the morning, but I promised to spend some time with Jeanie and Hope. I suppose there's no point in us talking about this again, but if you change your minds . . .' He bent and kissed his mother's cheek awkwardly. 'I'm sorry, Ma.'

He was almost at the door when his mother, lifting her face from her hands, said, 'And what about Jeanie?'

Ben stopped. He turned and took a step or two back towards her. His face was shocked.

'Jeanie? What do you mean – *what about Jeanie?*'

Olivia met his eyes steadily. 'Surely you realised. Surely you've known that she was in love with you, and that we all thought you felt the same about her, and about Hope, your goddaughter? So what are you going to tell *her* about this – this May person? Or haven't you even given that a thought?'

Chapter Nineteen

It was rare for Ben to sleep badly, but he tossed and turned all through that night, his mind a jumble of anxious thoughts. He was torn with guilt over having upset his mother and, therefore, his father who had looked to him to give her some comfort; at the same time, he was filled with resentment at their reaction to his news. Not that it was exactly 'news', he thought miserably, since he hadn't even asked May to marry him – and when he'd hinted at it a week or two ago she'd seemed almost dismayed at the idea, thinking that his parents wouldn't consider her good enough for him. But that could have been dealt with. It needed only for his mother and father to meet her and reassure her; and he'd taken it for granted that they would love her just as much as he did. How wrong I was, he thought bitterly.

In fact, their main objection appeared to be that he was 'too young'. *Too young*! Not too young to give his life in a war of someone else's making, not too young to defend his country, but too young to decide how live his own life – always assuming that he was allowed to go on living it. It's stupid, he railed silently as the hours ticked slowly by, it's *criminal* that we have to wait until we're twenty-one to do all the things we ought to be able to do, like vote – take charge of our own money, and get married. It wasn't fair!

And then there was Jeanie. His mother had been right there – it had never occurred to him that Jeanie had any aspirations in his direction. He'd known her ever since she came here from Portsmouth, pregnant, frightened and grieving for her sweetheart, lost at sea. His parents had taken her in then and looked after her with all the kindness he would have expected of them. They'd grown fond of her, just as he had himself, and he'd meant it when he told her that she was as good as a daughter to them. But for heaven's sake, he'd never expected to *make* her their daughter! Even that time when he'd kissed her, he'd never seen Jeanie as a possible wife. It had been just a moment of affection — a little more than casual affection, perhaps, but never developing into anything else.

At least it shows they're not snobs, he thought, faintly heartened. If they'd accept Jeanie, they wouldn't think May was beneath me. At least I can tell her that.

It still didn't mean they'd let him marry her before June, though. And it didn't make things any easier for him where Jeanie herself was concerned. If she really did have hopes of marriage sometime . . .

No! He couldn't believe it. He didn't want to believe it — it made everything even more complicated. But he knew that he would have to talk to her about it, and he would have to do so in a few hours' time — before he went back to Harrowbeer.

'. . . So you see, Jeanie, I'd really like to get married as soon as possible,' he finished next morning. 'But Dad and Ma — well, they just don't seem to understand.'

They were sitting on a fallen tree-trunk in a little wood at the edge of the village. Ben had had his breakfast alone, his father having already gone to the church to take early service and his mother being not yet up. Jeanie had offered him an egg as well as the Weetabix he'd eaten, but he'd refused. Afterwards, he'd asked her to come for a walk and she had left her work and called Hope from the garden.

They'd walked down the lane in silence, the little girl skipping in front of them.

'What's the matter, Ben?' Jeanie asked at last. 'I took your mother a cup of tea and she didn't look as if she'd slept a wink. I thought she'd want to come down and have breakfast with you, but she said no, and she didn't want me to take anything up either. There hasn't been bad news about Ian or Alexandra, has there?'

'No,' he said. 'I'm afraid I'm the one who brought bad news, Jeanie. The trouble is, I didn't think it was going to be bad news – I thought they'd be pleased.'

'Pleased about what?' she asked, after a tiny pause.

He looked at her, struck by the note in her voice. She knows, he thought. She knows what I'm going to say. And, immediately afterwards – Ma was right. She *did* think that maybe I might . . .

He couldn't finish the thought. For a moment, he wondered about simply saying no more. She wouldn't insist, not if he said it was family business. She wouldn't pry. But the idea slipped out of his mind as quickly as it had slipped in. He knew that he had to tell her.

He drew her over to the tree trunk and they sat down. Jeanie faced him and he met her eyes.

'I want to get married,' he said quietly. 'I've met someone in Devon that I want to marry.'

The pause was longer this time. He thought she turned a little pale, but her gaze didn't waver. After a moment, she said, 'I see.'

Ben ploughed on. 'She's called May. May Prettyjohn. She lives near the airfield.'

'Oh, so she's not a WAAF, then?' Jeanie said brightly. 'Somehow I thought you might fall in love with a WAAF.'

'No, she's not a WAAF. She's—'

'I expect she's a doctor's daughter or something like that. Or a nurse, like your sister?'

'No, she's nothing like that. She's just an ordinary girl, Jeanie. A bit like you, as a matter of fact. She lives in a cottage with her mother and father and grandfather. She doesn't have to join the Services because she's needed at home – her father's bedridden – but she does a lot of war work and she helps the wife of my Squadron Leader in the house. That's how I met her. And she's three years older than me, and that's all,' he finished a little desperately.

Jeanie looked away into the trees, where Hope was picking some early bluebells.

'A bit like me,' she said. 'Not glamorous or anything. Not posh. Just – a bit like me.'

Too late, Ben realised that this was the last thing she had wanted to hear. A smart, well-dressed girl from a 'good' family, someone who had been educated at an expensive school – someone like Alison Knight, for instance – she could have understood and accepted. She'd probably even expected it. But an ordinary girl, 'a bit like her' was almost an insult. He could see the thought in her mind: Why wasn't I good enough?

'Jeanie,' he said, reaching for her hand. 'Jeanie, please don't be upset.'

'I'm not upset!' She turned her head quickly, meeting his eyes. 'Why should I be upset? I'm pleased for you, Ben, I really am. I want you to be happy.' She turned away again. 'I just want you to be happy,' she repeated in a whisper, and he could hear the faintest of quivers in her voice.

'Oh, Jeanie,' he said helplessly.

For a few moments, neither of them spoke. Then she drew in a deep breath and faced him again. Her cheeks were still pale but her mouth was firm. He thought how pretty she was, and how brave in all that she'd suffered, and wished for a moment that he could have loved her. But he'd met her too soon, when he was too young to know what love was, and when she was too frightened and unhappy, and their moment had passed. It might have come again, but May had come instead and now it was too late.

'Tell me about her,' Jeanie said. 'And tell me about your mother and father too. Are they really against it?'

'Yes, they are,' he said. 'They're really upset. They think I'm too young and I haven't given it enough time, and they don't like her being older than me, and they want me to wait. But I don't *want* to wait!' he burst out. 'I've tried to explain to them – it's all different these days. Nobody has time to be engaged for three or four years like they used to be. You don't know what's going to happen in that time. You don't even know what's going to happen tomorrow. We've got to take our chance while it's there, Jeanie, or it might be gone for ever.'

'You don't have to tell me that,' Jeanie said quietly, and looked across the little clearing to where Hope was roaming amongst the bluebells, singing to herself. Ben followed her glance and felt ashamed. Jeanie and her sweetheart Terry hadn't been able to wait to share their love. They'd waited to get married, but they'd waited too long. By the time Terry was killed, Jeanie had been pregnant and the chance was gone for ever.

'I'm sorry, Jeanie,' he said. 'I wasn't thinking. But I don't want that to happen to us. To May.'

'Is it likely to?' she asked, and he knew she was asking the same question as his mother.

'No, it's not. We haven't "got" to get married, or anything like that. I haven't done anything wrong and I don't mean to. I just want to get *married*.'

'And you don't want to go against your parents' wishes. I can see that – your mother's in an awful state at the moment.' Jeanie paused. 'I'm really worried about her, Ben. She's not getting over Peter at all. She just seems to be sinking into a black pit and nobody can do anything to help her. If she'd only go to church, but she won't. She says there's no one there.' She sighed, her eyes troubled. 'I don't know what anyone can do to help. And yet, sometimes she seems just like she used to be – only *too* bright, if you know what I mean. And you get the feeling that she might break at any minute.'

'I thought this might help,' Ben said gloomily. 'I really thought she'd be pleased about it. And I don't want to hurt her any more, but it's my life, Jeanie, and we've got to face it – I could get killed too, any day. And I don't want that to happen and never to have been married to May. I really don't.' He squeezed her hand and thumped it lightly on the rough bark of the tree. 'So you see, Jeanie, I'd really like to get married as soon as possible. But Dad and Ma – well, they just don't seem to understand.'

Jeanie was quiet for a moment. She seemed calmer now, as if she had begun to accept the situation and was even trying to help him. She turned her hand over in his and said, 'So what will you do? Get married anyway?'

'I can't.' He looked at her with frustrated eyes. 'I'm not twenty-one until June. I can't get married without their permission.'

They talked for a little longer, without coming to any conclusion, and then Ben said, 'I'll have to go soon. I mustn't miss the train, but there's just one thing . . .' He hesitated and she glanced at him. 'Ma seemed to think – well, that we might – that you might think I . . .' He floundered, his face colouring, and she spoke quickly.

'It's all right, Ben. I know what you're saying. You don't need to worry about that.' She looked away into the trees where Hope had now gathered a bunch of flowers almost as big as herself. 'Just look at that kiddy!' She raised her voice a little. 'Don't pick any more, lovey, we'll never have enough vases for them all.' Turning back to Ben, she went on, 'I won't say I'm not fond of you, Ben. But I knew when you went away that you'd probably meet someone. I've always known that. And I expect this May's a lovely girl. I just hope she's good enough for you, I do really.'

'Trust my taste,' he said, grinning. 'And you'll like her, Jeanie, you really will.'

'Yes, I expect I will.' She withdrew her hand and stood up. 'We'd better get going, or you will miss your train. Come on, Hope.'

As the little girl ran towards them, Ben looked at her and said, 'Whatever happens, we'll always be special to each other, Jeanie. And I'll always be Hope's godfather.'

'Yes,' she said, and bent to take some of the flowers from her daughter's arms. 'You'll always be Hope's godfather.'

When they got back to the house, John had returned from church and Olivia was in the kitchen, looking pale but composed and preparing a packet of sandwiches for Ben to take on the train. She looked round as they came through the back door and smiled.

'There you are. I was beginning to wonder if you'd got lost. Have you had a nice walk?' She saw the bluebells. 'Oh, how lovely. Did you pick them all yourself, Hope? We'll have to find lots of vases to put them in.'

'I told her we probably wouldn't have enough for them all,' Jeanie said, going through to the scullery where such things were kept. She came back with two or three large glass vases in her arms and began to fill them with water. Olivia found a pair of scissors and started to trim the stalks.

'I love bluebells,' she remarked. 'And if you get them into water quickly, they last quite well. These will fill the whole house with their scent. You must have some in your room too, Jeanie.'

Ben stood watching a little helplessly as they bustled about. After a moment or two, his mother glanced at him and said, 'Why don't you go into the study and have a chat with your father, Ben? I'll make some coffee – you'll need something before you catch the train.' She gave him a bright smile and put her hand on his arm, guiding him gently towards the door.

Bemused, he caught Jeanie's eye and raised his brows. She shook her head very slightly and gave a small shrug, and he obeyed his mother and went out of the door and along the passageway to his father's study, which was just inside the front door so that visiting parishioners could pop in and out as they needed.

John Hazelwood was alone, sitting at his broad, cluttered desk and gazing thoughtfully out of the window. He glanced up as Ben looked round the door and waved his son inside.

'Come in, Ben. I imagine you have to leave soon.'

'In about half an hour.' Ben sat down and eyed his father cautiously. 'Ma seems better this morning.'

'You think so? Oh, she's brighter, certainly – but it doesn't usually last. When it wears off she'll be even lower, I'm afraid. However, it's probably a good sign that she can even make the effort.'

Ben felt guilt wash over him. 'Dad, I don't know what to say.'

'You've probably said enough already.' The vicar sighed and turned back from the window to face him. 'Oh, it's not your fault, Ben. You've got your own life to live and you couldn't know how this would affect your mother. I realise you expected her to be pleased, but the truth is that nothing can please her at the moment but having Peter back. It's not that the rest of you don't matter – you matter even more. But she's so exhausted by her grief that her mind just can't take in new ideas. She's confused. All her reactions are wrong, and she knows it and is even more distressed by it. And then there's Jeanie, of course.'

'I've never given Jeanie any cause to think—'

'I know you haven't. But she may have thought it all the

same, and that's partly due to your mother's encouragement. You see, with the rest of you away, Jeanie has been the only young person in the house and she's been with us so long now we look on her almost as a daughter. What's more, she's been such a tower of strength and such a comfort that I think your mother has made some assumptions that perhaps she shouldn't have made. But it's understandable, I think.' He looked at Ben as if pleading with him to understand.

'Yes, I suppose it is. I have talked to Jeanie this morning, Dad. Things are all right between us.' He met his father's eyes. 'You will like May too, you know.'

'Yes, I'm sure we will. But I'm afraid I can't give you permission to marry.'

Ben's heart sank. He had begun to think, from his father's sympathetic tone and his mother's apparent good humour, that they had decided to agree. 'Why not?'

'Because of your mother. Don't be fooled by this brightness of hers. As I told you, it could break at any moment. Bring up the subject of May and marriage again, and that will send her right down.' He compressed his lips, then said, 'Look, Ben, I know this is hard for you and I know you find it difficult to understand why she's so upset about this – I barely understand it myself – but take it from me, if you persist you could bring about a complete breakdown. At present, between us, Jeanie and I are managing to keep her head just above water. I really don't want anything else happening to upset her.'

'Yes,' Ben said in a dull voice. 'I can see that.'

'It's not so very long to wait, is it?' John asked persuasively. 'You'll be twenty-one in June. You can do as you like then.'

'Can I?' Ben asked. 'If it's going to tip Ma into a breakdown now, is it going to be any better in June? As you say, it's only two months away. Won't she be just as upset by my getting married the minute I don't need your permission? Couldn't that be even worse?'

'Yes,' John said quietly. 'It could. But that will have to be your decision.'

Ben stared at him. Then he turned on his heel and left the room.

Chapter Twenty

'Bombing targets are to be switched from now on.'

The Squadron Leaders on Harrowbeer Airfield sat listening as the new strategies were outlined to them at their briefing. 'We won't be aiming at German cities and factories any more. Our main target will be the French and Belgian rail system.'

'Railways,' Andrew said afterwards as they sat in the mess over pints of beer, passing the new orders on to their pilots. 'And not even the German ones. We all know what that means.'

'Invasion,' Stefan said. 'It won't be long now.'

'I can see that they want to prevent easy transportation for the enemy,' Ozzie Mason said, 'but won't that backfire on our troops? They won't be able to use them either.'

'Grow up,' Andrew advised him. 'Our men aren't going to be queuing up at the ticket office to buy day returns to Berlin! They'll have tanks and lorries and God knows what to transport them.' He filled the bowl of his pipe with tobacco. 'Wonder what old Bomber Harris makes of it.'

Robin Fairbanks strolled over to join them, a tankard in his fist. 'From what I've heard, he's not too pleased. Doesn't think an invasion will work. He says too many men will be killed, like in the First War and at Dieppe.'

'And not enough are being killed now?' Ozzie said cynically. 'Look at us – we take off night after night and only half of us come back. What more does he want?'

'He reckons we ought to go on flattening German cities with area bombing,' Robin said. 'I bet there have been a few up-and-downers between him and Churchill over this! And some of the Yanks agree with him – they think we ought to be going for the oilfields.'

'Well, someone's overruled them, then,' Andrew pointed out, 'because those are our orders. Probably Eisenhower. I think he's right, too – if we don't get rid of the transport facilities, the troops won't have a chance. The Jerries will be lined up on the beaches waiting for them with open arms.'

They stopped talking about it then and drifted into different conversations. Stefan sauntered outside to sit at the rickety trestle table that had been carried out, and after a few minutes Ben joined him. They smoked in silence for a while.

'Something is wrong,' Stefan said at last. 'You are not happy, I think.'

Ben gave him a quick glance. 'Is it that obvious?'

'Only to one who looks. Most people don't, but I've seen you when you think nobody is watching you. There's something on your mind – something you cannot resolve.'

Ben sighed. 'I don't suppose I'm any worse off than a lot of people. No, I know I'm a hell of a lot *better* off. I've got no right to be fed up.'

' "Right"? Does that come into it?' The Pole regarded him thoughtfully, then leaned forward. 'We each have a right to our own feelings. Sometimes it is the only right we have left.' He laughed suddenly. 'Right – left! Your English language is very strange at times.'

Ben grinned. 'I know. It's what makes it such a good language for puns and cryptic crosswords. Luckily, we can usually tell what the words are intended to mean.'

'You may be able to. It's sometimes confusing for us.'

Stefan paused. 'Do you want to talk about what is wrong, or should I mind my own big business?'

Ben grinned again. 'Just "business" is enough! I don't know, Stefan. I don't think continually chewing it over helps, really. Anyway, why should you bother with it? It's nothing in comparison with your problems.'

'That doesn't make it any less to you. It helps me too, to think about someone else for a while.' He waited for a moment, then leaned forward again. 'I think you should talk to someone. But if you don't want to talk to me, why not go to Alison? She's very sympathetic and very wise. I have shared some of my problems with her and she is a comfort.'

'I couldn't bother her. She's not far off having her baby.'

'And does that affect her mind? I think she would welcome your company.' The Pole gave him another quick look. 'I have seen other young men with the same look in their eyes that's in yours now, Ben. It comes when troubles grow too great to be borne alone, and it means danger. I would not want you to be one of those who do not come back.'

May was spending as much time as possible now with Alison. With the birth drawing nearer and with the squadron on almost permanent readiness, Alison needed company, and although she enjoyed walking to the cottage, she felt more secure at home. Hughie had been born a fortnight early, and she was a little afraid that this baby would be even earlier.

'How are you and Ben getting along now?' she asked one afternoon. 'Didn't he go home last weekend to see his mother?'

'That's right. She'm not well at all, he says. Still grieving over her other boy.' May chewed her lip for a moment, then said, 'I wanted to talk to you about that, but I've been putting it off. But seeing as you've brought the subject up . . .'

'What is it?' Alison, who had been lying back on the sofa, struggled to sit up. 'Is something wrong, May? He hasn't given you up, has he?'

'No. Leastways, I don't think so. But since he came back, well, he don't seem the same and that's the truth of it. There's something bothering him, I know that.'

'Have you asked him what's wrong?'

May lifted her shoulders. She was sewing a nightdress for the new baby, smocking it across the front with tiny stitches. 'I tried but he just sort of turned me aside. Changed the subject. And that's what worries me most,' she said, laying her work down and gazing at Alison with anxious brown eyes. 'Us've always been straight with each other. That's one of the things I've always liked about him. Now, there's something he don't want to tell me, and that can't be good, now can it?'

'No, it can't.' Alison looked at her thoughtfully. 'But it doesn't mean he wants to finish with you. I'm sure if that were the case he'd have said so.'

'I don't know,' May said. 'It's just that this is only since he went home. And I've been thinking . . .' Her voice faded and stopped.

'Thinking what?' Alison prompted gently.

'Well, there's this other girl, that lives with his parents. Jeanie, she's called. Got a little girl – he's her godfather. You can see what I'm worrying about, can't you? Suppose when he went back he realised it was this Jeanie he really wants? I mean, you know what Ben's like, he wouldn't want to hurt nobody. I know there's something upsetting him, something he don't want to tell me, and it don't need much of a brain to work out what it is, do it?'

'Oh, May, surely not! After all, he must have known her for years – she went to live with them before the little girl

224

was born, didn't she? I'm sure there can't be anything between them. He'd never have started to go out with you if there had been.'

'Well, if it's not that,' May said miserably, 'what is it?'

Alison could find no answer. They looked at each other for a moment, then she swung her legs off the sofa and heaved herself to her feet.

'I'm going to make a cup of tea,' she said firmly, 'and you're going to stop worrying about it. And the next time you see Ben, you're going to ask him straight out what's the matter. It's the only thing to do, May.'

'Yes,' May said, picking up her work again. 'Yes, you're right. I'll talk to him the very first chance I get.'

But her heart thudded uncomfortably at the thought. Suppose it really was all over between them . . . .

Ben thought about Stefan's words as he went through the next few days. They were now escorting the bombers over the new targets, attacking French and Belgian railways, and as he stared down at the long lines of track, glittering in the moonlight, he wondered how it had come to this – wiping out the vital links of a friendly country already suffering under German occupation. What sort of world were they creating – or, rather, destroying – and how could it ever be rebuilt once the war was over? The devastation he had seen, and taken part in, was almost too vast to imagine, and yet he knew that was only a small part of it. And all because of one man's evil ambition.

Yet if it hadn't happened, he wouldn't have met May. His love for her shone so brightly in his heart that it seemed impossible that it had come about through such evil. It was beyond understanding.

He thought about his mother and her pain. Somehow, she had been knocked off balance, and although his father was sure that she would slowly regain her health, he also believed that Ben's marriage could destroy it completely. Another thing that was beyond understanding, Ben thought hopelessly. It wasn't even a matter of waiting for his twenty-first birthday – she would still feel the same, still be as distressed. He might wait years before she could accept it. He might wait for ever.

And I *can't* wait for ever, he thought, driving his aircraft fiercely through the night sky. I *won't* wait for ever!

Yet he could not bear the thought of hurting the mother he had always adored. He could not face the possibility that he might drive her into a complete breakdown – a breakdown from which she might never recover.

He knew that Stefan was right in saying that his problems would affect his flying. But he didn't think they were making it more dangerous. Instead, he felt driven by a new anger, a frustration that he could take out on the German fighters. It was his duty to protect the Allied bombers, to drive off the enemy, to shoot down as many of their planes as he could. He took a ferocious pleasure in chasing the interceptors through the sky, in firing his guns and seeing his target suddenly burst into flames or spiral out of control into the ground far below. He thrust out of his mind the knowledge that there were men in these planes, young men like himself who were defending their country; to pilots in the sky, humanity took a back seat. The enemy was made of metal and wood, Perspex and fabric; skin, bone, muscle and blood could be forgotten – *had* to be forgotten.

That was what war did to you.

When he landed safely, he gave no thought to the dangers he had faced, merely felt joy as he claimed another 'kill', maybe two or three. All he wanted was a pint in his hand, a meal inside him and then to see May.

May. May. May . . .

As soon as he was on the ground, she filled his thoughts

once more, and the problem of his mother began to circle yet again in his head. Round and round and round, with no solution.

Since coming back from Hampshire, he had wanted desperately to talk to May about his mother and all that had happened at home, but he hadn't been able to find the right words. None of it would matter anyway, if she didn't want to marry him, and with all these problems in his mind he didn't know how to ask her. He was aware that if she had even the faintest idea that their marriage might cause problems, she would refuse and he wouldn't be able to persuade her.

In the end, he decided to take Stefan's advice and talk to Alison.

He cycled round one morning after a fairly quiet duty, when he knew that May would be working at one of her other jobs. Alison was indoors with Hughie, making Cornish pasties, and came to the door wiping floury hands on her apron. She smiled a welcome at Ben and invited him in, leading the way back to the kitchen.

'You'll have to let me go first,' she joked. 'You can't possibly squeeze past me now, I'm so huge. Sit down. I'll just finish this and then I'll make some coffee.'

'Don't hurry. I like watching. It reminds me of when I was a little boy, watching my mother make cakes and things.' A slight shadow crossed his face.

Alison noticed it but said nothing. She turned back to her work, rolling out the pastry and cutting it into circles which she covered with a mixture of minced meat, turnip and potato already prepared in a bowl. She damped the edges of the circles with a pastry brush, then folded them over into half-moon shapes and crimped them with the back of a knife. Then she dipped the pastry brush into a saucer of milk and brushed it over the bulging pastry.

'We always used to use egg to do this,' she remarked. 'It

makes the pastry look lovely and golden. But we can't afford to use eggs for that now, even in the country.' She lifted the pasties on to a baking tray and slid them into the hot oven, then dusted the flour from her hands. 'There, that's done. You'll stay and have one, won't you? I've done plenty. Andrew loves them, and I never know who he might bring home with him.'

'Well, if you've really got enough . . .'

'Of course we've got enough. You needn't worry about taking the rations – there's hardly any meat in them anyway. As May's mother would say, someone must have stood on top of Cox Tor to throw that in!'

Ben smiled, then said, 'As a matter of fact, that's why I've come to see you. To talk about May, I mean. I need some advice.'

'Oh.' Alison was at the stove, pouring hot water from the kettle into two cups with a spoonful each of Camp coffee at the bottom. She turned to look at him. 'Just a minute, while I get the milk.'

Ben waited while she went out to the meat safe by the back door and came back with a bottle of milk. She poured some into each cup and some more into Hughie's mug, then took the bottle back again. 'We'll take it into the front room. Carry it carefully, Hughie, and then you can come back for the biscuits. And you're not to eat any on the way! He will, all the same,' she added to Ben as they made their way to the living room. 'He thinks I don't know, but those crumbs don't jump up round his mouth all by themselves!'

Ben grinned, remembering doing the same thing himself as a small boy. All the little mischiefs and passing disobediences that he now realised his parents had known all too well and allowed him to get away with, while still making sure he understood right from wrong. And he was never, ever, allowed to get away with lying!

They sat down with their coffee and Alison glanced at

the clock on the mantelpiece. 'I mustn't forget the pasties. Now – what is it you want to talk about, Ben?'

He looked down at his cup, uncertain how to start, and after a moment, she said gently, 'May has talked to me a little, you know. She's told me what she feels about you.'

'Has she?' He looked up with sudden hope, then let his head droop again. 'That's not really the problem, though. I know how she feels – at least, I think I do. We love each other.' A flush crept up his cheeks. 'I want to marry her, Alison. But—'

'But it isn't that easy, is it?' She looked at him with sympathy, remembering the wait she and Andrew had been compelled to endure before they could announce their engagement. And then the long time before the wedding, with plans being made, parties held, the church and the reception to organise. 'It's not like it was before the war.'

'No, it isn't. And that's what my parents don't seem to understand. Well, Dad does – up to a point. But that's the least of the problems.' He shook his head slightly and fell silent again. 'To tell you the truth, Alison, I just don't know what to do.'

Alison waited a moment, then said, 'I'm not sure I will either, Ben. But if talking about it helps – and if I can make any suggestion – well, here I am. And it *is* why you came, isn't it?'

'Yes, it is. I've got to talk to someone or I'll go mad.' He bit his lip and then said, 'And that's the real problem, you see. I think – I think that if I marry May, my mother,' his voice shook but he took a deep breath and forced it under control, 'my mother will go mad.'

Alison sat quite still, feeling the shock drain all colour from her face. 'Going mad' was an expression a lot of people used lightly, but Ben's face and the tone of his voice told her that he was using it in its real sense. For a moment or two, she felt sick.

'I'm sorry,' Ben groaned. 'I shouldn't have said that. It sounds dreadful. I should have said she'd have a breakdown – the words Dad used. It doesn't sound so bad, but it's what he meant, I know. He really thinks she's losing her mind, and if I go ahead with this there'll be nothing anyone can do to help.'

'I can't believe it,' Alison said at last. 'Why should it upset her so much? She doesn't even know May. Is it because she's just an ordinary country girl?'

'No, it's nothing like that – I don't think it can be, anyway. She'd be perfectly happy if it was Jeanie – that's another problem, you see.' He explained about Jeanie and Hope. 'It never occurred to me that Jeanie might have any ideas like that, or that Ma might either. But apparently she's got it into her head that Jeanie's like a daughter to her now and the best way to keep her in the family would be for me to marry her. Hearing about May seemed to her like a betrayal, I suppose.'

'Why is she like this?' Alison asked. 'Is it just because of your brother, or has she always suffered from nerves?'

'No, she's always been wonderfully calm and strong. She never seemed to lose her temper or get really angry about anything, and we could always go to her with our troubles. So did most of the village.' He rubbed a hand over his face. 'I couldn't believe it when I saw how she's changed. I mean, when Peter died of course she was grief-stricken – we all were – but we expected her to get over it. As much as you ever do,' he added, glancing at Hughie. 'I mean, I know losing a child must be the worst thing that can happen to a mother, but so many people do these days and they do seem to get back to themselves after a while. But Ma – it's as if she's got stuck and she can't get out. And when I told her about May, it made her worse, not better. Dad thinks it could tip her right over the edge.'

'Oh, Ben. I'm so sorry.' Alison thought for a few

moments. 'So what are you going to do? Are you going to wait?'

'Well, I've got to, haven't I? I'm not twenty-one yet, so I couldn't get married anyway without their permission, and Dad won't give it to me. I can't really blame him. He's got to think of Ma. But it's my life too – and how long am I going to have to wait? How long have I *got*?'

'Ben . . .'

'Don't tell me not to talk like that!' he said savagely. 'You know as well as I do that I'm only safe while I'm on the ground. I could get killed any night. And we both know there's something big coming up – the Invasion. It'll be all hell let loose then, and none of us—' He caught her expression and stopped abruptly. 'Oh, God. I shouldn't be talking like this, should I, especially to you! I'm sorry. Maybe I'd better go.' He began to get up.

'No!' Alison put out a hand to stop him. 'No, Ben, don't go. You're absolutely right. We all know what can happen. We just have to live with it, put it out of our minds.' At that moment, an aeroplane roared overhead as it came in to land at the airfield less than a quarter of a mile away. 'As much as we can,' she added wryly.

Ben gave a rather twisted grin. 'As you say – as much as we can.' He sat down again. 'Sorry, Alison, I just get a bit het up over it all. I want to marry her *now*, you see – as soon as possible – because we don't know what's going to happen next. I tell you what, if I hadn't needed my parents' permission I'd have married her first and then told them. Though God knows what that would have done to my mother,' he ended gloomily. 'Oh, hell – sorry, Alison – I just don't know what to do.'

'What does May say about it?' Alison asked. 'I can't believe she'd want your mother upset.'

'No, she wouldn't. And that's the other problem. You see, I haven't actually asked her yet. Oh, she *knows* – I've told her I want to spend the rest of my life with her, but I haven't actually asked her to marry me. Not in so many words. I was going to do it when I came back, with the form filled in to say that I could. Then all I'd have had to do would be to persuade her and her parents. You see, I know they like me but I'm afraid they think that – that she'll be marrying out of her station. Not that I care tuppence about that!' he burst out. 'May's the best girl I've ever met. There'll never be anyone else for me.' His shoulders slumped again. 'But how can I ask her now? I'd have to tell her about my mother. I can't get married knowing that it would destroy her. And May might even say we'd better forget each other altogether. I couldn't bear that, Alison. I really couldn't bear it.'

He leaned forward in his chair, his elbows on his knees, and covered his face with both hands. Alison gazed at him, pity welling up in her breast. She could almost feel the turmoil in his mind, the violent swinging of his thoughts from one extreme to the other. The passionate commitment he obviously felt towards May, the overpowering desire to marry her at the first possible moment; all countered by the inescapable obligation towards his own mother. How could he ever live at peace with himself if he knew that his actions had driven her beyond reason?

'I think you ought to talk to May, all the same,' she said at last. 'I know you risk losing her, but at the moment *she's* frightened of losing *you*. I don't know what you're going to do about it all – I can't really see that you can do anything but wait – but you really ought to have things straight between you.'

'Yes,' he said. 'I think you're right.' He lifted his face from his hands. 'What do you mean, she's frightened of losing me? Has she talked to you about it?'

'Yes,' Alison said, hoping she wasn't betraying May's confidence. 'I can't tell you exactly what she said, but she knows there's something bothering you and she's afraid you may have changed your mind. That's really all I can tell you.'

'Afraid I've changed my mind!' he exclaimed. 'My God, that's the last thing I'd do. I tell you, Alison, if I lost May now and never saw her again, I'd never look at another woman. Never!'

Alison saw the expression in his eyes and knew that he meant it. She knew, also, that plenty of other young men – and women – had said just the same, and then some time later found that they could love someone else after all. But this wasn't the time to tell Ben that. He wouldn't believe her anyway.

'Talk to May,' she said quietly, finishing her coffee. 'Go and find her, and talk to her. She deserves to know the truth, and if I know May as well as I think I do, she'll be willing to wait for you. And if not – well, it's got to be resolved one way or another, hasn't it? You can't go on like this for ever.'

'No, I can't. And I don't want her upset either.' He sighed deeply and rose to his feet, and this time Alison didn't try to prevent him. 'She'll be on her way home now, won't she? I'll go to meet her. I don't have to be back at the airfield until four. We've got time for a good talk.'

Alison struggled to her feet. She opened her mouth to speak, then turned her head slightly, sniffing the air. They stared at each other and the same thought struck them both at once.

'The pasties!' she exclaimed, and pushed through to the kitchen. 'Oh, thank goodness – just in time!' She slid the tray of golden-brown crescents of bulging, savoury-smelling pastry out of the oven. 'Are you sure you won't stay and have one?'

Ben grinned. 'No, thanks. They look marvellous, but I think, on the whole, I'd rather meet May.' He reached out and touched her awkwardly on the arm. 'Thanks, Alison. Thanks a lot.'

He squeezed his way past the coats and mackintoshes hung along the passageway and let himself out of the front door. Alison watched it close behind him, then set the tray of pasties on the wire rack she had put ready on the kitchen table.

I hope I gave him the right advice, she thought. I hope I haven't made things worse.

Chapter Twenty-One

There was no time for Alison to worry too much about Ben, for that afternoon she had another visitor. As she cleared away the lunch dishes and put the rest of the pasties into the meat safe to keep cool, she heard a knock at the door and opened it to find Stefan on the step.

'Stefan! Come in. You should have come earlier – I made pasties and there were far too many. I suppose you're not hungry now?'

He smiled and shook his head. 'I had lunch in the mess. Lamb chops.'

'Oh, far better than you'd have got here! Come and sit down. I was just going to make a cup of tea – you'll have one, won't you?'

'Always the cup of tea,' he said. 'Yes, please. But let me make it. You sit down and rest. And how is this little man today, hm?' He rubbed Hughie's fair hair.

'Have you come to build a castle?' Hughie asked, and the Pole laughed.

'Yes, I will build castle with you. Now, you make your mother sit down. She needs rest. Put up her feet.' He guided them gently into the front room where Alison sank gratefully on to the sofa, then went out to the kitchen.

'I like Uncle Stefan,' Hughie observed, getting out his box of coloured wooden bricks. 'He builds good castles. And he plays nice music, too.'

'He does.' Alison leaned her head back and closed her

eyes, listening to the small sounds Stefan made as he moved about the kitchen, putting on the kettle, getting cups and saucers out of the cupboard, opening the back door to fetch the milk. He knows where everything is, she thought with a small shock, realising that this showed how often he had come to see her in the past few months. He seemed as much at home in the house as Andrew himself. More so, sometimes, during those late winter afternoons when he sat at the piano and played as the sky grew dark and the room was lit only by the firelight.

He came into the room bearing a tray with the teapot, a small jug of milk and the cups and saucers. He had brought Hughie's own mug as well, and had remembered the bowl of sugar-lumps. He set it all down on the low table by the sofa.

'Thank you,' Alison said, opening her eyes. 'What a treat, to be waited on.'

'Doesn't Andrew wait on you?'

'Oh yes, of course he does, when he's at home. But you know how busy he is – and then when he's here, he's tired. And I like to do things for him. It's my job!' She smiled at the tall Polish pilot. 'Do sit down, Stefan. You make me feel uncomfortable, having to look up at you.'

He lowered his long body into the armchair and leaned down to pick up one of Hughie's bricks. Every time he came, he built a different castle, and each one had its own story. Alison was never sure whether they were stories he had heard or whether he made them up, but they fascinated her almost as much as Hughie. They were true fairy tales – stories of many-turreted castles, with beautiful princesses who sat at casements brushing their long, golden hair and watching for a prince to come galloping on a white horse. Often, there was a black horse first, bearing a wicked king who would demand the princess's hand in marriage, and the prince would have his work cut out to save her. Or perhaps the story would be about the young prince himself, little and lorn, the last of the family with no lands to rule over, sent out into the world to make his own fortune. Or maybe there was really just one story, told from every different angle, so that you understood that each person in it had his own point of view, his own story to be told. Like in life, she thought. Like Ben and his parents, and May and hers. Like me and Andrew. And Stefan . . .

Perhaps everyone was like the princess, waiting for her prince to arrive; or like the prince, searching the world for his fortune and for love.

'How are you, Stefan?' she asked, thinking of all that he had left behind in his land of fairy-tale castles, where his family had spent their summers in a cottage beside a blue lake, with forests and mountains beyond.

'I'm well.' His silver-grey eyes smiled at her. 'And you? You look like a flower, Alison.'

She laughed. 'What sort of flower? An overblown chrysanthemum? But it's nice of you to say so, Stefan.'

'It's true,' he said. 'You look beautiful – like a rose, breaking from its bud. Being pregnant makes all women look beautiful.'

Alison blushed. 'I don't feel very beautiful,' she confessed. 'I feel fat and ugly and cumbersome. I feel as if I've got old all of a sudden.'

He came out of his chair and knelt before her, clasping her hands in his. 'Alison, you must never feel like that! Fat? No – it's simply the child you carry, the precious life you're keeping safe until it can live and breathe for itself. Ugly – not in the least. Beautiful, I tell you! And cumbersome – well, that will pass soon enough. It is just the way Nature has of telling you to rest, to save your energy for the child to grow strong.'

Alison felt her blush deepen. She looked down at their hands, clasped upon her knees beneath the swell of her belly. His fingers were long and slender, the hands of a musician. She remembered what he had told her about his violinist father and how he had taught them all to play an instrument. Stefan's had been the piano.

'Play something for me,' she said softly. 'Play something quiet that will remind me of peace.'

He went over to the piano and lifted the lid. As he always did, he let his fingers drift over the keys, as one might stroke a cat or caress a dog's head in greeting. Then he sat down and began to play.

The notes were clear and quiet and Alison leaned back in her chair and closed her eyes, letting the music flow across her mind, raising pictures of tranquillity – the primroses along the banks, the blossom on the trees, the call of the first cuckoo which she had heard only a day or two ago in the woods near Denham Bridge. She wondered what pictures it raised in Stefan's mind as he played – similar scenes, of lakes and rivers and mountains at peace, the countryside where he had spent those summer holidays he had described? And when he played the fiercer music, when the chords crashed together in stormy passion, what was he seeing then? She shivered.

At last he got up, stretching his long legs, and said that he must go.

'Come again soon,' Alison said, looking up at him. 'I like having you here, Stefan. And so does Hughie.' The little boy was already protesting that Uncle Stefan should help him build another castle, tell him a new story, play some more music – anything to keep him there a few minutes longer – and she felt rather like doing the same. She smiled at him, feeling suddenly shy, and he looked down into her eyes.

'I like coming here. I feel at peace with you, Alison. It's as if our minds meet. It's a rare thing to find, and a very precious one.' He took her hand in his and raised it to his lips. 'But for now, I must go. Don't get up. Stay there and rest.'

He ruffled Hughie's hair and bade him look after his mother. Then he moved softly to the door and was gone. They heard the front door close and the sound of his footsteps outside.

Alison got up from her chair. She put the hand that he had kissed against her cheek and looked into the mirror, trying to see what he had seen.

Trying to see why he had called her beautiful.

Ben walked slowly along the lane. The banks were studded with primroses the size of half-crowns, with patches of purple violets like dark splashes of wine between them. He picked a bunch, arranging them in his hands and pressing their soft petals against his face so that he could inhale their scent.

Overhead, a pair of squirrels chased each other through the fresh, bright green of new beech leaves. Across the parkland of the big house where May worked three mornings a week, he could see a dozen or so deer grazing. At that moment, the airfield was unusually silent, and with no roar of engines it seemed as peaceful as if there were no war at all. If only it were all over, he thought. Until now, he had been driven by the need to serve his country, to fight an enemy whose wickedness still probably wasn't wholly understood, to protect his land from the evil that had been stalking it for the past five years or more. But now, feeling himself a part of this tranquil landscape, he wanted it to be over. He wanted to settle down to a normal life with the girl he loved.

As he stood gazing over the bank at the deer, he heard footsteps coming along the lane and turned quickly, his heart thumping. In another moment, she was in sight – May, as pretty as her name, wearing a faded blue dress with white polka dots scattered over it, her arms, left bare by the short, puffed sleeves, round and smooth and already lightly tanned, her dark curls springing from her head. She saw him and stopped, her face flushing with delight, and he held out the flowers, unable for a moment to speak.

'Ben! Whatever be you doing here?'

'I came to meet you,' he said, finding his voice. 'I couldn't wait any longer. May, we have to talk. There are things I have to tell you.'

'Oh.' The pleasure faded from her face and she looked wary. Her glance fell to the flowers in his hand. 'You look as if you'm on the way to the churchyard.'

'They're for you.' He held them out and she took them a little reluctantly. 'May, what is it? What's the matter?'

'Don't know yet, do I? Depends what you want to talk about.' He could feel her withdrawal and his heart sank. I've made a mistake, he thought. She doesn't feel the same after all. Or maybe she just doesn't want to let it go any further.

'I want to talk about us.' He took her hand and tucked it into his arm, drawing her close, but when he bent his head towards her she turned her face aside so that his kiss fell on her cheek. 'May, whatever's wrong? Aren't you pleased to see me?'

'I'm always pleased to see you, Ben, you know that,' she admitted. 'But things haven't been the same between us just lately, have they? Ever since you went home.'

He looked at her, trying to see her expression, but she kept her face turned away and his alarm grew. 'That's what I want to talk to you about. Listen, May, can't we go somewhere by ourselves – now? Or do you have to go home? I suppose they'll be expecting you.'

She hesitated for a moment or two, then shrugged slightly. 'Well, I suppose 'tis best to get it over. I never did like dragging things out, specially bad news. I'll tell Mother we're going for a bit of a walk down to the village – there's some shopping I need to do anyway. I don't suppose it'll take long, whatever it is we got to say to each other.'

He looked at her, bemused, but said no more as they walked the rest of the way to the cottage. What bad news did she mean? He could think of only one thing and his heart sank. She's been thinking it over while I was away, he thought, and she wants to finish it. Oh, May . . .

They came to the gate where he had met her on the bright, frosty Christmas night, and May hurried inside. He heard the voices of her mother and grandfather and then she came out again, looking flushed. They set off down the footpath that led through the steep fields to the village.

'So what is it?' she asked presently. 'You might as well come straight out with it, Ben. No use beating around the bush.'

'Not here. Not until we can be private.' They came to a little cluster of trees and Ben took her in his arms.

'*This* is what I wanted to say,' he said, and kissed her firmly. 'And *this*. And *this*.' The third kiss took longer than both of the others put together, and when he ended it at last, they were both breathless.

'Ben,' she began, but he interrupted her.

'You can't say you don't love me, May! I know you do – I can feel it. You couldn't kiss me like that if you didn't love me.'

She stared at him. 'I never said any such thing. What are you talking about?'

'Oh, May,' he said hopelessly. 'I'm saying this all wrong, I know. I've been going over and over it in my mind, trying to make up the right words, and now I can't remember a single one. I'll just have to come right out and say it. May—'

'No,' she said, putting her fingers against his lips. 'I'll say it for you. You want us to stop, don't you? It doesn't matter whether we love each other or not, you've been home, and whatever happened there made you realise you've made a mistake. Well, I could have told you that all along. I tried, a few times. Us have had a lovely time, but that's all there is to it. It's all right, Ben. I understand. I'm not going to make a fuss about it.'

His brows drew together. He searched her eyes, then put up his hand to remove her fingers from his mouth. Holding them against his chest, he said, 'You're not making any sense, May. That's not what I was going to say at all. I don't want us to stop – ever. I want you to marry me.'

There was a silence. Then May said, in a whisper, '*Marry* you?'

'Yes,' he said. 'Didn't you know? You must have realised.'

'I didn't know what to think,' she admitted. 'I knew what I felt about you, but I wasn't sure . . . And then, when you went home and came back sort of different, I thought you'd realised it just wouldn't do. I thought you were getting around to telling me.'

'No,' he said, and released her fingers so that he could stroke her cheeks and wipe away the tears that had begun to wet them. 'No, that's not what I want to tell you at all. But . . . there is something, all the same.'

'What?' Her voice was touched with apprehension. 'What is it? Is it – is it Jeanie?'

'Jeanie?' He looked at her in surprise. 'What do you mean? Why should it be Jeanie?'

'Well, I don't know, do I? I mean, you've told me about her, how she lives with your mum and dad, and she's got this little girl, and you're her godfather. I just thought, I wondered – well, I wondered if you were *fond* of her, as well as – you know . . .' She floundered to a stop. 'I'm not sure what I do mean, now,' she finished hopelessly.

'I am,' he said, and gathered her close against him. 'You

were afraid we had an understanding, weren't you? Well, you weren't the only one. My mother thought that too.'

'Your *mother*?'

'Yes. That's why I need to talk to you, May. You see, I went back home for two reasons this weekend. One was because Dad asked me to, because he thought it would help Ma to see me. She's in an awful state still, May. She can't seem to get over Peter at all, and he thinks she might be heading for a really bad breakdown. And when I – well, that brings me to the other reason.' He glanced around. 'Let's sit down for a minute, shall we? The ground's quite dry.'

They settled themselves on the grass. Ben clasped May's hand in his and went on, 'What I wanted to do was get their permission to get married.'

'Their *permission*?'

'Yes. You know I'm not twenty-one yet. My birthday's in June.'

'But that's only a few weeks away!'

'A few weeks these days can be a lifetime,' he said quietly.

May bit her lip. 'You're not getting premonitions or anything, are you, Ben? You're not scared something's going to happen to you?'

'No, nothing like that. I just want to be married to you – now. As soon as possible. I love you, May, and I want you to be my wife, and I don't want to wait.' He sighed and looked across the valley towards the cottages climbing up the far side.

'But you hadn't even asked me!'

'I was going to ask you when I came home.' He gave her a quick, crooked grin. 'I was going to do it all properly – down on one knee, all that sort of thing. Flowers from the shop at the Leg O' Mutton. Even a bottle of champagne, if I could get hold of one. But – well, my parents wouldn't do

243

it. They wouldn't agree to sign the paper.' His shoulders slumped and he stared down at their clasped hands. When he looked up, she was dismayed to see tears in his eyes. 'They wouldn't even agree to think about it.'

'Oh, Ben.' For a moment, she felt only sympathy for his own misery. Then she remembered that this affected her too, and said, 'But even if they had – well, you didn't know for sure that I'd say yes, did you?'

His brows came together. 'No, not for sure. But you would, wouldn't you, May? You love me as much as I love you, I know you do. Why wouldn't you say yes?'

'Well, there's a lot to think about, isn't there? I mean, we're different. You're a vicar's son, you've been to a posh school, you *talk* posh, and I'm just an ordinary girl with a Devon accent. I haven't had the education you've had.'

'What's that got to do with it? I'm not going to test you on your maths or Ancient Greek.'

'No, but that's just it. I don't even know what Ancient Greek *is* – and all I know about maths is how to add up and divide and say my tables. All right, I know we'd never even mention things like that, but it's all the other things too – the things you take for granted and I don't know anything about. To tell the truth, I don't think my parents would be all that keen, either.'

'I thought they liked me!'

'They do. They like you very much. But they wouldn't want me marrying you, I'm sure. They'd think I was getting above myself.'

'That's just stupid!' he burst out, and May stopped abruptly, her cheeks colouring. He bit his lip and tightened his grasp on her hand. 'I'm sorry, sweetheart, I shouldn't have said that. Look, I think a lot of your parents, and your grandad too. They're the salt of the earth. And they're not stupid, not at all. Look at all the things your mother knows, the things she can do – cooking and sewing and making bread – they're far more use than being able to do trigonometry or algebra or parse Latin sentences. And the books your father reads. He's read far more than I have. He can talk about all sorts of things.'

'They'd still think I was getting above myself,' she repeated.

He didn't answer for a moment or two, then he said, 'But they'd come round, wouldn't they? They'd come to see that it's what we want, and they'd want you to be happy. I'm sure they'd agree in the end.'

'Maybe,' she said, sounding unconvinced.

'And you wouldn't need their permission,' he pointed out. 'You're old enough to do what you want.'

'And that's another thing,' she said. 'To start with, I wouldn't go against them – we'd have to wait until they were happy about it. And apart from that, they wouldn't like me being too old for you.'

'Well,' he said, trying to lighten the situation, 'we can't really do anything about that, can we.'

May ignored him. 'And they'd think you were too young anyway. They've already said as much.'

He quirked an eyebrow at her. 'You mean you've talked it over already?'

'Not in so many words,' she said, blushing. 'They've talked to me, though. They don't want us getting too serious.'

'It's a bit too late for that,' he said, and looked into her eyes. 'We are serious, aren't we, May? Both of us.'

'Yes,' she said, meeting his gaze. 'We are.'

He drew her close against him. 'May, darling, what are we going to do?'

'Can't we just wait until your birthday?' she asked. 'It's only a few more weeks and your mother and father might come round by then. Your mother might feel better –

people do get over things, in time – and mine would see that we're serious too. Things could be different by then.'

'Too different,' he said gloomily. 'Oh, I don't mean I think anything's going to happen to me, but – well, you know what it's like. Men going out and never coming back. I've been lucky so far, but . . . I just want us to be married, that's all. And that's the other part of it, the part I haven't told you yet. You see, my father's afraid that if we do wait, and get married in June when I don't need their permission any more, it could push my mother into a complete breakdown. She's so upset about it, and she can't be reasoned out of it because it's not really reasonable. He thinks it's because she knows that Peter will never be married, and she'd set her heart on Jeanie being her daughter, and – oh, I can't explain it, it's all mixed up, but he's afraid of her going right over the edge and never getting better. So, you see . . .'

'We can't get married,' May said. 'We can't get married until she's better. Perhaps we never will.'

'No!' he cried. 'No, don't say that. She *will* get better, as time goes on, I know she will. When the war ends – or sometime. But I can't do anything to upset her any more now. I couldn't have that on my conscience for the rest of my life.'

'No,' she said. 'No, you can't.'

Again, they sat wrapped in silence until Ben heaved a large sigh. 'Well, that's it, darling. That's what I wanted to tell you. It's up to you now. You might not want to wait for however long it takes. You might think it's all too difficult and we'd better say goodbye now, and stop seeing each other.'

May turned her face towards his. There were tears on her cheeks and her dark brown eyes were wet with more. But there was a determined set to her chin, and a firmness to her red lips.

'I'm never going to say that, my flower,' she said. 'Never in all this world. But there's something you ought to be saying to me.'

'Is there? What's that?'

'With all this talking,' she said, 'you've still never asked me if I'll marry you. I don't want you to go down on one knee or give me expensive flowers or nothing like that – that bunch of primroses and violets you picked for me is better than anything you can get in a shop. But I *would* like you to propose to me.'

He stared at her for a moment, then burst out laughing.

'Oh, May, May! I love you *so* much.' His smile faded and he took both her hands in his once more. Then he looked deeply into her eyes and said very seriously, 'May, my darling. I really do love you. Very, very much. Will you marry me? Will you be my wife?'

For a second or two, as she gazed back at him, he held his breath. And then her face broke into a beaming smile, and she threw both her arms round his neck and kissed him.

'Oh, yes!' she cried. 'Yes, I will – and I don't care *how* long we have to wait!'

Chapter Twenty-Two

They couldn't keep it a secret.

For the first few days, both Ben and May went around hugging it to themselves, thrilled with the shining promises they had made to each other. They considered themselves engaged now, but it seemed too new and precious to share at first. Then Ben said, 'You ought to have a ring, you know. Why don't we go into Tavistock tomorrow and buy one?'

May looked at him. 'I can't do that without telling the family first. I know I don't have to have their permission, but I think my dad would like to be asked. 'Tis only polite.'

'Yes. I ought to do that.' Ben thought for a minute, then said anxiously, 'What do you think he'll say? You told me he and your mum didn't seem too keen on the idea. You don't think he'll refuse, do you? What will we do then?'

'Cross that bridge when us comes to it, flower.' She took his hand. 'I don't think they'll be all that surprised, to tell you the truth. I've dropped a hint or two just lately, to put them in the way of it, like. I reckon they'll have chewed it over quite a bit when I've been out of the way.'

Ben grinned. 'So it's not exactly a matter of me asking, more just telling them they're right, is that it?'

'Well, us hopes so, don't us. Mind you, 'twas only a hint – but I caught Mother turning out some of my nan's old lace tablecloths the other day, the ones she was given for a wedding present and never used. She put 'em away quick when I came into the room, but I knew what she were doing all right.'

'That sounds promising,' he said. 'I'd better do it straight away. With things as they are at the moment, I never know whether I'm going to be able to get away from the station. I just wish we could be getting married instead of engaged, but there's nothing we can do about that.' He squeezed her hand. 'I do feel better about waiting now, though. Being able to talk to you about it and be properly engaged has made a big difference. I just want that ring on your finger now, so that everybody knows about it, and no big, husky Devon lad tries to take you away.'

May laughed. 'Not much chance of that! I know every Devon lad for miles around, and anyway most of 'em are away. Come home with me now, Ben, and talk to Father. And then we can go to Tavi first thing in the morning.'

It seemed to Ben almost as if he was expected at the cottage that morning. The living room was clean and tidy, with May's father sitting up in the big chair they'd set up for him. After coming downstairs for Christmas he'd announced that, since it was only his legs that were paralysed, he didn't see any reason why he couldn't sit in a chair just as well as in a bed, and old Mr Prettyjohn had altered his own armchair so that it had a longer part at the front for his son's legs to rest on. The bed itself was disguised as a settee during the day and they had even devised a way of transferring the invalid to it at night. William Prettyjohn was now much more part of the family, and his cheerful face and busy hands had quickly become an important feature by the big inglenook fireplace.

'Well, here's a sight for sore eyes,' Mrs Prettyjohn welcomed Ben when he and May came in through the back door. 'And how be you, my handsome? You'm looking extra smart this morning. Go in and say hello to my William and I'll put the kettle on.'

Ben did as he was told. William Prettyjohn looked up from the leather bag he was making and nodded. 'Mornin', young Ben. Bit of time off?'

'A few hours.' Ben sat down in the chair opposite. He felt unusually awkward, but William merely went on pushing his thick needle through the leather and drawing the thin strips through the holes. Perhaps I ought to ask him now, Ben thought, and cleared his throat.

'Here we be then, my flower.' Mrs Prettyjohn came bustling through the kitchen door with a tin tray on which he saw four cups and saucers and a plate of scones. 'Must've smelled these baking, you must. Grandpa's gone to do a bit of gardening for old Mrs Hubbard down in Buckland, so it's just us, all cosy. Here, Ben – take two while you're at it, save me passing it over again.'

Once again, Ben did as he was told. Still feeling shy and awkward, he sat eating the scones which for once tasted like dust in his mouth, and listening to the others talking. He replied when someone addressed him directly, but apart from that he was silent. He glanced at May once or twice and she gave him a reassuring smile, but his heart was thumping so hard he felt sure they must be able to hear it and he could only manage a faint, wavering grin back.

'What's that noise?' William asked suddenly, and he nearly jumped out of his skin.

'Oh, it's just Norman Philly, come with a load of logs. He said he'd be by this morning.' Mrs Prettyjohn jumped up and hurried to the back door. May got up too and followed her.

'I'll go and help.' She gave Ben a meaningful look and closed the door behind her.

William Prettyjohn picked up his work again and Ben stared hopelessly at the empty fireplace. For a moment, he entertained the thought of just not asking – of just letting it go, keeping the engagement secret and waiting until another day. Or week. Or even – but no, that was silly. Whatever was the matter with him? He could fly an aircraft over Europe, fighting the enemy, risking his life every night, yet he couldn't ask this man a simple question. He cleared his throat and the other man glanced up.

'Got a bit of a cold, have you, boy?'

'No,' Ben said desperately. 'As a matter of fact, there's something I want to ask you, Mr Prettyjohn.'

'Ask away then,' William said, stitching imperturbably.

'It's – it's just that – well, you must know that May and I are fond of each other.' He could feel the heat rising up his body, apparently from the ends of his toes to his ears. He went on rapidly, 'I mean, we're *really* fond of each other. We – we love each other, Mr Prettyjohn, and we want to get married. Well, engaged, anyway. I want to buy her a ring. I thought we could into Tavistock tomorrow and get it, but I thought I ought to ask you first and – and so, that's what I'm doing.' He stopped, feeling that he hadn't done this at all well. 'Would – would that be all right with you and Mrs Prettyjohn?'

William laid down his work at last and faced Ben gravely.

'You'm wanting to marry our May?'

'Yes,' Ben said, relieved to have it out in the open.

'And she wants to marry you, is that what you'm saying?'

'Yes, that's right.' Hadn't he made that clear?

'Well, I don't know as there be much I can do about it, then. She's of age, got the key of the door and all. Free woman.'

'I know, but it seemed only polite – a matter of courtesy,' Ben babbled, feeling his anxiety return and wondering if he had offended May's father in some way. 'It didn't seem right to just go and buy her a ring and then tell you.'

William regarded him thoughtfully. Then his face broke into a smile and he held out his hand. Ben took it in his, finding it surprisingly strong, and smiled back. It looked as if it was all right after all.

'Bless my heart, boy, don't look so worried. 'Tis just my way, to tease you along a bit – but if you wants our May and she wants you, there's nothing me nor Mrs Prettyjohn'll do to stand in your way. Though I won't say as we haven't had our doubts,' he added, looking serious again. 'There's a lot of differences between you, and you'll have to work at it, both of you. And you got to remember you'm still only a young chap, for all you'm doing man's work. Us'd both like to see you wait a bit before you ties the knot proper.' He saw Ben's face fall and went on more gently, 'But there, 'tis strange times and things has to be done different, I know. And like I say, May's a free woman, can make up her own mind and I dare say her will – always known her own mind, our May has, for all her looks so gentle and biddable. You'll find that out as time goes by.' He nodded. 'Whatever you decides between you, Mother and me will do our best to help. There.' He shook Ben's hand firmly. 'And now, if old Norman's finished unloading they logs, I'll get Mother to bring in a drop of Grandpa's elderberry wine so us can toast your future happiness.'

Ben started to get up out of his chair, but before he was properly on his feet the kitchen door opened and the two women came in. May was flushed and smiling and Mabel Prettyjohn was carrying the same tin tray, this time bearing four small glasses and a bottle of purple wine. Ben looked at them quizzically and she laughed.

'Us had an idea there might be something in the wind. So you'm going to be our son-in-law, be you?' She set down the tray and came over to kiss his cheek. 'And very welcome you'll be, though mind you, we had a lot of talking to do before us could make up our minds to it, what with May being older than you and you a vicar's son and everything.'

She poured the wine and handed it round, and William lifted his glass in the air. 'To May and Ben. Their future happiness.'

'May and Ben,' Mabel echoed, and they drank solemnly and then gazed at Ben with expectation. In some horror, he realised that he was meant to reply.

'You're not expecting a speech, are you?' he asked in dismay, and they all laughed. 'Well, I've never made a speech in my life, but I'm happy to propose a toast. To you all. To my lovely future wife,' he smiled at May, who dimpled, blushed and smiled back, 'and to my future parents-in-law. A finer couple never walked the earth.' He realised his blunder and flushed scarlet with embarrassment. 'I mean – oh Lord, I'm sorry. I just mean – well, I'll be very glad to be your son-in-law,' he ended, and buried his nose in his glass, wishing the earth would open up and swallow him.

William and Mabel roared with laughter and May came over and sat down beside him. He put his arm around her and she kissed his cheek. He realised with a sudden lightening of his heart that this was something new – that he could sit with his arm around May, in the presence of her parents, and it would be all right. The anxieties of the past few minutes evaporated and his face split into a smile that seemed to stretch from one ear to the other as he looked around the room.

'We're engaged!' he said in wonder. 'May, we're *engaged*!'

'I know,' she said, smiling at him. 'Isn't it lovely?'

The back door opened and they heard feet stamping on the floor and then the noise of someone pulling off a pair of boots. A muttering sound ensued, and then old Mr Prettyjohn appeared in the doorway and surveyed them with astonishment.

'What be going on here then?' he demanded. 'Drinking

and carousing in the middle of the morning? And be that my best elderberry wine, what I was saving for summat special, that you've opened up? Celebrating summat, are you?'

'That's right, Grandpa,' May said, getting up to kiss his wrinkled cheek. 'We're celebrating. We're celebrating something very, very special.'

Andrew came home late that afternoon, looking preoccupied. He had tea with Alison and Hughie and then said he had to go back.

'Can't you even stay to put Hughie to bed?' she asked in disappointment. 'We've hardly seen you lately.'

'Sorry, darling. You know how things are.' Everyone was aware now of the closeness of the Invasion. Yelverton was just outside the exclusion zone, but travel into Plymouth or anywhere along the coast was banned and the numbers of Allied soldiers, sailors and airmen were increasing every day. Camps were being set up wherever there was space, and khaki-coloured trucks, lorries and tanks were seen regularly rumbling along the roads and even the narrow lanes. The airfield itself had received several Canadian squadrons, and local pubs like the Leg o' Mutton and the Rock were filled with men every night. What with them and the Americans who were still at Bickham House, the whole area resounded with transatlantic accents. It was, Alison had thought once or twice, as if they had all been transported to Texas.

'I know,' she said with a sigh Normally, she tried not to let her feelings show, but her loneliness had increased just lately. She told herself that it was partly because of her pregnancy, but the nights when Andrew was flying seemed colder and more forlorn than ever before. She welcomed the visits of the other pilots – Robin, Ozzie, Ben and the rest – and spent as much time as possible with May, but still it was Andrew's company that she yearned for most. The only other times when she felt at peace were when Stefan was there, talking to her, telling Hughie stories or sitting at the piano, lost in his own world as his fingers roamed over the keys.

'It'll be over soon,' Andrew said. 'We're going to win this war, sweetheart, and it can't be much longer now. Once we're in France again . . .'

'There'll still be a lot of fighting. The Germans won't give in that easily, Andrew, you know they won't. Not after all this time. And France is a big country – and then there's the rest of Europe as well. It won't be over in five minutes.'

'We've got Russia on our side, though,' he pointed out. 'They're driving the Germans from behind. If we can just get them in a pincer . . .'

'It will still take months. Maybe even years.' Alison shifted uncomfortably in her chair. 'I'm sorry, I know I shouldn't talk like this, but I need you too. And with the baby so close as well . . .' Her eyes filled with tears.

'Oh, darling!' Andrew dropped on his knees beside her chair. 'Sweetheart, I'm so sorry. You know I wouldn't leave you if I didn't have to. I hate not being here, I hate not being with you at night. I realise how hard it is for you, I do really, but there just isn't anything I can do about it. Darling, please don't cry.' He took her face in his hands and began to kiss the tears away. 'You're all salty!'

Alison laughed a little. 'Sorry.' She felt for a hanky and wiped her cheeks and eyes. 'I didn't mean to do this, but – sometimes it just gets too much for me. I ought to know by now what it's like, being an Air Force wife, and, I know it's not as bad as being married to a soldier or a sailor, but all the same . . .'

'You're tired,' he said tenderly. 'You're tired and upset and you're having a baby. I ought to be with you. It's just not fair, is it?'

'Nothing's fair,' she said dispiritedly. 'And I feel so selfish, too. I mean, look at Ben with his mother having a breakdown over her other son, and look at Stefan. He doesn't even know if his family are still alive.'

'I know. He's told me how helpful you've been to him, letting him come here and talk and play the piano. But you mustn't let it get too much for you.'

'Oh, I don't. I like seeing him – and all the others, of course. I like the company. But it's you I want most.'

'You still see plenty of May, don't you?' he asked. 'It's all very well, all these rough pilots making themselves at home here, but it's a woman's company you need most.'

'May comes in nearly every day. She stays longer a couple of mornings and does the housework, but she usually drops in on the other days as well. She's a really good friend.'

'I wish your mother could come over again,' he said, 'but with all these travel restrictions . . . And she's so busy with all the war work she does.'

Alison drew herself up a little and gave him a slightly wavering smile of reassurance. 'Don't worry, Andrew. I'm all right, really. I just let it get on top of me a bit. I get lots of company really, don't I. I was just feeling sorry for myself. Don't take any notice.'

He smiled and kissed her. 'That's my girl. And you've got your bed booked in the maternity home, haven't you?'

'Yes, weeks ago.' Alison had decided against a home birth. Since it was so unlikely that either Andrew or her mother would be there, it had seemed best to go to the local maternity home in Horrabridge, two or three miles away. 'May's going to sleep in when it gets near the time and she'll ring the local taxi to take me in, and then take Hughie home with her to stay while I'm there. That's the worst part – I'll have to be in for a fortnight. I hope he'll be all right.'

'Of course he will. He loves being with the Prettyjohns, and I'll be around too. You're not to worry about that.' He kissed her again and then got to his feet. 'I really do have to be going now. I hate leaving you like this.'

'I'm all right.' She put up her hands and he took them in his to help her up. They stood for a moment with their arms around each other. 'Don't worry, darling. I was just being silly,' she whispered. 'Come in as soon as you can, won't you, to let me know you're home safely.'

'I will,' he promised. He held her for a moment longer, then let her go. She followed him to the door and watched him settle his cap on his head before stepping outside. He turned at the gate and gave her a wave, then strode away.

Alison stood there until he was out of sight. The evening was bright with the cool, clear light of late April. She thought of the mission he was on tonight – a flight over France again, probably, escorting the bombers which would rain death and destruction on the factories and railways below. She had a sudden chill of premonition.

Andrew always said he had 'had his crash'. But that didn't mean it couldn't happen again. Neither he nor his squadron could go on living charmed lives for ever.

Chapter Twenty-Three

All that night, the area around Yelverton resounded to the roar of aircraft. It was as if every squadron on the place was taking off. Probably they were, Alison thought as she lay in bed listening, still with the cold fingers of dread closing like a fist around her heart.

She tried to shift her bulk into an easier position. The baby seemed like a leaden weight inside her, with sudden bursts of furious activity when she most longed to rest. How many more weeks was it? Five? Six? If only I could know the exact date, she thought, it would help. But nobody seemed able to tell her that.

After a while, she fell into an uneasy sleep and dreamed she was walking in a jungle, an endless struggle through twining tendrils of thick green stems that twisted themselves about her and caught at her legs and feet. Somewhere nearby, she could hear lions growl and she tried to run, but the plants clung more tightly about her, bringing her sprawling at full length on the forest floor. Immediately she clutched at her stomach, afraid for her baby, and the lions snarled closer, their noise filling her ears until she woke in panic, finding herself bathed in sweat and the roar of aircraft sounding overhead.

It was just beginning to get light. Alison's mouth was dry and she struggled out of bed and felt for her slippers and Andrew's old camel-hair dressing-gown. She stumbled downstairs, still only half awake, and put the kettle on to make a cup of tea. The noise of the aircraft was diminishing and she wondered if they were all safely back home. She remembered her premonition of the evening before, and her dread returned as she stared anxiously out of the window. It's as if I know something bad's happened, she thought. I shan't be happy until I know he's back.

She took the tea back to bed with her, looking in on Hughie on the way. He was huddled down beneath his blankets, his thumb in his mouth, and she gently removed it. He grunted an objection and a tiny frown creased his brow as he pushed it back in. Alison smiled and left it there. Her mother disapproved of his thumb-sucking and had recommended a dummy, which she could remove when she decided he was too old for it. However, Alison had never liked seeing children with dummies in their mouths. Thumbs were natural, she said.

Back in bed, she piled the pillows behind her and leaned against them. Daylight was creeping in through the opened curtains and she could hear the birds singing. It was funny, she mused, how they always sang most at twilight – either at dawn or at sunset, when the darkness and the daylight blended into a soft blue-grey. At this time of year, the dawn chorus was just beginning, and in a few weeks it would be at its peak. In a few weeks, when her baby would be born.

Just then, she heard footsteps outside, in the quiet street. There was the click of the gate, then they came up the path.

Alison was out of bed at once. Forgetting her awkwardness, she thrust her feet back into the slippers and dragged the old dressing-gown around her once more. She was still struggling to tie the belt when she half tumbled down the stairs and saw the front door beginning to open.

'*Andrew*!'

Almost fainting with relief, she sagged against the wall and he leaped forwards and caught her just as she began to fall.

'Alison! What's the matter? Are you all right? It's not the baby, is it?'

'No,' she cried, clutching at his arms. 'No, it's nothing. It's not me at all – it's you. What are you doing here so early? When I heard someone walking down the road, I thought they were coming to tell me that something terrible had happened to you!'

'It's all right,' he said, holding her. 'It's all right, darling, nothing's happened to me. Come back upstairs and I'll make you some tea.'

'I've already made some. There's some in the pot, if you want a cup. But what are you doing here so soon? I heard the planes go over.'

She made to go towards the kitchen but he guided her firmly to the stairs and put his hand in the small of her back to urge her upwards. Bemused, she let him persuade her and then, when she was back in bed with the pillows piled behind her again, she looked at him more steadily and said, 'Something has happened, hasn't it? Something bad. That's why you've come straight home.'

'I'm afraid so,' he replied, and sat on the edge of the bed, holding her hands. 'It's something I knew you'd want to know straight away. And it's something I think we're going to need your help with.' He took a deep breath while Alison waited, her eyes fixed on his face, and then he said quietly, 'It's Ben. He didn't come back. We lost him on our way home.' He paused again and then said bleakly, 'We think he went down into the Channel.'

They went together to tell May. The air was loud with birdsong as they opened the cottage gate, but it seemed to Alison that there was a sadness in that song, a poignant quality like fragile glass just about to shatter. The colours of the garden seemed extra bright and the tin-mining chimneys away across the valley as sharp as pins.

May opened the door. She was dressed in her blue frock with the white polka-dots and puffed sleeves, and her face was eager and excited. Behind her, Alison could hear the chatter and laughter of the rest of the family. She glanced at Andrew, wondering how he would break the news, but before either of them could speak May had caught their hands and dragged them inside.

'Listen to this!' she exclaimed, her face alight with merriment. 'Dick White just called in and told us about it. You know the searchlight, over in the fields? Well, they've always got a sentry there, haven't 'em, and last night it seems he heard footsteps coming along the road as if someone was going to climb over the stile. So he said, "Halt! Who goes there?" just like he's supposed to do. But nobody answered.'

'May,' Alison began, but William had taken up the comic tale.

'Orders are that they have to challenge three times and if they still don't get no answer, they shoot,' he said. He looked so much better since he'd been living downstairs, Alison thought helplessly, but how was he going to look in a few minutes' time? She tried again to interrupt, but there was no stopping any of them. Grandpa was in his chair, wheezing with laughter, and Mabel herself was red in the face. William went on, 'So he did that, see, he asked three times, and whoever it was said never a word but just kept on coming. So he fired!'

He stopped, evidently expecting someone to ask what happened next. As Alison and Andrew stared mutely at him, he supplied the answer himself.

'And who do you think it were? Why, 'tweren't no one at all! And 'tweren't no ghost, neither.' He stopped again, fresh hilarity overtaking him, and when he finally managed to get the words out, the whole family erupted once more. Alison almost expected them to blow the roof off the

261

cottage with their mirth. 'It was Dick Hamley's old mare! Escaped from up Place Barton, her had, and gone wandering along the road, looking for some grass to eat.'

'I don't suppose Mr Hamley thinks it's funny,' May said, smiling, 'nor the sentry. But you've got to laugh, haven't you.' She looked at her friends properly for the first time, and her smile slowly faded. There was a moment of silence and then she said, in a completely different tone, 'What is it? What's happened?' She turned to Alison. 'Are you all right? There's nothing gone wrong with the babby, is there? Or Hughie?'

'He's all right,' Alison reassured her quickly. 'He's in with Mrs Potter, next door. And there's nothing wrong with me or the baby.' She stopped, not knowing how to begin . . .

'What?' May's voice sharpened. 'What, then? Tell me, for pity's sake.' Fear dawned in her eyes, followed by understanding. 'It's Ben, isn't it? Something's happened to Ben.'

'Oh, May,' Alison said, moving towards her. 'I'm so sorry.'

May sat down suddenly on her father's bed, and Alison lowered her bulk to sit beside her. She put her arms around May and Andrew, still standing, said quietly, 'He went down in the sea on our way back last night. It doesn't mean he's lost. He could still be picked up. A patrol went out at first light.'

'But they haven't found him,' May said in a dry, husky voice.

'No, not yet. But—'

May burst into tears. Her mother moved swiftly towards her and sat down on her other side. May turned away from Alison and buried her face against her mother's shoulder, and Andrew repeated what he had just told them. 'We'll keep looking. I'm going back myself as soon as possible, but

I wanted to come and tell you first. We'll do our best to find him, May.'

'Oh, Ben,' she wept. 'We were going to get engaged today.' She sat up and spread her hands out in front of her, staring at them. 'We were going to buy the ring.'

Alison gazed at her in dismay. 'So that's why you're all dressed up.' She glanced at Mabel and William. 'You knew about this?'

William nodded. 'Asked me for her hand last yesterday, he did, in the proper manner. Mother and me, us'd talked it over beforehand, see. Us had a pretty good idea what was in the wind and I won't say we didn't have no reservations, but as Mother said, when a couple of young things are in love there bain't much you can do about it. And Ben's a fine young chap, when all's said and done. So I was happy to give my consent, and they were going into Tavi this morning, on the bus.'

'Oh, I'm so sorry,' Alison said again, thinking how inadequate the words were. She put her hand on May's arm. 'I'm dreadfully sorry.'

'I won't never wear his ring now,' the girl said dolefully. 'And I was so happy when I got up this morning – and I never even knew he was gone. Why didn't I know? I ought to have *felt* it.' She sat up a little and laid her hand over her heart. 'I ought to have felt it here.'

Andrew squatted down in front of her and put his hands over her wrists. He looked into her face and said, 'May, we don't know yet that he's gone. I've told you, we've got planes out looking for him now and I'm going myself as soon as I get back. People have been rescued before. He's got a life jacket. A ship might have picked him up. Anything could have happened. You are not to lose hope.'

'Hope . . .' she said slowly, and a new expression came into her eyes. 'That's the name of that little girl – the one he's godfather to, that lives with his mother and father.

What about them? Someone ought to tell them. Oh, his poor mother!' Her own sorrow seemed to be pushed aside as she looked wildly from Andrew to Alison. 'He told me she's still grieving over her other boy – Peter. We couldn't get married yet because of it. This'll kill her!'

'We don't know yet that he's lost,' Andrew said steadily. 'But of course his parents will have to be told. A telegram will be sent.'

'A telegram,' she repeated in a hollow voice. ' "Missing" – is that what it'll say? Or "missing, believed killed"? Oh, that poor, poor lady.' She began to get to her feet. 'I'll go myself and tell her.'

'May, you can't!' Alison said. 'You can't go all the way to – where is it they live, somewhere near Southampton? And if she was really upset about Ben wanting to get married, how do you think she'll feel about seeing you?'

'It might help her,' the girl said stubbornly. 'She'll know when she sees me that I loved him proper. Anyway, I ought to go. If we were wed, that's what I'd do. It'd be expected of me.'

'It might be expected that she'd come to you, maid,' her father pointed out. 'But I don't suppose her will.'

There was a short silence. May sat down again, deflated, and began to cry once more. Andrew and Alison looked at each other.

'I'll have to go back,' he said, getting to his feet. 'I shouldn't really have come out, but I knew you'd want to know as soon as possible. We really are doing our best to find him,' he told May. 'Men have survived in the sea for hours – even days. If he managed to bale out . . .'

'Tell me one thing, then,' she said, looking up through her tears. 'Was the plane on fire?'

'No. It wasn't on fire. I promise you that.'

She nodded. 'At least he wasn't burned, then. That was

the thing he was most scared of, you know – being burned.' She covered her face with her handkerchief again and wept.

'I'd better go too,' Alison said quietly. 'I promised I wouldn't leave Hughie too long. I'll come back later, if you'd like me to.' She looked questioningly at Mabel, who nodded at her.

'That's right, maid. Come back later on. She'll be glad to see you then – us all will.' She turned her attention back to her daughter and Alison gave May's arm a last pat and followed Andrew to the door.

As they walked along the lane, hand in hand and sobered by all that had happened, Alison turned to Andrew and asked, 'Did you know that about Ben, that he was afraid of being burned?'

'No,' he said. 'I didn't. He never said a word about it to me. But he was a brave chap, darling. A very brave young chap.'

'Was,' she repeated slowly, and looked directly into his eyes. 'You think he's gone, don't you? You don't think he'll be saved.'

Andrew sighed heavily and then shook his head. 'No. To be absolutely honest, my darling, I don't think he had a chance.'

Chapter Twenty-Four

Ben was not found. By the time the dawn patrols were out, searching the area where he had vanished, there was no sign of him. A few scraps of floating wreckage were seen, but no more. Heavy-hearted and as upset by this death as he had been by Tubby Marsh's, Andrew reported him as 'missing, believed killed' and a telegram was sent to his parents.

Olivia was in the garden, sitting under the apple tree, when the boy rode up on his red Post Office bike. He went to the front door without seeing her and rang the bell. She was already getting to her feet when Jeanie opened the door.

'What is it?'

The boy turned. He was a Boy Scout from the village and she'd known him since he was a baby, being christened by her husband in the church font. He had red hair and a cheeky grin, but this afternoon his face was sober and uncertain.

'Oh, there you are, Mrs Hazelwood. I didn't see you.' He held out the brown envelope. 'It's for you.'

'For me?' She stared at it, not reaching out her hand, as if by refusing to take it she could make it go away.

'Well, for you and the vicar,' he said, an apologetic note in his voice. She wondered bleakly if he knew what was in it. He must know it was bad news. Telegrams always brought bad news. She took a step back.

'He's in the church.'

'Can't I give it to you, Mrs Hazelwood?' he asked. 'Only, I'm not supposed to take too long.'

Olivia looked at the envelope and then at Jeanie, who was white-faced. Slowly, she reached out her hand, then drew it back quickly, as if touching the envelope would contaminate her. She shook her head speechlessly, and tears began to slide down her cheeks. Her tall, gaunt figure swayed and Jeanie came down the steps swiftly and caught her. The boy dropped his bike and jumped to help her, and as they stood there in an ungainly huddle, the vicar himself came round the corner.

'What on earth?' He ran forward and took his wife in his arms. 'What's happened?'

'I brought a telegram,' the boy said, holding it out again. His freckled face was red with embarrassment and distress. Awkwardly, he bent to pick up his bike. 'I ought to be going but I've got to know if there's any answer.'

John took the envelope and looked at it. Slowly, he opened it and read the slip of paper, then he shook his head.

'No. No answer. You get back, Bobby.'

The boy gave a nod and turned away. He wheeled his cycle to the gate and then got on and rode off down the lane. Olivia and John looked at each other.

'Who is it?' she asked in a dry whisper.

'It's Ben, I'm afraid, my dear.' He heard Jeanie's cry and stretched out his other arm to take her into his embrace as well. 'I'm most terribly sorry. It's Ben.'

'He was our youngest,' Olivia wept. 'Our ewe-lamb. Our Benjamin. Oh, John . . .'

'I know.' He held her close. They were on the sofa in the drawing room and Jeanie, her eyes red and tears still slipping down her cheeks, had brought them a tray of tea. John thanked her and asked her to stay and have a cup with them, but she shook her head and went back to the kitchen. Olivia barely seemed to know that she'd been there.

'Drink this, my dear,' he said. He was having a difficult time holding back his own tears and could manage only if he distanced himself from his feelings. If he could just pretend this was happening to a parishioner rather than his own family, use his years of training and experience to batten down his grief and focus upon his wife's . . . It was the hardest thing he had ever done. The hardest, at least, since they'd had the news about Peter. 'Just a sip. It'll help you.'

'I don't want it.' She was too weak too refuse, however, and sipped obediently when he held the cup to her lips. Jeanie had put in several teaspoons of sugar, he realised when he tasted his own, yet Olivia – who hated sweet tea – didn't even seem to notice. Perhaps you didn't, when you really needed it. She drank some more and then waved it away and began to cry again.

'Oh, John! This awful, awful war. When is it going to end? When is it going to stop taking away all our children? When is God going to *do* something about it?'

'Oh, my dear.' He felt helpless. If she really had been a parishioner, he would have known what to say – all the usual things about God knowing best, working His purpose out, about having faith in Him, trusting Him . . . But none of these would do for Olivia, and he wondered suddenly if they would do for anyone. How did his parishioners feel, when he said these things to them? Did they listen out of politeness only, and respect for his cloth, while all the time inside they were rejecting his words? Would they really like to ask what Olivia would ask – how could a benign God let these terrible things happen? What was the point of trusting Him when at the very minute when you were on your knees in church, praying to Him, your own flesh and blood was being brutally murdered? It would be in vain, he knew, to point out that

God's own Son had died in agony on the Cross. The only time he had said that to Olivia, she had simply retorted that it just went to prove that there wasn't anything He could do, not really. If He existed at all . . .

And it was at times like this that John felt his own faith severely tested. He had told Olivia months ago that he had once almost lost it completely, but that it had returned to him. Now, with the loss of two of his boys, he wondered just how strong it was, and whether it would go on sustaining him. And what sort of faith it could be, to falter at his own loss, when he knew so many people had lost even more?

'Why don't you go upstairs and lie down for a while?' he suggested gently. 'I'll bring you some aspirin. You'll make yourself ill if you go on like this.'

'What does that matter?' she sobbed. 'What does it matter if I'm ill? Two of my children are *dead*, John!'

'And two of them are still alive,' he said. 'Hold on to that, my dear. And we don't know that Ben is dead. The telegram says he's missing—'

'Believed killed.'

'But not known for certain. There's still hope.'

Olivia withdrew herself from his arms and stood up. He rose with her, looking down at the face that had once been so serene but was now thin and lined and blotched with tears. Her fine, grey eyes were reddened and exhausted and her hair was lank. She looked like an old woman, and his heart went out to her even as he longed for the Olivia he had known and loved for so many years.

'Go and lie down,' he repeated, and she nodded wearily and went slowly from the room, her footsteps dragging as she climbed the stairs.

John watched her go, his heart filled with pity. His own grief welled up within him, but he thrust it down, telling himself he must wait, and went out to the kitchen where Jeanie was sitting with her elbows resting on the big wooden table, her head in her hands. She looked round as he came in and her lips trembled.

'Oh, Mr Hazelwood . . .'

'I know,' he said, coming to stand beside her and laying his big hand on her shoulder. 'It's a shock to us all.' He sighed. 'We all know it can happen at any time – we've known it all through the war – but it's still a shock. I'm very sorry, my dear. I know how fond you were of Ben.'

'It's not just me,' she said brokenly. 'It's Hope. He was her godfather and she loved him. Now she won't even remember him when she grows up. And it isn't even just her.' She looked up at him, her brown eyes filled with tears. 'I keep thinking of that other poor girl. The one in Devon that he wanted to marry. How is she going to feel, when she finds out? Will anyone even tell her?'

John Hazelwood stared at her. He had not given a thought to the girl Ben had wanted to marry – the girl he loved. He felt a great wash of shame as he realised that he didn't even know her name and address – he'd been so concerned with Olivia's distress that he'd never even asked. He had sent Ben away thinking that he didn't care.

May, however, did know the Hazelwoods' address, and wanted desperately to write to them. She talked it over with her parents and grandfather.

'I was Ben's fiancée. I know we didn't have the ring yet and I know they didn't give him their permission to marry, but we *were* engaged. You know we were. I ought to write to them. It would be rude not to.'

'That's right, maid, but it's poor Mrs Hazelwood I be thinking of,' Mabel said. 'Poor dear lady – her must be distraught at losing another of her boys. And if she were that upset about the idea of him getting married, a letter from you might upset her all over again. You know what his father said – that she were close to a complete breakdown. You don't want to make things even worse.'

'It seems wrong, all the same. It's not as if we were going to get married against their wishes. Ben was coming round to the idea that we'd have to wait till she could see things clearer. We wouldn't have done anything to hurt her.'

'And suppose she'd never come round?' William asked.

'Well, we could have crossed that bridge when we come to it. Anyway, it don't matter now, do it? It's never going to come to that. And I still think as I ought to write to them.'

'Why don't you just address the letter to the vicar?' her grandfather suggested. 'Let him decide whether to show it to her or not. Then you'd have done what's right without causing no more trouble.'

May turned and looked at him. He had been as saddened as the rest of them by Ben's loss, and seemed to have aged a year in the past week. But his eyes were as wise and kindly as ever and filled with compassion.

'Yes,' she said. 'That's what I'll do. After all, he'm a vicar and he'll know we weren't doing nothing wrong. I'll tell him all about it – how Ben and me first met, and how we used to go walking and sometimes went to the pictures together or a dance, and how we came to think so much of each other. I'll tell him how Ben asked me to marry him and how upset he was about his mother and how he wanted to help her, and I'll tell him we were going to wait until she was better, even though Ben wanted us to wed straight off. I'll tell him I'll always love Ben, however long I live. That can't hurt him, can it? None of that can hurt him. And maybe one day he'll be able to show it to Ben's poor mother as well, so she can see that Ben was happy with me, and how happy he made me feel too. Maybe that'll help her.'

Tears were sliding down her face as she finished speaking, and there were tears in the eyes of her three listeners. As she fell silent, her mother got up and came over to her, sitting beside her to take the weeping girl into her arms.

'That's right, my blossom,' she said softly. 'You tell him all those things. He'll know then that Ben chose a good girl to be his wife. Even that'll be a comfort to him, and let's hope to her as well. Poor dear soul,' she said, shaking her head. 'Losing two boys like that, and the other one still in danger – where did Ben say he was? In Italy?'

'They think he's at Cassino,' May said, and her mother folded her lips ruefully. They had all heard of the fighting at Cassino and the monastery which stood above it, and although Ian was a chaplain he would still be in danger. 'Oh, I hope nothing happens to him as well. I don't think she'd ever get over losing all three of them.'

'I don't know how any mother could,' Mabel said gravely, and gave her daughter another hug. 'There now, my flower, you get on and write your letter. Take your time over it, mind – it don't do to dash important letters off all in a few minutes – and I'll tell you what, you can use that lovely writing-pad Mrs Huccaby gave me for Christmas. I thought at the time, I don't know what sort of letters she thinks I write that I'd want such good paper for, what with there being such a shortage anyway, but you use as much of it as you like. I'll go and fetch it now.'

'I'll write it out in my old school exercise book first,' May said. 'There's quite a lot of pages at the end I never filled up. Then I won't waste any of it.'

She went upstairs to her bedroom and found the exercise book at the bottom of her cupboard. Sharpening a pencil, she sat down on the wide window seat and stared out of the window as she began to think what to write.

But as the memories crowded in upon her mind, she found the tears sliding down her cheeks again, and it was a long time before she could bring herself to set the point of the pencil on the rough school paper.

Chapter Twenty-Five

Andrew was now in charge of an extra squadron and was spending more and more time at the airfield, able to dash home only for quick visits. When he did come, he was exhausted and distracted, as if half his mind were still at the airfield or in the sky, and Alison knew that he longed to forget it for a few minutes and enjoy a brief period of home life. She made sure that, whenever he came through the door, she was ready for him, with a meal on hand, Hughie happy and contented and the home a pleasant place to be.

'Darling, I'm sorry,' he said, lying back on the sofa after a supper of shepherd's pie with spring greens from the garden. 'I'm not much help to you at present, am I – just when you need me most, too. But I can't get away any more than this.'

'I know. It's all right, I'm managing perfectly well, and Hughie's being so good.' They had put their son to bed together and Alison had left Andrew reading to him while she came downstairs to prepare the meal. 'And you don't need to worry about anything going wrong with the baby. The neighbours have all told me I'm to call on them straight away if anything happens, and May's a treasure even though she's so upset about Ben. She's being so brave about it.'

Andrew shook his head. 'I feel rotten about Ben. There was something special about him. He'd have gone on to do great things in his life. But then, so would so many others who'll never get the chance now. It's a foul business, Alison.'

'Don't think about it now,' she said softly, coming to sit beside him. 'Just let's sit here quietly together and try not to think about any of it. You need to rest.' She drew his head down to her breast and stroked his thick dark hair. 'It will all be over soon. It must be. The world can't go on like this for much longer.'

They sat together, their bodies close and warm. Inside, Alison could feel their baby moving, less vigorously now since there was much less room for it to kick its limbs. She took Andrew's hand and laid it across the swell of her stomach so that he could feel it too.

'New life,' she murmured. 'This is what you're fighting for, Andrew – this new baby, and Hughie, and all the other babies and children who need a peaceful world to grow up in. Never forget that. That's what it's all about.'

He didn't answer, and when she twisted her neck to peep at his face she saw that his eyes were closed and he had fallen asleep. She smiled and let her own eyes close, stroking his hair until she too had drifted into a contented doze.

'You're looking tired,' Stefan said when he came next day. He called in as often as he could now, even if only for a few minutes. 'You shouldn't be alone at this time.'

'It can't be helped. Andrew does his best, but when he does get home I feel I should be looking after him. I can rest at any time.'

'I don't like it, all the same,' Stefan said, frowning. 'You are near your time. Someone should be with you. Why can't your mother be here?'

'Because she lives at the opposite side of the country, and you know what travel is like now. All those signs saying *Is your journey really necessary?* And she has so much to do herself. It's not as if it's my first baby, after all. I know what to do when the time comes.'

'You will be going to a hospital, yes?'

'A maternity home,' she nodded. 'It's in Horrabridge – only two or three miles away. Bob Derry, who runs the local garage and uses one of his cars as a taxi, has told me that I'm to call him at any time, night or day. And May Prettyjohn's coming to stay with me at nights now, when Andrew isn't here. She takes Hughie out for walks too – that's where he is now.'

'I wish I could do more,' he said restlessly. 'You need a man to look after you.'

'I do have a husband,' she reminded him.

'But he isn't here!'

'He *can't* be here. It's not his fault, Stefan. There are plenty of other women in the same position, and look at all the friends I have. May, the neighbours in Milton Combe, you . . .'

'Ah yes,' he said, 'you do have me. I am your friend, Alison. I hope you know that, and I am happy to do whatever you want. You must only ask.'

'Thank you.' She smiled at him. 'Now, would you like a cup of tea?'

'I will make tea,' he declared. 'And look – I have brought you a present.' He produced a paper bag from his pocket.

Alison peeped inside. 'I can't take your chocolate, Stefan,' she said. 'You need it. And Andrew gives me most of his – I'll get spots if I eat too much.'

'Chocolate does not give spots. It is good for you. It has iron in it, good for blood. Please. I wish you to have.'

'All right, then. Thank you, Stefan. And it would be lovely if you could make the tea. But I really don't need to be waited on all the time. May looks after me very well and it's not as if I'm ill. It's a perfectly natural process, you know, having a baby.'

'And very hard work too,' he said. 'I know because my sister had a baby the year before I left Poland. I saw how tired she became and how her husband helped her. I know Andrew can't help you as much as he would like, and I am honoured to do what I can. I will go and make tea.'

He disappeared into the kitchen and Alison leaned back, thankful to be looked after despite her protests. She was beginning to feel weary of her pregnancy now. To begin with, it had been exciting and joyous, but as time went on and the war seemed to gather pace again, with her anxieties over Andrew growing sharper every night, her cumbersome body had become a burden to drag through the days. She felt awkward and ungainly, too big to sit in the armchairs, almost too big to share the bed with Andrew on the few nights he could spend at home. Too slow to take Hughie for walks, too tired to play with him as she would have liked to do. I just want it over now, she thought. I just want to be slim and energetic again, able to cope with it all.

Stefan returned with the tray of tea and they sat together in quiet companionship. After a while he got up and went to the piano, the soft, clear notes of a Chopin prelude drifted through the air and Alison closed her eyes.

All I want to do these days is sleep, she thought.

Stefan was still playing when May arrived with Hughie. May opened the front door and hesitated as she heard the music, but Hughie tore his hand from hers and ran in, shouting excitedly.

'It's Uncle Stefan! Uncle Stefan, guess what we found! We found a nest, a bird's nest, and it's got eggs in, blue ones. May says it's a robin's nest and the mummy bird will sit on them to keep them warm until the babies come out. Why doesn't she squash them? Do you know? Mummy, do you know why she doesn't squash them? Why couldn't you have laid an egg for a new baby? I could have helped you keep it warm.'

'I don't know,' Alison said, laughing as she struggled to sit up. 'I think it might have been a very good idea. Hello, May. I must have been asleep. It was so peaceful here, with Stefan playing the piano.'

'You did go to sleep,' he said, smiling. 'And very nice you looked when you were asleep.'

'I'm sure I didn't,' she said, blushing. 'Stefan made me some tea, May. I expect there's still some there, it should be quite hot. Where was this nest, then, Hughie? I hope you didn't disturb the mother bird.'

'No, she flew away just as we got there. We just looked at the eggs. May said we mustn't take any because it was like taking a baby robin and killing it. But I can show you where it is.'

'Next time we go out, then. Are you going to have some tea, May?'

'No, thank you,' May said, hanging her jacket in the passageway and coming through to the room. 'I'll make some more later on, when we have our supper. You'll be going now, I dare say?' she said to Stefan.

'Yes, I must go back to the station. We're on duty tonight.' He uncoiled himself from the piano stool and smiled down at Alison. 'I will come to see you again, though. If there is anything you want me to do—'

'It's all right,' May broke in crisply. 'I can see to anything Alison wants done. I know how she likes things.'

'Thank you, Stefan,' Alison said with a smile. 'It's nice just to have you here, you know that. And you make a very good cup of tea!'

'I've practised,' he said with a grin, and gave May a small nod of the head and a tiny bow. 'It's good to see you again. I'm glad you are here with Alison.'

He went out to the passageway and put on his jacket.

Alison gave him a last smile and May a brief shrug. Then he let himself out of the front door and went off along the road.

Alison glanced at May. 'Are you all right?'

'As well as I can be. Why?'

Alison hesitated. 'I know how you must be feeling. It's only a week or two since we heard about Ben and you've been so brave. You know, if you don't feel like coming here, you don't have to. I don't mind being on my own. Mrs Potter says I've only got to knock on the wall and she'll—'

'Don't talk so daft!' May snapped, and bit her lip. 'I'm sorry, I shouldn't have said that. But you know I don't mind coming here to spend the night. I like coming, and anyway I'd never sleep a wink, thinking of you here by yourself. It's just – well, I don't like that man. I never have.'

'Stefan?' Alison said in surprise. 'Why ever not? He's really nice, and so helpful. You heard what he said – if there's anything I need him to do . . .'

'Well, he didn't need to say that, did he? He knows I'm here. I just wonder why he comes so much. What does he want?'

Alison looked at her. 'I think he just wants company,' she said quietly. 'Someone to talk to about his own family. He hasn't seen them since the war began, you know. He doesn't even know what's happened to them. He just wants to be in a home.'

May sighed and picked up the tea-tray. 'Well, that's as maybe, but he's here a lot, isn't he? You don't want people talking.'

'They're hardly likely to talk about us with me as I am now!' Alison said with a laugh. 'Honestly, May! Everyone knows this is open house for half the airfield. There are always pilots in and out – most of the time, when Stefan's here, there are half a dozen others as well. It's what Andrew wanted – somewhere for his men to come and feel at home. I really don't think you need worry about gossip.'

'Maybe I don't.' May started towards the kitchen. 'But it's not me they'd be gossiping about, is it? All I want to say is, you ought to be careful. 'Twon't be long now before you're slim again, and with your hubby not here much . . . well, there's always someone with a nasty tongue in her head. I wouldn't like anyone saying things about you, that's all. I wouldn't like anyone to think you were carrying on.'

'Carrying on!' Alison exclaimed. 'Just because I try to be friendly to someone who's far away from his own home, and fighting for us as well? Surely nobody will think that. But if they do – well, let them! If anyone's got a nasty tongue and uses it that way, everyone else will know what she's like and won't take any notice. Isn't that true?'

'It is for most,' agreed May, 'but there's always those who say there's no smoke without fire. All I'm saying is, I know there's no fire, nor ever likely to be – but you wants to watch out that there's no smoke either!'

She went out to the kitchen and began to wash the cups Alison and Stefan had used, staring out into the garden as she did so. She didn't believe for one second that Alison was 'carrying on' with Stefan, nor that she ever would. All she knew was that if she and Ben were married, she wouldn't ever let another man make himself as much at home as that Pole had done.

If she and Ben were married . . .

Tears began to drip steadily into the washing-up water.

There had been no reply to the letter she had sent to John Hazelwood. It had taken her several days to compose it, writing on the few pages left in her school exercise book, reading the laboured sentences, trying again and rubbing them out until the paper was so thin you could see through it. Eventually she had managed a few paragraphs she was satisfied with and had copied them on to the lined writing-pad that her mother had given her, and posted them to Ashford. She knew there wouldn't be a reply for several days – maybe even a week – but as time went on she began to think that either the letter had never arrived, or they just didn't mean to answer. They didn't want to know her. They wanted to shut her right out of their lives – out of Ben's life. They wanted to pretend she had never existed.

It was like another little death. Like someone trying to wipe out the love she and Ben had shared; a denial that it had ever happened.

I just wanted to share it with them, she thought. I wanted to be able to go there and see where he'd lived, see the places he knew and the people he loved. I wanted them to know me, so that they'd know about that other part of him. If we can't do that, we've all lost something precious.

If Ben's mother hadn't been so distressed already, May might have tried again. But now, there was simply nothing more she could do.

In Ashford, the letter had arrived and been opened, as May had expected, by John Hazelwood. He had read it with pity for the girl who had written those stumbling lines, understanding the effort she had made and knowing what it had cost her. So they had got engaged after all, he thought. Ben had done the whole thing properly – asked her father, even though she was of age, and intended to buy her a ring. It was tragic that his crash had happened before he could do so, tragic that she had nothing to remember him by. John felt his heart go out to the bereaved girl and he longed to be able to do something for her.

There was nothing he could do, however. All she wanted was acknowledgement – to know that she was accepted as Ben's fiancée that John and Olivia would have welcomed her into the family. And as things were now, that was just not possible – might never be possible.

He knew he should write back. Common courtesy, as well as his own compassion, demanded that he should; yet he felt a powerful loyalty and compassion for his wife as well. He would have to go behind her back to write to May Prettyjohn, and he had never done that in his whole life. It would make a shadow between them and, in her present fragile state, it might be the shadow of the last straw.

I'll wait, he thought, folding the letter and slipping it into the pocket of his cassock. I'll wait for a sign.

Jeanie too was sorrowing over Ben.

I know he didn't love me the way I wanted him to, she thought, sitting in her room after Hope had gone to bed. I know he only thought of me as a sort of sister. But I thought he'd always be there, just the same – like a brother is. And he was Hope's godfather, too. I thought we'd always know each other, we'd always be special to each other. And now he's gone. I won't ever see him again.

Grief welled up in her heart and somehow it was mixed with the grief she had felt when her fiancé Terry had been killed. She had thought then that her life had ended, and never dreamed that worse was to come when she discovered she was pregnant. Terry would have married her if only he had been at home, but instead he had never even known about their baby. Her parents had been shocked and angry, and if it hadn't been for Terry's family in Portsmouth – for his sister Judy being in Ashford and knowing the Hazel-woods – she didn't know what would have happened to her and her baby. And she would never have met Ben.

If was a strange thought, that if Terry hadn't died, she would never have met Ben. And now he was gone too. The world seemed a very cruel place.

She looked down into the twilit garden and the pale

glimmer of blossom on the apple tree. A blackbird was sitting in the topmost bough and she could hear its liquid song filling the air. It was under that tree that Hope had been born, and Judy Taylor had been with her. She felt a sudden longing to see Judy again, and the rest of the Taylor family. Here at Ashford, with the vicar and Mrs Hazelwood so wrapped up in their own grief, she felt for the first time as if she were out of place. She wanted to go back to Portsmouth, to the small houses in the narrow back streets where she had grown up, to feel for a little while as if she were a child again and everything secure around her.

That's a laugh, she thought wryly, remembering how Portsmouth had been blitzed. But she knew that even the bomb damage wouldn't take away that feeling of security that a family could give. And then she remembered that she couldn't go home. Portsmouth was within the exclusion zone – nobody could travel in or out. It was as barred to her as if it were in a foreign country.

For a moment, despair descended upon her like a heavy grey cloud. And then she pulled herself together. There was nothing to be done about it. She would just have to wait until this Invasion they were all expecting was over, and go then. And in the meantime, she told herself sternly, I ought to be making myself useful, not sitting here with idle hands. I'll go and fetch the vicar's cassock and mend that hem he said was coming down.

Chapter Twenty-Six

Cassino, in Italy, finally fell in the middle of May. The news came through a few days later.

'You must feel very proud of your country,' Alison said to Stefan. 'It was the Poles who took it in the end.'

'And our flag is flying over the ruins of the monastery,' he agreed, looking at the newspaper she held. 'A shame that such a fine and ancient building should have to be destroyed first. And how many more are there? Towns like Cassino, like London and Coventry, like Warsaw – even like Berlin. The world will never be the same again.'

'It will be rebuilt,' she said. 'They're already making plans to rebuild Plymouth as a modern city, with wide streets and boulevards, quite different from the narrow streets and poky shops they had before. I know we'll all have lost a lot, but there must be gains as well.'

'Yes,' he said, looking at the newspaper again. 'But at what cost?'

Alison was silent. She knew that he must be thinking of his family. What had been happening to them during the past five long years? What would he find when the war was over at last?

Stefan laid the paper aside and turned to her. 'Let's think of something more cheerful. This may be the last chance I have to come to see you for a while.'

'Is that supposed to cheer me up?' she asked, laughing at him, and he smiled.

'I hope not. I just meant that we should spend these last hours more pleasantly together. The Invasion is very close now, you know.'

'I know,' she said soberly. The whole area was becoming like an armed camp, with American troops and vehicles advancing steadily towards the beaches. It must be the same all along the south coast, she thought, and wondered just how many thousands of men were going to cross the Channel.

'I think all our leave will be stopped,' he continued. 'Nobody knows just when it will be and they will want everyone on duty all the time. In any case, it is Andrew who you will want at your side now. This is going to be a difficult time for you, Alison.'

'I'm sure I'll be all right,' she said, wishing she could sound more certain. 'I've got plenty of people to look after me.'

'But it's your husband you need most. He's the one who should be with you at a time like this.' He moved to sit beside her on the sofa, and took her hands in his. 'I wish I could do more, Alison. I wish I could be here when he is not. Neighbours are all very well, May Prettyjohn is a good and stalwart friend, but you need a man with you.'

Alison turned her head and looked at him. Their faces were very close; she could see the afternoon light reflected in the silver sheen of his eyes. As she stared at him, they seemed to change, to deepen as the pupils grew wide and black, and she caught her breath. For a moment her heart seemed to pause, then start again more quickly. Then she drew back.

'I'm sure I'll be all right,' she said again, her voice shaking a little. 'You really don't need to worry, Stefan. I'm much more worried about you. You will take care, won't you? And if you're right about not being able to leave the station for the next few weeks – you will come and see me the first chance you have? And try to let me know that you're all right.'

Before she could say any more, he had kissed her cheek, so lightly that it was as if a butterfly had brushed its wings against her skin. Then he stood up.

'I must go now. I will see you again when all this is over. But I will be thinking of you, and hoping that all goes well for you.'

She pushed herself to her feet. 'Goodbye, Stefan. Take care. Please, take care.'

She hesitated, then lifted her hands to his cheeks. For a moment or two, he stayed very still. He took her wrists and held them lightly in his fingers; then he moved away.

'I'll see you again soon, Alison. I promise I'll see you again soon.'

Andrew came home that evening and told her the same thing.

'All leave's stopped from tomorrow. We're on readiness for D-Day.'

'D-Day?'

'It just means "Day",' he explained. 'H is for Hour and D for Day. Nobody knows the date. We won't know until it's here. But from now on, we've all got to be in position, ready. It's all or nothing this time, darling. If this one fails – well, God knows what will happen.'

'Oh, Andrew,' she said, tightening her hands on his. 'I'm afraid for you. If anything happens to you now . . .'

'It won't.' He smiled at her, and she saw that he was aglow with confidence and excitement. 'Nothing's going to happen to me – nothing.'

'You're looking forward to it,' she accused him, and he shrugged ruefully.

'Darling, I can't help it. It's my job, but it's more than that. We've been fighting our way through this war like an ant fighting through treacle. As fast as we gain ground in one place, we lose it somewhere else. But this is the big push. All the Services are working together to drive the Jerries back on their heels. All the countries, too – America, Russia and now Italy, and all the others who have joined in. This is going to be the moment that goes down in history, the moment when we really began to win the war. D-Day.' His eyes were gleaming, his voice low and fervent. 'It'll be talked of a hundred years from now. And I'll have been a part of it!'

Their eyes met and held. Alison felt a stirring within her, a strange, quivering feeling of excitement, as if she were sharing the emotion he had always told her he felt in the sky. That grand, soaring sensation that Stefan had described as 'dancing with the stars'.

'I wish I could come too!' she exclaimed impulsively, and her husband laughed.

'You will, my darling. Once this damned war's over, I'll take you flying with me. You'll know then what it's like.' He jumped up and caught her hands, pulling her to her feet. 'Let's go to bed. I just want to lie close to you and hold you. I want you in my arms all night, to give me something to remember while I'm flying. I want to be able to remember what every little inch of you feels like.'

'We'd better start at once, then,' she said with a smile. 'There are rather a lot of inches now.'

'And I love every one,' he said sincerely, putting his arms around her. 'I love every single one.'

It was three in the morning when she woke to find her nightdress soaked and the bed wet.

For a few moments, she could not think what had happened. Then she sat up and shook her husband's shoulder. 'Andrew! Andrew, wake up! The baby – it's started. My waters have broken.'

He shook himself as he surfaced from sleep, like a dog emerging from a stream. An instant later he was awake, sliding from the bed. 'Are you sure?'

'Yes. I'm soaked. Andrew, we've got to get to the maternity home quickly.'

'Right.' He was dressing already. 'Have you got your things ready?'

'My case is in Hughie's room. Oh – *Hughie!* What are we going to do?'

'It's all arranged, remember? I'll get Mrs Potter to come in and spend the rest of the night here, and I'll come back and tell May in the morning. She'll look after him then. Put on your dressing-gown, darling, and I'll give Mrs P a knock now. When she comes in, I'll go and get the car. We'll be on our way in a few minutes.'

'Andrew . . .'

'It's all right,' he said, holding his wife for a moment. 'Don't be frightened, sweetheart. Everything's going to be all right.'

'I'm so glad you're here,' she whispered, burying her face against his chest. 'I was so afraid it would happen when you were away. Oh, Andrew – if only it's born quickly. If only you could still be with me. I hope—'

'I hope so too,' he said, and took her wrists in his hands, pushing her gently from him. 'Now, you tidy yourself up and I'll go and knock up next door. I'll be back in a few minutes.' He gave her an anxious, searching look. 'Are you getting any pains?'

'No, nothing. I just feel a bit odd. Go on, then. But please don't be long.'

'I'll be back before you know I'm gone,' he promised, and took the stairs in three leaps. A moment later, she heard the front door open and then a furious hammering next door.

She stood by the bed, quite still for a moment, holding

her swollen stomach. It was happening at last. The baby was coming. If it came quickly enough, Andrew would be able to see it.

'You can stay in the waiting room if you like,' the Matron said doubtfully, 'but I don't think your baby is going to be born yet. There are no contractions at all.'

'But the waters have broken. Surely that means it won't be long?'

'I'm afraid it doesn't follow. Usually it means the birth is imminent, I agree, but I've known women go days – as long as a week – after the waters have broken. It's not very pleasant for the mother, because it means a dry birth and that can be more uncomfortable, but there's really nothing we can do about it. Babies have to come in their own time.'

Andrew gazed at her despairingly. 'There isn't anything you can do to speed things up?'

The Matron's lips stiffened. 'No, there's not. We only take those measures when the baby's overdue or there's some risk in waiting. Your wife's in no danger and neither is the baby, and it isn't due for another two weeks. So . . .'

'Two weeks!' he exclaimed. 'You won't let her go that long, surely?'

'Perhaps not as long as that, no. But as I've said, it's not uncommon for a woman to go several days, even a week, after the waters break.'

'All right, I get the gist.' He turned away, frustrated and dejected. 'I'll wait here for a while, but I've got to go back on duty at seven. I'll be able to see her before I go, won't I?'

'Probably. Unless she's already in labour, of course. We never allow husbands into the ward then.' The Matron saw his face and took pity on him. 'But I really don't think she will be. I'm sure you'll be able to see your wife before you go.'

Andrew went into the tiny waiting room and sat down.

He leaned forwards, rested his elbows on his thighs and let his hands hang down between his knees. His head drooped with the weariness that came from the sudden awakening and the anxiety of getting Alison here as quickly as possible, followed by the sharp disappointment of finding that the baby might not be coming yet after all. But Alison would have to stay here now. The Matron had said quite firmly that she couldn't be allowed home again, as labour might start at any moment and could be very quick. At least, he thought, she's safe. At least she'll be in the right place when it does start.

If only the baby could be born before he left . . .

Of all the people in the world that night, Alison and Andrew's new baby seemed to be in the least hurry. At six o'clock, there was still no change and Andrew decided that he would have to leave so as to have time to see May and Hughie before going back to the station. Matron allowed him into the tiny slip of a room where Alison was waiting in the high hospital bed, and he put his arms around his wife and hugged her against him.

'It's all right, sweetheart,' he murmured as she burst into tears. 'Everything's going to be fine. You're not to worry about a thing. They'll look after you in here, and Hughie will be perfectly OK with the Prettyjohns. You just rest and be ready for our baby when it comes.'

'*When* it comes,' she wept. 'I feel as if it's never going to come. It's like being teased – it's cruel, doing this and then not being born.'

'It's not the baby's fault,' he said, laughing a little. 'If you talk like that, it'll be afraid to be born at all. It won't want to arrive to a telling-off before it's even finished its first cry.'

'Well, no, of course I'm not blaming the baby,' she admitted, smiling through her tears. 'I don't know who I'm blaming. My silly body, I suppose, for not behaving as it should. Matron says it could be days before anything else happens.'

'I know.'

'And I've got to stay in bed all that time. She says my blood pressure's gone up as well.'

'Darling, they know what's best for you. And the doctor will be here later on too. You must do as they say.'

'I know. I will. I just wish – oh well, if wishes were horses, beggars would ride, that's what May would say if she were here. You will see that Hughie's all right, won't you? You must tell him where I am. He'll be frightened if he wakes up and I'm not there.'

'I will. I'm going to do that now. I'll go round to the Prettyjohns' straight from here and collect May and take her home. She'll be ready, won't she?'

'Yes. She knows it could happen at any time – any other night, she'd have been with me. And Mrs Potter will help too. We're so lucky to have such good friends and neighbours, Andrew.'

'We are.' He kissed her tenderly. 'Now, I'll come back and see you the first minute I can, and May will be here too. You're still not getting any pains?'

'No. I wish I were. I'd love to be having pains now!' She held him for a moment, then looked up, her eyes filled with tears but her mouth firm. 'Go on, darling. Go now. Quickly.'

He nodded, then gave her a last, quick kiss. His final glimpse of Alison was of a mound of white hospital sheets, pillows and blankets, and a face that was pale but smiling. At the door, he hesitated, half-inclined to go back, but she shook her head and waved him away. He closed the door and walked down the corridor.

Matron came out of her office as he approached. Her strong face was sympathetic.

'Your wife is in good hands, Squadron Leader. We'll take great care of her.'

Andrew nodded. 'I know. I'm sorry I was impatient earlier.'

She dismissed his apology with a quick wave of one hand. 'Don't apologise. It was perfectly natural. An anxious time for you both. Now, you have our telephone number, don't you? Ring later on this morning – say, at lunchtime – and we'll tell you if there's any news. And try not to worry. I'm sure everything is going to be all right. Your wife is a healthy young woman and she's already had one baby. I don't think there are going to be any problems at all.'

'Thank you,' he said, and shook her hand. Then he went out into the brightness of the spring morning and got into the little Morris 8.

His next task was to fetch May and take her home, to look after Hughie. After that, he would be back on duty. All leave would be stopped from the moment he drove through the airfield gate.

He had no idea when he would see Alison, or Hughie again. He had no idea when he would first set eyes on his new son, or daughter.

Chapter Twenty-Seven

It was two more days before Alison's baby was born.

During those two long days, Andrew was in a fever of impatience, anxiety and frustration. He went to see his Group Commander and even the Station Commander, but both said the same thing. 'Sorry, Squadron Leader. We can't give you leave to go and see your wife. You're not the only man in this position, you know. There are at least half a dozen whose wives are expecting to give birth soon, and more than that who have children they've never seen. We can't give you special treatment.'

'But she's only two miles down the road,' Andrew said desperately. 'I could be there and back in less than an hour. *Half* an hour.'

'It still wouldn't be fair on the other men,' he was told. And he had to admit that in his heart he knew they were right. Not that it made it any easier.

'None of us can leave the station,' he said later to Stefan as they sat in the mess, smoking and playing cards to pass the time. 'I realise that. It's just that she's so close . . .'

'I know.' Stefan was just as concerned. He had happened to be the only one in the mess, sitting at the breakfast table, when Andrew had arrived, anxious and unshaven, from taking Alison to the hospital. Dismayed, he had listened to the account of their hurried rush and the Matron's assessment of the situation. 'But it's taking so long. Can't they even give you some compassionate leave?'

'I asked,' Andrew said gloomily, 'but she's not in danger, you see. If she were, they might – but I can't be dishonest about it. It's not fair to the other men.'

'I don't really see that,' the Pole said. 'What good does it do to anyone else to deprive you? What harm would it do to them, to let you go?'

'It's about morale. And it's about being fair to everyone. It doesn't do to give men something to grumble about. They grumble enough as it is – we don't need to give them a real grievance as well!'

Stefan shrugged. If Alison were his wife, he thought, he would tear down the fences of hell, let alone an airfield, to get to her at this time. But Andrew was right. Nobody was allowed off the station now without special permission, and it didn't seem likely that this would be granted.

The worst of it was, as they all knew but didn't say, that Andrew might never see his baby. He might not live long enough.

Three times a day, he rang the maternity home. It was the first thing he did in the mornings, as soon as the Matron allowed. He rang again after lunch and again in the evening. On each occasion, he was told that nothing had happened. Alison was comfortable, and the doctor was satisfied. There was nothing they could do but wait.

'Wait!' he fumed, coming away from the telephone after lunch. 'She's been in there two days now. How long are we supposed to bloody wait? Why can't they *do* something?'

'They will if they think they should,' Robin Fairbanks reassured him. 'Look, Andy, I know it's hard but she's in the best place possible. You ought to be thankful you were able to take her in and see her settled. You'd be in an even worse state if she were still at home.'

Andrew glared at him, then conceded that this was probably true. 'All the same, it's actually started, hasn't it, so why can't they just move things along a bit? The baby must be ready to be born. I mean, it's got all its fingers and toes and everything. What difference will a day or two make?'

Robin shrugged. 'Don't ask me. I've never had a baby! But there must be some reason why it starts – some sort of trigger. Seems to me you've just got to wait for it and there's nothing else you can do.'

'I suppose so.' Andrew stared moodily out of the window. Across the road, the watchtower was already busy and beyond that he could see the bays where the planes were drawn up ready – Spitfires and Typhoons which had been flying the day before and taken over by the mechanics for maintenance during the night. Past the buildings and the hangars he could see the distant shapes of the Dartmoor hills – the rugged, escarpment of Sheepstor only a mile or two away, with the RAF transmitter on Sharpitor, and the smoother uplands of Cox Tor and Pork Hill further off. He thought of Alison's plans to go cycling and walking in the hills, plans which they'd not been able to fulfil. Maybe this summer. Or maybe next. The four of them, he thought. He with Hughie on the back of his bicycle, Alison with the new baby on hers. It would be old enough by then to use one of those little seats . . .

'Phone for you, Andy.' Robin's voice broke in upon his thoughts and he jerked round and hurried to the telephone in the corner.

'I never even heard it ring!' He grabbed the receiver and held it to his ear. 'Yes? Knight here – what is it? Is that the maternity home?'

'It's Matron here, Squadron Leader,' the calm voice said. 'I just thought you'd like to know that your wife has started her labour. She's been having slight contractions all night—'

'You didn't tell me that just now! Why didn't you say?'

'They were too slight to be concerned about. It could

have been just a false alarm. However, she's been examined now, and she's begun to dilate so—'

Andrew had no idea what this meant. He interrupted impatiently. 'How long will it be?'

'I can't tell you that, I'm afraid. Nothing seems to be happening very quickly as yet, but you can never tell. You'd better ring again at six, as usual.'

'At *six*? That's over four hours!'

'It's unlikely that anything will have happened before then. Please don't worry, Squadron Leader. Your wife is in very good hands and everything is progressing smoothly. We'll take great care of her.'

'I know. Thank you. I'll ring again at six, then.' He replaced the receiver and turned to face the others, who were all watching him expectantly. 'She's started, but they still seem to think it's going to take quite a while. God, I wish I could be with her!'

'You don't really,' Robin said. 'I know someone who saw his baby being born – it all happened very quickly and he had to deliver it himself. He said it was horrific.' He caught sight of Andrew's face and stopped abruptly. 'Anyway, I expect he was just laying it on a bit thick,' he mumbled. 'I don't suppose it's anything like as bad.'

Andrew gave him a withering look and returned to his position at the window. He stared out, trying to imagine what was happening to Alison at this moment. Oh God, he prayed, don't let it be too bad for her. Let it be over soon. Please, please let everything be all right . . .

'Scramble!'

The voice on the tannoy had barely completed the word before every pilot was on his feet and racing for the door. Most were wearing much of their flying gear already and the rest was being pulled on as they ran across the grass and tarmac towards the waiting planes. The mechanics were ready to help them get strapped into their seats, turn the propellers and whisk away the chocks, and within less than a minute the whole squadron was airborne and setting off for the coast.

In the tumult, Andrew almost forgot his wife, even now giving birth to their baby. He had no time to think; his brain had switched immediately into action, shutting out all other matters. But as he rose into the sky and steadied his aircraft, she slipped into his mind again and he cursed. He hadn't even had time to telephone.

Stefan too was thinking of Alison. He had been aware for some time that he was falling in love with her. He'd kept his feelings firmly locked away in his heart, knowing that she could never be any more than a friend, but as they'd exchanged tokens on that last day, he had seen in her eyes a deeper feeling than friendship, and had felt the sudden tension between them; and he'd known then that, whether she realised it or not, Alison was at least a little in love with him as well.

The knowledge had both shocked and delighted him. He was delighted because it was so long since he had felt that anyone loved him, and although he had had plenty of brief romances since he'd been in England, he'd never felt seriously in love with any girl. And he was shocked because he'd never had any intention of coming between Alison and her husband. He'd believed he could keep his love to himself. Now, he knew she was aware of it too – or, if she wasn't, she very soon might be.

I won't be able to see her again, he'd thought, the delight giving way to desolation. Not alone, anyway. I shall have to be very, very careful . . .

Suddenly, he realised that his aircraft wasn't lifting as it should. Almost at the end of the runway, it was still only half off the ground – and he was heading straight for the lump of craggy rock that marked the perimeter. Jerked back from his drifting thoughts, he fought to bring up the nose, let out a sharp breath of relief as it began to come up, then gasped as it dropped again. He screamed a curse as the plane teetered in the air, one wing dipping sideways. Even now, if he could just clear the rock – yes, he was almost there – he could do it. They were up . . . and then the tip of the propeller just shaved along the roughened edge. The plane tipped sideways, swung violently round, and dug its way into the ground.

Stefan looked up from his crazy position in the cockpit and saw the rest of the squadron passing overhead. He swore again in his native Polish and then passed out.

'Bear down,' the midwife said. 'You've got to help yourself here, Mrs Knight. Here – hold on to this towel.' She twisted a hand towel into a rope and fastened it to the iron bedhead. 'Now, pull on that and bear down hard.'

'I can't,' Alison moaned. 'I can't do it any more. Can't I have a rest?'

'Only if Baby says so, I'm afraid.' The nurse looked round as the door opened and Matron popped her head in. 'It's going very slow, ma'am. The pains are still five minutes apart, but they're so strong. She's getting proper worn out.'

'There's nothing we can do about it.' Matron came in and looked down at the sweating figure on the bed. She laid one hand on the swollen abdomen. 'Listen to me, Mrs Knight. Your baby will come in its own time and not before. There's no use fighting this, you just have to let yourself go with it. Try to relax . . .'

'I *can't* relax!'

'. . . and just bear down as the pain asks you to do. That's what it is, you see – it's the only way your body has of telling you what to do. Bearing down will make you feel more comfortable, and each time you do it your baby will be a little closer to being born.'

'It hurts!' Alison screamed.

'I know, but it's Nature's way. It will all be over soon and you'll have a lovely baby.'

'I don't want a baby! I just want this to stop!'

Matron nodded. She'd heard it all before, and she knew that once the baby was born Alison would forget – or deny – that she'd ever said such things. 'It will all be over soon,' she said, patting Alison's hand, and then turned her head sharply as they heard a commotion outside.

'Whatever's going on? Stay here, Nurse. I'll be back as soon as possible.' The older woman hurried out, closing the door behind her, and Alison began to groan again as a fresh wave of pain crept up her body and tightened its hold, like an iron band, about her stomach.

'What's happening?' she panted as the wave receded. 'I can hear a man's voice – is it Andrew?'

'Are you expecting him to come?'

'I want him to come. Is he here? Let him come, please. I want him!'

'No!' the midwife exclaimed, shocked. 'Of course he can't come in here. In any case, I don't think he's here. Now, you stop worrying about your husband, Mrs Knight, and think about yourself and your baby. It'll be here soon.' The sound of voices outside grew louder and she glanced over her shoulder a little anxiously. It certainly didn't sound like the usual subdued murmur of visiting time, yet why else would a man – several men, by the sound of it – be here? Apart from husbands and workmen like plumbers or handymen, the only male visitors were the local doctors. These voices didn't sound like any of those.

Matron came in again. Her lips were folded with disapproval. She looked down at Alison, who was tensing her body as the contraction began again.

'Do you happen to know a Polish pilot?' she enquired rather frostily. 'I believe his name is Dabrowski.'

'Why, that's Stefan!' Alison screwed up her face as the pain swelled around her. 'Stefan!' she screamed. '*Stefan!*'

'Mrs Knight – please!' The appalled midwife turned to Matron, who drew herself up with displeasure. 'Please, you really mustn't call out like that. Why, he might hear you.'

'I *want* him to hear me,' Alison sobbed, her body sagging again. 'I want him to hear me, I want to see him. I want somebody with me.'

'*We're* with you.'

'I want someone I *love*,' she cried. 'I want someone who loves *me!*'

Matron took a breath and spoke in a stern voice. 'Mrs Knight, be quiet at once. You don't know what you're saying. Now, forget about what's going on outside, or who's there, and concentrate on why you're here. You're having a baby. That's all that matters. Stop behaving like a silly girl and calm down. The pains are there for you to work with. Stop fighting them. The sooner you do that, the sooner your baby will be born, but if you carry on like this you may even harm it. Do you understand?'

'Yes, Matron,' Alison whispered.

'I should think so, too. Now, I'll go and sort out whatever's happening outside while you and Mrs Phelps here get on with your work. And when I come back, I shall expect to find that this baby is very close to being born, and there'll have been no more of this silly behaviour. The idea!' she said to herself as she left the room. 'The very idea!'

Stefan had been taken to another room. He was lying back on a narrow hospital bed when Matron came in and gave him an icy look. He summoned up his most charming smile.

'Madam, I have to give you my thanks for taking me in. My plane crashed . . .'

'So I understand,' she said. 'What I *don't* understand is why you were brought here. Surely there's a hospital on the airfield?'

'There is. I do not know why I was brought here.' He tried the smile again. 'They didn't ask me, you see. I was not conscious.'

She stepped forward and laid a professional hand on his brow. 'Well, you seem to be now. But I suppose we'd better keep you for a while, to make sure there's no concussion, at least until one of your own doctors can come and attend to you. It's most irregular, however. This is a maternity home, not a casualty clearing station.'

'I know. I'm very sorry.' The smile was even more winning. 'However, I promise not to have a baby to cause you more nuisance.'

'Really!' she exclaimed, but he saw her lips quiver very slightly, as if the ice had begun to thaw a little. 'You will not be permitted to be a nuisance,' she went on firmly. 'A nurse will come along to examine you and attend to your injuries, which seem to be very slight, and you'll then stay in this room until a doctor can come. Please don't detain my nurses longer than you have to.' Her look told him that she knew all about Polish pilots and their ways with nurses. 'As I've already explained, this is a maternity home and we have a patient in labour at this very moment.'

'Ah, yes,' he said. 'And I believe she is a friend of mine. Mrs Knight, not so?'

Matron's disapproving frown returned. 'It *is* Mrs Knight, as it happens,' she said coldly, 'but that's none of your business. Your job is to recover from whatever injuries you sustained when you crashed your plane,' the tone of her voice left him in no doubt as to her opinion of his flying capabilities, 'and return to the airfield. Obviously we'll do our best to see that that's as soon as possible. Now,' as they heard a cry from the room nearby, 'I must get back to my real patients. Excuse me, Mr Dabrowski.'

She turned and swept out of the room with a rustle of starched uniform, and Stefan lay back on the bed. In truth, he felt much more shaken than he had allowed her to see. The crash had hurt his pride more than his body; although his head throbbed and he felt bruised and sore all over, he knew there were no serious injuries and his most urgent desire was to get back to the airfield and take up another plane. He was furious with himself for the accident and knew that it would mean a carpeting from the Station Commander, but he knew also that he was too good a pilot to be grounded, and with the Invasion imminent they would need every man they could get.

There was no use in letting his impatience get the better of him, however. No Service doctor would leave the station until all the aircraft were back – not for a pilot who had nothing much wrong with him – and however desperate the need, there would be no flying for him until he had had that carpeting and another plane was made available. Meanwhile, here he was, ludicrously put to bed in a maternity home, and with Alison herself giving birth to her baby only a few yards away. What Andrew would have given to be in my place, he thought wryly.

The door opened and a young nurse came in. She looked no more than eighteen or nineteen, with a small, freckled face and ginger curls escaping from her cap. She was already blushing as she came through the door, and when Stefan smiled at her the blush turned a fiery red.

'Have you come to examine me?' he enquired.

'Matron told me to make sure you had no serious injuries and to attend to those you had.' Timidly, she came closer to the bed, stopped just beyond arm's reach, and looked at his face. 'Can you tell me where it hurts?'

'All over,' he said seriously. 'I think both my legs may be broken. Do you wish to see?' He began to push down the bedclothes.

'I'll look at your head first. Matron said there may be some concussion. She didn't say anything about broken legs.' Warily, she came close enough to touch him and he obediently bent his head so that she could part his hair with her fingers. 'You've got some lumps but there doesn't seem to be any bleeding. Is it tender?'

'Only a little, but then you have such a gentle touch.' He turned his face up towards hers. They were very close now and he saw the panic in her eyes. 'Don't be afraid, little nurse, I'm not going to hurt you. Have you not dealt with men before?'

'I'm training to be a midwife,' she said primly, stepping back.

'Still, some of the babies you deliver must be boys.'

'Of course they are.'

'Well, they will be men one day. We were all babies once, you know.' He saw the bemused look on her face. 'It's all right, little nurse. Perhaps I am concussed, after all. Are you going to look at my other injuries?'

'You haven't really broken your legs, have you?' she asked doubtfully, and he laughed and shook his head.

'No, I'm not badly injured at all. Just bruised and scratched. I was very lucky. A few cuts here and there – perhaps you should wash and dress those – but nothing more. I promise to behave.' His eyes danced and she began to relax and smile tentatively back at him. 'And then I may have a little favour to ask of you.'

'A favour?' She was cautious again. 'What is it?'

'That I will tell you when you have finished. By then, I hope we will be friends. Don't look so concerned, little nurse. Now, shall I be quiet while you dress these terrible wounds of mine?'

'I think you'd better.' She clearly didn't know quite what to make of him and although he enjoyed teasing her he was reminded sharply of his sister Krystyna, who had been just as shy and timorous before her marriage. He sighed, wondering how she was now and whether her Jewish husband were still alive. Whether even Krystyna herself were still alive . . .

'You're looking sad,' the nurse said quietly as she bathed the cuts on his arms and shoulders. Most of the damage seemed to have come from the cockpit as it shattered around him, and from jagged edges catching his skin as he was dragged out of the wrecked plane. As Matron had said, though, it was largely superficial and he would soon be taken back to the airfield.

'I was thinking of my family in Poland,' he said. 'You remind me of my sister.'

'Oh.' She stopped her work and looked at him. 'I'm sorry. Do – do you ever hear from them?'

'Not since the war began and I left my country. I often wonder . . .' He left the words unsaid. 'I'm sorry. I didn't mean to make you sad as well.'

'Everyone has something to be sad about these days,' she murmured.

'Even you?'

'I've lost an uncle and a sister,' she said. 'My uncle was a soldier. He was killed at Dunkirk. My sister was a Wren and a bomb hit the barracks where she was stationed. There were nearly twenty of them killed that night.'

'A sister!' he said. 'That is dreadful for you. She was older than you?'

'Three years.' She looked more closely at a gash on his shoulder. 'This is going to need stitches. I'll tell Matron.'

'One moment.' He lifted his hand to stop her and she paused. 'May I ask my favour now?'

The girl hesitated. She had relaxed during their conversation, but now her wariness returned. 'What is it?'

'The woman in labour now – Mrs Knight. She's a friend. Her husband is my Squadron Leader. He hasn't been able to see her since she came in – all leave's been stopped and we're on duty day and night.' He leaned up on one elbow, anxious to persuade her. 'If I could just see her for a few minutes, so that I can tell him when I go back to the airfield.'

'But she hasn't been delivered yet! Matron would never allow it.'

'For just a moment,' he pleaded. 'And perhaps by the time I leave, her baby will have been born. What objection could there be then?'

'Only husbands—'

'But her husband can't be here! It's forbidden for him to leave the airfield. And I *am* here. She would want to see me, I know it. And Andrew – Squadron Leader Knight – he would want it also, I am sure. When he finds out I've been here,' he put his head on one side and gazed at her, 'he will be disappointed if I can tell him nothing. So disappointed.'

The nurse glanced nervously at the door behind her. They could hear Alison's groans and the voices of the midwives urging her on. She chewed her lip and then made up her mind.

'I'll try. That's all I can promise. If Matron or one of the others were to find out, I'd get into terrible trouble, so it'll have to be when she's on her own, and that won't be until the baby's born now. But if there's a chance – well, I will try.'

'Thank you.' He lay back on his pillows and she slipped out of the room.

Silently, Stefan joined his voice to those of the midwives in encouraging Alison and her baby in their battle. With the nurse gone, he began to be more aware of his cuts and bruises, the aches of his body and the throbbing in his head. He felt sick and shaken, but he knew it would pass. His more pressing desire was to see Alison.

He knew that he hadn't been strictly honest with the nurse. He did want to see Alison for Andrew's sake, so that he could report on her and, with luck, the baby. But most of all, he wanted to see her for his own sake. He wanted to be with her. And, when he'd heard her call his name, he had known that she wanted him too.

Chapter Twenty-Eight

The baby was born at last, just after five o'clock in the morning.

The whole maternity home seemed to relax once it was all over. It was a small home, with just two wards and a few private rooms, and there were fewer than a dozen new mothers in at the time. Stefan, by now stitched and waiting for transport back to the airfield, was in a fever in case he was whisked away without having a chance to see Alison; but once the birth was over and she and the baby had both been bathed, the corridor fell silent. After a few minutes, the little nurse slipped into the room.

'I think it would be safe now. They've given her a cup of tea and gone to have their breakfast. You'll be very quick, though, won't you?'

'I will. Don't worry.' He swung his legs off the bed and padded towards the door, not stopping to put on his shoes. Apart from that, he was fully dressed. 'Keep watch for me, will you? If anyone comes, knock on the door and I'll jump out of the window!'

'Don't be silly.' But she stationed herself nervously by the door and he slid into the room.

Alison was propped on her pillows. The bedclothes lay oddly flat over her body and he realised he had been subconsciously expecting her to be the same size as when he had last seen her. Her eyes widened as she looked up at him and then her face crumpled with tears.

'Alison!' In two strides, he was beside the bed, cradling her against him. In the same moment, he realised that she was holding the baby against her, wrapped in a creamy-white shawl. 'Sweetheart, don't cry. You've got your baby – you should be happy.'

'I am,' she sniffed, wiping the tears away. 'It was just seeing you – I felt so lonely. Andrew can't come to visit me and I don't know when we'll be together again – and then you were here and it seemed like a miracle.' The tears flowed again but she was smiling as well. 'Oh, Stefan, it's so lovely to see you!'

'Ssh,' he said, bending to kiss her cheek. 'Nobody must know I'm here. Matron would probably have me shot. I can only stay a few minutes. Show me your baby. Is it a boy or a girl?'

'It's a girl.' Proudly, she drew aside the folds of the shawl and he looked down at a face that was neither red nor wrinkled, but creamy and smooth, with pale blue eyelids tightly closed so that long dark lashes lay like fans on the downy cheeks. The head was covered with black hair, still damp and wavy.

'She's exactly like Andrew,' he said in astonishment. 'I never believed it before, when people told me that newborn babies could resemble one of their parents.'

Alison nodded. 'She is, isn't she? There's not a scrap of me in her.'

'I expect she will have your beautiful nature,' he told her seriously, and then kissed her again. 'I am so pleased to be here. It is a privilege.'

'But why are you here?' she asked. 'Andrew can't come, so how did you manage it? And you've been here for hours. I didn't think Matron allowed—'

'Matron had no choice.' He tapped one of his bandages and her eyes widened again as, for the first time, she really took in his appearance. 'I crashed my plane and they brought me here. There was some confusion at the airfield gate – so much was going on, so many planes taking off – and this was the nearest place with medical facilities. It was just luck – for me, good luck.'

'You crashed your plane? But are you really all right? Was anyone else hurt?'

'It was just me. I clipped the Rock. The aircraft is broken, but I am just a little bent.' He smiled at her. 'I shall be in trouble, no doubt, but they'll find me another plane. I will be back in the air by tonight. But for now – it is good that I can be here with you. I can tell Andrew that he has a beautiful daughter, as well as a beautiful wife.'

'Oh, Stefan,' she said, and leaned her head against him.

They stayed quiet for a few moments and then he said, 'I will have to go soon. There is a little nurse keeping watch for me – I don't want to get her into trouble.'

'No, you mustn't do that.' As he straightened up, she reached up her free hand and slipped it round to the back of his neck, drawing him down again. 'Stefan, I'm so glad you were here. If it couldn't be Andrew – well, there's nobody I'd rather have.'

A little more pressure on the back of his neck, and his lips met hers. They kissed; a brief touch of the lips. And then there was a soft knock on the door and she let him go. Hurriedly, he straightened and moved away, then he turned back again.

'The baby's name – what is it to be?'

'Caroline,' she said, and then, after a tiny pause, 'She's going to have three names. Caroline Morag Stephanie.'

'You've seen Alison?' Andrew echoed. 'You've seen Alison *and my daughter*?'

Stefan had returned to the airfield to find most of the squadron safely back. Two had been lost – Brian Summers, and a new pilot who had been with them only a week or two. Stefan himself had been checked by the station doctor and seen the Group Commander about the crash. When he came back to the mess, the first thing he had done was seek out Andrew and tell him what had happened.

'It was just luck,' he began, but Andrew wasn't listening. He'd telephoned the maternity home the minute he had landed and discovered that he was a father again, and Matron had told him the weight of the baby and the names Alison had chosen. For a moment, as he listened, he was bemused, and when he heard that Stefan had actually been in the little hospital while Alison was giving birth he had felt as if his world were dropping away from him.

'They won't let me off the station,' he said bitterly. 'I can't even go two miles to see my own wife, and you waltz in as if you were the King himself. And she's even named the baby after you! It's crazy. I don't understand it.'

'It was just an accident,' Stefan said, trying to explain. 'I didn't ask to be taken there. I didn't even know that was where I was, until I came to my senses in the bedroom. Then I heard her voice . . .'

'What do you mean, you heard her voice? She was in labour.'

'Yes,' Stefan said. 'She was in labour. She was crying out. Calling for you,' he added in the hope that this might mollify his Squadron Leader.

'Calling for me? Oh, my God – my poor Alison. And me not there.' Andrew began to pace up and down the mess. '*I* ought to have been there, not you. It's all wrong. Oh, this bloody war!'

Stefan waited. He didn't know what to say. He had thought that since Andrew couldn't see Alison or their baby himself, he would be glad that a friendly face had been there with her, glad to hear at first-hand what the baby was like. Instead, he seemed angry – angry with Stefan.

There was no reason, Stefan thought uncomfortably,

why he should be angry about the accident that had taken the Pole to the maternity home at just that critical moment. But if he knew the feelings that Stefan had towards his wife, he would have every justification. He might think Alison the most lovable woman in the world, but that didn't mean he wanted other men loving her.

And I do love her, Stefan thought. All these months when I've been visiting her, talking to her, building castles with Hughie and telling him stories, playing the piano – all this time, I've been falling in love with her. I should have realised what was happening and stopped before it was too late. But I didn't. Perhaps I didn't want to realise it.

'I'm sorry,' he said at last. 'I didn't mean to take myself where I was not wanted. It wasn't my wish. But I was there – and of course I wanted to see her. And I think she was pleased to see me too.'

'I'm bloody sure she was!' Andrew burst out. 'She named our baby after you, didn't she!' He stopped by the high mantelpiece and leaned his elbow on it, biting the side of his thumb.

There was an uneasy pause. Then Stefan said, 'I think when a woman has just had a baby she is at the mercy of her emotions. She probably regrets it already. You do not have to call the baby that name. I will understand.'

Andrew turned and came over to him. 'No, it's all right, Stefan. If that's what Alison wants to call the baby, she shall. You've been a good friend to us, after all – especially to her. Keeping her company all these weeks . . .' His voice trailed off and he hesitated, as if suspicion had touched his mind. Then he shrugged it away. 'I know you're a man of honour. You won't have taken advantage of the situation – I don't think that for a moment. It's just – well, it's so bloody *disappointing*.'

'I know,' Stefan said quietly. 'And I am very sorry.'

They stood in silence for a moment or two and then

Andrew heaved a deep sigh and said, 'Well, you'd better tell me. How is she, really? Matron said she was fine but you know what these nurses are – they say you're "comfortable" when you're half dead. And tell me about the baby, too.'

Stefan smiled, relieved but unable to push away his guilt completely. 'Alison is very well. Tired, but she had a difficult night. All she needs is a good sleep. She is looking beautiful. And so is the baby.'

'Is she? Is she really?' Andrew seemed to have forgotten his anger. 'What's she like? Does she look like Alison? Is she like Hughie? He was like a snowball when he was born.'

Stefan laughed. 'No, she's not like a snowball, not in the least. And she is not like Alison either. In fact, she looks very much like you.'

'Like Andy?' Robin Fairbanks asked, joining them with a pint of beer in each hand. He gave one to Andrew and one to Stefan, then turned away to pick up his own. 'I thought you said she was good-looking?'

'Who sent for you?' Andrew demanded good-humouredly, then turned back to Stefan. 'What do you mean, she looks like me? I thought all new babies looked like Winston Churchill.'

'This one doesn't. She looks like a princess. Pale, smooth skin and thick black hair just like yours.' He winked at Robin. 'It seems impossible, doesn't it, that a baby can look like Andrew and yet be beautiful?'

'Impossible? I'd say it was a blooming miracle.' Robin lifted his pint. 'If you ask my opinion, the poor kid's going to need all the help she can get. Anyway, let's drink to a long and happy life for her. To – what did you say her name is?'

'Caroline,' Andrew said. 'Caroline Morag.' He paused, glanced quickly at Stefan, then added, 'Stephanie. Old Dabrowski here's going to be her godfather.'

'Is he, by Jove?' Robin raised his eyebrows and lifted his glass to Stefan, who hoped he didn't look as astonished as he felt. 'Well, here's to you, old boy, as well. And here's to the proud daddy.'

'To Andy!' the others shouted, and Stefan realised that the whole squadron had gathered about them. 'Andy and Alison and their new sprog.'

Stefan drank with them, thankful when the conversation was directed away from himself. He moved away and stood by the window, looking out at the twilight and thinking about the picture Alison and her baby had made in the white hospital bed.

Robin Fairbanks came and stood beside him.

'It's a bloody shame old Andy can't get out to see them, you know,' he remarked quietly. 'It must sting a bit, to know that you were there instead. But I dare say he's glad, on the whole. I'm sure *she* was.'

'I hope so,' Stefan said, thinking of the soft touch of her lips on his. 'I hope so.'

May came in to see Alison as often as possible. For the whole two weeks she was in the home, Alison was not allowed to put a foot out of bed. She fretted and railed against it.

'I feel perfectly well now. I'm sure I could manage. And I'm going to have to, once I get home again. I'm just getting weaker, lying in bed all this time. It's silly.'

'You've got to get over the birth,' May said, putting a small brown-paper parcel on the bed. 'It's hard on a body, having a baby. You've got to get your strength back.'

'I've *got* my strength back,' Alison grumbled. She had been feeling tearful and crochety for two or three days now. 'Look at women in Africa and India. They have their babies while they're working out in the fields. They just go behind a bush for a while, then come out and carry on working, with their babies on their backs. They don't stay in bed for a fortnight.'

'Well, they're different,' May said. 'Open your present. It might cheer you up.'

'I'm perfectly cheerful, thanks,' Alison said ungraciously, but she unwrapped the brown paper, smoothing it out carefully so that it could be used again. 'Oh May, they're lovely!' She held up a tiny pink knitted jacket and a pair of minute bootees. 'Have you knitted these since the baby was born? Wherever did you get the wool?'

'That little shop in Yelverton,' May said, smiling with pleasure. 'I saved some of my coupons and the lady put by some pink and blue baby wool for me, so that I could have the right colour. Mother knitted them, though. I haven't had much time myself.'

'No, of course you haven't. You've been looking after Hughie as well as doing your other work. Well, say thank you to your mother for me until I can do it myself.' Alison gazed in admiration at the little garments. 'They're so tiny, aren't they? I can't believe Hughie was ever that small. How is he, May? I hope he's not missing me too much.'

'He's getting along fine. We keep him busy most of the time so he doesn't have time to miss you, and when he goes to bed he's asleep the minute his head touches the pillow. He's been helping Grandpa in the garden, and I took him down to Double Waters this afternoon – he walked all the way there and back and hardly complained at all. We saw the herons on their nests, and a dipper, and a kingfisher! And he found a shiny stone on the old mine-dumps there. He thinks it's a diamond, but Father says it's called marcasite.'

'It sounds as if he's having a lovely time,' Alison said wistfully. 'I wish I could come home, May. I'm missing him so much.'

'I know. But the time will soon pass, and you've got to

313

get to know little Caroline as well. You'll soon be back and then you'll have your own family all around you.'

'Will I? I hope so. But with everyone getting ready for the Invasion . . . well, I've got a nasty feeling about it, May. I'm so afraid that something's going to happen to Andrew.' She stopped and looked at her friend with wide, frightened eyes. 'I might never see him again. He might never even see his baby!'

She burst into tears, and May immediately moved closer to comfort her. She put both arms around Alison and drew her close, patting her shoulders and murmuring. Alison turned her head so her face rested against May's breast, and sobbed as if her heart were broken.

'I'm sorry, May. I'm being so selfish, especially after you've lost Ben. But that's just made it worse – it's made me realise all over again how dangerous it all is. I can't stop thinking about it. I try, I really do – I tell myself how lucky he's been so far, what a good pilot he is and all that – and then I think about Ben and how good *he* was as well, but how it didn't make any difference in the end. And I wonder just how long anyone can go, being lucky, and . . . oh, it all goes round and round in my head, and I feel like a prisoner in here, and Andrew's a prisoner on the station. We're only two miles apart but we can't see each other. And then I think how he may fly off one day and never come back, and it starts all over again. I can't seem to stop it.' She lifted her head and looked at May with red-rimmed eyes. 'And you're doing so much for me, looking after Hughie and bringing me lovely presents and all I can do is snap and grumble and be a grouch and then cry all the time. I don't know what's the matter with me.'

'You've just had a baby,' May said soothingly. 'It often takes women like that. And you've got plenty to grumble about, too. Everything you say is right, after all. It's awful for you.'

'It's awful for everyone,' Alison sniffed. 'Not just me. There are plenty of people worse off than I am. You are, for a start. You've lost your fiancé before he even had a chance to give you a ring, and you'll never have his babies. And I shouldn't be saying things like that!' she burst out as May's eyes filled with tears. 'I'm just making it all worse.'

'No, you're not. You're saying what's true. And I'll tell you something, Alison – it might sound funny, but I'm glad to hear somebody saying it, because most people are frightened to. And if I say anything like it, I just sound sorry for myself. But it is true. We never had a chance to get married or – or to love each other properly – and I'll never have his babies. But nothing's going to happen to Andrew, and even if it did, at least you'd have Hughie and Caroline.'

'I know.' Alison found a hanky under her pillow and wiped her face and eyes. 'I'm sorry, May. I'm just being selfish. You won't want to come and see me any more if I go on like this.'

'Of course I will,' May said stoutly. They both looked round as a bell began to ring in the hallway between the two wards. 'I'll be here every day, until you can come home. You don't need to worry about that. But I'll have to go now – that's the end of visiting time.'

'Next Tuesday,' Alison said as May bent to kiss her. 'That's when I'm coming out. A whole week away – it seems more like a year.'

'It'll soon go by,' May told her, and gathered up her things. 'I'll take this brown paper away with me, it'll come in useful again, but I'll leave the jacket and bootees, shall I? I tell you what, I'm looking forward to seeing the little dear in them. I just wish I could see her now.'

'I do too.' Husbands were the only ones allowed to see the babies before they went home, which seemed to Alison to be a dreadful waste. Because Andrew couldn't come, she was the only one who would know what Caroline had looked like during these first two weeks of her life.

Except for Stefan, of course. He had seen Caroline when she was less than an hour old.

She watched May walk down the ward and turn to wave goodbye. Alison lifted her own hand and fluttered her fingers, and then turned back to her own thoughts.

Stefan. Somehow, he had become inextricably entwined with her thoughts about Andrew. And her fears that she might never see either of them again were even more intense.

Dusk was gathering in blue shadows as May walked back from the maternity home. Once, this walk across a neck of the moor and through deep, leafy lanes would have been a peaceful stroll, with no sound other than the evening song of blackbirds, thrushes and robins as they prepared to roost for the night. Now, the air was filled with the sound of aircraft; their engines running as they waited to take off, the roar as they lifted into the sky, the distant growl as they set off on yet another bombing raid.

Much of the moor where she had once roamed so freely was fenced off too, buildings crowded where once there had been nothing but gorse, heather and grass. The ponies and sheep that had grazed there had been pushed aside, and tarmac roads and runways criss-crossed the land. And even the roads themselves were busy with traffic – heavy vehicles on their way to the coast, lorries filled with soldiers camping at the roadside. The atmosphere was tense with waiting; there was the air of a country holding its breath as the preparations were made for a new and, perhaps, ultimate chapter in the whole troubled story of this war.

May felt as if dusk were gathering in her heart as well. She could still not quite believe that she would never see Ben again. She had had no time to come to terms with his loss, no time to search her own heart and grieve. Alison's situation had taken over; you couldn't turn your back on a baby being born, or on the woman giving birth, especially when she was your best friend. And that was what Alison had become. In the short time since she and Andrew had moved into the cottage at Milton Combe – less than eight months – May had found in her a companion and confidante such as she had never known. She couldn't quite understand it – they were from such different backgrounds, their whole lives had been different and in normal circumstances they would barely have met. Yet because of the war, they had come close together. Probably the same thing had happened to many girls and young women – finding themselves in one of the Services, mixing with others that they would never have known in Civvy Street, and finding out that class and background had little to do with character. Friendships were being made during these years that would last a lifetime.

And people had fallen in love. People like her and Ben.

At the gate to the cottage, she paused. The airfield was behind her now, out of sight, and for a few moments there was silence. Looking down into the valley, she could just see the turret of the little church, and far beyond that the glitter of the River Tamar as it widened out into Plymouth Sound. The sun had disappeared in a glory of flame and apricot and the first stars were pricking the pale blue sky. The birds had almost stopped singing and there were just a few sleepy twitters from the hedgerow.

Her heart ached at the beauty of it. A beauty that Ben would never share now. A beauty that she would have to live with, alone, for the rest of her life.

Chapter Twenty-Nine

When Jeanie found the letter in John Hazelwood's cassock her first instinct was to put it aside unread. She was laying it on her washstand, to replace when she had finished her sewing, when she noticed the postmark and realised that it came from Devon.

She hesitated. Anything from Ben's Squadron Leader or the Station Commander would have been in an official envelope. And she didn't think it could have come from one of Ben's fellow-pilots – the handwriting didn't look like a man's. It wasn't a very educated hand, either – in fact, it looked rather like Jeanie's own handwriting.

It must be from May Prettyjohn.

That poor girl, Jeanie thought with a sudden rush of sympathy. She must be feeling as bad as I do. Even worse, because it was her that Ben wanted to marry. And she's written to the vicar, too. I wonder if he's answered her?

She didn't think it was very likely. The letters the vicar had replied to were always kept in a pigeonhole in his bureau. He was very careful about that, as he'd explained to her once when she was cleaning his study, because it was important to know which letters you'd answered and which were still waiting. If he'd replied to May, her letter would be there.

Jeanie looked at the envelope. It was a private letter. It was nothing to do with her. Yet she couldn't help feeling, allied with her own grief, a pity for the girl who had written it. We both loved him, she thought, and we've both lost him. And if the vicar can't bring himself to answer, *someone* ought to. It's not fair, leaving her like this. It's cruel.

Before she knew it, her fingers were opening the envelope. She smoothed out the folded pages and began to read.

By the time she had finished, tears were pouring down her cheeks.

That poor girl, she thought again. She really loved Ben – you could tell it from the way she wrote about him. And he loved her as well. They ought to have been allowed to get married. It was wrong to stop them. *Wrong*.

Her heart was beating fast as she folded the letter and put it back into its envelope. She picked up her needle and cotton, but her hands were shaking too much to put the thread through the eye. She laid them down again and stared out of the window into the garden. Under that apple tree, she had first met Ben. Under that apple tree, she had given birth to her baby. None of it had been easy for her, but at least her engagement to Terry had been a happy one, recognised by both families. And although her pregnancy had almost caused her parents to disown her, Terry's family had stood by her and it had all come right in the end. And, best of all, she had Hope to remind her of him. If no other man ever wanted to marry her in the whole of her life, she would always have Hope.

May Prettyjohn had none of that. She didn't even have Ben's ring to keep by her heart. She didn't have the right to come to Ashford and be welcomed by his family. She'd never known the joy of loving him fully, and she would never have his baby.

I can't leave it there, Jeanie thought, looking down into the twilit garden. The apple blossom had begun to fall, carpeting the grass beneath with snowy petals, tinged with softest pink. She could hear the grunting of a hedgehog as it snuffled along the foot of the hedge while overhead a pale sickle moon had risen into the sky. In the distance, she could hear the throb of aircraft.

I *can't* leave it there, she repeated to herself. I've got to do something about it.

It was several days before she could decide what to do. Her first thought was to go down to Devon and see May Prettyjohn for herself. Talk to her, try to help her to understand how things were at the vicarage. But the girl knew that already – Ben had told her, and they'd agreed not to marry until his mother could accept it. He'd asked her father's consent to marry her, and they'd been going to buy a ring, but that was as far as they were going, for the time being.

Even that, Jeanie knew, must have been hard for Ben to accept. He'd wanted so much to marry his sweetheart, and he'd wanted to marry her soon, before his twenty-first birthday, just in case something happened to him. It was as if he had known.

All through the war, he had been confident that nothing would ever happen. He'd been bright and brave and daring, filled with courage and a sense that nothing could ever touch him. He'd told her once that you had to feel like that – what was the word he'd used? Invincible? – or you wouldn't be able to do the job. But he'd lost that feeling, perhaps when he'd fallen in love. He'd realised what he had to lose. And so, just as if it had to happen, he'd been killed.

Oh Ben, she thought, the tears starting yet again. My poor, poor Ben . . .

'Jeanie, are you all right?' The vicar's voice startled her as she stood at the kitchen sink, her hands in the cooling washing-up water. 'You've been standing there for over five minutes without moving a muscle. I was beginning to think you'd been turned to stone.'

Jeanie moved round and his expression deepened to concern as he saw the tears on her cheeks.

'I'm sorry,' he said. 'Is it Ben? I forget that you're as upset as we are.'

'I don't expect I am,' she said, taking a saucer from the water and standing it on the draining-board. 'He was your son. You're bound to be much more upset than anyone else could be. Except . . .' She hesitated. She'd quickly discarded her first idea, to go and see May – she could no more go to Devon than she could go to Portsmouth – and had realised that she had no choice but to speak to the vicar himself. Perhaps now was the moment.

She took a deep breath. 'I've got to talk to you, Mr Hazelwood. It's about Ben. It's – it's serious.' She saw the look on his face and added hastily, 'It's all right – it's not the same as it was with Terry. But I really do need to tell you something.'

He searched her expression carefully. Then he nodded and said, 'You'd better come into the study.'

'I'll finish the washing-up first.' She tried a little laugh. 'Mustn't waste the water!'

He smiled back at her. 'Come as soon as you're ready. And – don't look so worried, Jeanie. Whatever it is, I'm sure we can sort it out.'

He left the kitchen and Jeanie returned to her work. I hope he can, she thought. But it all depends on Mrs Hazelwood, and that poor lady really isn't in any fit state to sort anything out.

'Well, now,' John Hazelwood said when Jeanie was sitting nervously opposite him on the edge of one of the sagging armchairs by the fireplace. 'What is it that's worrying you?'

The study was quite a big room; its walls were lined with bookshelves crammed with books, and it contained a few chairs and small tables and a large desk at which John composed his sermons and did all the paperwork involved in being a vicar. In the corner was the bureau which held his correspondence, and this was the only tidy part of the room, the one thing that the vicar was meticulous about, and the most sacrosanct piece of furniture there. The shelves, tables and even some of the chairs overflowed with papers and books, and the door was hung with robes and cassocks.

'You're not going to be very pleased about it,' Jeanie began hesitantly. 'I told you it was about Ben. It's nothing wrong,' she added quickly, still afraid that he might misunderstand. 'I mean, nothing wrong that he did. It's me.' She bit her lip and then said, 'I read the letter May Prettyjohn wrote you.'

John stared at her. 'You read her letter? But how did you come across it? I've kept it in my bureau. Surely you haven't been looking through that. You know that everything in there is confidential.'

'No! No, truly I haven't. But you left the letter in your cassock pocket. I was mending the hem and I found it.' She looked at him pleadingly, aware of the painful colour in her cheeks. 'I didn't read it to start with – I knew it would be wrong. But I saw where it was from and I guessed it was her, and – well, I just couldn't seem to help it.'

'I think you could have helped it, Jeanie,' he said gravely. 'I think you must admit that.'

'Well, yes, I suppose I could.' She looked down, feeling the tears hot in her eyes, realising for the first time what he must be thinking. They had taken her into their home, cared for her, treated her almost like a daughter – and she had let them down. By this one, simple act, she had let them down. She raised her eyes again and said, 'I'm really sorry. I know I shouldn't have done it. But I did, and – and I can't forget it. I've got to talk to you about it.'

John was silent for a few moments, his brows drawn

together in thought. Then he said, 'Yes, all right, Jeanie. We can't pretend you haven't seen it. But what exactly do you want to talk about?'

'Well, I know it's none of my business but – I was fond of Ben too, you know. I was really fond of him. I've got to admit I was a bit upset when I heard about this other girl, but when he talked to me about her, I could see he really loved her. And when I read the letter I could see she loved him, too. And I wondered – I just wondered if anyone had written back to her. Because I could do it, if you'd like me to.'

'You?' he said in surprise.

'Yes, why not? You see, I know what she must feel like. I lost my boy too. Only his family were good to me – they took me in when I needed it and found me this place with you, and helped me to keep Hope. When you look at it like that, I'm a lot luckier than May Prettyjohn. Me and Terry might have done wrong, but we made each other happy, and he died knowing what it was like to love me. And *I* know what it was like, too.' She looked at him a little defiantly. 'I know people say that was wrong, but I can't ever be sorry about that. And I've got Hope, and she's a part of him for ever. I know I shouldn't be saying things like this to you, Mr Hazelwood, what with you being a vicar and everything, but as it's turned out I'm not sorry about any of it.'

Again, he took a moment or two to answer. His voice was still quiet, as he asked, 'Are you saying that Mrs Hazelwood and I have treated this girl badly, Jeanie? That we've been wrong all this time?'

'I wouldn't dare say that, Mr Hazelwood. You're a vicar. I'm just saying what happened to me.'

'But your fiancé's family were good to you – those were your words. They stood by you and took you in. My wife and I haven't done those things for May. In fact, we didn't

323

even reply to her letter until a week ago. I *have* written back, Jeanie, you'll be pleased to hear. At least I've done that.'

'I'm sorry, sir,' she murmured, her eyes falling. 'I've been talking out of turn. I'd better go – there's things I ought to be doing.'

She began to get up but he lifted a hand to stop her. 'No, Jeanie, don't go. I didn't mean to reproach you. I think you're quite right. We haven't done as we should by this poor girl. Even my letter – well, it was just a note, really, polite and formal, thanking her for writing. With no thought for her feelings, no sympathy for her loss. I'm ashamed of it.' He placed his hands on his knees and stared down at them. 'You've made me ashamed.'

Jeanie was shocked and dismayed. 'I didn't mean—' she began, but again he stopped her.

'I know you didn't. But you were right. We've been very remiss.' He sighed deeply. 'I've been so wrapped up in my own sorrow, and my wife's health, that I've grievously omitted to think of what poor May was going through. You've been wiser and more compassionate than I, Jeanie. I'm glad you read that letter.'

'Glad?' she whispered.

'Yes, glad. Otherwise I might have gone on, pushing it from my mind, ignoring the pain she must be feeling. What sort of a man of God am I?' he demanded bitterly. 'What sort of guidance can I give, when my own sins are so black?'

Jeanie didn't know what to say. She had never seen the vicar like this, except when in the pulpit, denouncing evil. She wished she had never spoken to him about May's letter. It's just what Mum always says, she told herself. Good never comes out of doing wrong. Only, when she thought about her daughter Hope, she could never quite believe that – unless what she and Terry had done wasn't wrong after all . . .

And if it hadn't been, perhaps reading May's letter wasn't either. Perhaps good might come of it yet.

'I don't see that you're that bad,' she said to the vicar. 'It's not as if you can't put things right, after all.'

He stared at her, half amused by her words, half incredulous. 'What do you mean?'

'Well, you know her address, don't you? You could write again. Or I could,' she offered again. 'She seems a nice person. Why don't you let me do that?'

He shook his head. 'No. You're quite right, this is something I must do myself. Not that it wouldn't be a very nice idea for you to write to her as well,' he added. 'You're of an age, after all, Ben was a special person to you both and you of all people can understand just how she must be feeling. I think she would very much appreciate hearing from you. But Olivia and I must play our part as well.'

'Mrs Hazelwood?' Jeanie queried doubtfully. 'Do you think she's well enough? I don't think May would want to upset her any more.'

'No, I'm sure she wouldn't. But I've come to the conclusion lately that it isn't doing my wife any good to let her go on in this way. If we allow her to go on hiding from the truth, she'll never be able to face the rest of her life. She'll always stay in this shadowy world she seems to be living in now. And it seems to me that the shadows are growing deeper every day . . .' His voice faded and he seemed to be staring past Jeanie at a future he dreaded; then he turned his head and looked at her properly again, smiling apologetically at her bewildered expression. 'I'm sorry, Jeanie. I don't suppose I'm making any sense to you. Look, if you want to write to May, then please do so with my blessing. Explain how things are here if you like, but tell her I'll be writing again soon, properly, and tell her my prayers are with her.' He sighed. 'No, even that I should be doing myself, and I will. You just write her a friendly letter of your own.' He fell silent again and Jeanie began to rise uncertainly to her feet. He looked up then and added simply, 'And thank you.'

'What for?' she asked. 'I haven't done anything.'

'You have,' he said. 'You've brought me to my senses. You've shown me the error of my ways. I shall have to spend quite a long time on my knees, praying for humility, after this.' He grinned at her. 'Don't look so worried. In fact, if anything, you're the answer to my prayer. I've been waiting for a sign and I think you may be it!'

Jeanie left the study, not at all sure that she liked being called an answer to a prayer, or a 'sign'. But you had to make allowances, she told herself, when someone had suffered like the vicar and his wife had. Losing two sons, one after the other – it was bound to make them go funny for a bit.

Anyway, the main thing was that he didn't mind her reading May's letter and he didn't mind her writing back. And he was even going to write again himself.

Jeanie felt a lot happier for knowing that.

Chapter Thirty

D-Day was declared on the day that Alison came out of hospital.

All through the previous night, aircraft had been roaring in and out of the airfield and everyone knew that it must have been the same all along the South of England – thousands of flights being made across the Channel to protect the ships and bomb the targets on the French coast. At the same time, the English beaches were crowded with ships and landing craft, taking the great Army which had been camped in streets and lanes for the past fortnight or more, to make this massive attack that was designed to crush the German forces at last. It would not be over in a week, nor even in months; yet everyone hoped that this was the beginning of the end of the war.

'It's as if they were never here,' May said, fetching Alison in Bob Derry's taxi. 'All those Americans over at Bickham have gone – all the tents, everything. The children were up there right away, seeing what had been left behind. And they've been talking about it all morning on the wireless, saying that this is the biggest invasion there's ever been. There's been parachutists going in, and gliders, and all sorts.'

'Gliders?' Alison echoed in surprise, and May nodded.

'Huge great things, big enough to carry tanks. Well, that's what I've heard, anyway. I suppose it's true,' she added a little more doubtfully, 'but you never know these days, do you, with all the propaganda and everything.'

It was not only France that had been invaded. The Americans, moving purposefully through Italy, had taken Rome, driving the Germans back from the city after months of strategic planning. It really looked as if the tide had turned.

'It's a shame Andrew can't be here,' May said as the taxi drew up at the door of the Knights' cottage and she helped Alison out of the car. 'It don't seem right, coming home with your new baby and no husband to greet you.'

'It can't be helped.' Alison paid Bob and he drove away while May opened the front door. She stepped into the hallway and drew in a sigh of thankfulness. 'Oh, it's *so* nice to be home. And I can't wait to see Hughie again. It seems like months – Oh!' She gave a little cry of joy as the door to the living room opened and the little boy peeped out. 'Hughie! Goodness me, you've grown! Come and see your little sister.'

She held out the white-swathed bundle in her arms. Hughie looked suspicious and backed away, and Alison turned to May with a laugh. 'Hold the baby for a minute, will you? I want to give my big son a big cuddle.'

May took the bundle and carried it carefully into the front room, where her mother was waiting impatiently to see the new arrival. A cradle had already been placed across two dining-chairs but May didn't put the baby inside. Instead, she sat down on the sofa beside Mabel and together they gently parted the soft, lacy shawl and gazed down at the small face.

'Oh, the dear of her,' Mabel breathed. 'What a little pretty. Look at that little face – just like a flower. And Caroline be such a lovely name, too. What did you say the others were?'

328

'Morag, after Andrew's granny,' May said. 'And Stephanie.'

'Oh, that's pretty too. Three names!' she said to the baby. 'Three nice names to choose from when you'm grown up. Who's a lucky little girl, then?'

Alison bent to hug Hughie. 'Are you pleased to see me again, then? Have you been a good boy for your Auntie Mabel and Uncle William? I bet you've had a nice time staying in the cottage. Tell me what you've been doing.' But Hughie hid his face against her neck and refused to speak.

'He'm a bit overwhelmed by it all,' Mabel Prettyjohn observed comfortably as Alison brought him into the room. 'He'll come round soon enough. And how be you, Alison? You'm looking well.'

'I'm fine. I could have come home a week ago, but they won't let you put your foot to the floor for a fortnight. I'm sure it's not necessary.' She saw the cradle. 'Oh! Look at that! It's beautiful.' She touched the carved wood. 'Wherever did it come from?'

''Tis our family cradle,' Mabel said proudly. 'Been in the family this past eighty years or more. It were made for my father when he were born and us've used it for every babby since. We got it out while you were in the hospital and William's dad polished it up a bit and brought it round last night. You don't have to use it, mind,' she added quickly. 'Not if you don't want to. You might want summat a bit better than an old cottage cradle.'

'I can't think of anything better,' Alison declared, stroking the rich dark oak. 'It's lovely. I was just going to put her in a drawer until she was big enough for a proper cot. Oh, look – it rocks, too. She'll sleep like a – well, like a baby, in that.' She turned to take her daughter back from May, and laid her amongst the soft blankets. 'There. She didn't even open her eyes. Thank you very much.'

Mabel got to her feet. 'I'll make a cup of tea, shall I? The kettle's on. And then I'm going to go home and see to things there, but May can stop with you for a while. She'll sleep here as well for a few more nights if you want her to.'

Alison shook her head. 'I'll be all right. And perhaps now they've started the Invasion, Andrew will be allowed to come home again. I'm longing for him to see Caroline.'

''Tis a crying shame he couldn't come in to see you at the hospital,' Mabel said, taking another peep at the baby before going out to the kitchen. 'Him being only a mile or two away, and all. But there, we've all had a lot to put up with in this war.' She cast a quick look at May and bit her lip. 'I'm sorry, flower, I didn't mean to remind you.'

'It's all right, Mother. I don't forget Ben anyway. He's in my mind all the time. It's a relief to hear someone else talk about it now and then.' As her mother left the room, followed by Hughie, she said to Alison, 'People are frightened to talk about things like that, you know. They say they don't like to upset you, as if you're not upset anyway, but what they really mean is that they don't want to see you being upset. They'd rather it was all pushed away, out of sight. I *want* to talk about Ben. I want to be upset, in a funny sort of way. Or perhaps I just want to be *allowed* to be upset. I can't forget him that easy, and I don't want other people to either, but maybe that's selfish of me.'

'I don't think it is,' Alison said. 'I think you have a right to feel whatever you like. There hasn't been any news at all?'

'Not as far as I know,' May said sadly. 'But then, they wouldn't tell me, would they? It's his parents they'd write to. And all I've had from them is a note from his dad, saying thank you for what I wrote. As if I were a stranger.' Her voice held a touch of bitterness. 'We loved each other, Ben and me. We were *engaged*. But there, I suppose with his mother the way she was, I can't expect anything more. I just wish I knew what it was they thought was so bad about me, that's all.'

'Oh, May—' Alison began, but at that moment Mabel came back into the room with cups and saucers on a tin tray, followed by Hughie carefully bearing a plate of biscuits, and there was a little flurry of activity as they found somewhere to put their cups and persuaded Hughie that the baby didn't want a biscuit.

'She's too small yet. She just drinks milk. But later on, when she's bigger, she'll be able to play with you,' Alison told him. 'You'll have some lovely times together.'

'She's not having my bricks,' he said. 'She can have that purple donkey Auntie Mabel knitted me. I don't like it any more.'

'Well, that's generous,' Alison said as they all laughed. 'I expect she'll like it better than bricks, anyway.'

Mrs Prettyjohn drank her tea and then said she must go. She had her menfolk's dinner to prepare, and after that she was going down to Buckland to the Women's Institute meeting. There might be fighting going on all over the world, but life at home still had to continue, and the WI was an important part of it.

'You don't have to stay all day,' Alison said to May. 'I mean, I'd like you to, of course, but I'll be quite all right on my own if you've got other things to do. You've already given up a morning's work to be here.'

'I don't mind that. There wasn't much for me to do anyway.' May hesitated, then said, 'As a matter of fact, there's something I want to talk to you about. It's about Ben.' She paused again. 'Well, it's about his mother and father, really. I was wondering if I ought to go and see them.'

'Go and see them?' Alison repeated. 'But why? Do you think it's a good idea?'

'I don't know. That's what I want to talk to you about. I

mean, you know that sort of people better than me. Do you think they've taken against me because I'm just an ordinary girl? D'you think they think I'm a gold-digger or something? I'd just like to let them see it's not true – not for myself, but for them. It must be awful for them if they think that Ben – well, that he wasn't really happy that last day. I'd like them to know I really did – *do* – love him. I thought it might help. But I don't really know – it might make everything worse.' She stopped and looked at Alison with anxious brown eyes. 'What do you think?'

Alison felt helpless. 'I don't know, May. I really don't know. It might not even be you – his mother was already ill, wasn't she? She was upset over his brother being killed. It seems to me as if she can't cope with anything just at the moment, and if you turned up unexpectedly . . .'

'It would make everything worse,' May finished quietly. 'Yes, I can see it might. But leaving it like this, it just seems so wrong. It's not *finished*. And I can't seem to settle until it is. I feel as if I ought to meet them, just so that we can sort of know each other a bit. I mean, I know they wouldn't want to go *on* knowing me – without Ben, there'd be no point. But it seems wrong that we should never even see each other. I feel I ought to do it. For Ben.' She fell silent for a moment, then added in a low voice, 'It's the only thing I can do for him, now.'

At last, Alison was left alone. The afternoon had been a busy one, firstly with Caroline needing her feed immediately after lunch, then with a succession of neighbours popping in to see her. Alison had been surprised by the interest shown. She'd spoken to them all at different times, as she'd walked along the road with Hughie, but hadn't dreamed so many were interested enough to make a special visit. By the time May left, just before tea, she felt quite exhausted and hoped that nobody else would come.

'There,' she said to Hughie, shutting the door after the last visitor had left. 'Wasn't that nice! And hasn't your little sister been good? She hasn't cried at all yet.'

'She hasn't done anything,' Hughie observed. 'Only sleep. And she had her milk.' He cast a curious glance at his mother. Alison had been slightly shocked by May's suggestion that he should see Caroline having her feed, and it had certainly appeared to surprise him, but on consideration she thought the country girl was probably right. It was a natural thing, not to be hidden away as if it were a matter for shame, and in any case it would be difficult to manage without Hughie ever seeing what was happening. After the first day or two, May had said, he would take it for granted. He'd seen that litter of kittens up at the farm feeding from their mother, after all. There really wasn't any difference.

'Except that I don't have six of them,' Alison had said with a laugh. 'Thank goodness!'

It was nearly time now for Caroline's next feed. She made Hughie a drink of orange juice first and put two biscuits on a plate for him before settling him down with his Rupert book. Then she drew the curtains and switched on the wireless.

The six o'clock news was just beginning as she unbuttoned her blouse. As she took Caroline in her arms and put her to her breast, Alison heard the measured tones of the BBC announcer tell how D-Day had begun and the invasion of France was now under way.

Where was Andrew in all this, she wondered as the baby suckled and Hughie murmured the story of Rupert Bear's adventures to himself. Had he been flying all night, all day? And Stefan too, and the rest of the squadron – how were they faring? It seemed so strange, so wrong, to be within a few minutes' walk of the airfield and yet know nothing of what was happening there. I might as well have stayed in Lincolnshire, she thought suddenly. At least I'd have had my parents there. Friends are all very well – and the Prettyjohns have been wonderful friends to me – but it's family you really need at times like this. And a tear dropped from her eye on to the baby's face, making her jump and lose the nipple from her mouth.

'It's all right, sweetheart. I'm sorry – there, that's better.' The baby began to suck again. I'm being sorry for myself, Alison thought. That won't help anyone.

All the same, she felt suddenly very lonely, in the cottage by herself apart from two small children. For the past fortnight, she had been in the company of a dozen or so other women, as well as the nurses and visitors who came in during the evenings, and before that she had had either Andrew, Stefan or the other pilots dropping in. Now, suddenly, there was no other adult than herself and for a moment or two she was panic-stricken.

Then she pulled herself together. Nothing's any different from before Caroline was born, she told herself sternly. In fact, it's better, because I'm not pregnant any more. I'm strong, fit and well, and full of energy. I've got my lovely baby girl and my sturdy little boy, and as soon as this horrible war's over and Andrew can be at home with us all we'll be a proper family, living a proper life. An ordinary life.

Caroline had finished feeding. The news was over and a music programme had begun. Alison buttoned up her blouse again and fetched a clean nappy from the pile on top of the dresser. She changed the baby, laid her in her cradle and put the used nappy in a bucket in the kitchen.

'You've been a very good boy,' she told Hughie, lifting him on to her knee. 'We'll just sit here for a while together before you have your bath, and you can tell me all about what you did when you stayed with Auntie May. Did you have a nice time?'

He nodded and leaned against her, sliding his thumb into

his mouth. He seemed to have overcome his suspicion of the baby, she realised with relief, and cuddled him against her, filled with a surge of love for him. I missed him so much when I was in the hospital, she thought. I'm never going to leave him again. I'm not going to leave either of them.

The room was very quiet. For the first time that day, there was no roar of aircraft. If only she could hear Andrew's footsteps coming down the road, she thought longingly. If only she could hear the gate click as he opened it, and his key in the lock of the front door.

But there was no sound of footsteps. All that could be heard through the open window was the twilight song of the birds.

The days following D-Day were just as busy at the airfield, with both bomber and fighter pilots working round the clock, coming off duty only to eat and sleep while the mechanics worked on the aircraft to get them ready to fly again. The men lost all count of the days and seemed to live in a haze where flying was the only reality and they felt awake and alive only when they were in the air.

Andrew, however, could not forget that he had a wife and two children less than a mile away, and that he had not even seen his baby yet.

'It's a bloody farce,' he said to Stefan as they ate their dinner one night. 'I could walk there and be back in half an hour. I know the boss says it'd be a bad example to the other blokes, but every last one of them would understand. D'you realise, that baby's nearly three weeks old now and I don't even know what she looks like. And what makes it worse is that *you've* seen her.'

'I know. I'm sorry. I didn't mean—'

'Oh, for God's sake, I'm not blaming you. It's just the way things happen.' Andrew threw down his knife and fork. 'I can't eat any more of this. I'm going outside. A walk round the airfield might cool me down a bit.'

He pushed back his chair and strode out of the room. The other pilots looked up and then glanced at Stefan.

'He's upset,' Stefan said awkwardly, and Robin Fairbanks nodded.

'Don't blame him, either. But it's not good – he's walking on a knife-edge at the moment, and you know what that means. He could crack up – he wouldn't be the first. Or he could have an accident.'

Stefan looked grim. 'It's so stupid. All he needs is half an hour with his family.'

'I know, but he'll get it soon.' Robin cleared his plate. 'This pace won't keep up for ever. We'll get some leave soon, we're bound to, and then he'll be able to go home. At least he *can* go home – there's plenty of chaps here who won't be able to. Look at Jock, for instance. He lives right up in the north of Scotland. Hasn't been home since last Christmas and probably won't get there till next Christmas.'

'And I,' Stefan said, 'don't even know if I have a home to go to.'

Robin gave him a quick look. 'No. Sorry, mate. I forget that sometimes. Maybe Andy does too.'

'There's no need for him to remember,' Stefan said. 'Everyone sees their own problems. There's no reason why mine should be more important to him than his own.'

Robin pushed back his chair, rather more quietly than Andrew had done. 'Well, I'm going to get a bit of shut-eye. I've no doubt we'll be flying again pretty soon. You'd better do the same.' He walked out and after a moment or two Stefan followed him.

The grey, dismal weather of D-Day and the few days after it, had cleared. The moon was waning now and the stars shone brightly. In the bays, bunkers and blister

336

hangars, aircraft engines grumbled as the mechanics tested them, but nothing could be seen apart from their silhouettes against the dark blue sky. Yet to Stefan, it seemed as if all his senses were sharpened, as if he could hear and see more clearly than ever before; as if the darkness of the night meant nothing. He felt that he could have made his way across the darkened airfield without stumbling, knowing exactly where his feet were taking him, and that when he sat in the cockpit of his plane he would be more bird than man.

He was aware of a strange light-headedness, hardly knowing whether he would rather fly or walk. We're all treading on the edge, he thought. Any one of us could tip over at any time.

He walked slowly between the darkened huts and buildings, past the hangars and workshops, past the inspection pits and the parachute packing shed. He walked past the ammunition store and past the air-raid shelters, past the anti-aircraft guns and the searchlight mountings. Every now and then, he would encounter someone else strolling in the dark – a couple of pilots, a mechanic or two, a group of WAAFs. For a brief space, the skies were quiet. It was as if the world were waiting.

But we've finished with the waiting, he thought. The war is more furious now than it has ever been. In a few months, perhaps it will be over. And what then?

What of his family – his parents, his brothers and sisters? Where were they now, and what had been happening to them all this time? And his home: did it still exist, or had it been destroyed?

He leaned against the wall of a hut and gazed into the sky, thinking of the people he had loved so much. Would they ever be able to come together again? Would they ever be able to take up their lives, as they had been before this terrible nightmare began?

Andrew walked all the way round the perimeter fence.

It was like being in prison, he thought. Looking out at the world through barbed wire, watched by sentries, deprived of your liberty and freedom. Out there, only yards away, was the world you were fighting for, yet you weren't allowed any part of it. A prisoner who had committed no crime.

He wasn't really looking for a way out. For one thing, he knew that the fence was patrolled regularly and maintained, so there would be no holes or even weak points. But if there had been, he would have been strongly tempted to use it. The frustration that had been simmering within him for weeks now had reached boiling point and he didn't know how much longer he would be able to keep it from erupting. His only release was when he was in the sky, watching the bombers rain destruction on the enemy, or engaging in deadly battle himself with the Luftwaffe. Then he could use all his fury in the way he had been trained to do, taking a dark pleasure in sending each Heinkel or Messerschmitt spiralling into the sea or exploding on the ground. He ignored the risks he took, wanting only to achieve as many kills as possible, wanting only to get this bloody war over so that he could go back to Alison and his children, wanting only to see the baby whose early days he had already lost for ever.

It made no difference that he was certain to see her before long, that this ban on leave must be over soon. It made no difference that thousands of men – soldiers, sailors and other airmen now in France or Italy, Africa or the Far East – were away for even longer and were missing years of their children's lives. Andrew was consumed by his own pain and misery. It was like a thick fog in his brain, blinding him to everything else but the need to kill, for only when enough aircraft had been shot out of the sky could he return to a normal life.

He came back to the mess and went straight to his room, without speaking to anyone, and flung himself on his bed. Perhaps he could sleep until it was time to go on duty again. Until it was time to kill . . .

Chapter Thirty-One

The restriction on local leave was lifted next morning.

It was announced as the squadron was at breakfast. The attacks on France were just as intensive and duties would be round the clock, but during off-duty time the airmen and women would be allowed to leave the station. Liberty had been restored.

'Why couldn't they have said so yesterday?' Andrew demanded in frustration. 'I could have dashed over to see Alison before going on duty. There isn't time now, dammit.'

'You can go this evening,' Robin said. 'Not long to go now. You just need to kill a few more Jerries first.'

'Don't worry, I will,' Andrew growled. 'Bloody Hun has kept me away from my wife and kids long enough. Anyone unfortunate enough to get into my sights today has a very nasty shock coming to him.'

He got up and marched out. The others looked after him, and Stefan said, 'It will be a good thing when he has seen his wife and baby. He is in a dangerous condition.'

'Aren't we all,' Robin said sombrely. 'But at least we're driving 'em back. If they're not on the run now, they soon will be. Maybe this time, it really will be all over by Christmas.'

'They've been saying that since the whole bloody shambles started,' someone else chipped in. 'I suppose it has to be right eventually. And at least we can go out and have a few beers this evening. I'm for the Leg o' Mutton myself – anyone joining me?'

They made their way out of the mess, beginning a discussion on the merits of the local pubs as they did so. There was a feeling of jubilation at the prospect of joining normal life outside the wire once more. But there was still a day's work to get through before freedom was granted; in less than half an hour they would be on readiness, and soon after that in the air. The holiday atmosphere was tempered with the grim determination that gripped them all once they were in the cockpit.

Andrew was trembling as he got into his plane. The fury that had been boiling up inside him had not been lessened at all by that morning's news; instead, he felt a bitter rage for the time he had lost. When he took off, it was with a burning determination to kill.

The Channel was massed with shipping. Troops were still being taken over, and the injured brought home. The air too was full of traffic as the bombers and fighters flocked to the coast of France and more wounded were brought back in Dakotas. And through them all, like angry wasps disturbed at their nests, buzzed the enemy aircraft, piloted by men as determined as Andrew, fighting as he was for their country and their way of life.

Off the shores of Normandy, he could see the Mulberry harbours, created by concrete caissons that had been towed across. Andrew himself had seen these being built on the South Coast of England months ago, and wondered what was going on. They had looked like huge buildings then, rearing high on the shingle of beaches like Stokes Bay and Southsea, and none of the pilots had been able to imagine what they were for. Now, looking down, he could only marvel at the vision of the men who had thought of such an idea and been able to persuade those in command to carry it out.

The beaches themselves were more crowded than they had been since the very different days of Dunkirk, exactly four years earlier. Andrew was still haunted sometimes by the vivid, sickening memory of thousands of soldiers, stranded amongst the dunes, driven to the very edge by the Germans and waiting for the little ships which were their only means of escape. He had been flying a Spitfire then and had fought desperately to prevent the strafing and bombing coming from the Luftwaffe. It was at Dunkirk that he had first understood the horror of war. Four years ago, he thought with a grinding sense of hopelessness. Four long, hellish years, and still the world seemed bent on destruction.

Death and destruction were still to be seen, down there on the beaches and in the fields, the villages and towns beyond. He could see craters where bombs had fallen, ruined vehicles, buildings ravaged by fire, some still burning. He could see the shreds of parachutes caught in trees and, once or twice, the parachutist himself, still dangling from the branches. And he could see the Army itself, making its purposeful way through the countryside, with every man equally determined to bring an end to this nightmare that had gripped the world for so long.

A voice yelled in his ear and he jerked his head round to see a Junker approaching fast from the sun. Immediately, he hauled on the joystick and the Typhoon's nose lifted like a rearing horse, so abruptly that it almost stood on its tail. He missed the German plane by a hair's breadth, passing directly above it and firing as he went, and when he looked down, he saw a ball of flame spiralling earthwards.

That's one, he thought with savage delight, and turned to search the sky for more. Alison and the children, the reason for his rage, were thrust to the back of his mind, but the fury itself remained and drove him into the attack. He forgot that he was on escort duty, with bombers to defend, and broke away from the formation to search for his own prey. For the next half-hour he hunted through the sky, firing at everything that flew, not even bothering to count his kills. He felt like a fox, let loose in a coop of chickens; nothing mattered but the frenzy of killing, nothing mattered but to leave no enemy aircraft flying, no enemy pilot alive.

There was nobody to see when he was finally shot down. Nobody to see whether he lived or died.

Three fighter pilots failed to return to Harrowbeer that afternoon: Robin Fairbanks, a Canadian by the name of Nick Petrie – and Andrew Knight.

'They still might come back,' Brian Summers said as those who had returned gathered in the mess. There was always a period when pilots who had ditched and been rescued, or forced to land somewhere else, might phone in to report. But as time went on, no telephone calls came and they knew that the three men had been lost or, at best, taken prisoner. They looked at each other and knew that someone must go and tell Alison.

'It had better be you, Stefan,' Brian said awkwardly. 'You know her pretty well, don't you?'

'We are friends, yes.' The Pole nodded slowly. 'I will go. I'll go tonight. She'll know that we're allowed out on local leave again; she'll be expecting him. We can't leave her worrying all night.'

He went back to his room and bathed and shaved. He dressed with care in his best uniform; it seemed important to treat this occasion with respect, not to go in flying jacket with open collar and crumpled shirt. Then, with a heavy heart, he walked out of the gate and along the country lane towards Milton Combe.

Alison was waiting in the front bedroom, sitting in the

window to watch the road. She knew that Andrew would be with her at the first possible moment. For quite a while, she had kept Hughie up to see his father, but as it grew later she saw his eyelids drooping and put him to bed. At any moment, she expected to hear the ring of Andrew's bicycle bell and the click of the door as he opened it. Her heart beat fast with excitement and she felt as if she were a young girl again, ready for her first date.

From her open window, she could see across the fields towards the Cornish moors. The chimneys of the old mines stood out in sharp relief against the deepening apricot glow of the setting sun, and the air seemed to echo with birdsong. The airfield was quiet and she felt as if the world were momentarily at rest. This is what it'll be like when it's all over, she thought. Quiet and peaceful, with women waiting for their men to come home from a day's work and the children fast asleep in bed, safe from all the fighting. In a few months, perhaps, this is what it will be like . . .

The sound of footsteps caught her ear and her heartbeat quickened. She could not yet see who was walking along the road, but the steps were firm, although slower than she would have expected from a man hurrying home to see his wife and child and new baby. When they stopped at the front gate, she leaned forwards to look down from the window.

It was Stefan.

As he laid his hand on the gate, he glanced up and saw her. Their eyes met and Alison felt a numbness spread over her body. She heard a roaring in her ears and felt sick and dizzy; as it cleared she found her hands clinging to the windowsill so tightly that she had almost to prise them away. She stared down at him, wanting him to smile at her, to reassure her, to tell her that Andrew was coming – he had work to do, he'd sent Stefan on ahead, anything – but his face was as frozen as hers. Dumbly, she turned away

344

from the window and went with heavy steps down the stairs to let him in.

He was at the door when she opened it. They looked wordlessly at each other and then he stepped inside and took her in his arms.

'Oh, no,' she said in a muffled voice. 'Please no . . .'

'He didn't come back,' he said, holding her close. 'Nobody saw what happened – he went off on his own after some Junkers. We were over France . . . He may be quite all right, Alison. He may be perfectly all right.'

'Over France,' she repeated dully. 'He crashed, over France.'

'Nobody knows for certain. We have to wait.' He steered her gently towards the front room and sat her on the sofa, then placed himself beside her, holding both her hands. 'We mustn't lose hope.'

'He crashed over France. Over France.'

'It's different now,' he said. 'There are thousands of Allies there. If he went down close to a camp . . . They have field hospitals – he could have been helped at once. He may not even be injured. You mustn't give up, Alison. He'll be back, I'm sure of it.'

'Yes, of course he will,' she said without conviction, and then, her eyes suddenly bright with anger: 'It's so unfair! All this time he's been safe only a mile or so away and not allowed to come and see his own baby, and the very day he *could* come, he goes down! Why? Why do these things have to happen? It's as if someone hates us, and wants us to suffer! What have we done to deserve it? What have we ever done?'

She burst into tears and he pulled her into his arms again and held her head against his chest. He could feel her slim body shaking and realised that this was the first time he had seen her since the night Caroline had been born. The cruel irony of it struck him yet again; that he was the one who had been with Andrew's wife that night, he the first to see the baby, and now here he was, comforting her at the worst moment of her life.

He sighed and rested his head against her hair, feeling its silkiness on his cheek, feeling his love for her warm his heart and body. It was a forbidden love, he knew that. He could never take advantage of it, even though he had believed once or twice that Alison was close to returning it. But always, Andrew had stood in the way. Stefan had no doubt that Alison loved her husband and would never betray him. And even now, if Andrew were indeed lost and never came home, he would still stand in the way. It would be a very long time before Alison could open her heart to another man.

He felt a sudden anger with himself for even allowing these thoughts into his mind at such a moment. They must be forgotten, thrust into some darkened recess and locked away. He must never, never allow Alison to know what he felt about her; he must be a friend to her and nothing more.

Alison's sobs subsided at last and she drew back a little, wiping her face with the handkerchief Stefan held out to her and drawing in deep, shuddering breaths. Her mouth twisted in an attempt at a smile and she said, 'I'm sorry. I've made your jacket all wet.'

'It's all right,' he said, still holding her. 'It doesn't matter about the jacket. It doesn't matter about anything else at all. I just want to be here to help you. Cry again if you want to.'

'I probably will,' she said with the ghost of a smile. 'I'll probably cry a lot. But I've got to think of the children too. He never even saw Caroline. He never even had a glimpse.'

'I know. But I'm sure he will see her, you know. I don't think Andrew will be so easy to kill. He's alive somewhere in France, I feel certain of it, and he'll come back to you. You must believe that, Alison.'

'I'll try.' She took in another breath and looked at him.

346

His heart twisted a little. In her grief, she had never looked more lovely to him; he longed to comfort her but knew that he was already doing all he dared. She asked, 'Would you like a cup of tea?'

'Yes,' he said, 'but I'll make it. And I've brought something to put in it – something to help with your shock.' He took a small bottle of brandy from his pocket and set it on the small table. 'It will do you good.'

Alison smiled faintly. 'All right. But I mustn't have too much.' She glanced at the clock. 'It's almost time for Caroline's feed.'

'Perhaps I should go.' He hesitated in the doorway. 'I'll make your tea and then leave.'

'No!' The sharpness in her voice startled them both and she gasped and then went on more quietly, 'No, please don't go. Stay with me, Stefan. I – I don't want to be alone. Not tonight.' Her eyes were enormous as she stared at him, and he hesitated again, then went back to her and laid his hands on her cheeks. For a moment, their eyes met, and then he let her go.

'I won't leave you alone,' he said in a low voice. 'I will stay, as long as you want me to.' There was another moment of silence and then he went out to the kitchen to make the tea.

Alison sat very still. She gazed out of the window at the gathering twilight. It was time to draw the curtains and turn on the lamps.

She knew she would not hear Andrew's footsteps coming down the road now. Perhaps she would never hear them again.

After sharing the tea Stefan made, Alison went upstairs to feed Caroline. The baby was asleep again by half-past ten, and she laid her in the wooden cradle and covered her up.

347

As footsteps sounded on the stairs, she turned to find the Pole standing at the door of the bedroom.

'May I see her?' he asked softly, and Alison nodded. He came to stand beside her and they stood together, looking down at the peaceful face.

'She is even more beautiful than before,' he murmured.

'I know. And the image of Andrew – that dark, curly hair, and those huge eyes. I'm sure they're going to be brown, like his. If only he could have seen her just once!'

'I know. It's all wrong that I should be the one.' He reached down and touched the baby's cheek with one fingertip. 'It's like satin. She's perfect.'

Alison moved away from the cradle. 'She'll sleep for hours now. She's such a good baby – hardly ever cries. Hughie was a monster at this age.' Her voice trembled a little. 'I'll just go and make sure he's covered up. He's such a fidget, he throws his bedclothes off all the time.'

Together, they went into the next room, where Hughie lay in a tumble of sheets and blankets, his fair skin flushed and his hair damp. Alison straightened out his bedclothes and removed the top blanket, then smoothed back the damp curls. Hughie snuffled and muttered something, then turned away, shrugging the blankets over his shoulder and burying his face in his pillow.

'Nothing wakes him now,' she observed, 'but when he was a baby we hardly dared move. I suppose they're both used to noise, with all the planes going over.' Memory washed its pain into her heart again and her mouth trembled. 'Oh, Stefan . . .'

Once again, he took her in his arms. They stood together, her head against his chest, as she struggled to control herself, then she looked up at him and said, 'You won't go, will you? You'll stay with me?'

'All night?' he asked doubtfully, and she nodded. 'Alison – you have to think about what people will say.'

'I don't care what anyone thinks, or says!' she burst out fiercely. 'I need someone with me. I need *you*. You've been such a comfort to me all these months, coming to see me in the afternoons and evenings when Andrew couldn't get home, and then being with me the night Caroline was born, and now, when I need you most. I can't be alone tonight, Stefan, I can't! Please stay.'

'Yes,' he said after a moment. 'Yes, of course I will stay. I don't have to be on the airfield until the morning. I shall watch over you.'

Chapter Thirty-Two

May was out early that morning. All night, she had listened to the aircraft coming and going, and wondered whether Andrew had managed to get home yet. Her mind was filled with sorrowing thoughts of Ben as well, wishing that he could be one of those still flying. Except that then she'd be worrying over the danger he was in . . .

As the sun rose, sending fingers of golden light slanting through her curtains, she gave up trying to sleep and slipped out of bed. She was working at the Barton this morning but didn't have to be there until eight. There was time for a walk before the rest of the family stirred.

In peacetime, she would have walked up to the common and strolled on the short, springy turf amongst the grazing sheep and Dartmoor ponies. But the airfield had spread itself over all her favourite walks, and since Ben had been lost it made her heart ache to see the clutter of buildings, the hangars, the bays and shelters and the long wire fence. Instead, she turned along the lane and walked down the long hill to Lopwell, where the River Tavy became tidal. There had been a mill here in earlier years, and May remembered the pleasure steamers that used to come up the river. They'd been good days, she thought, gazing down at the quiet waters – everyone walking down together for the Sunday School and church outings to Calstock, then coming home late in the evening, sunburned and tired, to sing their way through the darkening lanes. Would those days ever come again, or did they already belong to an era that was past? The war had changed and taken away so much; had it taken away that old way of life, for ever?

She walked back through the village, nodding to a few other people also out early, and went up the hill towards Alison's cottage. She wouldn't intrude, she told herself, but it would be nice to see if Andrew had managed to get home. However, as she came within sight of the cottage, she saw the front door open, and a tall man, wearing uniform, emerge and stand talking for a moment on the step.

May stopped. So Andrew had come home, she thought, and felt a warm surge of pleasure for her friends. She waited, not wanting to interrupt their farewell, and then a frown creased her brow.

The uniform the man was wearing was that of the Polish Air Force. It wasn't Andrew at all.

It was Stefan Dabrowski.

Before she could move, Alison came out of the door and walked down the path with the Polish airman. They stood at the gate and May, frozen with shock, saw him take Alison in his arms and kiss her. Then he strode quickly away along the road, and Alison turned and saw May.

'Oh, May,' she said, and burst into tears.

May stared at her. She could think of nothing to say. Disappointment welled up inside her, together with the bitter taste of betrayal. Not that Alison had betrayed her, exactly, but her obvious betrayal of her husband had turned all May's feelings for her upside down. She hardly knew which way to turn.

Alison held out her hands, as if begging her friend to come closer. But May felt as if her feet were nailed to the spot. She shook her head disbelievingly and found words at last.

'I don't understand. What be going on? What was that Polack doing here?'

'Don't call him that! It's a horrible word. Stefan's my friend, May. He came to – to . . .'

'I don't think I want to hear what he came for,' May said stiffly. 'He looked as though he'd been here all night.'

'He was.' Alison began to cry again. 'Oh May, the most awful thing.' She covered her face with both hands and May stared at her in bewilderment. 'It's Andrew. He's missing. May, Andrew's missing and Stefan came to tell me. They don't know what happened to him. Nobody saw him go down. They waited to see if he would phone in, but he never did.' She curled her fingers into fists against her cheeks, and then pressed them to her mouth. 'He's gone. And he never saw his baby. That's the worst part about it – *he never even saw his baby*!' The tears broke out again and this time May took three swift steps towards her and took the other girl in her arms. She felt Alison's body shaking against her and cursed herself for the thoughts she had harboured. Even if she'd thought a few times that the Pole was getting too friendly, it was obvious that Alison felt no more than friendship for him. It was Andrew she loved, and now she had lost him, just as May had lost Ben.

'Oh, you poor love,' May said, holding her close. 'You poor, poor love.' She drew her back through the gate and along the path to the door. 'Come back inside now and tell me all about it. I'll make you a nice cup of tea.' Crooning and murmuring, she led her friend into the front room and sat her down on the sofa. There were some blankets and a pillow there, as if someone had spent the night on it, and once again she felt ashamed of her thoughts. She pushed the blankets aside and then, on second thoughts, wrapped one round Alison's shivering body.

'I've just had some tea,' Alison said dolefully. 'Stefan made it. I feel as if I've been drinking tea all night. He came to tell me yesterday evening. I thought, when I heard him arrive, that it was Andrew. But as soon as I saw him, I knew.' She raised anguished eyes to May's face. 'He's gone, May! He always said he'd never have another crash, but I was always afraid he would, and I knew that if he did, he wouldn't – wouldn't – sur-survive.' The words hiccoughed painfully out of her and she began to gasp as if she were losing her breath. 'May! I can't – I can't – I can't breathe!'

'It's all right.' May took her flailing hands and held them tightly. 'It's all right, flower. Just try to breathe slowly, one breath at a time. That's it – that's lovely. Now another one. Slowly, now, there's no rush. There, that's better. Lean against me. Let yourself go soft. Now just breathe gently, that's all you've got to do. There.'

Gradually, Alison relaxed and her breathing became easier. The tears still flowed down her cheeks but the terrible, painful sobbing had ceased and after a few more minutes May laid her gently back against the pillows and wrapped the blanket more closely about her. As she drew away, she saw that Alison's eyes were closing.

Tired out, poor soul, she thought compassionately. I dare say she didn't sleep at all last night, and she'd have had to be feeding the baby as well. Us'll have to be careful she don't lose her milk. Well, she can sleep now for a bit. I'll get Hughie up and give him his breakfast in the garden, he'll like that, and there'll be no need to disturb her until the baby wakes up. She should get another hour or so, at least. And I'll run down to the phone box and let them know at the Barton. I can't leave her by herself today.

She crept out of the room, closing the door softly behind her, and went quietly up the stairs. But before she went into Hughie's room, she stood for a moment on the landing, looking out of the window and trying to take in the news she had just been given.

Andrew Knight, gone. And Alison, like so many other

young women, a widow. It was enough to break your heart – if it hadn't been broken already.

Andrew's Group Captain came to see Alison later that day. They sat in the garden, where Hughie was playing on the scrap of lawn old Mr Prettyjohn had left when he had dug it over for vegetables. The lettuces were growing well, and the young tomatoes were neatly tied against twigs gathered from the hedges. Beetroot and radishes were showing leaf, and there was a patch of fresh earth where Alison had dug out some new potatoes only yesterday. She'd been going to cook them for Andrew's supper.

Alison's tears had dried now and she felt a strange, icy calm as she sat in the old garden chair watching the officer's face. She knew that when he was gone she would probably weep again, but for now she was determined to maintain her dignity. Tears were only for friends to see, and then only at the very worst moments.

'I can't tell you how sorry I am,' Group Captain Stanton said. 'Andrew was a fine pilot and an excellent Squadron Leader. He'll be very much missed. But we mustn't give up hope. I'm sure Dabrowski told you that nobody actually saw him go down. We don't know that he was killed. He may well have escaped – it's not unknown, not unknown at all. And if he did . . .'

'If he did,' Alison said tonelessly, 'the Germans will probably catch him. And they'll kill him.'

'Not at all. They're far more likely to take him prisoner.'

'Do you really think so?' she demanded with sudden vigour. 'I've heard the stories – parachutists shot as they come down, pilots killed in their burning aircraft, or just left there, struggling to get out. And suppose he was injured again? Are they really going to treat him properly, with our soldiers driving them back? Are they really going to give him a bed in one of their field hospitals, when they must have hundreds of their own men wounded? And even if they do, we'll probably bomb it,' she added forlornly. 'It would be better for Andrew if he *were* killed when the plane went down.'

'My dear,' Stanton said helplessly, 'you mustn't talk like this. You mustn't even think it. We must always keep up hope.'

'I know.' The baby, asleep nearby, stirred and whimpered, and Alison leaned over to rock the cradle. 'I'm sorry to behave like this,' she said. 'It's just that I do know what happens. And I know how unhappy Andrew was in the past few weeks.' She lifted her eyes to his. 'He never saw his baby, Group Captain Stanton. She's almost a month old and he never saw her. It was cruel, doing that to him.'

'There was nothing we could do about it. Orders—'

'Oh, I know all about *orders*!' she exclaimed. 'My father was a Colonel in the Army. He served in the First World War. I grew up knowing about *orders*.' She stood up and lifted the baby into her arms. 'There – isn't she beautiful? Our little Caroline. At least I shall have photographs of her daddy to show her as she grows up. And now she's due for her feed, so . . .'

'Yes, of course.' The man got to his feet and stood awkwardly for a moment. 'I really am sorry, Mrs Knight. And I'm afraid there will be a few formalities, once we're certain . . . But as I say, there's no certainty at all at the moment, and I myself feel sure that Andrew will come back. People do, under the most extraordinary circumstances.'

'I know. Through Spain. I've even met one or two.' She settled the baby securely in the crook of her left arm and held out her right hand. 'Thank you for coming, Group Captain. It was kind of you to take the trouble.'

He bowed his head and left. Alison stood for a few more minutes holding her baby against her, looking down at the face that was so like Andrew's, with the furrowed brow of babyhood beneath the black curls. As she gazed down, the blue-tinged eyelids lifted and Andrew's eyes seemed to stare back at her, almost as if they were trying to tell her something.

'What is it, my sweetheart?' she whispered. 'What is it you want to say to me? What is it that you know?' And then, feeling even more strongly that it was Andrew himself who was trying to speak to her: 'Where are you now, my darling? What happened to you?'

But there was no reply. The eyes squeezed tightly shut and Caroline opened her mouth instead and began to cry, and the moment that had seemed almost like a strange, brief flash of communication had passed.

Feeling more alone than she had ever felt in her life, Alison sat down to give the baby her feed.

Chapter Thirty-Three

The roses that Olivia had insisted on keeping, when the rest of the garden was dug over for vegetables, were at their best as John Hazelwood took the path that led to the church. The apple tree was covered in tiny fruits and had begun to drop them on the patch of grass where Hope had been born, and the path was bordered by lavender and rosemary which brushed against the skirt of his cassock and sent their aroma into the soft morning air. He felt the sun on his bare head and looked up into a blue sky with just a few small clouds hovering anxiously around the edges, and wished that the world were really as peaceful as it seemed at this moment.

He had written to May Prettyjohn three days ago, pouring out his sympathy and compassion for her in their shared loss. Trying his hardest to see her as the girl Ben had loved, a girl who would have shared his and Olivia's lives as well as Ben's and would have been the mother of his grandchildren, he had known a deep feeling of shame that it had taken Jeanie to show him the way. As he posted the letter, he couldn't help wondering if he would ever hear from her again. Perhaps, having lost Ben, she would think his family had no more interest in her; perhaps she would read the letter he had written and then simply throw it away.

Well, it was done. And he needed to tell Olivia about it.

He opened the door to the church and stood for a moment letting his eyes get used to the shadowy dimness and the cool air on his face. A shaft of coloured light streamed through the east window and flung its rainbow pattern on the stone floor, and a vase of white roses glowed on the altar. Their scent wafted through the little church and as he breathed it in, he realised that there was someone else already here. A bowed figure, sitting in the front pew, hunched as if in prayer.

John stepped back, not wishing to disturb the person, and made his way quietly round the side of the church towards the vestry. As he came level with the front pew he glanced sideways, wondering who it was who had come so early to pray and, to his astonishment, saw that it was his wife.

He stopped abruptly, half-inclined to go to her, and then reminded himself that she was as entitled as anyone else to worship privately and undisturbed. But as he started forward again, she raised her head and their eyes met.

'Olivia,' he said quietly, and she got up and came towards him. 'Olivia, what are you doing here?'

'What *should* I be doing in a church?' she asked, and he shook his head a little, feeling bemused.

'It's just that you haven't been here for so long. I was surprised – but very pleased, my dear.' He took her hand. 'I hope this means that you're feeling better.'

'I don't know,' she said. 'I don't know if I'll ever feel better. Perhaps I feel different, though. Changed in some way.' She sat down again and he took his place beside her, looking into her face. Her eyes were fixed on the coloured window above the altar and some of its light fell on her cheeks, touching them with iridescence. Her grey eyes were steadier than he had seen them for some time, and her lips firmer. He felt a sense of relief, yet reminded himself that her sadness must still be there. Nothing could change the fact of their loss of two sons.

'How do you feel changed?' he asked gently.

'I don't know, quite. As if I've come out of a thick fog,

perhaps. There are still misty patches but I'm beginning to see again.' She turned to him. 'You've changed, too. I can feel it. Something's happened in the past few days and you're different. And that's made me different too.'

He stared at her in shock. '*I've* made you change?'

'It's not quite like that,' she said, 'but we've always been so close, haven't we? Our feelings have always been shared in some way. Do you remember when I was expecting the children, and you were the one who was sick in the mornings? And how you felt my labour pains? I think it's been the same now. We've been feeling each other's pain. As long as neither of us could break free of it, the other one was trapped as well. But in the past few days, I've felt almost as though a knot has been untied inside me. And I know it's partly to do with you – your face is different. A few wrinkles have been smoothed out.' She shrugged a little and looked up at the brilliant colours of the window again. 'Or maybe I'm finding my way back to my faith, as you said I would.'

'I hope you are,' he said, and leaned forward to kiss her cheek. 'And you're right – something has changed.' He paused, weighing it up in his mind. Once he had told her, there would be no going back; they would have to discuss the whole thing. And he didn't know if Olivia were yet strong enough. Then he saw her face and knew that he had already gone too far to draw back. He took a deep breath and said quietly, 'I wrote to May Prettyjohn.'

There was a brief silence. She looked away from him, towards the altar and its gleaming vase of roses. She lifted her chin a little and stared up at the stained glass of the window with its image of Jesus with a small white lamb carried over His shoulder. Then she turned back.

'The girl Ben told us about?'

'Yes. She wrote to me, you know. I didn't show you the letter – I didn't wish to upset you. She wanted us to know that she was thinking of us, and to tell us how upset she was. And there was something else.'

Olivia prompted him to go on. 'What else, John? What did you think might upset me so much?'

'She told me they were engaged,' he said. 'Ben asked her father the night before he was killed. They were going to buy the ring the next day.'

In the dim light, he could see the colour drain from her face. She swayed a little and he tightened his arm around her. 'Engaged!' she breathed.

'Yes. They weren't going to get married yet, though. Not until you were happy about it. She made that very clear. They wanted everyone to know that they planned to marry, that they belonged to each other, but that was all. They were going to wait for you – for us.'

'And suppose I never agreed?' she asked. 'Would they have waited for ever?'

'I think, in time, you would have come round,' he said gently. 'You've always wanted our children to be happy. And perhaps once we'd met her . . .'

Olivia interrupted him. 'There wasn't any reason why they *should* have married, was there, John? They hadn't done anything foolish?'

'I'm sure they hadn't. And the girl isn't in any kind of trouble, I'm convinced of that. Just sorrowing and grieving, and wanting to share it with us. She seems a very nice girl, Olivia. And Ben loved her.'

His wife sat silently for a while, then she said, 'I always hoped that he and Jeanie . . .'

'I know, my dear. And I think Jeanie hoped that a little, too. But there's a wise head on those young shoulders. She made me realise that I was wrong not to write back to May, and—'

'*Jeanie* did? You talked about it with Jeanie?'

'She came to me. She confessed that she'd come across

May's letter in my cassock pocket, when she was mending the hem, and had read it. She offered to write back herself, or even go to see her once the travel restrictions were lifted. I knew then that I had no choice. We can't ignore this poor girl, my dear. She would have been our daughter-in-law. She would have been mother to Ben's children. We can't pretend that she doesn't exist.'

'No, we can't.' Olivia was quiet again, then she said, 'I'd like to be on my own again for a while now, John, if you don't mind. I hadn't quite finished what I was doing here.'

He paused, his hand on her shoulder, then got slowly to his feet. He had no idea now why he had come to the church; perhaps it was simply to ask for guidance for himself. In any case, he had found far more than he had been searching for, and his heart swelled with gratitude and relief. After a moment, he turned and walked slowly out of the church, leaving his wife with her head bowed again in the darkness.

Outside, the brightness and the heat came almost as a shock. He stood for a moment or two feeling the warmth of the sunshine on his face, and then he went back to the house.

When the letter arrived at the Prettyjohns' cottage, May took it out into the garden to read.

She didn't open it at once. She sat on the old bench her grandfather had made, hidden from the house by the raspberry canes, and turned it over and over between her fingers. It was in a white envelope and felt thick and bulky, as if it contained several sheets of paper. She knew that it must be from John Hazelwood, although she hadn't expected to hear from him again. She felt half afraid to open it, sure that once she had done so, her life would change in some way, with no going back.

361

You'm being daft, May Prettyjohn, she admonished herself, and put her thumb under the corner of the flap.

Half an hour later, she came back into the cottage. Her mother, who was sitting at the kitchen table polishing the brass candlesticks that she'd inherited from her grand-mother, glanced at her.

'Be you all right, maid? You look upset.'

'I'm all right.' May sat down on the wide windowsill and leaned her head against the thick wall. 'I've had a letter from Ben's father.'

'Ah. I thought that might be it. And what do he have to say, my flower?'

'Oh, he's been very nice. He says he's glad that Ben was happy during his last few weeks and that he'd found someone to love and who loved him as much as I did.' May's voice shook a little and a tear crept down her cheek. 'He says he's sorry he didn't answer properly when I wrote to him, but he was worried about Ben's mother. I knew that, of course. Ben told me all about her and I didn't want to upset the poor lady any more than she had been already. But now Mr Hazelwood says that he felt he had to write. He says it was wrong of him not to do it before.' She shook her head a little wonderingly. 'He'm a vicar, Mother, and he says he was wrong! And he says that the girl they've got living there, the one Ben told us about – Jeanie – she wanted to write to me herself. He's put a note in from her.' She took a separate sheet of paper from the envelope and looked down at it. 'It's a nice little note, too. I think I'd like Jeanie.'

Her face crumpled and the tears began to flow in earnest. Mabel Prettyjohn left her polishing, wiped her hands on a damp rag, and came over to put her arms around her daughter.

'There, there, my pretty. You have your cry now, it'll do you good. Let it out, let it out.' Gently, she removed the letter from May's fingers, where tears were already beginning to blur the ink, and laid it on the table.

'I shouldn't keep on like this,' May sobbed, trying to stem the flow. 'It's weeks now – I should be getting over it. I keep trying to pull myself together, but every now and then it all comes over me again. And when I read this letter . . . It's such a nice letter, Mother. And I shan't ever know them now, not properly, like I would have if Ben – if Ben . . .'

Mabel patted her shoulder and rocked her in her arms. 'And it hasn't helped, knowing that Alison's lost her man as well, has it? Made it all the worse.'

'There's been so many of them,' she wept. 'Ever since the airfield opened. So many pilots have come to Harrowbeer and been killed, and they'm all so young, too. Just boys.'

'I know. It's war. 'Tis always the same in war.'

'Well, why can't they stop it?' she cried with sudden anger. 'Why can't they find another way to sort out their arguments? 'Tis nothing to do with us ordinary people – none of us wanted it. They didn't ask us if us wanted to go to war, they just *told* us. But we'm the ones getting killed, not they politicians. It's us – people like Ben and his brother, and Andrew, and all they other brave men. It isn't fair!'

'Life isn't fair whoever you are,' came William's voice from the other room. 'You don't have to be at war to know that.'

The two women looked at each other and May wiped her face and went through the door to where her father sat propped in his chair, his useless legs on a stool in front of him. 'I'm sorry, Father,' she said quietly. 'You'm right. I should be ashamed.'

'No, maid, there's no need for that. I didn't mean you to take it that way. I just wanted to say that it don't matter who or what you are, you can't expect things to go the way you want them. Sometimes they do, and sometimes they don't, and all us can do is carry on as best us can. You have your cry out, maid, like your mother says, but after that you just got to pick yourself up and get on with things. There's no other way.'

'I know.' She sat on the edge of the bed, now in its daytime guise of sofa, and took his hand. 'I know, and I'm trying. It was just getting this letter that started me off again. It's so nice. And it all seems so sad. Such a waste.'

'Ah, I won't argue with that, maid.' He patted her hand. 'All I can say is, 'tis not for us to fathom why things are as they are. Nobody's ever worked that out, as far as I can see. All us can do is keep smiling.'

'Yes,' she said, 'you're right.' And proved it by giving him a tremulous and still slightly tearful smile. 'I'll go and help Mother with the dinner. We'm having pasties and I promised to make the pastry.'

She went back to the kitchen and picked up her letter. Later on, she would take it up to her bedroom and, perhaps, read it again. After that, she would put it away in her little box of treasures, with the snap Ben had given her of himself standing on the wing of his aeroplane.

She didn't think she was likely to hear from the Hazelwoods again.

'I suppose you'll go back to Lincolnshire,' Stefan said. He was in his usual chair, a cup of tea beside him and Hughie on the rug at his feet. Apart from Caroline, asleep in her cradle, it was as if nothing had changed since those winter afternoons when he had called to talk to her about his life in Poland. Yet everything had changed. Nothing would be the same again.

Alison stirred. The fine weather had disappeared and the thick, misty drizzle that so often hung around the high ground of Harrowbeer was falling outside. It was too warm and muggy to light a fire, yet the brightness of a few flames would have cheered the dismal afternoon. It wouldn't have warmed her heart though, she thought sadly. There was a chill there now that would never thaw.

'Not yet,' she answered. 'I couldn't let Andrew come back and find me not here.'

Her mother had written to her as soon as Alison had let her know that Andrew was missing, begging her to come home if only for a week or two. She would come to Devon as soon as she could, she said, but for now wouldn't it be better for Alison to be at home, where there were plenty of people to look after her and the children? But Alison had made the same reply: she could not leave Harrowbeer until she knew for certain what had happened. She could not let Andrew come home – as she still prayed he would – to an empty house.

The Group Captain had come to see her again after that first day and they had discussed all the possibilities. Men had been apparently lost before and then returned. Some had managed to get back from France, brought across the Channel at great risk by fishermen and landed on some dark, lonely beach. But the beaches were now mined, wired off and guarded, and anyone landing along the south coast would risk being blown up or shot.

There were other ways of getting back. If you could reach a safe house, you might be passed along, like a particularly dangerous parcel, until you reached Spain where you would be out of the reach of the Germans and could be brought more safely across the Channel. Alison herself had known two men who had returned this way. One had told her how, with several other men, he had been hidden for three weeks in the home of a notary in Marseilles, not allowed to look out of the windows in case he might be seen, not allowed to flush the lavatory in case he might be heard. Eventually, he had been taken to another house, and then another, and then on a long trudge across the Pyrenees and into Spain. When he finally reached England, he was given a few days' leave and then returned to duty.

'You believe he will come back,' Stefan said, half in question, half statement, and she nodded.

'I have to.' *Until we know for certain, we must never give up*, the Group Captain had told her. 'It may sound silly, but I feel that as long as I keep my hope alive, I might somehow help to keep Andrew alive too. If I let it go, I'll be taking away whatever chance he might have.'

Stefan glanced down at Hughie and rested his hand on the fair hair. 'I know just what you mean,' he said quietly. 'I, too, must keep on hoping for my own family. But it's very hard, when you know all too well what might be happening.' There was a moment's silence, then he said more strongly, 'But for Andrew, I believe there is much hope. Nobody saw him go down. And if he did die, it would have been as a hero. He has been a great flyer, Alison. You will always be able to tell your children that, whatever happens.'

They were silent for a few minutes and then she asked, 'What will you do when it's all over, Stefan? Will you go back to Poland? Some of the others have been saying they'd rather stay here.'

'Who knows? Some are afraid to go back, for fear of what they may find. And if the Russians have control – well, we know them of old. They are no better masters than the Germans. If we could bring our families here – if we still have families . . .' He paused, his face shuttered. 'And then there are those who have found a different life in this country. Those who have married, or want to marry English girls. I don't think they will want to take their wives to Poland, not as it must be now.'

'What would you do?' she asked. 'You're a musician. Will there be any orchestras?'

He gave a short laugh. 'Oh, I think my music will now be for my pleasure alone. The world will have other things to consider as it sets itself to rights after the catastrophes of the past five years. We will all find ourselves living very different lives from those we expected to live. This war has changed everything.' He looked at his hands, at the long, sensitive fingers. 'I shall probably find myself laying bricks to help rebuild this poor broken world, but whether that will be here or in Poland, or in some quite different country, I have no idea.'

'Oh, Stefan,' she said, looking down at the castle Hughie was building. 'It's all so sad.'

He nodded. 'But I know that you say every cloud has a silver lining. If it had not been for this war, I would never have come to this place.' He hesitated. 'I would never have met you.'

Startled, she looked up and met his eyes. They were very dark, with just a rim of pale, glittering silver. She felt her heart twist a little and then she looked away.

'Play the piano for me,' she said. 'Play something strong and powerful, something that makes me think about winning wars. Something that will make me feel that it will all come out right in the end, and Andrew will come back, and you can go home to Poland and find your family again.'

He got up and went to the piano. Lifting its lid, he sat down and let his fingers stray over the keys. Hughie scrambled to his feet and went to stand beside him, watching his hands intently. Then the music began.

As the notes of Rachmaninov's Piano Concerto No. 4 filled the room, she lay back in her chair and thought of Andrew, soaring high in his plane; and seemed to see, through his eyes, the destruction that lay below.

Chapter Thirty-Four

By the middle of June, London and the south-east of England were under attack once more and people were having to take to the air-raid shelters they had thought would no longer be needed. The flying bomb had arrived.

The first few had been mentioned briefly in the news as 'gas explosions'. But as more and more occurred, it was impossible to dismiss them and soon everyone knew about the stubby-winged pilotless 'aircraft' that had been seen flying from the direction of Calais.

'They say you can tell the sound of their engine from any other sort of plane,' May said when she came to clean through for Alison one morning. 'But it's when the engine stops that you need to take cover. They just come straight down then, and if you're underneath you don't stand a chance. And they're big, too – big bombs, I mean.'

'I know,' Alison shivered. 'One of the pilots told me they carry a ton of explosive. And they've got a new sort of engine, too. That's why it sounds different – he called it a buzz-bomb.'

'Well, they can buzz off as soon as they like,' May said, polishing the piano. 'I thought we were doing all right, what with the Invasion and everything, but now we'm right back to the Blitz. I tell you what, I sometimes wonder if it'll ever be over.'

She went out to the wash-house at the back of the kitchen, where Caroline's nappies were boiling in the old copper. With a pair of large wooden tongs, she fished them out and dumped them in an enamel pail to take back to the kitchen and rinse, dropping another pile in to take their turn. By the time they were all done, there was a row of snowy nappies fluttering on the washing line, and Alison called her in for a cup of tea.

'It's time we had a break,' she said. While May had been washing and cleaning, she had been baking rock cakes and preparing vegetables for her and Hughie's dinner. 'When we've had this, I'll walk back with you. I've got a book for your father.'

'Oh, he'll be pleased with that. He was saying last night he didn't have nothing to read. He liked that last one you brought him from the library.'

They walked along the road, pushing Caroline in her pram while Hughie stumped alongside. Bob Derry's taxi passed them, with two people inside, and they stood back against the hedge as it went by. To their surprise, it stopped at the gate of the Prettyjohns' cottage.

'Whoever can that be?' May asked. 'Us don't know many people rich enough to pay for taxis.'

She quickened her steps as the car doors opened and the strangers got out. Bob Derry got out too and they stood talking for a moment while he was paid; then he drove back towards the airfield, giving May and Alison a cheerful wave as he went. The man and woman turned to greet them.

'Good morning,' the man said. 'You must be May Prettyjohn.' He came forward, holding out both hands, and May took them uncertainly. 'I'm so glad to see you, my dear. My name's John Hazelwood. And this,' he indicated the tall, silver-haired woman standing at his side, 'is my wife Olivia. We're Ben's mother and father.'

May stared from one to the other. Her skin felt suddenly cold.

'Ben's mother and father? But – I don't understand. I didn't know you were coming. You didn't say . . .'

'I know,' he said quietly. 'It was all rather sudden, you see. We decided we must come and tell you in person, and—'

'Tell me what?' she broke in, and tore one hand away to put it to her cheek. 'What's happened? Why have you come?'

Olivia stepped forward. She laid her hand on May's arm and spoke in a quiet, steady voice.

'My dear, we've had news of Ben.' Her voice shook suddenly. 'He's coming home. He's all right. May, Ben's all right.' Her voice broke and tears began to stream down her cheeks.

John Hazelwood let go of May's other hand and put his arm round his wife's shoulders. His own mouth trembled in the depths of his beard, but there was joy in his eyes. He looked from May to Alison and then to Mabel and old Mr Prettyjohn, who had come to the cottage door, and nodded his head.

'It's true. We've heard from the War Department. He's back in England already. He was hurt when his plane went down in France and a local farmer found him and took him in. They kept him at the farmhouse and the local doctor attended him. He had a broken leg – the man set it well enough, from what we can gather – but they couldn't move him for some weeks. Then they brought him through Spain and now he's in hospital in Cornwall. We're on our way to see him.' He looked at May with kind eyes. 'We couldn't go without telling you.'

'Ben,' she whispered. 'Ben's alive? He's in Cornwall.' She turned and stared across the fields to the hills over the valley.

'You can come with us, if you like,' Olivia told her. 'Mr Derry's coming back to collect us in an hour.' Tears slipped down her cheeks but her eyes remained steady. 'We want you to come with us.'

Alison glanced towards Mabel Prettyjohn, who stepped forward and held out her hand.

'Come you indoors,' she said in her warm voice, as rich as Devonshire cream. The kettle's boiling and I reckon us could all do with a cup of tea. There's fresh bread out of the oven, and some good home-made butter and a bit of cheese to go with it, if you've got the fancy. I dare say you've had hardly a bite past your lips since morning, if you've been on the train.' She glanced at Alison. 'You too, maid. There's plenty to go round.'

Alison glanced at the Hazelwoods. 'Thank you, Mrs Prettyjohn, but I think I ought to go home. This is your family business.'

'And aren't you one of the family then, as good as?' She looked at the Hazelwoods. 'This is Squadron Leader Knight's wife, Alison. She knows your Ben well.'

'He used to come to our house quite a lot,' Alison explained. 'But I really think I will go, all the same. I'll just leave this book for your father, May – you can drop the other one in at any time. And – and let me know if you go to see Ben. I'd like to send him my love.' She turned away quickly and set off back along the lane, with Hughie trudging beside the pram. The others looked after her and Mabel clucked her tongue in self-reproach.

'There, if that wasn't proper thoughtless of me. Her own hubby's been missing this past week or more,' she told the Hazelwoods. 'And the babby not six weeks old – never saw the little mite, he didn't. Poor Alison, she's been a brave little maid, but it's hard for her, and it don't matter how pleased you might be to hear of someone else's good fortune, you'm still going to wish 'twas yours.' She urged them along the path to where old Mr Prettyjohn waited, leaning on his stick. 'Well, there's nothing we can do about that; 'tis you and young Ben we must be thinking of. And May, here. 'Tis wonderful news for her.'

The girl was still standing at the gate, her hand resting on the top bar as she stared across the valley. Her face was as ashen as if she had received bad news rather than good, and her cheeks were wet.

'I can't seem to believe it,' she whispered. 'I can't seem to take it in. Ben, still alive, down there in Cornwall. I thought he was dead. I thought I was never going to see him again . . .'

'I'd already begun to realise how wrong I was,' Olivia told them as they ate their simple lunch. 'I seemed to have lost everything – my two sons, my faith, even my reason. And all I could think of was that I'd sent Ben away unhappy. He'd come to us to tell us he'd found you,' she looked at May, 'and we sent him away. *I* sent him away.'

'He understood,' May said quickly. 'He knew how unhappy you were. He didn't want to hurt you.'

'I know. But that made it all the harder, somehow. He – a boy of twenty – understood *me*, but I wasn't prepared to understand him. What sort of a mother was I? I had so much guilt to live with. I felt so far away from everything I'd grown up with – my faith, my family, even my husband. I felt as if I were drowning.'

'Oh, my dear,' John said quietly. 'I don't think I ever realised just how bad it was.'

'I didn't want you to. I don't think I knew it myself. But that morning, I suddenly felt as if I needed to go back to the church. I hadn't set foot inside it for so long.' She touched her husband's hand and he turned it over and gripped her fingers. 'It wasn't easy. It was almost like stepping off a cliff over a deep sea. But as soon as I walked through the door, I knew it was the right thing to do. And then, as I sat there trying to find my way back, trying to make my peace, John came in and told me that he had written to you.' She looked at May again. 'He told me that he'd heard from you, and that you'd told him you were engaged the night before Ben was lost.'

'We wouldn't have got married without—'

'I know. But that doesn't matter, not now. What mattered to me most was that my son had been happy. For that last evening, those last few hours, he was happy. I knew then that we must come and see you.'

'But you didn't know he was all right.'

'Not then, no. That news came a few days later. That's why we're able to travel, you see – we can go down to Cornwall to see him. And you can come too.' She withdrew her hand from John's and held it across the table to May. 'Will you come, my dear? Will you come with us and see Ben?'

'Oh, Mrs Hazelwood,' May said, half laughing and half crying. 'How can you even ask?'

They went as soon as their meal was over. Nobody had eaten much, so Mabel made sandwiches with the leftover bread and cheese, and wrapped them in greaseproof paper. She was anxious about their journey until the Hazelwoods told her that they could catch the Plymouth train in Yelverton and then change for Penzance. The hospital Ben had been taken to was in Falmouth, and they would be able to put up for the night in a hotel there. They would take a room for May as well, and waved away any offers to pay for her.

'It's our invitation,' John said firmly, 'and besides, Ben would never forgive us if we didn't do this.'

It seemed to May incredible to be talking about Ben in this way again. Incredible that he was in England, less than a hundred miles away. Incredible that in a few hours she would be with him, talking to him, able to look at him and

373

touch him again. And not much less incredible that his parents were here, that so much had changed in the space of just a few hours.

She ran upstairs to pack a few things for the night. In a short while, Bob Derry would be back to take them to the station in Yelverton. She remembered that she was supposed to have gone to work that morning, and that someone would have to let her employers know what had happened. They would understand, she knew. And there was Alison, too – Alison, walking home alone to face a bleak future without her husband. Perhaps he'll come back too, May thought with sudden hope. It would be so wonderful if Alison could know the same joy as she herself was feeling at this moment.

She paused with her hand on the lid of the little suitcase – the only one the family possessed, bought when her father was in hospital after his accident. Yes, it *would* be wonderful if Andrew were to come home, but she knew that it wasn't very likely. And somehow, now that Ben had returned, it seemed even less likely.

You couldn't have two happy endings.

Chapter Thirty-Five

'So May's gone down to Falmouth with Ben's mother and father,' Alison told Stefan. 'It's wonderful, isn't it? A fairy-tale ending.'

'Truly, a fairy-tale ending,' he said soberly, and met her eyes.

'I'm very happy for them,' she said. 'I really am.' Her voice shook a little but she went on determinedly, 'How could I not be?'

'Of course you are. I would not expect anything else. But it's hard for you. Very hard.'

'I can still hope,' she said, though her tone was forlorn. 'Nothing's changed about that. I've still got just as much hope as I had before.' She looked away from him, out into the garden. Hughie was in bed and Caroline in her cradle. It was late in the evening but twilight had only just began to fall and the air was still alive with the sound of birds. Swallows swooped high and low between the trees, swifts screamed thinly high above; martins twittered at their nests tucked beneath the eaves, and a blackbird sat on top of the washing-line pole, his lungs almost bursting with the force of his song. 'Andrew's alive somewhere, I know it. After all, if Ben can come home, so long after everyone had given him up for lost, why not Andrew as well? They're not the only ones. Others have done it. Some have taken weeks, months, to get through France and find a safe way to

Spain.' She turned and looked at him, her eyes huge. 'I've got to believe it.'

He nodded slowly. 'Yes. Of course you have.' He looked down at his hands, linked loosely together and hanging between his knees. He seemed about to say something else, and then to change his mind. The silence grew, seeming to envelop them both, and Alison watched him uneasily, half-afraid of what he might say when he did bring himself to speak.

'You've been such a help to me, Stefan,' she said. 'All those weeks when Andrew was so busy, and now since he's been missing . . . I don't know what I would have done without you. I was already so upset that he'd never been able to see Caroline and then, when you came to tell me he was lost . . . I don't think I managed very well, but I'd have been much worse without you to help me.'

'Nobody could have been braver,' he said. 'I just wanted to be here, to do whatever I could to help.'

An aircraft passed overhead. It was a rare night off for Stefan and he had come early, stayed for supper and was now sitting back in the armchair. Alison was on the sofa and the last rays of the evening sun were casting a warm golden light into the room. The war was still being fought all over the world but the Germans were being pushed through Italy, and the Red Army, thrusting its way through Lithuania, was advancing on Warsaw. It seemed that, at last, the Allies were driving the enemy back on all fronts.

Stefan was following the news about Warsaw with great interest. 'If there's a chance of liberation, the Poles will rise up,' he told Alison. 'I'm afraid there will be much more bloodshed before this is over, but we won't be beaten.'

There was great excitement too over the Gloster Meteor, a new aircraft which was powered by turbo-jet. Alison had seen one, flying over Harrowbeer; it had streaked across the sky so fast that she barely had time to catch a glimpse of it, and the sound of its engines seemed to follow it, so that when you heard the noise and looked at the sky, the plane had already passed.

'Of course, the Germans have one, too,' Stefan said, when she spoke of it. 'The Me262. But at least we can fight them on equal terms still.'

'We don't have the flying bombs though,' Alison observed. 'There's still such a long way to go before it's all over.' She paused, then added, 'And when it is, you'll go away. Whether you go back to Poland or stay in England, you'll move away from here.'

'Perhaps,' he said, looking at her. 'Perhaps not. Who knows what any of us will do? It's going to take a long time before life returns to the way it used to be. If it ever does.'

'No,' she said. 'It never will. Things have changed too much.' The garden was filled with shadows now and the birds were finally falling silent. 'I still believe that Andrew will come back,' she said at last, 'but I know I will have to make plans as though he won't. I've got two children to think of. I suppose, if the war ends and he doesn't come home, I'll go back to Lincolnshire. And yet – I'll be so sorry to leave this place.' She thought of the first day she had come to Harrowbeer and stepped out of the Morris 8 to gaze out over the rolling moorland. 'It was so exciting to see hills and valleys. I wanted to explore it. I wanted to go walking and cycling all over the whole of Dartmoor – to go down to the beach, to the little coves and bays. None of that has happened, yet I've fallen in love with the place and I don't want to leave it. I'd like to stay here for ever.' She turned back to him and smiled a little. 'That must be difficult for you to understand. You've always longed to go home, to Poland.'

Stefan's face was in half-darkness now and she could not read his expression. But there was a strange tone in his voice as he answered her.

'I have longed to go home, but mostly I long to see my family again. As to staying there – I'm not so sure. You see, I've fallen in love as well. And I don't want to leave, either.'

'It was so lovely to see him again,' May said when she came to have a cup of tea with Alison a few days later. 'I just couldn't believe it was true. I wanted to keep touching him to make sure it wasn't a dream. I even asked Mr Hazelwood to pinch me once!'

Alison laughed. 'And did he?'

'No, but he patted my hand and said he felt the same way. And none of us knew whether to laugh or cry, so we did a bit of both. And then, do you know what Ben's mother and father did? They went out and left me by myself with him. I thought that was so kind of them. In fact, it was kind of them to take me with them at all, and pay my fare and for my room and everything. They'm lovely people, Alison.'

'I thought that too.' Alison had met them again when they brought May back to Milton Combe. They had insisted on taking the whole family and herself out for dinner to the Rock Hotel, where they were staying overnight. Even William had gone along, carried in through a back door and settled in   chair. It was the first time he had been out   since his accident but he was determined th   ot be the last.

'I like being in the pub ag   remarked as the sixth person to spot him left the table after coming over to talk. 'I'll be getting old Bob Derry to bring me over a few more times. Or I could roll down the hill to the Who'd Have Thought It!'

'Just when I thought I'd got him where I could keep my eye on him, too,' Mabel said resignedly, and they all laughed.

It had been a happy evening, and Alison had determinedly thrust away all her anxieties about Andrew in order to enjoy it with them. May's face had been alight with joy, and it was clear that the Hazelwoods had taken her to their hearts. They had invited her to go and stay with them when Ben was released from hospital, which would be quite soon; the RAF doctor at St Mawgan, the station near Newquay, had examined him and pronounced him fit to be sent home on convalescent leave as soon as the plaster was off his leg. He would be back on active service as quickly as possible, but it was decided now that they would be married before that.

'Where's the wedding going to be?' Alison asked now. 'At Ashford, in their own church?'

May shook her head. ''Tis going to be here in Milton Combe, because of Father, mostly. He might have big ideas about going to the pub, but he'll never be able to travel all that way. And there's only Ben's sister who can come anyway, with his other brother still in Italy.' She gave Alison a shy glance. 'You'll be coming, of course?'

'I'd love to. Are you having bridesmaids?'

'My cousin's little girl, it'll be a treat for her and there's an old party frock of mine will do for a pretty dress for her. Mother's going to put some frills and ribbons on it, and we'll have plenty of flowers for bouquets. And when I was in Tavistock yesterday I found some lovely muslin in the curtain shop. I thought I could make a wedding dress out of that. Of course, us can't have no icing on the cake but Ben says he don't like icing anyway, so that's all right. And Mrs Hazelwood says I can have her mother's wedding ring. Isn't that nice of her?'

'It's very nice. I'm really pleased for you, May. You deserve to be very happy. Are you going to stay at home afterwards?'

'Well, there's not much else we can do, really, is there?

Mother says we can move into her room seeing as there's the double bed there and Father's downstairs now, and she'll move into mine.' May blushed. 'I don't know what we'll do once the war's over. Us'll just have to take that when it comes.' She got up and took the cups out to the kitchen to wash them. 'Do you know, if it hadn't been for you I wouldn't never have met Ben. It was at that party you had before Christmas when us first saw each other. And then on Christmas Day, he came walking down the lane and I invited him in.'

'You'd probably have done that anyway,' Alison said. 'I think you two were meant to meet. You were meant to be married too. Nothing will get in the way now.'

'I hope not,' May said, pausing with her hands in the sink. 'I really do hope not . . .'

Alison didn't see Stefan again for over a week. She spent her time as usual, looking after the children and the house, working in the garden and walking in the lanes. She called at the cottage to talk to William Prettyjohn about books and ask Grandpa's advice on vegetable growing, or to help Mabel with the sewing for the wedding. She was usually at home in the late afternoon, so that any of the pilots who wanted to drop in for tea would find her there, and in the evenings she listened to the wireless or read.

There was plenty to do, and yet there was always that emptiness at the back of her mind; the emptiness of being without Andrew, and the torment of not knowing whether he were alive or dead.

She missed Stefan too. After that last evening, as they'd sat late with the dusk gathering in the garden and the shadows finding their way into the house itself, she had heard nothing from him. He had got up rather abruptly after his remark about not wanting to leave, and left without his usual last cup of tea or cocoa. At the door, he had touched her cheek with one finger, and then turned away. She had stood at the door, watching him disappear into the dusk, feeling strangely disturbed, as if he had been trying to tell her something she had not understood.

He was probably worrying about his family, she decided eventually. The information about the Red Army advancing towards Warsaw wasn't wholly good news for a nation that had suffered under the Bolsheviks before. And it was so long since he had heard anything of his parents, his brothers or sisters that he must be almost afraid to find out. They might none of them have survived; he might feel even more alone than he did now.

It was a surprise, then, to meet him walking along the road when she was out on one of her afternoon walks with the children. She quickened her step towards him and saw his face light up and then, unaccountably, close down again.

'Stefan! Where have you been all this time? I've missed you.'

'Alison.' He stopped and took her hand, bringing it to his lips in the way that he always did. 'I've missed you too. But I thought it best . . .' He didn't finish and she felt a small frown crease her brow.

'What did you think best?'

'Never mind. It's of no importance now.' He ruffled Hughie's hair and peeped into the pram at Caroline, then said, 'Are you out for a walk?'

'Yes, we're going for a picnic. It's such a lovely afternoon. Why don't you come with us? I've made plenty of sandwiches.' She saw his hesitation and said coaxingly, 'We could go as far as the river if you came too. It's too far for me to push the pram on my own, and the hill's so steep on the way back.'

They walked along together and she told him about the plans for the wedding. 'I'm sure you'll be getting an invitation. Ben says he's asking the whole squadron.'

'Indeed, he already has. And we are going to give him a guard of honour as he and his bride come out of the church. That's a secret, though,' he warned her. 'You're not to tell them.'

'I won't. Oh, it's lovely to have something nice happening for a change.' They reached the river and found a grassy spot on the bank to settle down. While Stefan took Hughie down to a little beach to paddle and throw pebbles into the water, Alison lifted Caroline out of the pram and laid her on the old blanket she had brought with her. The baby kicked her legs and gurgled at the gently moving leaves above, stretching her hands out as if trying to grasp them and pull them down.

She's grown so much already, Alison thought, watching her. She was smiling and laughing now, an oddly deep-throated chuckle that made everyone else laugh too. She still had the thatch of soft, dark hair, so much like Andrew's, and her eyes had darkened to the same brown as his. She was totally the opposite of fair-haired, blue-eyed Hughie; people would find it hard to believe they were brother and sister, as they grew older.

Stefan came back and threw himself down on the blanket beside her. They sat watching Hughie, who was sitting on a rock staring intently into the water.

'What's he looking for?'

'Fish. We saw some very tiny ones – I don't know the English name for them.'

'Minnows, I expect. Or sticklebacks – they have little spikes on their backbones. He's not thinking of catching some for tea, I hope.'

'He's *thinking* of it,' Stefan said. 'I don't think there's much risk that he will succeed.'

They sat quietly for a little while and then he said, 'I have something to tell you, Alison.'

'Oh?' She felt her heart bump. She was suddenly not at all sure that she wanted to hear what he was about to say.

'There is a Polish squadron coming to Harrowbeer soon – probably in the next week or two. I am going to join them.'

'Oh,' she said. It wasn't what she'd been expecting to hear, although she could not have said what that was. 'Well, you'll be pleased about that, won't you? To be back with your own countrymen.'

He inclined his head. 'That will be good, yes, although I shall be sorry to leave our squadron. I have made many good friends there. But I shall be leaving Harrowbeer too, Alison. The new squadron will be going to another airfield and I shall be going with them.'

'Oh,' she said again. She looked down at her hands, looped around her drawn-up knees, and felt at a loss as to what to say next. She was conscious of a feeling of loss, as if something she'd hardly known she valued was being taken away from her. Lamely, she said, 'I'll miss you.'

'I'll miss you too, Alison.' He paused and she looked up and met his eyes. They were very dark. Her heart jolted and she felt a sudden anguish.

The silence lasted no more than a heartbeat. Then he got up abruptly and stood over her, holding his hand down to help her up. She gripped his fingers and he hauled her to her feet. She stood close to him, her hand still clasped in his, and laid her other hand on his shoulder. She could feel his breath on her cheek.

'Stefan—'

'No!' he said sharply, and let go of her fingers. He stepped away so suddenly that she staggered. 'This is not what you want.'

'I don't want you to go away. I'll miss you so much.'

'And I will miss you. More than you know.' His darkened eyes found hers again. 'I have to tell you, Alison, that I asked for this posting. It was my choice. When I heard that the squadron would be here . . . I knew it was time for me to go back to my people.'

Alison stood very still. On the rug, Caroline kicked and chuckled, and down by the river Hughie had picked up a stone to throw into the water. She felt a great sadness settle over her. Sitting down again, she rested her forehead on her knees.

Stefan came back. He squatted in front of her and touched her on the shoulder.

'You do understand why, don't you?' he said, and she nodded without looking up.

'I have great feeling for you,' he said. 'I have always had it. I knew I must never say this to you – I should not be saying it now – but I think we should be speaking the truth to each other. If you had not been married . . .'

'Yes,' she said. 'I know.'

'You feel it too. You know that if you had not been married—'

'But I am!' she exclaimed, looking up at last. 'I *still* am. Andrew's alive, I know it. And even if he weren't . . .'

'And that,' he said quietly, 'is why I must go away.'

They looked into each other's eyes and he laid one palm along her cheek. Alison closed her eyes. Then he took his hand away and when she opened her eyes again, he was by the river with Hughie again, pointing at something in the water.

After a while, he came back and they ate the sandwiches Alison had made. They drank water from a bottle and Caroline had her feed while Stefan took Hughie for a walk. After that, they climbed the hill back to the cottage.

'I won't come in,' he said as they reached the door. 'Thank you for a beautiful afternoon, Alison.'

'Will I see you again before you go?' she asked, looking into his face.

He hesitated, then said a little too quickly, 'Oh yes. I expect so.' But she knew from the expression in his eyes that he would not come back.

'Goodbye, then,' she murmured, and he took her hand and kissed her fingers, his lips warm and tender on the tingling skin.

'Goodbye, Alison, my friend. My very dear friend.'

He walked away along the road, but although Alison stood watching until he turned the corner, he did not look back.

Chapter Thirty-Six

The wedding day was fine and warm, and the villagers of Milton Combe turned out in force to see May Prettyjohn, in a billowing cloud of white muslin, go through the church door to marry the tall young RAF pilot who had come back, seemingly, from the dead.

The church was filled, and those who couldn't get in lined the path through the churchyard to cheer her and wish her well. Inside, flowers blazed from the windowsills and beside the lectern. On the altar stood a vase of golden roses.

John Hazelwood, who was to officiate, stood on the chancel steps waiting, his prayer book in his hands. Ben, with his old friend Tony Sinclair beside him as best man, waited nervously in the front pew. Behind him sat his mother, his sister Alexandra and Jeanie. Hope was to be a bridesmaid along with May's little cousin, and they had come down in the farm trap – which had been scrubbed clean and decorated with flowers – with May and her grandfather. William himself had been brought into the church on the bier more commonly used for coffins, and was now in the front pew on the other side, ready to give his daughter away, but she was to enter the church on Grandpa's arm. Mabel, sitting beside her husband, was looking her best in a pink costume that she had had since before the war and a hat she had made herself.

Alison sat just behind them with Hughie and the rest of

May's family; Caroline had been left with Mrs Potter next door. She glanced across the aisle at Ben and gave him a small smile, and then the soft notes of the organ changed to the dramatic bars of 'The Wedding March'. The bride was here.

The congregation stood up. Ben, visibly trembling, turned to watch his bride approach, and Alison's heart turned over at the expression on his face. She glanced at his mother, saw tears glimmer on Olivia Hazelwood's cheeks, and felt a warm gratitude for the older woman's sake, that her son had come home.

May, carrying a bouquet of yellow roses that echoed the colour of those on the altar, came slowly up the aisle, leaning on her grandfather's arm. Her dark curls were piled on her head and the radiance of her smile shone through the drift of muslin veiling her face. She stopped at the chancel steps and turned to Ben, and there was a moment of silence as, with a look that needed no words at all, they pledged themselves to each other.

John Hazelwood waited until they turned back to him, and then began to speak in a resonant voice that rose to the rafters and filled the church with his own personal joy.

'Dearly beloved, we are gathered together . . .'

As Stefan had promised, there was a guard of honour outside the church when the newly married couple emerged, and a burst of cheering and a shower of rose petals. May, her veil thrown back and her face rosy with laughter and happiness, ran with her husband beneath the arch of swords and posed for a few photographs. With almost no film available, only one or two people had cameras, but William had insisted on having the photographer from Tavistock to record the occasion.

Alison stood in the background, her heart filled with pleasure at her friends' happiness, and yet still touched with her own pain. As she had watched and listened to the service, she had not been able to help remembering her own wedding to Andrew and the joy she had felt – their hopes for the future, their plans and their dreams. But as swiftly as the memories entered her mind, she thrust them away. This was a day for rejoicing; she could cry later, when she was alone.

At last the congratulations and good wishes came to an end. Those who were going to the reception at the Prettyjohns' cottage began to set off up the hill, while May and Ben climbed into the trap and clattered off ahead of them, behind the old black pony. And as Alison stood with Mabel and old Mr Prettyjohn, waiting for the crowd to disperse so that William could be helped from the chair that had been placed by the church door, she noticed a man in RAF uniform walking down the narrow village street. His dark, tumbled hair was so much like Andrew's that as she saw him she felt her heart stop.

He could not be Andrew. He was too thin. And one sleeve of his uniform was pinned, empty, across his chest. But as he came closer and began to search the crowd, as if looking for one particular face, she knew the truth, and began to run.

'I went down behind the German lines,' he told her as they sat in the front room of the cottage later that evening. Hughie, worn out with excitement, was in bed and Andrew had at last relinquished Caroline for her evening feed. Now she too was in her cradle, snuffling gently in her sleep. 'I was damned lucky – a French farmer saw the plane go down and got me out. My left arm was pretty badly crushed but the local doctor saw to it pretty well, though he couldn't save it. They kept me in their loft for weeks. They could have been killed if I'd been found, but they wouldn't give me away. I owe them everything.'

'I can't believe it,' Alison said. Tears came to her eyes again. 'I'm sorry, darling, I can't stop crying. It's been so awful – I tried to believe that you'd come back, but it was so hard at times. And it was all the worse that you hadn't seen Caroline. It was all so unfair.'

'Well, we know life isn't fair, don't we,' he said. He slipped his right arm around her shoulder. 'All the same, I'm glad I've still got one of these to hold you with. You'll have to make sure you always sit that side of me.'

'But how did you get back?' she asked. 'What did the French family do?'

'Well, the Jerries are being driven back all the time, you see, so after a while we were in Allied territory and it was safe for me to come out. As soon as that happened they contacted the nearest Army camp and I was collected, taken to a field hospital and once they were satisfied with me I was sent home with the next batch of wounded soldiers. And here I am, back again like a bad penny.'

'Not a bad penny,' she said, leaning against him, feeling the warmth of his body. 'A gold sovereign.' She understood now what May had meant by saying she had needed to keep touching Ben to make herself believe he was really there. 'Oh Andrew, I'm so glad you're back. I'm never going to let you go away again!'

'Don't think there's much chance of me going, anyway,' he said a little ruefully. 'By the time I've persuaded the RAF to let me fly one-handed the war'll be over.'

'I hope it will,' she said, and then lifted her head. 'Listen.'

The air was filled with the sound of aircraft. They got up and went to the door. The golden light of sunset bathed the sky and tinged the feathery clouds with apricot and gold. A squadron of Spitfires flew over in tight formation.

'That's the Polish squadron,' she said quietly. 'Stefan

must be in one of the planes. He told me he was going with them. He's left Harrowbeer, Andrew.'

Andrew slipped his arm around her and held her tightly against him. The Spitfires were on their way west, into Cornwall. As the two watched, the last one dipped its wings and then flew away into the burnished distance and, with a pang of sorrow, Alison wondered if she would ever hear from Stefan again; whether he would ever find his family; whether he would even survive whatever was left of this terrible war.

They turned to go back inside, their arms still wound about each other's waists. The sound of the aircraft died away, and Alison heard the blackbird once again; and the shimmering sky was filled with the liquid joy of his song at twilight.